CRYSTAL
WAR

Other Novels by Joshua Palmatier:

The "Ley" Series:

Shattering the Ley
Threading the Needle
Reaping the Aurora

The "Well" Series:

Well of Sorrows
Leaves of Flame
Breath of Heaven

The "Throne of Amenkor" Series:

The Skewed Throne
The Cracked Throne
The Vacant Throne

The "Crystal Cities" Series:

Crystal Lattice
Crystal Rebel
Crystal War

Anthologies from Zombies Need Brains:

After Hours: Tales from the Ur-bar
The Modern Fae's Guide to Surviving Humanity
Clockwork Universe: Steampunk vs Aliens
Temporally Out of Order * Alien Artifacts * Were-
All Hail Our Robot Conquerors!
Second Round: A Return to the Ur-bar
The Modern Deity's Guide to Surviving Humanity
Solar Flare * Submerged * Guilds & Glaives * Apocalyptic
When Worlds Collide * Brave New Worlds * Dragonesque
The Death of All Things * The Razor's Edge * Portals
Temporally Deactivated * Galactic Stew
Derelict * Alternate Peace * Noir
My Battery Is Low and It Is Getting Dark
Shattering the Glass Slipper * Artifice & Craft * Game On!
Skull X Bones

CRYSTAL

WAR

A Novel of the Crystal Cities by

Joshua Palmatier

Zombies Need Brains LLC
www.zombiesneedbrains.com

Interior Design (ebook): ZNB Design
Interior Design (print): ZNB Design
Cover Design by ZNB Design
Cover Art "Crystal War"
by Justin Adams

ZNB Book Collectors #39

First Printing, Zombies Need Brains Edition, June 2025

Print ISBN-13: 978-1940709703

Ebook ISBN-13: 978-1940709710

Printed in the U.S.A.

PART I

BROVETTO

Chapter One

"So that's Brovetto."

Dalton stood with ex-Councilor Varenov, Lane, and the leader of the Brovettan rebels, John Senn, on the wayfare before the city. The refugees that had fled Iandolo—both Brovettan and those from other Crystal Cities—formed a makeshift camp in the predawn light on the elevated road behind them. It had grown in size as they traveled, until it now stood at over a thousand souls, all haggard and hungry, all exhausted.

But their goal was in sight.

Like Iandolo, Brovetto was built on a massive plateau high above the harsh and desolate Flatlands below. But that was where the resemblance ended. This city was low and wide, only five levels high. Instead of towering spires of lucent reaching into the heavens, there were squat buildings with rounded domes surrounded by walls and turrets, all rising toward an off-center complex of buildings that housed the governmental offices and army barracks. Obscured by darkness, he could only pick out odd angles and edges at first, outlined by the few sources of lucent light brightening the night. Iandolo would have been vibrant with lucent—in the towers, at mid-level, even some on the edges of the lower levels. Brovetto was the reverse, the bands of lucent few and far between. The lack of lucent was unsettling, even though Dalton had known to expect it based on everything Varenov and John had told him of the city on their way here.

But when the first rays of dawn touched the buildings, he sucked in a sharp breath. "It looks…dead."

"It nearly is," Varenov said.

"What you saw hidden in the depths of the lower levels of Iandolo—in the streets the gangs run and the dead zones near the hub—all of that is here, but on the surface." Senn waved a hand at the crumbled buildings, the cracked lucent. "This is what has become of Brovetto after years of neglect and the constant incursions from Iandolo's army. Once we depleted our mines of lucent, then of any other valuable ores, we were abandoned."

Varenov frowned. "It's not as simple as that."

"But it is."

Lane made a strangled noise. "Stop it. Both of you." She nodded toward the slowly emerging city, the ruins a burnished gold. "We're going to reach its waygate today. What should we expect?"

No one spoke.

Dalton faced Senn. "You were here most recently."

Senn shrugged. "But that means nothing. Prefect Arctus and the Iandolan Army more or less rooted out all of the main rebel locations while he was here. I'm certain a few members have survived, but not many. I fled with those I could find before Arctus was finished. From what I heard while in Iandolo, he gutted the governmental structure here, since they backed Terrial's attack at the Lyceum. I don't know who's in charge now. Likely someone from Iandolo, perhaps even someone from the army."

Dalton turned to Varenov. "And what about you? Will they recognize you as Councilor?"

"It's possible. I don't know if the Council sent out reports about my removal and arrest. But even if those reports were never sent, there were refugees fleeing ahead of us. Whoever is in charge in Brovetto will have heard of the uprising, of the breaking of the waygate, of Erilyn's activation of the Warding. They will be expecting us."

"By now, they would have seen our group from the walls," Senn added.

Dalton mulled it over, but it was Lane who spoke up first.

"I think we should have my mother approach them first. If they aren't certain about her status as Councilor, perhaps we can get in that way. The refugees may not have thought to tell them of her slated execution."

"It may be enough to at least get all of these people inside the gates," Varenov said. "We can't survive much longer out here on the wayfare. We're barely surviving as it is."

"And if not—" Lane crooked her hand. "—we can always force our way in."

"Let's hope that's not necessary."

"You're assuming that once we're close to the city your magic will work," Senn said. "You haven't been able to use it on the wayfare."

Lane's hand fell. "That's true. But why wouldn't it? It worked for the mages of the Iandolan Army when they were here."

"I don't know. But even now, all of you are underestimating how bad off the streets of Brovetto are. Even you, Varenov. It's ten times worse than when you were here last."

"Regardless," Varenov interceded, "it's probably best that you lay low, Lane, at least at first. No need to reveal all of our secrets. Let them think we are merely refugees."

"There are going to be stories from those that came before us," Senn said. "Of what she did at the waygate. They're going to be searching for her."

"Then we can only hope they don't know what our daughter looks like."

Dalton shifted to catch Varenov and Senn's attention. "I'll send Nic and Picall ahead of us to scout out the gate and the walls. We'll make a decision on how to approach the city then. They may simply be letting all of the refugees in."

Varenov nodded, although it was clear she didn't believe him. She and Senn retreated, heads bent together, their conversation intense, Lane and Dalton following a few paces behind.

"You don't really believe they'll be letting everyone in, do you?" Lane asked.

Dalton sighed. "No. I expect the gates to be closed and that we'll need your help getting them open."

They entered the edge of the camp through the loose ring of guards, people beginning to stir. Most were bedded down as comfortably as possible on the stone of the wayfare, bundles of meager possessions used as pillows, blankets pulled tight against the night's chill. Their faces were gaunt and hollow, but they were still alive. With the help of Maupin and the tullers, who had brought what food they could from the tull and hunted the Flatlands along the way when possible, and with what provisions had been stored along the way at regular waypoints, they'd managed to feed everyone with strict rationing. They'd only lost six people enroute—four to wounds received during the fight to escape Iandolo and two more to the harshness of the journey and the elements. Others had simply vanished, either walking away in the middle of the night or throwing themselves over the edge of the wayfare to the Flatlands a thousand feet below.

Dalton's stomach growled as they passed the wagon that held all of the remaining food stock. He nodded at Arch, the bartender and his mercenaries already doling out the meager breakfast to those awake. Some bowed their heads to Dalton and Lane as they clutched the small bowls to their chest; others merely stared as they passed. Dalton had learned to ignore it all, although it still made him uncomfortable.

"Your mother's hopes that you can lay low are pointless," he said, motioning to all the attention they were drawing. "Everyone here knows who you are."

"Do you think they'd betray us?"

"It only takes one."

"True." Lane glanced around them. "But do you notice a difference this morning? Everyone is a little more energetic, more animated."

"Because we're almost there. They likely haven't thought about what might be waiting to greet us."

They reached the wagon that had been converted into a medical unit, the bed covered with a rough tent to keep the sun off of those recovering. Lane snagged Dalton's arm to halt him, forced him to face her.

"How's Devon doing?"

"More or less the same as when you saw him last."

"He knows we don't blame him for anything that happened when he was in Havvelan's hands, right?"

"He knows. We've said it enough times. But he doesn't believe it."

She clenched her hand in frustration, hatred flickering across her face, then focused on Dalton again. "Maybe once we reach Brovetto, once he's all healed up…"

Dalton gave her a strained smile; Lane deserved at least that. "Maybe."

She squeezed his arm. "I'll get our gear together." Then she headed off to their own pallets.

Dalton rounded the end of the wagon, to where the folds of the canopy lay closed, but paused. Shoulders bent, he gripped the wood of the wagon's back panel, struggling to regain control. Straightening, he scrubbed at his face and eyes with one hand, glanced around to see if anyone had noticed his momentary lapse, then hauled himself up and through the flaps into the wagon bed.

Nic and Raven looked up as he entered, Nic reaching for his knife before recognition hit. Raven barely flinched. Devon lay in one of the pallets. Two others were occupied—one with a man who'd succumbed to heat exhaustion during the travels the day before and the second with a woman with a low-grade fever that hadn't broken yet. A fourth was Raven's, although Dalton rarely found her using it.

Dalton checked in on Devon first. The erstwhile Science student was asleep, his face still bruised and scuffed, but the marks were fading. His torn ear still looked like gnawed gristle, but hadn't gotten infected. The swelling around his eye had receded.

He ran his hand through Devon's sweat-matted hair, traced his fingers down the side of his face. Devon stirred, groaned in irritation, which made Dalton smile as he pulled away and let him settle again.

"He's healing faster than I am," Raven said quietly.

Dalton took a seat beside Nic, the other two shifting to make room. "Yet you're the one up and about. I've even seen you outside the tent, walking with the others."

"I'm a Regular. I can't sit in this wagon tent all day. I get restless."

"And irritable," Nic said. "Downright grumpy, which is dangerous for everyone." He jutted his chin out toward Devon. "No change. Moans in his sleep. Cries out once in a while. Quiet when he's awake."

"I didn't expect anything else." They sat in silence for a long moment before Dalton stirred. "Where's Picall?"

"Guard duty."

"Find her. We're going to reach Brovetto today. I want you two to check it out before we get there."

Nic stood, Raven a heartbeat behind. When the ex-gang member gave her a questioning look, she said, "I'll come with you."

Dalton ignored the silent communication that passed between them before they both climbed out of the wagon. As soon as they were gone, he slid down and lay next to Devon, draping one arm over Devon's side. When he tensed, Dalton tightened his hold and kissed the back of Devon's neck, until Devon shuddered and relaxed.

They lay like that for ten minutes, Dalton listening to the camp waking up. Devon whimpered and stiffened against his chest, then jolted awake with a choked cry, gasping. His hand fumbled for Dalton's, clenched tight as he calmed.

"Nightmares again?" When Devon didn't answer, he added, "The tower?"

"Favian was trying to get me to reveal more about the mage sigils, about the Source and the Outcome. I'd already told him everything, but he didn't believe me. So he ordered Arctus to bring me your eye." He twisted inside Dalton's grip, until he could see Dalton's face, one hand raised so he could brush his fingers over Dalton's eyes. "When he tossed it on the floor before me, I woke up."

"I'm fine. It was just a dream."

"I can see that. But it was so real. Not just the dream, but when I was really there, in that room, tied to that chair. When he pulled back the cloth and revealed that toe, told me it was yours, I...I believed him. I could feel you, in that other room. Knew you were being tortured, being mutilated, all because of me."

"It wasn't me. I wasn't there."

Devon's face crumpled as he fought back guilt and tears. "I know that now," he choked out, voice thick with phlegm. "I do. But I still told them everything—about the double pyramids, about the sigils we learned from the Brovettan mages, about what Lane had discovered on her own. Everything." He clenched his eyes closed. "I betrayed you all."

Dalton pulled Devon's head into his shoulder. "You didn't betray us. None of us think so. Not even Lane. She said the Iandolan mages were already learning the Brovettan mages' sigils. They used them to defend the internment camps, when they captured her. The cantrip? They used that to try to kill us during the executions at the Pulpit. And both cantrips and lightning when we were trying to escape the city." He pulled back, caught Devon's gaze, made certain he was listening. "You didn't give them anything they didn't already know or wouldn't have figured out eventually on their own. At most, you helped them make the connections faster, that's all."

"But—"

"No. There's nothing more to say. Besides—" He kissed Devon's forehead and sat up. "—you didn't tell them everything. You didn't say anything about how you can fix lucent, right?"

"Favian only asked about the magecraft."

"Then he doesn't know as much as he thinks he does. Now get up." He stood and held out a hand. "We're going to reach Brovetto today and from what I've seen, we're going to need your help."

Devon hesitated. "But...Lane."

"You're going to have to face her eventually. You can't cower in this wagon forever."

It hurt to see Devon flinch, but Dalton quashed the urge to let him stay. He gave a silent sigh of relief when Devon reached up and gripped his hand.

When he stepped down from the wagon, he found Lane waiting for him, their pallets and satchels clutched in her hands. But the moment she saw Devon emerging behind him, she dropped them and dashed forward, colliding with an audible thump.

"Careful," Devon gasped. "I'm still healing up."

Lane didn't appear to hear, her grip tightening, tears in her eyes. "You bastard, making me worry like that." She pulled back, checking him all over, sending an uncertain glance toward Dalton as she did so. He merely shrugged.

"Lane," Devon said, catching her shoulders to draw her attention. His voice caught, but he continued. "Lane, I'm sorry. I'm sorry I wasn't stronger. I'm sorry I told them about what we—what you—discovered."

Lane shook her head. "It doesn't matter. They would have found out eventually anyway. I'm sorry they did this to you."

"They didn't hurt you, did they? They told me—"

"No," Lane interrupted sharply. "No, they didn't hurt me. Not like they did you and a few others they were holding. They needed me for something else."

"The execution. Dalton told me."

"And a failsafe. In case they couldn't get you to talk."

Guilt twinged across Devon's face again and Dalton started forward, but they were interrupted by the arrival of Varenov.

"Devon! Good to finally see you on your feet." The ex-councilor gave him a curt nod as she passed out dried strips of meat to all of them from her pouch.

Dalton bit off a chunk of his. "Lizard," he muttered as he chewed. "My favorite." He noticed Devon had already finished and handed the rest of his over.

"Senn has spread the word," Varenov said, the camp around them already beginning to shift forward. "We're headed out."

"I sent Nic, Picall, and Raven ahead."

"Good."

Mindell's daughter appeared, the healer himself already climbing into the seat of the wagon.

"Did you want to ride?" she asked Devon.

He glanced at Lane, then Dalton. "I think I'll walk. For as long as I can."

"Let me know when you get tired. You can join my father on the driver's bench."

She climbed up into the back of the wagon, slapping its side. A moment later it lurched into motion.

Dalton grabbed Devon's shoulder. "Let's find out what Brovetto has to offer us."

* * *

Nine hours later, a shout rose from the front of the group of refugees. Devon perked up on the bench to the healer's wagon, then glanced down to where Dalton kept pace at its side.

"They're calling for you, Dalton."

"Stay here," he ordered, then began to jog forward, the rest of the refugees grinding to a weary halt around him, most simply collapsing where they stopped.

He found Varenov, Senn, Lane, and Maupin waiting for him, Nic and Raven trotting in from the direction of Brovetto. The city walls filled the horizon, shimmering in liquid heat waves, maybe an hour distant at their current pace. The city itself barely rose above the walls, a blister on top of the plateau. Having only lived in the towering city of Iandolo, Dalton felt as if the city were missing, the place where it should stand achingly vacant.

He arrived at the same time as Nic and Raven, Senn motioning with one hand. "Report."

Nic shot a glance at Dalton, but straightened. "The Luminesque waygates are closed and there are soldiers on the walls. They're expecting us."

"However," Raven added, "there are no refugees outside the walls waiting to get in. I'd wager that they've been letting those who came before us inside and have only closed the gates recently."

"Probably because of the size of our group," Varenov said. "We're large enough they may see us as a threat."

"Where's Picall?" Dalton asked.

"She stayed behind to see if they reacted. We're fairly certain they saw us checking it out. There aren't really any places to hide on the wayfare."

"Then we should send someone to speak to them," Varenov said. "Reassure them we aren't the forefront of an army, that we're merely refugees."

"It has to be you, Varenov," Senn said. "Whether they recognize you as councilor or not, you're still the best negotiator we've got."

Varenov stared toward the far walls, then nodded. "I'll need a minimal escort. Dalton and Maupin as guards, along with Picall when we reach her. None of you have Iandolan uniforms—that alone will tip them off that I'm no longer officially a councilor—but it can't be helped."

"What about me?" Lane asked.

"You need to stay here," Senn said, "with me, in case we need to force our way in."

"Why aren't you going?" Dalton asked.

"We can't risk anyone recognizing me, knowing I was part of the rebellion from before. Those of us here in the group are going to try to blend in with the other refugees. I've already spread the word."

Lane was clearly unhappy, but agreed with a quick, "Be careful," to her mother and Dalton before retreating with Senn, Nic, and Raven to get the rest of the refugees prepared.

"Any particular words of wisdom?" Dalton asked Varenov as he, Varenov, and Maupin headed out at a brisk pace intended to outdistance the group behind them.

"Nothing springs to mind."

Twenty minutes later Picall emerged from the heat shimmer, standing to one side of the wayfare, tuller staff cocked to one side. She joined them without a word. Ten minutes after that, they came within sight of the waygate.

Like that of Iandolo, the gate was a massive construct of metal and lucent, although here it was a burnt umber in color, unlike the vibrant blue of the gate Lane had broken in their escape. Dalton judged the gate and walls were smaller than that of Iandolo's as well. Pennants snapped from the parapet and soldiers could be seen watching them from above.

"Nothing has changed since Nic and Raven left to report," Picall said. "Some activity up above when they saw you approaching, but—"

A sharp metallic clang cut her off and a moment later one side of the gate began to open, wide enough to allow a group of ten soldiers dressed in the maroon and white of Iridesque to emerge. Dalton and Maupin stepped forward, but Varenov restrained them, bringing their group to a halt.

When the Iandolan guards approached, Dalton noted the green and gold armband—the colors of Luminesque—wrapped around their upper arm. They were in a standard protective formation, but when they halted ten paces away, those in front parted and a prefect stepped forward. He held himself stiffly, face narrow, eyes hard, puckered scars along one cheek. He scanned all four of them, brow pinched in uncertainty, then focused on Varenov.

"Councilor Varenov," he said with a slight nod.

"Not a councilor any longer, Prefect Burdock."

A tension in the prefect's shoulders eased slightly. "So we have heard—from the refugees we've already received and our most recent reports from the Council and Prefect Arctus." Burdock's gaze shifted behind them. "May I assume that those with you are refugees as well?"

"They are. Some of them are wounded, all of them hungry."

"I can imagine. I'm surprised you made it all the way from Iandolo with this many."

"We lost a few along the way."

Dalton didn't see Burdock signal, but the nine other soldiers began to spread out to either side of them. Picall reacted instantly, skipping backwards and bringing her staff to the ready. Dalton and Maupin drew their swords, Dalton pulling Varenov in behind him. The soldiers tensed, their arc half complete.

"Hold!" Burdock commanded, and all of them halted, weapons steady.

Burdock took a step toward Varenov. "I will allow them within the gates on one condition—that you surrender yourself."

"Don't," Maupin said. "They'll kill you. Or send you back to Iandolo so Havvelan can finish what he started."

"Maupin, Dalton, Picall, stand down," Varenov said. "I knew this was the likely outcome, especially once I recognized Prefect Burdock. He has always been loyal to Arctus. I suspect that's why he was placed in charge here in Brovetto." She drew herself upright, as regal as if she were still a councilor. "You will allow them entry? Feed them and provide healers for the wounded?"

"Of course."

"Then I agree."

Dalton's hand clenched tight on the handle of his sword. "Varenov—"

She shot him a glance and shook her head. "This is the only way. Maupin, Picall, head back to the refugee group. Tell them they've agreed to let us in. Don't tell anyone on what condition."

With clear reluctance, Maupin backed toward Picall, then both tullers retreated, wary at first, then at a run.

Dalton sheathed his sword and sidled closer to Varenov. "What are you doing?"

"Ensuring that everyone gets inside the gates. None of them will survive much longer trapped outside." At Dalton's look, she added, "I may not officially be a councilor for Luminesque, but I am still responsible for protecting them."

Consternation crossed Burdock's face, but he motioned to his men. "If you will follow me."

Varenov didn't move. "Not until all of the refugees are inside Brovetto."

The two glared at each other until Burdock relented. "Very well." He turned and issued orders to two of his men, both heading back into the city at a run. Shortly after, the gate opened wider.

They waited, the small group edging to one side as the sun began to set. Dalton wiped sweat from his forehead, felt the grit that had stuck there, and fidgeted, trying to capture Varenov's gaze. But she ignored him.

Then the refugees arrived, Dalton surprised to find Maupin and Picall leading them, with Nic, Arch, and Raven urging everyone forward around the three wagons. Arch's mercenaries and Maupin's tullers were scattered throughout the group, Senn's rebels blending in with the regular refugees, both the Brovettans they'd freed and those regular citizens from all of the other Crystal Cities that they'd accumulated those first few days' march from Iandolo's broken and Warded gates. He nearly missed Senn, walking with a woman and two children, one of them held in his arms. Lane was helping an elderly man with a cane, although she cast her mother a surreptitious worried frown. When he didn't see Devon, Dalton inadvertently stepped forward, until he caught a hand wave from Mindell indicated he was inside the tented wagon.

As the last of the refugees filed through the gates, Burdock said, "After you, Varenov."

They entered, Dalton staying close to Varenov's side. The refugees had been herded into the center of the plaza, surrounded by ranks of Iandolan soldiers.

"What is the meaning of this, Prefect Burdock?" Varenov demanded as the gates behind them began to close.

"I'm afraid, Councilor Varenov, that—like all of those who came before you—everyone is under arrest."

"For what?"

"For being insurrectionists."

Varenov spun on him. "These people are not insurrectionists! Most of them are Brovettans, simply hoping to return home. The rest are citizens that got caught up in the upheaval in Iandolo and fled for their lives!"

"Agreed. And I have no doubt that some of them are indeed insurrectionists, the instigators of that upheaval. Until I am certain which are which, you are all under arrest."

The gates rumbled shut with a hollow boom.

"Welcome to Brovetto, councilor."

Chapter Two

Varenov watched in mute anger as Prefect Burdock's soldiers moved on the crowd of refugees in the square. A squad seized Maupin, Picall, Raven, Nic, and Arch, those who had led the Brovettans and others into the city, and escorted them off to the side. The others began dividing the refugees into two groups, herding them toward two large buildings on either side of the gates—an army barracks and an armory. People began to protest, some vociferously, many struggling, but they were all exhausted and there were too many soldiers. She caught sight of Mindell on the medical wagon, Cerelle and Sadie, a few others, but not Lane or John.

Dalton stood at her side, hands clenched. She could feel his tension.

Facing Burdock, she asked, "You promised to aid them."

"And I will," Burdock answered. "They are citizens of the Crystal Cities, after all."

From the main thoroughfare behind him, a slew of carriages arrived. One of them pulled up beside them. Burdock stepped forward and opened the door, motioned with one hand. "After you, councilor."

She glanced to the side to see Maupin and the others forced into the other carriages. Nic looked her way with a dark frown.

Turning back, she gave Burdock a similar look, then stepped up into the carriage. Dalton and Burdock joined her a moment later with another captain, who slapped the roof before they were all settled, the carriage lurching into motion.

She shifted in the cramped quarters, the carriage jolting over a rough patch of stone. "Where are you taking us?"

"The governmental buildings on the Fifth Level, to the councilor's quarters actually. They're currently unoccupied."

"They've been unoccupied for nearly twenty years."

"True. But isn't that your fault, councilor? You were the representative of this province, yet you rarely traveled here."

"I felt I was helping the Brovettans more by being in Iandolo, where I could influence the other councilors."

"And yet, look at the city you left behind." He motioned toward the window.

She hesitated, then pulled the curtain aside.

People filled the streets, stepping into shops or pausing at carts pulled up along buildings, but everyone looked weary and worn down. Nearly everyone was gaunt, their clothes hanging off of them, as tattered and worn as their faces. They stared at the carriages as they passed, some fearfully, others with hatred. Many buildings appeared abandoned, even on this main thoroughfare, some with vacant windows or doors, a few with walls or roofs collapsed inwards. Active lucent was rare, the streets lined with oil lamps instead, their harsh smell prickling her nose. Varenov had seen places like this in Iandolo, but they were all in the lower levels, and even then the people had appeared more robust. But she knew she hadn't been deep inside the city. Not as deep as Lane and Devon and the others had been. She'd only seen the surface.

They passed a marketplace, more active and energetic than the streets, giving her hope, then a park. But as they passed up through the levels, nothing much changed. When they finally reached the Fifth Level and Burdock motioned her and Dalton out, she noted that even the governmental buildings had rough edges—cracks in the stone and scars along rooftops and around windows. Black char surrounded the double doors into the hall, residual signs of the fighting that had gone on when Prefect Arctus had come to purge the city of the rebels who'd fallen in with Terrial and attacked Iandolo. Inside, the results of the fighting were more evident, with doors torn from their moldings, additional signs of mage fire, cracked walls, and broken lucent.

Maupin, Arch, Nic, Picall, and Raven were led inside, then taken off to the left. Soldiers moved forward to separate Dalton and Varenov, but Dalton stiffened, hand moving toward his sword.

Varenov placed a hand on his arm. "Don't. Go with them. We don't want any trouble. Everything will be fine."

He gave her a troubled look, but didn't resist when they took him off in the same direction as the others.

When she turned back, Burdock gave her a tight smile and preceeded her up the curved stairs in the foyer. Here, some of the lucent still worked, a few flickering, but most intact and glowing brightly. Veins of it swirled up the wall in blue and yellow.

Upstairs, down a long hall, Burdock stopped before an open door and motioned her inside, where a chair sat at the end of a long table.

"Have a seat, Councilor Varenov. We have a lot to talk about."

* * *

"I can get us out of here within minutes," Lane said, stepping forward and raising one hand, but her father restrained her.

When she twisted herself free, he said, "They have your mother hostage."

"My mother wouldn't want that to stop me."

"That's true, and we'll use your talent if necessary, but right now we have other, less violent, means."

"What do you mean?"

Senn glanced around the barracks where they'd been herded by the Iandolan soldiers, then motioned her to one side. The group had been split between two buildings to either side of the gates. The wagons had been taken to the armory across the way. Lane had tried to follow them, hoping to reach Devon, but the soldiers had moved too quickly, dividing the rest of the group into two. She'd been caught up with Senn and the families they'd pretended to be part of and escorted into the old barracks. Maupin, Picall, Raven, Nic, and Arch had been singled out and led off with her mother and Dalton toward the governmental buildings—all of those that had acted as leaders when they'd arrived. She'd seen Cerelle and Sadie near the wagons earlier and assumed they'd been taken in with them, but she didn't know where any of the others were.

Senn drew up near three men, all Brovettan, who gave curt nods. One of them turned away, strode off a few paces, and kept an eye on the Iandolan soldiers around the barracks still getting the captives situated as the other two sidled closer.

"What's the situation?" Senn asked.

"We lost a third of us to the other group, but some of Maupin's tullers can make up for that. They should be willing, since they hauled off Maupin himself."

"Good. What about Arch's mercenaries?"

The two glanced at each other and the second man said, "We can approach them."

"And Mouse?"

The first man snorted. "He's already outside. You can't keep him locked up."

"Then for now, we wait. See who else you can gather up."

The two men nodded, then drifted away, the lookout headed in a different direction.

Irritated, Lane asked, "What was that all about?"

"Planning." When she crossed her arms over her chest, his mouth twisted into a faint smile and he shook his head. "Just like your mother." Then he faced her. "Neither your mother nor I thought we'd walk into Brovetto and take over, so we planned ahead."

"You knew we'd be arrested?"

"We thought it likely, yes."

"So what's the plan?"

"Right now, one of my men—Mouse—has slipped out of the barracks. He's good at things like that. He's going to head into the city to see if any of our rebel friends are still around. I don't think there will be many, but they couldn't have all been caught or killed. Once we know what kind of support we'll have from the outside, we'll figure out our next move."

Lane remained silent for a moment, troubled, then: "You said 'walk into Brovetto and take over.' Is that the end goal? To take over?" She couldn't help letting an edge of accusatory anger creep into her voice. "That's what you want isn't it? To seize control? Like you did with our attempts to help the Brovettans as soon as you arrived in Iandolo."

Her father rubbed at his eyes with the fingers of one hand, pinched the bridge of his nose. When his hand fell, he stared off toward the roof of the barracks, collecting himself, then turned back.

"That wasn't what we wanted in the beginning, all those years ago. We just wanted regular meals, a decent place to live. That's what we were fighting for. Peacefully, at first. It's why your mother got involved. But nothing changed, no matter how much we protested or begged. Things only got more desperate. So we started to fight back. That's when your mother got disillusioned. When the protests became violent, she pulled away—from the group...from me. I knew I was losing her but I couldn't see any other option. And I couldn't just..." He grasped at the air with both hands, then let them fall. "I couldn't just let it go. Not for her. Not when there were so many here starving, killing themselves just to survive.

And for a while, the violence worked. Things improved, because others began to pay attention to those living in the slums. We stopped the violence because things got better, but that faded. Without the reminders, without the threat, it's easy for people to forget.

"So we started up again, pushed harder. We wanted *change*, not just a few placating words and an empty promise that lasted only as long as the breath taken to make it. *Real change*. And with every action we took, your mother stepped farther and farther away. Until we went too far, or pushed too hard, and triggered a response from the Council."

"The raid led by Favian."

Senn nodded. "The group's intent was to capture Councilor Orland and demand change from the Council. The Iandolan Army that had been sent to protect him found out about it and when they interceded…it all went to hell. Orland was killed, among others, which they blamed on us, of course. Our group managed to escape in the aftermath, for the most part, shocked at how brutal it had all become. Both sides were reeling. Your mother saw an opportunity and she took it, never thinking that the Council would end up appointing her as Orland's replacement. She'd simply seen a chance to end it all without violence—improve conditions for those in Brovetto and allow Iridesque a clean way out of the debacle.

"But as before, the attention and aid faded over time. Oh it took longer, much longer, but our group never really went away. The core of it remained, always in the background, and eventually we began to emerge again, this time with a mage."

"Terrial."

"We thought it would give us an advantage, especially when she began training other mages. We never expected her to break away on her own and offer her mages to the leaders of the government at the time, who had their own ambitions. The idiots."

"So they attacked Iandolo, triggered the Warding, and nearly seized control of the Crystal Cities. I don't see how that justifies why you need to take over here, now. It would seem to be the reverse."

"Because none of them were Brovettan! We haven't had anyone leading Luminesque who was Brovettan for decades! *We* are Brovettan. *We* should be the ones making decisions about our own city!" He threw up his hands in frustration. "Our city is controlled by the Council. And our representative on the Council has been a pawn of Iandolo for as long as anyone here can remember. We need to break that cycle. And unlike those that used Terrial to create the Warding, we aren't trying to take over all of the Crystal Cities. We just want control of our own."

Some of the stiff anger bled from Lane's shoulders. Since her father's sudden appearance in Iandolo, she'd kept her distance, even on the enforced journey from Iandolo to Brovetto along the wayfare. She'd avoided him, had resented his arrival, caught off guard because her mother had led her to believe that her father was dead. His first action had been to seize control of Maupin's operation to rescue the Brovettans. That had become his main focus. It hadn't seemed as if he wanted to connect with her, his own daughter. He'd cared more about breaking down the internment camps. That hadn't changed even after Lane's capture, according to Nic.

So she'd avoided him, shoved him away whenever he tried to approach her to talk. He'd said more to her in the last ten minutes than he had since he'd first arrived in Iandolo. His presence put her on edge, but at least now she understood a little better why he'd been so intent on the Brovettans' plight before.

Still wary, she asked, "And how are you going to do that? How are you going to take over?"

"First, we're going to have to eliminate the Iandolan guard that Prefect Arctus left here."

Lane didn't like the word 'eliminate,' but she didn't have time to protest as someone called out her name. She turned to find Proctor Arrend and a cadre of the Lyceum students and proctors he'd brought with him headed toward her.

"Lane!" Arrend repeated. His gaze flicked toward her father. "And John Senn. Good to see you both." He drew up close, the proctors and students—Lane recognized Jillian, Itch, and Alan, along with a few of the younger mage students—shuffling to a halt behind him. He glanced around surreptitiously. "I presume we don't intend to stay here?"

"And why is that?" her father asked.

"Because none of us fled Iandolo with the hopes that we'd be arrested in Brovetto and sent immediately back."

"We can help," Jillian said. "We want to help."

Alan and Itch nodded.

Arrend gave the History student a strained look. "As Jillian says, we want to help. The proctors with us are mostly Arts and Humanities, but we do have a few War students and mages." He looked at Lane pointedly. "They can be taught."

Her father looked the group over with a frown. "I'm not certain—"

"Listen up!" someone shouted from the front of the abandoned barracks.

A man in a captain's uniform climbed up onto one of the few chairs scattered around the room amongst the pallets along the walls. Those in the hall, clumped in fearful and uncertain groups, slowly fell silent. Behind him, in the open space before the doors, soldiers appeared and began to set up tables and chairs in two tiers.

"You are all under arrest," the captain began, then raised a hand at the sudden grumble from everyone gathered. "We know most of you are simply refugees from the recent troubles in Iandolo, but we also know there are insurgents among you that caused the uprising in the first place. If you know of any of these insurgents, it would be best if you pointed them out to us immediately." He paused, glancing around. Lane wanted to shrink back, but her father didn't budge, stood perhaps a touch straighter. There was a restless shifting around the suddenly silent room, glances thrown in all directions, but no one spoke up.

"Very well," he said, and motioned with one hand. The soldiers in the first tier sat and set out paper and ink, while others moved into the crowd. "We're going to interview each of you one at a time. Provide your name, occupation, and any family with you. We will ask you additional questions about the unrest in Iandolo. Any weapons you have on you will be confiscated. If you know of any insurgents among you, this will be your last chance to point them out. We know many of you are wounded and that all of you are hungry. After you've been questioned, we will provide a healer, if necessary, and food."

The doors opened, guarded by a squad of soldiers on either side, and others were escorted in. A group of four began setting out medical supplies on one of the tables in the second tier, while the others began pulling loaves of bread, apples, and other assorted foods from baskets and crates brought in behind them.

The scent of fresh baked bread struck Lane like a hammer. Her gut seized and her mouth flooded with saliva. She nearly groaned. Many of those gathered took an involuntary step forward.

The captain smiled.

The soldiers that had moved into the crowd of refugees each singled out someone and drew them forward. A few resisted, at which the soldiers became more forceful. One woman cried out and wrested herself free, stumbling to the ground. As a Brovettan tried to help her up, two additional soldiers stepped forward and shoved the man back, snatching the woman up and hauling her forward to one of the tables, throwing her to her knees before it and standing behind her to keep her there.

Lane noticed men and women scattered throughout the room casting furtive glances toward her father, a few adjusting position to indicate their swords or knives, but he signaled back with a shake of his head, then turned slightly toward Lane and Arrend.

"This complicates things."

"Should we do something?" Arrend asked.

"Not at the moment. But you should be prepared to act if necessary." He looked at Lane in particular. "Your mother may be a hostage, but that doesn't mean she's powerless."

* * *

Varenov settled herself into the single chair, back stiff, hands in her lap. She eyed Burdock across the length of the table. "What do you intend to do?"

Burdock placed both hands on the table and leaned toward her. "Send you back to Iandolo, to face your delayed execution."

"That may be harder than you think, but I didn't mean with me. I meant with the refugees."

The Prefect hesitated, then pushed himself back upright. "My men are processing them now."

"Processing?"

"Each will be interviewed. The insurrectionists will be rooted out and returned with you to Iandolo to face judgment. Those that are true refugees, whether Brovettan or not, will be allowed to stay."

"Easier said than done."

"Oh, I believe we'll find someone willing to point out those responsible."

Two Iandolan soldiers entered with trays of cheese, bread, and sliced apples. A third poured two glasses of wine. Then all three departed.

Burdock waved to Varenov's tray and glass. "Eat. Drink." His voice grew harder. "And tell me everything that happened in Iandolo that led you to this."

Varenov shifted forward and rested her clasped hands on the table but didn't touch anything. "It's simple. After Arctus left to come here to purge Luminesque of the conspirators who allied with the mage Terrial, the Council decided to round up and imprison all of those of Brovettan blood."

"Imprison?"

Varenov narrowed her eyes. "That's not what the Council called it, of course. They sequestered them in established zones at different levels of the city. I objected to this plan, vehemently, but I was overruled by the other councilors. Others also disagreed and the zones were attacked and the Brovettans freed. The Council concluded I had helped those who aided the Brovettans and so I was arrested and slated for execution."

"And did you help them?"

"I helped the Brovettans who'd been forced into the zones. The living conditions were deplorable and the soldiers ostensibly guarding them were treating the Brovettans like animals. *Less* than animals, actually. I had no contact with those that eventually freed them. Or, at least, freed most of them."

Burdock frowned. "Iandolan army soldiers were guarding them?"

"Supplemented by those who'd volunteered or been recruited into the new War colleges that were initiated shortly before you and Arctus left for Brovetto."

"But they could not possibly have been fully trained—"

"They weren't."

They stared at each other, Burdock's brow creased in consternation, and Varenov drew in a sudden breath of comprehension.

"You've heard none of this before now, have you? You haven't been getting reports from Arctus. You only know what you've managed to gather from the refugees that arrived before us."

"What happened after you were arrested?" Burdock asked, voice sharp. "What happened at the execution?"

Varenov allowed herself a thin smile. "Arctus attacked the gangs in the lower levels because they aided the Brovettans—were actively hiding those that escaped—and in retaliation, the gangs interrupted the execution. I escaped in the confusion, but by then the entire city had erupted into chaos. There was fighting on every level and everyone not fighting was either hunkering down to ride it out or attempting to flee. I joined up with a group attempting to flee…and now I'm here."

"Your departure wasn't as simple as that. Iandolo closed its gates. You destroyed them!"

"I didn't destroy them. My daughter did. To set us free. To set everyone in the plaza who was attempting to flee free."

"And then what? Your daughter created a Warding to keep the Iandolan Army from following you?"

"No, the Warding was released by someone else. But yes, it allowed those that escaped to run without being hounded by soldiers. And yet, I don't think you've realized exactly what that Warding means for you."

Burdock stiffened. "What do you mean?"

Varenov stood. "No one in Iandolo knows how to bring down a Warding. Those that brought the one holding the Lyceum before are here now, with me. And yes, I'm certain that someone at the college—Proctor Favian, perhaps—will eventually figure out how to take it down, but in the meantime, no one can leave Iandolo by the Brovettan gateway. Not Arctus.

Not Havvelan. And certainly not the Iandolan Army. You're cut off, Prefect. Whatever forces you have here are all that you've got. There won't be any reinforcements from Iridesque. Not within the next few weeks. Probably not within the next few months. You're alone."

Burdock bristled. "Hardly alone. I have a full contingent of Iandolan soldiers here. What do you have? A smattering of insurgents? Refugees?"

"I have my daughter."

Burdock faltered, but rallied. "We have our own mages stationed here."

"Can they stand against her? She defeated the mage who set up the first Warding around the college, after taking that Warding down. She destroyed the lucent gates in Iandolo to get here. Can your mages deal with that?"

Burdock didn't answer, so Varenov leaned forward.

"Your men are *processing* the refugees right now, Prefect. My daughter is down there, among them. And all she needs is a reason."

* * *

"We can't let them do this," Lane said. She paced back and forth behind a shield of men and women her father had slowly assembled as the Iandolan soldiers continued their interviews. "It's like the quarantine zones all over again."

"You need to calm down." Senn motioned toward the front of the building, where the two tiers of tables stood. "Some of those they've interviewed are getting food and medical attention."

"And some of them are being led off to one side, under guard. Most of them are your men, or Maupin's or Arch's."

"I see that. But not all of them. They're singling out anyone who looks like they can fight, or had weapons on them when they were searched. A few made it through their questioning. No one has given us up yet."

"And how long is that going to last? We can't let what happened in Iandolo happen again here. We need to do something!"

"Like what?"

One of the Brovettans being questioned suddenly shouted, "You can't! I'm a citizen of the Crystal Cities! Just a merchant for shard's sake! Look at me!" He leaped up from where he'd been kneeling in front of the table, head snapping around in desperation. For a moment, his gaze locked onto Lane's.

Then two soldiers closed in on him from opposite sides. With a cry, he lurched toward where those that hadn't been questioned yet were huddled in groups, but one of the soldiers tripped him. He landed hard, face smashing into the stone floor, and before he could recover they were on him. Each grabbed an arm and hauled him upright, blood dripping from a broken nose. He moaned as they began to drag him toward the others that had obviously been singled out as insurgents.

"Lane—" Senn began.

But she'd had enough. She pushed past her father and through the small group that surrounded them, out into the open area that had formed between those who'd escaped Iandolo and the soldiers. One of the guards shouted a warning and within a breath every soldier in the room had tensed or drawn a weapon, a few of them dashing toward her.

Drawing to a halt, she sketched out the base sigil and said, "That's enough."

The guards that had headed toward her staggered to a stop, shifting uneasily. Behind her, she heard movement and caught some of her father's men fanning out to either side of her, blades bared if they had them. The soldiers surrounding those already singled out closed ranks to keep them there, while everyone else remained where they were.

"I see we've finally flushed some of you out."

Lane's gaze centered on the captain as he moved forward, his men shifting position behind him. She waited until he was ten feet away, then raised her hand slightly. "No closer, unless you want to burn."

The captain paused. A few of his men continued changing position but he stilled them all with a gesture. "You do realize we have our own mages here, don't you?"

Behind him, near the door, a man edged into the light. He was dressed like one of the soldiers, not in the gray robes mages usually wore in the army, but his hand was crooked exactly like Lane's, the base sigil already set.

Lane smiled. "Hello, Cole. How'd you get stuck with this assignment?"

"Recent graduate, as you know. Luck of the draw."

The sound of shouting and running feet came from outside, then the doors to the barracks were flung wide open, a contingent of Iandolan soldiers flooding in, including another mage, older than Cole by at least ten years, one Lane didn't recognize.

The captain took another step forward. "I presume you are Lane Illea, Varenov's daughter. We've been looking for you."

"Here I am. Who are you?"

"Captain Silleac."

"You need to stand down, Captain Silleac. Let us go. Before this escalates."

Silleac chuckled. "Why would I do that? We have your mother."

"We didn't fight our way out of Iandolo, out of the internment camps, the towers, only to be imprisoned again here. My mother would agree with me."

"My mages can deal with you. My soldiers can handle the rest."

"Are you certain about that?"

Her father's voice startled her, almost made her lose the form she held.

Senn stepped up beside her, motioned toward the two mages. "I'm certain they've heard of what Lane has done, perhaps even seen it themselves on the grounds of the Lyceum. Since then, she's fought against mages at the internment camps, in the lower levels, even broke open the gates of the outer wall. Can your mages match that?"

Cole's eyes widened and he fidgeted, but the other mage held steady.

Silleac shrugged. "Let's find out."

Lane swore and began her secondary sigil—a shield, to protect those around her from whatever Cole and the other mage threw at her—as Senn shouted out orders and all of the men and women with weapons surged forward. Screams erupted and the refugees near the tables dropped to the ground, some still clutching bread in their hands. The men already separated out and under guard leapt onto their captors.

Lane focused her attention on the older mage. As she finished the form, the shield rising from the stone floor in an arch of scintillant light, the other mage completed a fire sigil, flames roaring toward her. A few of the soldiers flattened themselves to the ground moments before it would have struck them, while others rushed into a protective formation around the mage, one Lane recognized from the Lyceum. The fire hit her shield and exploded outwards in a fan before sputtering out. Senn's men were engaging the Iandolan soldiers on either side of the edge of her shield, holding them back.

Lane had completed the base form and started a fire sigil of her own when someone bellowed, "Hold!"

Lane paused, most of those fighting closer to the entrance to the barracks doing the same, including the mage, but kept her hand crooked. Three figures stood silhouetted by the open doors—a guardsman, the prefect—

And her mother.

When the fighting to either side of her shield continued unabated, the prefect took a few steps forward and roared, "I said HOLD!"

Slowly, the clash of swords, grunts, and cries of pain died down, the soldiers pulling back from the shield. Men panted, cursed, or winced at wounds. One or two were kneeling or prostrate, either unconscious or moaning. A few were bleeding.

Silleac strode up to Prefect Burdock and protested, too softly for Lane to hear the words, but his demeanor was clear. Burdock raised a hand to quiet him, his gaze raking across the shambles of the barracks.

Lane's shield chose that moment to die. As its light drifted upwards and faded, she found herself exposed. Burdock noticed her immediately.

"Stand down, Lane. Your mother and I have come to an agreement."

"What agreement?"

"A truce, of sorts. We'll let you and all of your refugees into the city, unmolested. No questioning, no interviews. We'll even provide medical treatment and food."

Everyone around the room shifted, the refugees with murmurs of hope, the soldiers with rumblings of disapproval.

Lane kept her eyes on Burdock. "In exchange for what?"

"We maintain control of the governmental buildings and the gates. And you hand over your mother and the leader of the insurrectionists, John Senn."

Lane's gaze shot to her mother, who straightened and gave her a slight nod, her mouth pressed into a thin line. Protests rose from around the room, on both sides.

"You can't do this," Silleac spat. "We have them. We can take them all down now!"

"Are you certain of that, captain?" Burdock's voice was sharp but calm.

Silleac bit off what he was going to say next and turned away.

Lane felt her father's presence at her side, caught Arrend's profile on the other, but she ignored them both.

"What do you intend to do to them?" she asked Burdock.

"Hold them until someone from Iandolo arrives. Or until I hear word from the Council."

"Why should I trust you?"

"I can't give you a reason to trust me. Not one you'd believe."

"Then why shouldn't I simply take control myself right now." She motioned with her crooked hand and a significant number of those assembled flinched.

"Lane," Arrend muttered, her name loaded with warning.

Burdock nodded. "Based on what your mother has told me, I have no doubt you could. But how many of us are you willing to kill in order to seize control? How many of my men? And how many of your fellow refugees—or Brovettan citizens—would die during the attempt? Don't forget, I have half of your group still under guard in my armory."

Lane hesitated, teeth clenched, her gaze flicking back and forth between Burdock and her mother. She desperately wanted to talk to her.

"You have to accept the offer," her father said.

Lane nearly choked in disbelief. "You'd allow yourself to be taken? What if he's lying? What if he hurts you? Kills you?"

"I agree you can't trust him, but if you and Devon and the others are free, then you can figure out another way to take control."

"He'll have control of the gates," she countered. "We might have the run of the city, but we're essentially prisoners regardless."

"That's never stopped you before."

She shook her head. "He's going to try to get the upper hand the entire time."

"And you'll be doing the same. It's a stalemate."

He backed off slightly, some of his men close. They edged forward in concern and he began speaking to them heatedly.

Lane ground her teeth together, then asked Arrend, "What do you think?"

The proctor hesitated. "I think your mother has agreed to this in order to save you and the rest of the refugees. And that she's confident you can fix it."

Her father returned. "I've ordered my men to follow your lead, whatever you do."

She sucked in a steadying breath, then muttered, "Fine. Let's do this."

Stepping forward, all of Burdock's soldiers tensing at the movement, she said, "Pull all of your men out into the plaza. We'll follow. And tell them to release everyone from the armory as well."

"Captain Silleac, have everyone fall back." When Silleac didn't move, he said more forcefully, "Fall back."

With a grunt of disgust, Silleac motioned to his men, all of them edging away from the refugees. Lane's mother gave her a terse nod, then retreated with Burdock. Everyone waited until they'd left, then looked toward Lane.

"Grab whatever you can of what was left behind," Lane said, finally lowering her arm. "Then head outside. Maupin's and Arch's groups, guard everyone else as best you can."

They moved fast, gathering up the food and whatever medical supplies were lying about while Lane, Senn, Arrend, and a few of the others shifted to the door. Outside on the plaza, in the deepening dusk, Burdock was coordinating the release of the others from the armory, wagons already being herded onto the plaza, away from the gates. Torches were being lit, even though most of the lucent here in the plaza still appeared to work.

"Where are we going to go?" Lane asked as they watched. "I don't know this city."

"My men do. They'll find you and the others a place to hide. Most likely somewhere in the Burn, then maybe the Narrows after that."

"Why there?"

"Harder to track you in the Narrows. The streets are utter chaos. Half of them don't even have names."

"And then what?"

"Then you figure out how to get me, your mother, and the rest of Brovetto free."

Lane snorted.

As soon as the armory was empty, the refugees from there milling around the wagons, Lane and the others emerged from the barracks and joined them. She didn't see Devon or any of the others, but night was falling fast, the clouds overhead already a burnished orange-gold.

"Are you certain about this?" Lane asked as she, Senn, Arrend, and a few others faced Burdock, Silleac, her mother, and her escort. Their mage stood off to one side.

"I trust your mother. And I trust you."

Lane turned to one of her father's men, Vasill, his second in command. "Get them into the city. Make certain they're safe."

Vasill nodded and began calling out orders, the refugees behind breaking up into small groups and heading out into the streets that branched off from the plaza. He made certain some of the fighters remained behind though.

"I believe you owe us an insurrectionist," Burdock said, his eyes on the refugees already leaving.

"I'm right here."

Her father stepped forward and was seized immediately, led off to one side, near her mother.

"You took five others away with my mother," Lane said.

Burdock smiled. "Consider them additional collateral in our agreement, to keep the peace."

"That wasn't the agreement," her father spat.

"It is now."

Lane took a step forward, but Arrend caught her arm and she noted that their mage already had his hand raised, had already completed the base form.

"Go, Lane," her mother said. "We'll be fine."

Arrend pulled her back, the others falling in around her protectively. She resisted at first, then forced herself to break eye contact with her mother and stumbled along with them after the refugees.

* * *

As they were manhandled toward two waiting carriages, Senn muttered to Varenov, "This wasn't the plan once we were inside."

"That would never have worked. I had to improvise."

He glanced back to where Lane and the refugees had vanished into the outskirts of the city. "Let's hope she can pull them all together and save us."

"It doesn't matter what happens to us," Varenov said. "All that matters is her and Brovetto."

Chapter Three

"What do we do now?" Lane asked.

She stood at the burnt-out husk of a stone window, a slew of the refugees already moving in and cleaning up the detritus of the fire that had swept through the building—through this entire area, thus giving it the name the Burn. More of them could be seen in the streets outside in the patchwork of torches and moonlight, wagons pulling into cleared areas or halting in the middle of streets. Camps were being set up in the jagged remains of charred, collapsed brick walls and jagged shards of lucent, the buildings they'd been a part of destroyed.

She turned to face Arrend, Vasill, and the two men who'd apparently been assigned as her guards, and motioned to the destruction around them. "This is worse than the lower levels of Iandolo."

Before either of them could answer, Devon stumbled through the open doors of the trading house, Cerelle and Sadie behind him. As soon as he saw her, he rushed towards her.

"Where's Dalton?"

"Prefect Burdock has him," Lane said. "Along with Nic, Maupin, Picall, Arch, and my parents."

He gasped as if punched, but hardened immediately. "We have to get them."

Lane reached for him, found him trembling. She shot a glance at Cerelle, who merely said, "He shouldn't be moving around so much yet."

"I'm fine." Devon drew in a breath, then said again, more forcefully, "We have to get them."

"And we will, as soon as we figure out how. Right now, Burdock is using them as insurance, to keep us in check."

"Can't you—" Cerelle crooked her hand and waved it about.

"He didn't say so explicitly," Arrend said, "but the moment she tries, Burdock will likely kill everyone he has hold of."

"Then why did we let them take them?" Devon demanded.

"We didn't have a choice!" Lane snapped.

Arrend stepped forward, both hands raised. "We're all exhausted and stressed, from traveling the wayfare and the fact that we've had no sleep. We can't do anything about this tonight. I suggest we all find some place to rest and we'll deal with this in the morning."

"This wasn't the plan," Vasill said.

Lane and the others turned toward him. "What do you mean? What plan?"

Vasill fidgeted, glanced at the two guards, who shrugged. He sighed. "Senn didn't think we'd even make it through the gates—not without using force—but if we did, he thought we'd be arrested and held. His plan was to get Mouse out, have him round up as many of the old rebels in our group as he could find, and then have them break us out. He didn't expect them to start questioning us, or to pull some of us away from the others. It was supposed to be simple."

"Did my mother know of this plan?"

Vasill nodded. "She thought they'd take her away, but she was willing to sacrifice herself if the rest of us could get free."

"Of course she was," Lane said under her breath, but she focused on Vasill. "Where's Mouse now?"

He shrugged. "He hasn't reported back yet."

"Will he be able to find us?"

"Everyone in Brovetto will know where we are before dawn. If they aren't aware already."

"Right." Lane rubbed at her eyes with one hand, pinched the bridge of her nose. "Let me know as soon as you hear anything from Mouse."

"Of course."

"You should have just burned them all," Devon said, "before they had a chance to take any of us."

Lane shot him a glare, but the sharp retort on her lips died when she caught sight of the fear edging the anger on his face. Instead, she forced herself to take a deep breath and said, "You don't mean that. It's what Havvelan would have done. Or Favian."

At the proctor's name, Devon flinched, one hand involuntarily reaching toward his mangled ear. But Lane was heartened to see shame creep over his anger.

Arrend was right—they were exhausted. Burnt out. She could see it in everyone's faces.

Someone cleared their throat and she turned toward the sound, tensing, only to find two tullers standing off to one side, far enough away that Vasill's men hadn't shifted to halt them, but clearly wanting to approach. It took a moment for Lane to recognize them—Unsel and Vash, the tullers who'd helped them extricate some of Maupin's informants when the persecution of the Brovettans within Iandolo had begun. Unsel's hair was grayer now, his hazel eyes more drawn, and Lane would hazard there were more scars on his cheeks as well.

Vasill's two bodyguards shifted to block them, but Lane said, "It's all right. I know them."

Unsel stepped forward, Vash a few paces behind. Both gave her a deferential nod.

"What do you need, Unsel?"

He gave a strained smile. "That's what I came to ask you."

Lane's eyebrows rose.

"With both Maupin and Picall being held by the Iandolans…" he began, but trailed off, spreading his hands open with a shrug.

"It's fallen to us to take care of you," Vash finished.

Unsel gave her a dark look, but spoke to Lane. "If you need anything from the tullers, just ask."

"Thank you." She watched them retreat toward a far corner of the room, where a small group had already finished hollowing out their own space amongst the rubble. She recognized many of them, including Gillian, the Historian. Many of them had joined their group as they fled along the wayfare, ascending from the Flatlands up one of the numerous natural supports, bringing food from the tull.

"Lane."

She faced Devon, arms crossed. "What?"

"About Dalton—"

"We can't do anything about him or the others right now, Devon."

"I know, I just—" He raised a hand and she noticed how much it shuddered, realized that Devon wasn't trying to push her into action like before, that he wasn't angry, that he merely appeared…lost. "You don't understand," he said, his voice ragged. He wasn't even really looking at her. "In the towers, I thought he'd been captured, was convinced they were torturing him. I betrayed everything for him. Everyone. And they never had him." He finally met Lane's gaze. Behind him, Cerelle and Sadie traded looks. "But now, they *do* have him. I don't think I can take it."

She grabbed his shoulders, forced him to really look at her. "We will get him out. We'll get all of them. Do you hear me?"

He hesitated, then nodded.

"Here," Arrend said, suddenly appearing at their side carrying two steaming cups. He handed one to Devon and one to Lane. "Some tea. The tullers are a little more practiced at impromptu camps and already have some ready. Careful, it's hot." He ushered them closer to the window, where Vasill and the others had arranged some pallets. He settled them in, motioning Cerelle and Sadie closer as well with a look. "I'll be back with more for you."

As soon as Lane sat and took a sip, the extent of what had happened since that morning fell across her shoulders and back with an ominous weight. She sighed heavily, took another longer sip, breathed in the steam. It smelled of mint, the aroma tainted by the omnipresent scent of char from the ruins around them. "Mmm, it's delicious."

Arrend returned with cups for Cerelle, Sadie, and himself. He leaned in and muttered something to Cerelle, her slightly confused expression smoothing out before she urged a reluctant Sadie to sit beside Devon.

For a moment, all of them simply sat and drank in silence. Devon yawned, his tea already half gone, while Cerelle and Sadie merely sipped. Lane didn't think Arrend had touched his yet.

Lane scanned the room, noted Vasill and his guards had begun some sort of watch. All of the rest of those who'd claimed space within the building were already asleep or hunkered around small fires, conversing in low tones.

Her mind spun around again to her mother and father. "How are we going to get them out?" she muttered, frowning.

"I don't think that matters right now," Arrend said. "You—all of us—need to rest."

She turned to him, his words somehow muddled and distant.

And then her fingers started tingling.

She swore, holding her mostly empty cup out in front of her, and spat, "Gillian."

Arrend said something else, but she didn't catch it. Instead, Cerelle was there, catching her and her cup as her body sagged, laying her down on the pallet. As she tucked a blanket around her, Lane saw Sadie doing the same for Devon, the mathematician already asleep.

She tried to rouse some anger, but the tea took full hold and she felt herself slip away.

* * *

She woke with a jolt...and a mild headache. Her mouth felt dry and tasted foul, but the exhaustion had lifted. She sat up, worked a kink out of one shoulder, and glanced around.

Sunlight streamed through the window, revealing more char and soot than had been visible the night before when they'd arrived. It already stained nearly everyone's clothing. The camp was already bustling, people cleaning, cooking, mending, and repairing. Devon was still unconscious on his own pallet. Cerelle looked up from where she sat a few paces away, alone, needle and thread poised over rent cloth, and smiled. Only two of her father's men remained on guard.

Lane glared at Cerelle. "Don't ever do that to me again."

"Don't look at me. It was all Arrend."

Lane scoffed, then glanced at Devon. "Is he all right?"

"He will be. He got a heavier dose, from what Arrend tells me. He'll likely be out for a while."

"Where is everyone?"

Cerelle waved a hand. "Out and about. Vasill has taken control of Arch's men and they and your father's group are setting up watchers and patrols around our makeshift camp. He reported in a short while ago and said many of the Brovettans who were with us on the wayfare have already departed, searching out family and others they know in the city, but we still have a sizable contingent from Iandolo who don't have connections here. Everyone who stayed is still settling in. Unsel and Vash have taken it upon themselves—with the help of the tullers—to find food and water. They've already sent out scouting groups into the city, with a few of our mercenaries in each group, just in case."

Lane's eyes widened, then shot toward the window. "Already? How late is it?"

"Around the sixth bell."

Lane swore. The tea had kept her under longer than she'd thought.

She rubbed her temple. "And Arrend?"

"I wondered when you'd ask." She went back to her stitching, but nodded toward a far doorway, nothing more than an empty arch now. "Go see for yourself. He's back there with the rest of the proctors and students from the Lyceum."

Lane frowned, but rose and picked her way through the debris and scattered pallets and people who'd found refuge in the building, her two bodyguards following behind. Many of the people gave her a quick smile or nod as she passed. She was shocked at how much the interior had been cleaned since last night, only the largest of the debris still remaining, even most of the soot and char scrubbed away, at least from the areas in use. Stones had been used for firepits and impromptu seating, although most of it appeared to have been removed completely.

As soon as she reached the doorway, she heard the activity. Stepping through, she found the courtyard outside filled with people—or perhaps it had once been a large warehouse, with only low walls remaining on all sides. Arrend stood to one side, directing everyone as they moved and placed stones, building up and leveling off the walls. Another group was working on what was obviously going to be a communal oven, a distinctive dome already taking shape. One of the Humanities proctors from the Lyceum that had joined them was overseeing that project. And in a space cleared off to one side, another group of people were clearly practicing basic fighting maneuvers under Alan's watchful eye. Not all of those participating were from the college though; some were men and women from the caravan, of all ages. Lane picked out some Merchant, Arts, and Mage students as well.

"Alan's taking it a little too seriously, don't you think?"

Lane turned, surprised to find Jillian standing next to her, a board, papers, and stylus in one hand. Her bodyguards shrugged when she glanced at them; they must have recognized the Historian and let her approach. She sighed. "What's going on?"

"Proctor Arrend felt we all needed to keep busy and decided we should help with the rebuilding of the Burn, but also should take our studies back up as best we can. We've been 'slacking off' too long, what with the rebellion and fleeing for our lives and whatnot. So he divided us up into groups, proctors and students alike. Some of us are helping with the clean-up and construction. Others are training. Once Alan started working with his group, some of the others from the caravan asked if they could join in. After what happened at the gates with Prefect Burdock, no one is feeling particularly safe at the moment."

"That's because we aren't safe. Not really." Lane eyed Jillian. "And what are you doing?"

The Historian waved her papers and stylus. "What I was trained to do—record events as they happen."

Arrend noticed them and headed over. "I've got people working on the—"

"You drugged me."

Arrend took in her rigid stance, the arms crossed over her chest. "It was a simple sleeping draught."

"From Gillian?" At Arrend's nod, she said, "Gillian isn't the best at judging how much would be 'simple.' I know from experience."

"Both you and Devon needed it, Devon in particular. I could tell you'd both continue to push yourselves until you collapsed, and everyone here would have let you, because they're all exhausted and terrified themselves."

"Don't do it again."

"Of course not."

Lane didn't believe him, but she let her arms drop. "Where's Vasill? Cerelle said he was setting up a patrol?"

Arrend motioned toward one of the openings in the courtyard wall. "I'll let him explain. As I started to say, I've got people working on the ovens here, which I think should be a communal area..."

Lane listened as he explained the initial plans, but her focus was on the streets and the people as they headed into the area surrounding the husk of the merchantile where they'd settled last night. Wagons had been pulled to the side of the streets and people were busy clearing the roadway, stacking stone to one side. A few were already using the stone to shore up walls, some using mortar the color of soot to fix them in place. The numbers were thinner, as Cerelle had warned her, but not as much as she'd expected. The group had taken over essentially three square blocks and nine buildings, the most intact in the immediate area. Clotheslines had already been strung, horses stabled in what had once been a shop. She could smell roasting meat, although she wondered what it could be. Definitely not lizard.

Then she noticed Vasill ahead. Her father's second made a sharp gesture, her two bodyguards reacting instantly, pulling her, Arrend, and Jillian to a halt.

"He doesn't want you to approach," one of them said.

Vasill was already moving toward them. When he was close, he said, "In here," and drew them into one of the crumbling buildings on the side of the street.

"What's wrong?" Lane asked.

Vasill didn't answer immediately, leading them instead through the outlines of the inner rooms, over debris, toward a corner wall facing the cross-street they'd been approaching with the gaping hole of a window still in it. He halted a few paces away from it, to one side, took a quick look through the window, then grunted, facing them.

"I knew Burdock releasing us into the city was too good to be true. Take a look through the window, carefully, so you won't be seen."

Lane shifted forward, Arrend at her side, to where Vasill had stood a moment before. "What am I looking for?"

"Second building down, across the street, the one with part of the second floor still intact."

Lane found the building, made of brick, what used to be a tenement she guessed. The street sloped downwards here, so she could see into the windows of the second floor. She still wasn't used to how flat Brovetto appeared to her, with no towers reaching into the sky and everything located on individual levels.

"I don't see anyth—" Movement cut her off and she stilled, Arrend drawing in a sharp breath behind her. "Someone's there, in the building. At least two people."

"Burdock's soldiers," Vasill said, pulling them back, out of the line of sight. "We've found at least five other places where they've taken up position around the Burn, all fairly hidden. There are likely more."

"A guard," Arrend said.

Vasill nodded. "I've set up a patrol, our men clearly visible. But I've put a few hidden watchers of our own in place to keep an eye on these men. So far, they haven't done anything to the groups that have left to get food or those returning to their own families in Brovetto, which makes me think they're only interested in certain people from our camp."

"Like Lane."

"And Devon. Probably others. We don't know how well-informed they are about our leaders. They likely picked out some of us when we were held in the armory and barracks, but they could have gathered information from those they're holding as well."

Lane wanted to protest that none of them would reveal anything, but then thought of Devon and what he'd revealed under torture in the towers.

Vasill touched her shoulder to catch her attention. "You should stay near the center of the camp, keep yourself out of sight whenever possible." When she stiffened, he added, "Your father ordered me to keep you safe."

"I can't stay here forever, not if we're going to get the others out of Burdock's grip."

"We're already working on that."

"What does that mean?"

"It means that there are ways out of the Burn besides the streets."

Lane considered pressing him on the details, but decided to wait. "What about the rescue itself?"

"That hasn't been our top priority—"

"Why not?"

Vasill heaved a sigh of exasperation and rubbed his forward with the heel of one hand. Only then did Lane wonder if he'd taken a moment to rest himself last night. Based on the ragged edge to his voice and the bruising beneath his eyes, she'd wager not.

"Listen," he said, hands raised toward her, "I know it's your father and mother being held—and who knows what the others mean to you—but we haven't even been here a day yet. Even without the watchers, people are going to notice any movements we make in the city, and word will get back to Burdock. With the watchers…well, we're going to need to be discreet. But this is our city and we know its secrets. Most of them. Even then, nothing is going to happen overnight. Once Mouse returns and we know more about what our resources are here, then we'll be able to plan."

Lane restrained herself from her first response, but before she could form a second, she heard someone climbing the debris from behind. All of the rebels tensed, her two guards stepping to flank the low walls around the door into the back room. Vasill moved a step in front of her, a knife appearing in his hand. Arrend and Jillian backed out of the way.

Then Cerelle stumbled into the entrance, catching herself on the remains of the doorway with a curse. The guards relaxed as her gaze settled on Lane.

"There's someone from the city here to speak to you," she said.

"Burdock?"

"No, not from the Iandolan army, from the city of Brovetto itself."

* * *

When they entered the gutted merchantile hall again—they needed to come up with something else to call it, Lane thought—she found a delegation of four people waiting for her, led by a woman with a hard Brovettan face tanned by work in the harsh sun. She carried herself stiffly, her gaze angry, although she was dressed in meager clothes. Her eyes were a steel gray, the planes of her face edged.

She stepped forward the moment she saw Lane.

"What do you think you're doing here?" she asked.

"Trying to survive."

The curt answer brought the woman up short. She glowered as Lane moved to where someone had arranged some of the larger debris into a seating area, almost like the Council chambers back in Iandolo, but on a much smaller—and rougher—scale. She frowned as Cerelle tugged her toward the central seat, facing an array of stone blocks. Lane resisted, but Cerelle gave her a look and prodded her into position, Arrend arriving with tea. He smirked at her raised eyebrow but said nothing. Her bodyguards took position to either side of her, standing, but she gestured both Cerelle and Arrend toward stones nearby. As the delegation settled into the seats before her, the woman holding back at first, finally giving in at a soft word from one of the others, Lane shot a glance toward the back of the hall where Devon still slept.

"No help from that quarter," she muttered to herself, then faced the Brovettan woman seated before her. "Who are you?" The words came out harsher than she'd intended and the woman stiffened.

"My name is Maureen Turing and I've come to find out your intentions here in Brovetto."

"No, you've come to tell us what we can and cannot do here in Brovetto when we haven't even been here a full day yet."

Maureen's companions fidgeted at the bluntness, but Maureen didn't react.

Lane leaned slightly forward. "Are you the governor?"

"Not officially."

"So you hold no true power here."

Maureen's chin lifted. "The people of Brovetto—the *true* citizens—follow my lead."

"And what have you told them to do?"

"Nothing. I've told them to do nothing. Those of us who have lived here for years have suffered under the hands of the 'Brovettan government,' nothing but a pawn of the Iandolan Council, for decades. That in and of itself was harsh, but tolerable. Then the rebellion started and things got worse. Fighting in the streets. Assassinations. It brought the mages and the Iandolan army down upon us. When they left, I thought the worst was over. For a while, it seemed true. But then those the Iandolans had left in control here decided they could seize control of Iandolo itself and that brought the wrath of the Council in all its strength down on us. The purge of the government here, of the city…" Her voice caught and she struggled for a brief moment before regaining control. "It was bloody and it was brutal, but it was cleansing. When the Iandolan army left, leaving Burdock in charge, all of us were terrified of what would happen next. But Burdock surprised us. He stabilized the city, used his garrison to help rebuild key sections, repaired the water supply. He's kept his soldiers in check, kept them from harassing us. He's allowed us to regroup and begin to move on."

"And you don't want us to mess that up."

Now Maureen shifted forward. "You don't know what we've been through for the past year, for the past twenty years! This is the most stable, most peaceful, the city has been in decades, including those years after Councilor Orland was killed. The streets may have been quiet then, but tensions were still high. We like this new arrangement beneath Burdock. People are beginning to hope again, beginning to live again."

"Even though it's beneath Iandolo's heel?" Arrend asked. "Burdock is essentially your governor now. The Council hasn't even set up the pretense of a government for you. There is only you and the Iandolan army."

"Better that than the corrupt and ambitious government we had before Arctus and his army arrived."

Arrend shook his head.

"You're wrong though," Cerelle said into the silence, surprising Lane. "Have you not spoken to any of the refugees from Iandolo once they've arrived? We do know what you've suffered over the years. Or at least we've had a taste. Brovettans in Iridesque were never treated equally, but after the Warding attack..." Cerelle pressed her lips together, then waved a hand. "Why do you think we're all here?"

Maureen remained silent, eyes on Cerelle, but the other three refused to look at any of them. Which meant they *had* spoken to some of the refugees, heard the horror stories, and still they were here, speaking to Lane.

She sighed. "You asked what our intentions are. When we left Iandolo, our only intention was to escape, Brovetto our only chance. Even outside the waygates, we were only looking to survive. But then Burdock took several of us prisoner."

Maureen nodded. "We heard."

"Then you should know that we intend to get them back. After that...I don't know what we'll do. Most of those with us only want some peace, like you."

"You can't stay here," one of the men with Maureen said. "Maureen, tell them—"

Maureen raised her hand and the man fell silent. "I understand why you came here and that you'll need to stay long enough to get those Burdock has taken back, but Connor is right. You can't stay after that."

Lane drew breath to protest, but Maureen forestalled her with a look.

"As you say, we have spoken to the refugees as they've arrived and they've told us enough stories about those last few days and weeks within Iandolo to know that the Council will not simply let all of you go. Especially you, Lane Illea, daughter of Councilor Varenov and, more importantly, rogue mage. Every moment that you remain here brings Iandolo and its army closer. They will hunt you down. I don't want you in Brovetto when they do."

She stood, those with her hastily following suit. Lane waited until they had reached the door to the makeshift hall before saying, "No matter what Burdock has done up until now, he is still Iandolan. Eventually, he will turn on you in favor of Iridesque. That is where his loyalty remains."

Maureen paused to listen, but did not turn back before exiting.

"We can't leave," Cerelle said immediately. "Many of those with us won't be able to survive another journey along the wayfare like that. And besides—"

"Where would we go?" Arrend cut in.

"But you know she's right," Lane said. "Havvelan won't let us go. As soon as he frees the waygate to Luminesque, he'll be coming for us. I just don't think it's going to matter much to him whether we're here when he arrives or not." She let the words settle for a moment, then faced Arrend. "As for where we could go, there are two other wayfares out of Luminesque—one to Radimansque and the other to Scintillesque. And there's the Flatlands. There are options. But for the moment, at least, we have a reprieve. They aren't going to force us to leave until we have the others back."

"They shouldn't be able to force us to leave in the first place," one of the guards muttered, but they dropped their gaze when Lane stared at them with a frown.

A low groan came from behind them and Lane spun to see Devon pushing up from where he'd slept, one hand rising to his head. "What happened?" he croaked out, his voice nothing but gravel.

"Cerelle, get some water," Lane said. She was already halfway to Devon's side, kneeling down beside him in the next breath.

He blinked up at her, scrubbed at his eyes. "Lane? I feel awful. My head is pounding."

Lane glared up at Arrend, who'd come up behind her. "I told you Gillian isn't good with dosage."

Cerelle arrived with a pitcher, water sloshing from the rim as she poured a cup. She handed it to Lane while Arrend helped Devon straighten into a seated position.

"Drink this." She held the cup, even though Devon raised his hands to hold it as he drank. He took a sip, then began to gulp it, enough that Lane pulled it back and told him to slow down. The more he moved, the more stable he became, and Lane was forced to grudgingly admit that he looked better—less exhausted, skin flushed instead of wane. The tremble in his arms and hands had faded.

After a moment, he pushed the cup back and wiped his mouth. "I'm good. Even the headache is fading."

"Dehydration, most likely," Arrend said.

Lane rolled her eyes, but focused on Devon. "You've been asleep for most of the day, Devon."

"Really?" He glanced at Cerelle, at Arrend, at the guardsmen and the others within the hall, still groggy, but then he remembered, his gaze latching back onto Lane as his eyes widened and his hands clutched at her. "Dalton! We have to get Dalton back."

"We don't even know where he's being held yet."

"I do."

Everyone turned at the voice to see a short, thin man, barely over five feet tall, standing a few steps behind Lane's bodyguards, smiling. Both of them startled—one swore—as if they hadn't known the man was there.

"Oskar Standish, but everyone calls me Mouse." He gave an ostentatious bow. "I found them. I found them all."

Chapter Four

"He's keeping them in the governor's mansion," Mouse said.

"In the cellars?" one of Vasill's men asked.

"No, in the state rooms."

"That doesn't make any sense," Vasill said.

All of those gathered—Vasill and few of his men, Unsel and Vash, Arrend, Cerelle and Sadie, Devon, and of course Lane herself—contemplated in silence for a moment.

"No," Lane said, "it makes perfect sense. How many men does he have here in Brovetto?"

"Maybe five hundred soldiers, about the same for support staff."

"Not that many soldiers, really. Some will be on rotation on the gates—remember there are three of them. He's got some keeping an eye on us here, then there are those patrolling the city. He's not going to be using the Brovettan guardsmen for that. Which means he has few men remaining for any other type of duty. Certainly not enough to police a cell block in one of the city prisons, or any other building for that matter. He'd have to keep the prisoners close, so everything's centralized, which means the governor's mansion, where he's set up his base of operations."

"She's right," Mouse said. "As far as I can tell, the Iandolan army has only seized control of the barracks and armories surrounding the three gates and the governmental buildings on the Fifth Level. He's left all of the other buildings to the city patrols."

"Then we're going to have to find a way into the governor's mansion," Devon said.

Vasill stirred. "Senn had all of us scout out various ways into and out of the Fifth Level. He knew we might need access at some point. The problem is none of us have checked them out since Prefect Arctus came with the army for the purge. I don't know how many of those access points have been compromised."

"How did you get in?" Unsel asked Mouse.

The man gave a crooked smile and shrugged. "Through the main gates."

"I don't know how he does it," Vasill said, "but we can't sneak a group of us, even a small group, through the main gates." He glanced at Lane. "Especially you. And I assume you're going to demand to be part of the group."

"Along with me," Devon said.

Vasill nodded without comment. "Then we need another way in." He glanced at some of his men. "We'll need a few days at least to scout out a route. And to find a way to get you, Lane, out of the Burn without Burdock's watchers noticing. Until then, you should stay out of sight."

"No, I don't think so. I think I should do the opposite." At his surprised look, she added, "I should make certain they see me everywhere. Make them think I'm going to stay within the Burn, follow Burdock's rules. Make the guards relax."

"Very well." Vasill turned to Mouse. "How much of our old network is left?"

"Almost nothing. Prefect Arctus was thorough."

Vasill grimaced. "Then we'll have to do this ourselves. Mouse, grab a half dozen men and find a way into the Fifth Level. Arctus couldn't have rooted out all of our old routes."

The escape artist motioned to two of the men flanking Vasill and all three left, Mouse snagging a few more men on the way out.

Then Vasill faced Lane. "I'm going to double your guard. If you're going to be roaming the Burn, I want you protected."

"And what will you be doing?" Lane asked as he stood.

"I'm going to find us an unobtrusive way out of the Burn."

* * *

Varenov started when the lock clicked in the door, the sound sharp in the relative silence of the room where she was being held. She tensed as the door swung open and Prefect Burdock strode in, stepping to one side as a flurry of guards entered behind him with a small table, two chairs, and dinner settings for two, including tapered candles.

Varenov raised an eyebrow at the Prefect.

"I trust the accommodations are acceptable?" Burdock asked.

Varenov glanced around the room. It contained a bed—not a cot or a pallet, but an actual bed with blankets and pillows—along with a desk, chair, armoire with nothing in it, a dresser with a vase of water and a basin for washing, and the small settee where she currently sat. The desk contained paper, a quill with ink, and a small arrangement of flowers. "Sparse, but not spartan." She returned her gaze to Burdock. "Certainly more than I expected in terms of a cell. Are the others being held in similar rooms?"

Burdock drifted toward the glass doors that looked out onto a balcony and a view of the city beneath. "Perhaps not quite so large, but definitely not what most would consider a cell."

"Havvelan and Arctus would be appalled."

Burdock faced her. "Were you not kept in the towers when you were captured?"

Varenov snorted a laugh. "We were kept in the towers, yes, but Havvelan saw fit to have some of the rooms…modified."

"But you were a councilor."

"To Havvelan, as soon as I 'betrayed' the Council, I was no longer a councilor. He wanted to make certain I knew that." She thought about how they'd found Devon, along with some of the other rooms they'd opened in that hallway. "Although what I endured there was nothing compared to some others."

Burdock frowned, but his attention was caught by those setting up the table behind them. "Would you join me for dinner?"

Those at the table lifted the domes from the assorted plates and the aroma of seared meat and spices filled the room. Varenov's stomach clenched, then growled. He mouth flooded with saliva. She swallowed it down and said faintly, "I haven't had real meat since we fled Iandolo. Since before that actually. Havvelan's service in the cells wasn't this…generous."

Burdock moved to pull one of the chairs out, gestured to it with one hand. "Have a seat."

Before Varenov could move, he shifted to the other chair and sat. One of the guards poured two glasses of wine. Burdock picked up a knife and fork, began to cut into his steak.

"It's not a trick, Varenov," he said, before taking a bite and chewing. "Eat. I apologize for the portions. We are on rather strict rations here in Brovetto."

Varenov rose slowly. Burdock continued to eat as she settled into her own chair. She watched him for a moment, then reached for the wine, taking a sip, before picking up her own utensils. The knife was sharp and she twirled it thoughtfully in her fingers before beginning to cut. There were numerous guards outside the door and she knew nothing about wielding a knife aside from eating.

The portion was small, she realized. Perhaps only three bites. But there were roasted carrots and some kind of cream sauce drizzled over it all. She couldn't remember tasting anything so delicate.

After a few bites followed by chewing in silence, she rested her wrists on the edge of the table. "What is the meaning of all of this?"

"All of what?" Burdock motioned for more wine.

"All of…this," Varenov said in exasperation, her gesture taking in the room, the food. "This is not how the Iandolan army or the Council treats prisoners. At least not the current Council."

"You forget that we are in Luminesque. The Council has left me in charge here."

"You're still beholden to Prefect Arctus and the Iandolan army."

Burdock remained silent, slicing the carrots on his plate, but not eating them. Finally, he placed the knife and fork aside, leaning his elbows on the table, hands clasped before him. "You're right. But in the last day or so since your arrival, we've been questioning not just your companions but some of the other refugees as well. It's become clear that the reports we've been getting from Iandolo and the Council since Prefect Arctus left me in charge here have been…"

"Lies?"

"Less than forthcoming. For example, your imprisonment in the towers. The reports merely stated that the Council had declared you a traitor, that you'd been apprehended, and were being held in the towers until you could be executed."

"All of which was true."

"But lacking details. Especially considering the importance of the charges. There was no mention of what you'd done that had forced them to declare you a traitor. When Prefect Arctus left with my unit as part of his army, you were still a member of the Council in good standing as far as I knew. A contentious member, but nothing hinting at traitorous."

"Quite a bit happened in Iandolo after you left."

"So I've determined. I have the Council's version of events, at least up to a point. I'd like to hear your version."

"Even if it's nothing but traitorous lies?"

"Indulge me."

Varenov stared at him over the table, trying to judge his sincerity. He was frustratingly hard to read. Was he toying with her? She had no evidence the others weren't being tortured even now, that they were even alive. Look at how they'd lied and manipulated Devon in order to get information from him.

But in the end, it didn't matter. She wanted to tell him. Having him hear the truth of what had happened in Iandolo couldn't make their situation here any worse.

"Very well," she said, setting her own knife and fork aside. "It began with random attacks on our Brovettan citizens living within Iandolo. Attacks that I suspected were being orchestrated..."

* * *

Devon jerked out of sleep with a cry, hand reaching for his mangled ear before he even became aware of the hall around him. A few fires burned in the tuller camp, laughter and low conversation drifting toward him as figures moved in the dark. The night sky opened like a void overhead, outside the tarp they'd erected over their end of the hall, scattered with stars. He stared up at them, his heart calming, until his hand dropped from his ear.

"Nightmare?"

He gasped and spun toward Cerelle, sitting in the dark a few pallets away. Sadie gave him a nod of acknowledgment from the space on Cerelle's other side before rolling onto her side, back to him.

"What was it this time?" Cerelle asked. "The towers?"

"No. Yes." Devon pulled himself into a seated position, half facing Cerelle. "It was about Dalton. What they might be doing to Dalton."

"And what were they doing to Dalton? In your dream."

Devon hesitated, the vestiges of the dream coming back with sick clarity. "They had him laid out on a table, tied down with thick ropes. His bare chest was riddled with lacerations, crusted with blood, skin flushed with fever and infection. His hands were mangled, fingers broken. They'd pulled out his fingernails, the skin beneath raw and angry. He was sobbing, trembling. When a figure stepped forward bearing an iron glowing white-hot, he began to thrash and screamed, 'What do you want? What do you want? Ask me anything!' But the figure—I don't know who it was, I couldn't see—said nothing. They hadn't asked Dalton anything, not since the start. It had only been pain heaped atop pain. The figure leaned forward with the iron, raised it to Dalton's face, close enough he could feel the heat, and then they pressed it against his ear—"

Devon sucked in a hitched breath, clenched his eyes closed until he'd calmed himself.

"That was it. That's when I woke up."

Cerelle shifted position. "That's progress then."

"What do you mean?"

Cerelle shrugged. "You spent most of the trek along the wayfare dreaming of what had been done to you by Havvelan and Favian in the towers. Even when those nightmares began to fade, you replaced them with recriminations for what you'd revealed under torture. But now you're afraid for Dalton. It isn't about you anymore."

"And that's progress?"

"Yes, it is."

Devon stood abruptly. "Where's Lane?"

"One of the new walls collapsed. She went to see if she could help. A couple of the refugees were injured."

He hesitated only a moment. There was no way he was going to get back to sleep. "I'm going to go find her." He reached for his satchel, the one carrying only essentials. Cerelle stood as well, dusting herself off with a curse about grit and soot collecting everywhere.

"Where are you going?" Devon asked.

"With you, of course. Lane isn't the only one who warrants an escort here."

He frowned but didn't protest.

They made their way through the hall, Unsel waving as they passed by, Vash giving a nod toward Cerelle.

Outside, the courtyard was empty except for a few souls sleeping near the communal oven. Devon moved into the street, tension thrumming through his body. For the past five days, he'd followed Lane and Arrend around as she surveyed all of the activity going on in the Burn. They'd visited the communal oven to check on its progress, the rounded kiln nearing completion. The walls surrounding it had been shored up and leveled off and those workers had moved on to other buildings and repair work. Training of the Lyceum students had continued in the courtyard as well, Alan working with the War students and anyone else who wanted to learn basic fighting skills. Lane had worked with some of the mage students, all young enough they were still working on basic forms, nowhere near the point where she could begin teaching them Devon's double pyramid version of the mage structure. They'd roamed the streets, greeted the refugees that had decided to stay with them, commented on the stone houses they'd restored or begun to build from scratch. One entire square had been sectioned off for gardens on one side, a makeshift marketplace on the other. On the fourth day, a few vendors from the city had ventured into the Burn with their wagons—a tinker, another selling produce. Lane had made certain to converse with them all, and to wander the streets where Burdock's men were watching, although she never stayed long.

The entire time, Devon could think of nothing but Dalton and Nic and the others, imprisoned as he had been imprisoned in the towers of Iridesque. He'd helped with the rebuilding occasionally, moving stones, clearing debris, but mostly he'd fretted and stewed.

He needed to move, to take action, do *something*. He'd been stagnant for nearly a week since Dalton was captured and the raw, contained anxiety was twitching in his arms and fingers.

"Where did the wall collapse?" he asked.

"I didn't hear, but if there were injuries…"

"The hospital."

He started toward the building they'd set aside for Mindell, his daughter, and any of the Humanities students that had come with them. Tents had been erected inside the arched doors where they'd been able to clear away the rubble. Activity outside one of them led them to the left. They found two of Lane's guards outside. As soon as they recognized Devon and Cerelle, they stepped aside and motioned them in.

Mindell stood next to the bed, hands hovering over the arm of a young girl who lay unconscious, his eyes closed. The arm was bruised and swollen. Another patient, a man, lay on a second bed on the other side, head bandaged, although a trickle of blood had seeped out from beneath it and run down to the corner of his eye. Lane stood behind Mindell with the other two guards.

Devon took a step forward. "Lane—"

She shot him a glare and he fell silent, focused on Mindell instead.

The healer drew in a slow breath, then exhaled, his hands dropping to his side. He blinked, registering Devon and Cerelle's presence with a frown, then said, "It's not broken, merely bruised. She was lucky. I'll do what I can, but it will still take a few days before the swelling will begin to subside. Her father on the other hand—" He shifted away from the girl to the man with the bandaged head. "—he took a pretty hard blow to the head from one of the stones. That kind of trauma is harder to handle. We'll have to see if he's got a concussion once he comes around again. I don't dare do anything until then except dress the wound."

"Do what you can, Mindell."

Lane turned and motioned everyone except the healer out of the tent. Once outside, Lane rubbed her eyes and pinched her nose. Even in the light of the torches and lanterns that lined the rows of tents, he could see the bruising beneath her eyes, the tension at the corners. He realized that he may have been following her around these last few days, but he hadn't been paying any attention to her, hadn't noticed whether she was sleeping or not, whether she was eating or not. He hadn't been paying attention to anyone since…since Iandolo, since he'd been captured. Even on the wayfare, when everyone had been suffering, and here.

He glanced at Cerelle, who's brow furrowed in confusion. When he said, "Progress," she nodded as if she understood.

"Were those the only two hurt?" Cerelle asked Lane.

"No, but the others weren't as serious. None of them were brought to the hospital."

"You look exhausted," Devon said. "Maybe we should return to the hall, try to get some sleep."

Lane gave him a weak smile. "The only reason I came out to check on them was because I wasn't sleeping when the news arrived. I doubt I can sleep now."

"What if I asked Gillian for some tea?"

Lane's look was blistering, but cracked into a weary chuckle at Cerelle's smile. "It's reaching the point I might have to take you up on that offer."

Before any of them could make moves toward the hall though, Vasill appeared in the arched door, flanked by two of his men.

"There you are." He scanned all of those nearby, then took a step closer and lowered his voice. "I think we've found an alternate way out of the Burn."

* * *

"We've been ignoring it since we arrived," Vasill said as he led Devon, Lane, and the rest through the darkened street, back toward the hall but angled slightly away. "Mostly because the cistern is dry, so what use could it be? But then one of my men asked what was down there when we passed by it. We decided to take a look."

"A cistern?" Lane asked.

"You've seen them in Iandolo. The large circular basins that capture rainwater for the city's use?"

"I know what a cistern is, Vasill. I'm just not certain how it's going to help us get out of the Burn undetected."

"I was skeptical as well, but wait until you see it." He'd begun to slow, then motioned toward his guardsmen carrying the torches, who promptly smothered them. Night folded in upon them as they halted to let their eyes adjust. "The cistern here is close to the edge of the area we've claimed. Burdock has watchers posted near enough I don't want to use any lights. It might draw their attention."

Devon glanced back toward the heart of their claimed section of the Burn, surprised at how easy it was to pick out the halls and homes and camps of the refugees by the flickering fires and illuminated windows and doors, especially with the rest of the Burn surrounding them a flat black. The silhouette of a figure or two passed in front a few of the fires as he watched.

Then he turned his back to the lights, focused on the darkened street before them, blinking to take away the afterimages of the fires from his eyes.

"Everyone able to see?" Vasill asked and, when no one answered, he stepped forward, moving slower now. "This way."

They crept down the street, the debris underfoot making the trek treacherous. No one had set up near this section, since there was nothing much left of the buildings except mounds of stone. Until they reached the next intersection and the rounded stone wall of the cistern emerged from behind the rubble.

It rose to about ten feet high, the sides smooth, although there were sections where the stone had flaked away or where chunks had broken free. Vasill led them around its side until steps appeared, spiraling up to the top, where they discovered that the wall of the cistern was nearly ten feet thick. Debris lined the rim. Devon accidentally kicked a chunk of stone that skittered to the inner edge and vanished over the side into the pitch-black depths below. He moved up to listen to it fall but heard nothing.

Cerelle tugged at his sleeve. Vasill had begun to circle around to the right. Beyond him, the levels of Brovetto rose, each marked by graduated levels of light. On their level, to either side of the Burn, there was the yellow-orange of flames, sparse and scattered. On the next two levels, the islands of light were closer together, but by the fourth there were a few signs of lucent. Only on the Fifth Level was the lucent prevalent.

It was the first time Devon had noticed how much smaller Brovetto was than Iandolo. Not only were there fewer levels, with those levels wider and farther apart, but the city was maybe only a fifth of the size. It felt tiny, almost insignificant.

No wonder those from the outer cities entered Iandolo with such awe. And no wonder those that came ended up feeling lost.

Vasill suddenly knelt and pointed to a set of steps leading down into the cistern on the inside wall in a spiral, like those on the outside, but these were narrower and vanished into obscurity twenty feet down. "It descends for approximately fifty feet. Use the wall for support. There are no railings."

Then he led the way, the rest of them trailing behind, Devon following Cerelle, a couple of the guards behind him. The deeper they descended, the less light they had, until Devon was feeling his way forward more with his hands and feet than with his eyes. Those in front of him became nothing but an occasional flicker of movement, and then only scuffs of sound. His chest tightened and he began to sweat, the darkness reminding him of the room Favian and Havvelan had kept him in within the towers. When they weren't there, there'd been no lucent, no flame. He'd been kept in utter darkness. He fought to control his breath, which had quickened, to steady his heart, but when he bumped into Cerelle at the bottom of the steps he nearly screamed.

"Can we light a torch?" Lane asked from the void ahead. "Are we deep enough?"

"It's safer not to just yet," Vasill asked.

"What about my lucent?" Without waiting for a response, Devon pulled his satchel from his side, began rooting around inside. He shoved aside papers, an ink bottle, until his fingers brushed up against the crystal lantern. "I've got it."

"Try it out, but shield it as much as you can."

Devon cupped his hands around it to block the light as much as possible, then flicked it on.

It sputtered, almost exactly like a candle, then steadied, but Devon frowned. "That's not as bright as it usually is." He glanced up at Lane, her and the others visible in the greenish light, their faces washed out and blurred.

"I thought you were dimming it somehow," Lane said.

"No."

"It's for the best," Vasill said, already turning away. "No one should be able to see that from above. There's a tunnel—or rather, what was a pipe for the water—over here."

As they moved around the edge of the bottom of the cistern, lines of lucent within the walls of stone reflected the thin light from the lantern. Devon traced some of the veins with his fingers and, when they reached the tunnel and paused, pushed himself into it. It was all dead, although not due to any flaws in the threads that he touched here. There was something damaged farther down the line, down the tunnel Vasill was leaning into.

"Where does it come out?" Lane asked, moving up beside Vasill.

"There are a couple options—"

"Show me."

The two faced off against each other, until Vasill shook his head and muttered, "Just like your father," under his breath. "Follow me."

They entered the tunnel, forced to hunch down since the rounded pipe was only five feet in diameter. The curved bottom was just uneven enough that Devon had to brace himself with one hand as they edged forward. In the tight confines, the lantern threw long shadows ahead and behind and any sounds echoed both forward and back. All along the pipe, Devon's hand brushed against lucent, a faint tingle spreading through his fingers at each touch. He'd expected the cistern and pipe to be dank, to smell of water and possibly mold, but instead the walls were dry and gritty, some kind of mineral deposit flaking off in his hands and crunching beneath his feet.

They reached a junction, Vasill turning left. The descent into the cistern had completely disoriented Devon, so he had no idea which direction they were heading now. The tunnel continued, widening slightly. After what felt like hours, broken only by a few hissed questions from Lane and blunt answers from Vasill, they reached a small room, this time with three other pipes leading away in various directions.

As they all spread out and straightened up, Vasill pointed to the three pipes. "The one on the right goes up to the next level. That one takes you farther around this level and the other leads to another empty cistern outside of the Burn."

"Up," Lane and Devon said together.

They headed right, Devon positioning himself behind Vasill and Lane this time. They wove through some type of massive hydraulic system built of chambers and doors and pumps and lucent. Again, most of the lucent Devon checked was dead but undamaged. The pipe began to climb after that, the floor becoming a series of steps, until it ended in a massive sealed door.

"Can we get it open?" Lane asked as Devon edged past her, placing his hand on the lucent embedded in the door. As soon as he touched it, it burst into life, blue light threading around the door and into the walls on either side. The metal of the door was cold and vibrated beneath his palm.

"I don't think we want to do that," he said, closing his eyes as he felt his way through the lucent. Lines shot out in all direction except down into the tunnel they were in, as if something were blocking it, although again he sensed no damage. He focused on the sections where the lucent from below merged with the active lucent here.

"Why is that, Devon?" Cerelle asked.

He opened his eyes, pulling his hand away from the door. "Because there's water on the far side, probably enough to flood this entire tunnel and kill us all."

Lane faced Vasill. "Then how are we supposed to get out?"

Vasill pointed up.

A vertical shaft drove straight upwards, the rungs of a ladder protruding from one side.

They ascended, reaching a trapdoor at the same time Devon's arms began to ache from the exertion. He shouldn't have been trembling yet—he'd climbed hundreds of such ladders in Iandolo—but he hadn't been doing much of anything since being captured. And who knew how long it would take to recuperate from the stress his body had endured beneath Favian and Havvelan's hands.

They emerged inside a small room filled with pipes and valves, some of it clearly damaged. Panels were embedded in a few of the walls, pathways of lucent snaking out from central nodes. Some of the lucent was cracked, several of the buttons missing.

Vasill and Lane headed for the door in the far stone wall; Devon moved toward the panel.

"Careful," Vasill said as Lane grabbed the door handle. "It's night, but we're on the Second Level now. There are more people here."

Devon ran his hand across the panel, touched the lucent. Some of the threads that were whole were still active, in various shades of blue, green, and purple. Most in the bottom half of the panel were dead or damaged. An entire section of one pathway had been pried free; he could see the scarring where whoever had taken it had scraped their prybar against the metal to get beneath it.

He followed a few of the pathways that were active. The blue one led down to the door containing the water below.

"Devon, come look at this," Lane said, catching his attention.

He pulled free from the lucent and moved to where Vasill and Lane had the door cracked open. A few of the guards moved aside, while Cerelle came up behind him so she could peer over his shoulder. Lane took the lantern from him and shifted to one side so it wouldn't be seen through the door.

It opened onto a wide square, an inactive fountain at the center, the stone statue there depicting a flock of rising birds. Stalls and carts lined the square on the two sides Devon could see, flaps pulled down and tarps tied tight for the night. A few guards—or the owners themselves—slept on pallets and one stall still had a regular lantern lit inside, chinks of flame visible through the cracks in the wood and the edges of the cloth awnings. Buildings rose up behind the stalls and carts—what looked like tenements—and the third side opened up onto a street.

Devon risked ducking his head outside to check to either side of the building they were in, Vasill muttering a curse beneath his breath before Cerelle snatch at his shirt and pulled him back inside.

"We're inside a small stone building that appears to take up this entire side of the square. I didn't see anyone set up on this side though. Anyone exiting from this door is going to be conspicuous."

"Unless the square is full of customers," Vasill said. "We've watched this door for the last few days. Peak activity is around midday, where the square can get crowded. Unfortunately, there are also city patrol watching the streets, even at night." He gave Devon a warning look.

"So we can get out here, if we're careful."

"A few of the other tunnels are possibilities as well, but none of them get us this close to the Fifth Level. We're on the steepest side of the plateau Brovetto is built on. The levels rise quickly here. If Mouse can find us a way in somewhere near here, even a few levels up, we won't be exposed for long."

Lane contemplated the door, then Devon, before returning her attention to Vasill. "Then all we're waiting for now is Mouse."

"He said he was going to check in tonight."

"Then we'd better be there when he arrives."

Lane turned toward the door that led down into the tunnels, but Devon forestalled her with a "Wait," and a hand on her arm. He motioned her toward the panel. "You need to take a look at this."

"What is it?"

"As far as I can tell, it's a map of the water system that provides the city with water. This path here is what we used to climb up to this level. This blue line leads to the door we discovered below with the water behind it."

Lane scanned the panel more intently. "I'm not seeing whatever it is you're seeing."

"The cisterns we've found on Level One are all dry. In fact, the entire level is dry, along with parts of Level Two. The few people that are surviving there, including us, are using basins and barrels and other sources to collect rain water for drinking and cooking and watering gardens and such. Some are even trekking into the upper levels to fill buckets and water sacks to bring back down."

"And?"

Devon waved at the grid in frustration. "I don't understand why there isn't water in the lower level already."

Lane pointed to the missing section of lucent on the panel. "Clearly there's been some damage to the system."

"But that only affects this one set of tunnels, this section of the lower level. There's no damage to these sections here and here that I can see. There should be water running to those parts of the city. Their cisterns should be full. But they're not."

Lane frowned, gaze flitting over the pathways once again, this time with purpose, before shooting back toward Devon. "You're saying the water to the lower levels was turned off on purpose."

"It wasn't because of damage. I'd wager that all of this happened *after* the water was cut off."

"Burdock?"

"No," Vasill said, stepping forward. Devon had forgotten the rest of them were there. "The water in the lower levels stopped long before Burdock. Before even Prefect Arctus arrived for his purge of the government and the rebels."

"How long ago?"

Vasill glanced at his fellow rebel guards, then shrugged. "Maybe ten years ago. We were told that the lucent powering the system had been damaged and that in order to preserve what we could, the lower level would have to be abandoned. You're saying that's not true?"

"Not based on what I saw of the lucent on our way up here."

Vasill swore, pacing away from them, staring into the darkness of one corner a long moment before turning back, his jaw clenched. "It must have been a way to manipulate us, to get the people of Brovetto into the upper levels."

"But why?" Cerelle asked.

"Control," Lane said. "Isn't it always about control?"

"It significantly restricted our food supply," Vasill said. "Most of our largest fields were in the lower level. The years following the abandonment were disastrous. Thousands starved. Based on what I've seen of the city in the last few days, it's still having an effect."

"And confined to fewer levels, you'd be easier to patrol. If they were trying to root you out…" Devon let the thought hang in the angry silence.

Lane faced him. "Can you fix it?"

"I can probably remove the blocks to the cisterns in the lower levels right now, but it would flood our route up here. As for the destroyed lucent—" Devon shrugged. "I'd have to find pieces of lucent large enough to replace what's missing. The pieces that are fractured should be easy to repair."

"What do you mean 'repair'?" Vasill asked.

"We need to get back to the hall," Lane said, already moving toward the door to the tunnel. "In case Mouse returns."

Vasill hesitated, looking back and forth between Devon and Lane's back as she ducked into the tunnel, then muttered something under his breath and followed her.

Chapter Five

When they emerged at the base of the cistern, the sunlight was sharply slanted, revealing only the upper part of stone above. Devon had doused his lantern as soon as they saw the vague outline of the opening ahead. They ascended the stairs, Vasill forcing them to wait while he poked his head up above the rim, then scouted out the surrounding area to make certain none of the Iandolan watchers were about. They traipsed back to the merchantile hall they'd made their base of operations.

They found Arrend, Sadie, Unsel, and Vash waiting for them.

"What did you find?" Arrend asked as soon as they stepped through the threshold, the tuller camp to one side, a contingent of students and proctors from the Lyceum to the other, everyone within earshot turning.

"Possibilities," Lane said, then motioned everyone toward the far end of the hall where they kept their sleeping pallets. All of those that had become Lane's impromptu council settled onto the stones arranged for Maureen's visit except for the guards, who stationed themselves before the meeting to watch those already within the hall and those who might come in. The tullers and those from the college returned to their evening activities. The scent of roasted meat filled the hall, making Devon's stomach clench. Vasill sent a guard to gather and pass out food and drink to everyone.

As soon as everyone was settled, Lane said, "We have a way out of the Burn. There are various exits, but the most significant comes out on the

Second Level at a marketplace, as close to the Fifth Level as we're likely to get from here."

"So we'll be able to get the others free?" Sadie asked. Her hand twisted on the handle of her knife in agitation.

"If Mouse can get us onto the Fifth Level."

"He'll find a way," Vasill said.

"Then we'd better prepare. Vasill, gather up a small group of your men, no more than ten. Devon and I will be going——"

"Sadie and I as well," Cerelle said.

Lane hesitated, but nodded. "Very well. Unsel, Vash, Arrend, you should ready those here in the Burn in case things don't go as planned. And warn Mindell. We won't know what condition they'll be in once we find them."

"Of course." The three shifted off to one side, toward the tullers, already deep in discussion.

Vasill stood. "Any specific requirements of the men I choose?"

Lane thought for a moment. "Anyone familiar with that section of the city, if possible."

"None of us are familiar with the Fifth Level."

"Then whoever you feel would be useful."

As he headed out, Cerelle and Sadie moved in closer.

"So what do we do until Mouse arrives?" Cerelle asked.

"Rest if you can," Lane said, rubbing at her forehead. "He might not even show up tonight."

"I'm going to see if I can hunt down some stray lucent," Devon said. "There must be some in all of this debris. I've seen some being tossed aside."

"I'll go with you," Sadie said.

Cerelle settled in next to Lane as Devon and Sadie left the hall, Sadie grabbing up one of the lanterns. Outside, the sun lit up the western horizon in vivid orange and yellow, a dark band of clouds moving in from the northwest. Lightning illuminated them from the inside, a few bolts snaking down toward the Flatlands. Stars were already appearing to the east.

"I think some of the workers were stashing the lucent they found over here," Sadie said. "They've been separating it out of the general rubble."

"Why?"

Sadie shrugged. She led him out of the courtyard and across the street, to where a small building had been used as a dumping ground for all of the stone and other debris that had been cleared from the streets and the buildings currently in use. Most of it was heaped up in the back, but off to one side lay a small section dedicated to lucent. Sadie set the lantern on the remains of the building's stone wall and they both knelt down before the pile.

Devon grunted as he began to sort through it. "Mostly fragments and splinters."

"There wasn't much left of anything in the Burn. And likely anything significant has been picked over."

Devon held up a small section of red, finger-length, its ends jagged, but its interior clear of the black smoke that typically permeated dead lucent. He tucked it into his satchel, then tossed aside a bunch of pieces that were no bigger than the tip of his little toe, all in various shades of orange, green, and blue. Most were coated with a thin film of ash and char.

"You seemed a little agitated earlier, in the hall. Anxious," he said as he dug deeper into the lucent.

Sadie was silent for a time, picking through the pieces, presenting Devon with anything she thought might be worthwhile, then she said in a rough, angry voice, "I'm tired of it all. Tired of Iridesque using us, abusing us, ordering us around, incarcerating us like they did back in Iandolo. I thought we were free of that once we left, once we were on the wayfare. It was better there, even though we were struggling, starving. We were free.

"And then we arrived here, Brovetto, and the first thing they do is throw us all into the barracks and armory. They begin questioning us, sorting us out, searching for the troublemakers. It would have been the internment camps in Iandolo all over again if Lane hadn't intervened. And even then the army managed to keep eight of us hostage.

"It needs to end. Not tomorrow, not a week from now, but *now*."

She chucked a piece of lucent into the heap, crystals scattering at the force, and stalked off to one side, shoulders hiked, breath controlled but heaving.

Devon rose slowly, approached from behind, but halted a few paces away. He tried to think of something to say, but Sadie spoke again before he found anything appropriate.

"You were there in the zone, so you know something of what it was like, but you don't truly understand. Because you weren't there when they kicked open the door of your house with no warning, when they burst into your apartment, grabbed whoever was nearest, and slammed them into a wall or a table, or kicked their chair out from beneath them. You weren't there when they rounded you all up, not giving you time to grab anything of value, anything to cherish, and thrust you into the streets to lead you to the zone, or herded you into wagons already filled to capacity and dumped you into the middle of the internment camp."

She turned to face Devon again, arms crossed over her chest, hands holding her own shoulders, as if she were containing herself. Her gaze met his and held.

"It must end, Devon. Here, in Brovetto, and everywhere else as well. We need to get our friends free from Burdock, yes, but it can't stop there. I don't want what happened to me and Cerelle and all of the others who were put in the 'quarantine zones' to happen again. For those that made it out and for those that didn't. For the families that were separated. For the families that were destroyed. *It must end.*"

Devon stilled at the intensity in her voice, at the rage he saw in her eyes. He'd been focusing on himself, on Dalton and his own personal pain, but there were larger implications to what had happened in Iandolo with the internment camps, what was happening here in Brovetto.

Thunder rumbled out of the west and both he and Sadie turned to see that the storm had moved significantly closer. The sun had set far enough that the massive anvil of its leading edge could only be seen when lightning flared across or behind it. Gusts of wind had begun to blow dust around the hollow of the building, hinting of violence, and Devon's skin prickled with pent up energy.

"This storm is going to be nasty," he said, grabbing for his bag. Sadie had already snatched the lantern.

They raced back to the merchantile hall, the wind intensifying. In the street, the refugees that had stayed in the area were shouting out warnings, everyone grabbing anything loose or free and stashing it away, parents herding kids inside tents or shelters. Dust skirled around them all, grit getting into Devon's eyes and mouth. He spat to one side as they entered the courtyard, Arrend at the door to the hall ushering people inside.

"Head to the back of the room," the proctor shouted. "Under the canopy!"

"What canopy?" Devon asked. As far as he knew, the hall was exposed to the sky, the roof burned away.

But as he ducked under Arrend's arm, Sadie in front of him, he found the tullers unfurling swaths of tarps across wooden supports that had been rigged between what remained of the walls. Vash and Unsel were monitoring those lashing the tarps to the struts, the stone, the ground, the tarps layered and overlapping so that water would be funneled away from the interior. Tullers were standing on the tops of their wagons to secure some of the flaps. Devon marveled at the engineering—obviously planned out well ahead of time—but then Arrend shoved him from behind toward the back of the room.

He found Lane and Cerelle huddled with a group of tullers and refugee children and parents, all of their own possessions pushed against the back wall. Someone had covered the windows from the outside, the waterproofed fabric sucked in and out by the wind with sharp *whump*s. The canopy had already been completed here, the apex of the sloping fabric attached to the highest point of the wall above.

"It's moving in fast," Devon said as he tossed his satchel with the rest of their pallets. He motioned to the canopy. "I didn't even notice them working on it."

"You've been a little distracted," Lane said. "They started working on it the first day here. Before the work on the oven and courtyard began."

One of the tarps got away from its handlers and began snapping back and forth. It slashed a man across the face and he screamed as he fell from the wagon he was standing on, but a woman snatched the flailing fabric and brought it back under control with the help of two others. Unsel shouted, "Lash it down there! On that post! That's right," while Vash helped the injured man to his feet. He held a hand to his face, blood trickling from between his fingers, but when he pulled it away Devon could see it was merely a cut above his eye, deep enough to leave a scar. Two other tullers came forward with bandages and led the man to one of their wagons, Gillian already mixing up some kind of poultice.

As soon as the last tarp was tied down, Unsel eyed the intricate structure that covered the entirety of the hall, then nodded and made his way toward Lane, people stepping aside as he approached.

"That was the last of it. It should hold." He hesitated and glanced up as a burst of wind shuddered through the tarps with an odd whirring sound. "And it should keep us dry. Mostly."

Another gust, more violent than the first, and Devon flinched and ducked down. "If you say so."

Unsel grinned and moved away, the tullers now focusing on their fires inside the room.

"What's wrong with you?" Lane asked. "It's just a storm."

"In Iandolo, when a storm like this was coming, all I had to do was retreat into the deeper part of whatever level I was on. Instant shelter from wind, rain, whatever it decided to throw at us. Same thing at the Lyceum, if you went deep enough into one of the dormitories or halls. We can't do that here." He waved around the room. "It feels...exposed. Even with the canopy overhead."

"Wait until the rain starts," Cerelle said.

Devon glanced at her with a frown.

"It's going to be a while before it ends," Lane said. "Everyone may as well settle in."

They all found a space, Devon sitting on the ground, back against one of the stones they'd been using as benches. Sadie and Cerelle fell in on either side of him, while Lane began moving among the rest of those sheltering with them, chatting with mothers, fathers, kneeling down to distract and calm weeping children. Devon watched in silence, winced at every snap of the tarps or rumble of thunder. He could tell the storm was moving closer by how sharp the sound of the thunder became.

The rain came sudden and not with a spattering of droplets but with a torrent. The sound of it striking the tarps overhead startled even the guards, someone crying out in terror. Devon swore under his breath, at the same time as thunder cracked and sizzled, close enough he felt it shudder in his chest. He found himself pushing into the stone at his back, as if he could force himself inside it, his breath coming in short gasps. Cerelle twined her fingers through his and he squeezed them tight.

"It feels like the storm is right there," he murmured.

"That's because it is," Cerelle answered, and he was heartened to hear the tremor in her voice. He wasn't the only one being affected by the storm.

Then he did a quick scan of the people nearby and asked, "Where's Vasill?"

At the front of the hall, the tarp securing the door to the courtyard was torn aside and Vasill and six other guards stumbled into the hall, falling to their knees, water and hail sluicing off of them. Unsel, the closest, shouted to the rest of the tullers, who converged on the flailing flap at the door, Unsel himself kneeling beside Vasill, helping him rise. None of the guards appeared hurt.

Devon rose when he saw Lane making her way to Vasill's side. The rebel shrugged off Unsel's steadying hand, wiped the water from his face, and straightened.

"Report," Lane said.

"I managed to secure five before the storm hit. We were trying to make our way back here through the deluge when we ran across him." Vasill stuck a thumb out at the sixth man, who gave a nod.

"Mouse," Lane breathed.

"I've found us a way in," Mouse said, then stepped forward. "Shall we go?"

"In this?" Devon asked, startled. Even Vasill frowned, glancing back toward the storm.

"No one will be on the streets," Mouse countered. "Not even guards."

"He's right," Vasill admitted. "It would solve the problem of exiting the pump house into the market on the Second Level."

"But what about the tunnels?" Lane asked. "Won't they be flooded?"

Devon considered the schematic he'd seen in the pump house. "Only on this level. Once we start climbing, we should be out of it."

Lane considered the newly-secured door flap, all of those nearby watching her. She clenched her jaw as thunder crackled overhead. "Let's go get our people. Cerelle—"

"Already ahead of you," Cerelle interrupted, handing over a cowled robe to Lane, another to Devon and Vasill. Sadie was handling the other guards and Mouse. "It will help protect against the rain, at least a little."

Devon raced back for his satchel, then shrugged into the robe, joining the rest as they gathered around the doorway. The tarp shuddered with the wind and apprehension crawled up Devon's back, tingled in his arms, but before it could build Vasill gave a nod and the tullers pulled the flap aside.

Rain splattered against Devon's face as Vasill and two guards charged into the storm, Lane and Cerelle a step behind. Devon sucked in a breath and followed, Sadie at his side, the other guards behind.

He gasped at how cold the rain was, then flinched as pebble-sized hail struck his chest and shoulders. Lane and the others ahead were already mere shadows in the deluge. The courtyard and streets were flooded with water at least an inch deep, his boots instantly soaked through, the bottom edges of the robes immediately saturated, dragging down as if hemmed with weights. Lightning flared to the right, the crack of thunder nearly simultaneous, followed by two more strikes ahead. He spluttered as the rain lashed up under the cowl, but didn't slow. Someone ahead shouted, but he couldn't hear the words.

Then they were at the base of the cistern, circling up the stairs to the top. Sheets of rain cloaked the levels above from view, driven by ferocious winds. Devon swore as they made their way to the interior steps, hunching down at the exposure to the elements, until they were descending, the smooth stone slick enough he had to steady himself against the wall to one side.

The bottom of the cistern held water ankle deep, but rising. Water poured from spouts all around the edges, funneled in from the streets. Everyone splashed their way to the main tunnel. By the time they reached it, the water was halfway up Devon's calves.

"Go, go, go!" Vasill shouted, standing to one side of the tunnel and shoving them all as they passed. When he slapped Devon's back, he added, "Lantern!"

Devon fumbled for the satchel, trapped beneath his robes. He cursed, but managed to get a hand into the pouch and pull out the lantern. It sputtered to life, still weak, like before, but it was enough to see by, especially now that they were out of the rain.

They sloshed forward, reached the cross tunnel and turned left. When they reached the junction, the water had risen to above Devon's knees, but only a trickle of water came out of the pipe that led up to the pump house.

"Now we go up," Lane said.

Vasill led the way. Water trickled down Devon's face, dropped from his sodden robes, the material like dead weight, but he knew they weren't done with the storm yet. By the time they passed the mechanical pumps and reached the sluice gate, he was breathing hard and his legs ached.

Everyone was gasping when they staggered into the pump house. Cerelle tried to wring out the sleeves and bottom of her robes, the others following suit as Vasill checked the door with Mouse.

"The storm's lessened a little," he said, then turned to Mouse. "Do you know where we are?"

Mouse snorted. "Of course." Then he frowned. "We'll need to circle a little farther north around this level."

"Lead the way."

"No, wait," Cerelle said. She tilted her head toward Devon. "Some of us need to recover."

Devon realized he was the only one still trying to catch his breath. He forced himself to straighten, to control his breathing. He would never have been this drained back in Iandolo, before the torture, but he could feel his arms trembling. "I'm fine," he managed with a steady voice. "Let's go get Dalton and the others."

Lane's forehead was pinched in concern, but she nodded and motioned toward the door.

They stepped out into the vacant marketplace, thunder rumbling overhead. But the violence of the storm had lessened by at least half. They could see the empty street off to the left and chinks of light through the closed shutters of windows and a few doors. All of the lanterns on the streets were doused though, whether from the rain or on purpose Devon didn't know. But there was enough light from the lightning and other sources that he doused his own lucent lantern and put it away.

Mouse sprinted across the street and the others followed, everyone trying to look everywhere at once. He didn't pause on the far side, slowing only enough that everyone could keep up. They kept to the main thoroughfare, hugging the buildings, trying to keep out of the storm. But the rain came down in sheets, the wind blowing it in all directions. It dripped from Devon's cowl as they moved, from his nose, and he gave up wiping his face free of it.

Ten blocks further on, those in front of him halted and pulled into a side street. As Devon followed, frantically gesturing to those behind, he saw a contingent of Iandolan guardsmen ahead talking to a couple citizens. One of them motioned in their direction.

Without a sound, Mouse took them down the side street, cutting right at the next intersection, but slowing as they reached the cross street the guards had been on. Peeking around the corner, he motioned everyone across, then followed. Devon looked towards the guardsmen, but they were lost in the rain, the intersection too far away.

After that, Mouse wove them through lanes, intersections, and alleys, the streets becoming less uniform and more brambly and narrow. They curved off in odd directions, had random corners and dead ends, and met at strange angles. The buildings were haphazard as well, some with second or third floors hanging over the lower levels or completely covering the street below. Devon fought back a sense of claustrophobia, the architecture making everything feel tight and constricted, and realized this must be the section Vasill had called the Narrows. Yet it also cut down on the intensity of the rain and wind. He had no idea how Mouse kept track of where they were. Within three twists and turns of the road, his sense of direction was completely destroyed.

Then, halfway down a narrow, three guards stepped into the street ahead of them. One of them turned, then shouted and pointed. A whistle sounded, the usual piercing tone garbled by the dampness.

"This way," Mouse said, surprisingly calm. He dodged into the alley they'd just passed. With a glance upward, Devon realized they were delving closer to the walls of the next level. He could see the heights above. Unlike Iandolo, Brovetto's levels weren't stacked one atop the others, but were rather tiers built into the plateau they were on.

Then he had to focus as Mouse was leading them through successively sharper turns, cutting into the next street, then the next, following a curve, then slipping into a narrow so close and hidden Devon nearly missed it. His shoulders brushed the stone sides and the enclosed space echoed everyone else's gasps and harsh breathing. Someone cursed and then they spilled out onto another street. More whistles sounded, from two different sides, and Mouse paused to listen, still calm. Devon's heart thundered in his chest; his breath hitched.

Someone shouted, although Devon couldn't see anyone.

Mouse stepped into another narrow that curved out of sight ahead. As soon as they rounded the bend, they ran up against a dead end, a stone wall that was clearly part of the plateau, although it had been chiseled smooth.

"What in bloody hell, Mouse?" Vasill spat.

Without a word, Mouse pushed on the brick of the building that abutted the wall. Stone ground against stone, but a portion of the wall fell back.

"Inside," Mouse said. "Quick, before anyone sees."

Vasill ducked in first, followed by two other guards, then the rest, Mouse coming in last. With Vasill's help, the two shoved the hidden stone door back into place.

Devon had already dug his lantern out again and flicked it on.

They were in a store room of some kind, musty with disuse. A few crates with straw sticking out through the cracks were stacked to one side, but otherwise the room was empty.

"Now what?" Lane asked. "Those were Iandolan guardsmen. Do they know who we are? Do they know what we intend?"

"I don't see how," Vasill answered.

"They weren't all Iandolan soldiers," Mouse said. He had worked his way through the group to the crates. Climbing on top of them, he reached for the ceiling, pushing upwards.

A section of the slats popped up and he pushed it aside, looking around at the rest. "Who's first?"

Vasill stepped forward. "What is this place? It wasn't one of the rebels' hideaways. I would have remembered."

"No. Most of those were rooted out and destroyed by Prefect Arctus and the army. This was a little hideaway of my own."

"Used for what?" Vasill asked as Mouse stepped down from the crates and Vasill climbed up. He scanned the far side, then reached and hauled himself up and into the opening with a grunt.

"Smuggling." At their startled looks, he grinned. "Not everything I did was for the cause."

They could hear Vasill moving about for a moment, then his face appeared and he reached through toward Lane. "You're next."

Lane stepped up and Vasill grasped her upper arm, then heaved. The rest of them followed suit, the guards steadying everyone from below or helping Vasill from above.

The second room had a lower ceiling with additional crates stacked at the far end.

"Wait, if the room below was for smuggler storage, what was this room for?" Devon asked as Mouse scrambled up last without aid.

"The real storage room," the escape artist and now confessed smuggler answered distractedly as he moved to the opposite wall, the one set against the plateau. "I've always found it best to have layers upon layers of deceit in place. It gives me the most options when plans get skewed." He shoved against the back wall, hard, and the entire section caved inwards, stones falling into an open space beyond.

He turned back. "Not where I'd anticipated entering the mines, but it will have to do."

Lane and Vasill shifted forward, Devon a step behind. He felt a cold draft from the ragged opening that reminded him of the sublevels beneath Iandolo.

"Are there skrill?" he asked, holding his lantern up to the darkness. It carried the same taste of grit and hollowness as the skrill mines.

"Not this high up," Mouse said. "They prefer the lower levels." Then he climbed through the hole, reaching back for Lane's hand.

"Will this screw up our plans?" she asked as she stepped through.

"No. But we will have to climb."

They emerged into a short tunnel that emptied out into a massive manmade cavern carved from the rock of the plateau itself. Devon's lantern faded out within ten feet, although he thought it was a little brighter than it had been in the Burn. Still not at full strength. The immensity of the room couldn't be seen, but he could feel the emptiness before and above them, even if he couldn't see the ceiling or far walls.

"Allow me," Lane said, then completed a sigil.

A ball of white light formed before the group and began drifting out in front of them, rising slightly. Lane created two more, sending them diagonally off to either side of the first.

Within fifty feet, massive columns appeared, reaching up into the darkness, and not long after, the ceiling. Unlike the floor, the ceiling was ragged and rough, the columns expanding the last twenty feet into a funnel shape.

"The columns are the only things holding up the upper level here," Mouse said. "Brovetto mined every last possible resource out of this plateau. It's merely a husk now, all of the lucent, all of the ore—everything has been extracted from its heart."

They stood in silence for a moment, the orbs drifting farther away, revealing more columns, an entire expanse of empty space.

Then Mouse stepped forward. "This way. We'll need to run to make up some time."

They ran, their robes weighted down with water muffling the sounds of their progress. Weaving through the columns, Mouse led them diagonally deeper into the mine, Lane creating spheres of white light along the way. The chamber they were in ended, a short tunnel leading to another, then another. The further they progressed, the rougher the contours of the mine and the older the stonework. They passed a metal wagon tilted onto its side, scattered buckets, piles of stone debris from collapses from the ceiling. In one section, water poured from a crack above, creating a stream that runneled away into the darkness. Based on the track it had worn in the floor already, it had been active for a while.

A wall appeared in the light ahead, stairs carved into its side. Devon groaned, his legs already rubbery, but Mouse began scaling them without pause. Within moments, though, the entire party slowed as part of a step broke free beneath Vasill's foot and tumbled the twenty feet to the mine floor below. Everyone edged closer to the wall to one side, hand out for balance. More stone broke free the higher they went, Sadie and some of the guards swearing as they caught themselves. In one section, an entire chunk had fallen away, only a thin ledge a foot wide available. Devon pressed his back into the stone behind him, thinking of the path beneath the towers he'd taken with the Regulars to rescue Lane or the Corlian Shaft he'd been forced to scale with Nic when taken captive by Carbolen. Neither had seemed as dangerous as this.

After what felt like an eternity, the stairs entered a vertical mining shaft, enclosed on both sides, and Devon's heart calmed, the open pit of the mine no longer yawning to one side. He heard some of the others breathe sighs of relief as well. Lane's orbs were no longer effective, so he broke out the lucent lantern and they ascended, moving a little quicker now.

The stairs ended abruptly a short time later, emerging into a rough tunnel. Mouse gathered them all close.

"We're on the Fourth Level now, beneath the Fifth. We're going to come out in one of the walls surrounding the governmental buildings. From there, we'll have to pass through a few streets to reach the governor's residence where they're keeping Varenov and the rest. It should still be dark, if it isn't still storming."

"And there's no way to get us closer to where they're being held?" Lane asked.

"Not that I could find."

"Then this will have to do. Everybody prepared?"

Everyone adjusted weapons, loosened catches. Devon dug into his satchel and found the dagger Nic had given him ages ago in Carbolen's hall. Mouse drew Vasill and a couple of the guards off to one side, speaking to them quietly. The rebel leader's face was grim, but he nodded in understanding.

Then Lane turned back. "Ready."

Mouse jogged a short way down the tunnel, halting at what appeared to be a random location, the tunnel continuing on before them. He motioned to the left wall, an opening overhead. "This is where we climb."

He reached for stones that jutted from the wall, pulling and stepping up, using them like a ladder. As soon as he did so, Devon recognized the pattern of their placements. He vanished into the opening above, what Devon had assumed was some kind of air shaft for ventilation.

Vasill and two other guards followed, then the rest. The muscles in Devon's legs and shoulders burned as he drew himself upwards, but he grit his teeth against the pain. Air gusted past him as he entered the narrow shaft, smelling of fresh rain. The scent spurred him on. He hadn't realized how dry and dusty the mine had been.

He came up behind Cerelle in a narrow room, the others packed close before him, vents in the stone to one side clearly leading to the outside. He could feel the gusts of wind coming in from them. Ahead, Vasill and the two guards were peering through an opening lit from beyond by lantern flames, the burnished yellow light flickering. Cerelle gestured for him to douse the lantern. Vasill gave a hand signal to the two guards—four fingers, then two with a motion to the right. Both nodded. Voices filtered through, followed by laughter—

Then Vasill and the others were moving, slipping through the hole with shocking speed. Someone shouted, there was a clash of blades, grunts, the crash of a table or chair being knocked over, pottery shattering, then a gurgle. Something slumped to the floor. Then there was only heavy breathing, a sharp, pained gasp.

Mouse had slid up into the opening, but now waved them forward.

The room beyond was a shambles, Vasill and the guards standing over the bodies of six soldiers, four Iandolan army, two clearly Brovettan city guards. They'd been playing cards, the floor littered with them, the table overturned, shards of tankards mixed in with spilt ale and splashes of blood. Two hadn't even made it out of their chairs.

Lane looked over the bodies grimly, focused on Mouse with disapproval. "Was there no other way?"

"I'd hoped the room would be empty when we arrived. The rain must have driven them inside."

"We always knew there may be bloodshed involved," Cerelle said.

"Think of how many they killed in the internment camps," Sadie added.

Lane didn't seem mollified, but she said, "Let's go find our people."

Mouse nodded, moved to the door, opened it a crack to peer outside. Devon and the rest picked their way around the room.

"It's clear," Mouse said. "Head to the shadows in the lee of the building straight ahead. We'll circle around it on the right. Stay clear of the windows."

Everyone nodded understanding and then they were rushing through the door into the courtyard beyond. The rain hadn't stopped, but had lessened to a drizzle, water still pouring from roofs and the wall behind in waterfalls. The courtyard and streets ahead were lit with scattered torches and a few lucent globes. The governor's manse loomed to their left, the gates to the right, and straight ahead a building with multiple windows shuttered against the weather and lit from within lay half in shadow.

The group darted across the open space of the courtyard and ducked into the darkness, broken only by what light came through the cracks in the shutters. As they skirted around the building, Devon heard raucous conversation and realized it was the Iandolan army barracks.

At the corner, Mouse checked the street beyond, then signaled them across to the curved base of the wall of the manse. He led them around its edge until he came to a rustic door, clearly used for servants for deliveries. It was locked, but within moments he'd picked it.

Then they were in, racing into a corridor with storage rooms off to either side packed with crates and barrels and sacks of rice and produce. The air hung heavy with spice and oils and cured meats. They skirted the kitchens, the noise of rattling pans, chopping, and sharp orders following them, finally exiting into a foyer beneath a set of stairs to the second floor. Firelight and voices came from the room beyond. Mouse gestured up and to the left. They ascended, Vasill and the guards taking the lead. They saw no one in the hall above or the corridor beyond, only doors to various rooms, lucent sconces lighting the way. The walls we cracked and scarred in places, signs of the purge led by Prefect Arctus months before. A few of the lucent lights were dead. But Devon was focused on Mouse, his breath coming in short gasps, his chest tight. The rebel smuggler indicated a grand double door at the far end of the hall and Vasill, Lane, and the others swarmed forward, Lane with crooked hand.

Vasill tested the door—unlocked—and then they burst through into the room beyond, everything strangely quiet, the only sound their footsteps on the stone floors and the rugs beneath the furniture. The guards fanned out, Vasil in front, Lane, Cerelle, and Sadie a step behind him. Mouse and Devon hung back.

Devon scanned the room, taking in the luxurious bed, the table and chairs, the settee and desk off to one side. The doors to a balcony stood closed against the storm, rain spattering against the glass. The only light came from outside or spilled in from the corridor behind them, the room drenched in shadows.

"There's no one here," Devon said, the words choked with disappointment. He tried to swallow down the fear that followed. "Dalton—"

"This doesn't even appear to be a cell," Lane said, turning toward Mouse, her hand falling. "Are you certain—"

"This is where your mother was being kept," Mouse said. "I swear."

"She *was* kept here," a voice from inside the room said.

Everyone spun, blades raised, as someone rose from one of the chairs, hidden before by its back.

"Burdock," Lane said, as he stepped into the light.

The prefect focused on her. "Your mother was kept here, but I'm afraid, at Captain Silleac's insistence, they've already been moved."

Chapter Six

"Where is she now?" Lane asked, stepping forward, hand raised again.

Vasill and the other guards fanned out to either side, circling around the prefect.

"I'll take you to her. I'll take you to all of them. That's why I'm here."

Lane hesitated. "And why would you do that?"

"Because I've had some long and meaningful conversations with your mother and father, a few with the others as well. They've been most revealing."

"About what?"

"Iandolo. The Council. What happened there while Prefect Arctus and I were here in Brovetto with the army, rooting out the insurgents. And also what those insurgents were attempting to do here in Luminesque itself."

Burdock hadn't moved, even though Vasill and his men had nearly surrounded him. He hadn't even reached for the sword at his side.

"You expect us to believe that you've had a change of heart?" Cerelle asked.

"No. If I were in your position, I wouldn't believe it either. Right now, you're thinking this is some sort of trick, that I'm playing you for time, stalling while Captain Silleac flanks you from the stairs—" Mouse dodged out into the hall with Sadie at his heels. "—but I assure you that's not the case."

Everyone waited, tense, until Mouse and Sadie returned. "Nothing in the hall or on the stairs."

Lane faced Burdock again.

The prefect kept his hands in clear view. "What the Council did in Iandolo to the Brovettans is in violation of the Founders Pact. Everything I have heard from the refugees we've taken in, from your mother and the others, confirms it. Everything I've witnessed since I took over here in Luminesque points to similar violations done by either the Council or its councilors in the past. Even the correspondence—or lack of correspondence, rather—and the vague orders I've received from Iandolo suggests that everything I have heard is the truth."

"None of this matters," Vasill said, moving in close to Burdock from the side, blade ready. "We came for the others. Tell us where they are."

"Captain Silleac wanted them moved as soon as he heard there was suspicious activity on the Second Level at the start of the storm. We transferred everyone to rooms in the servant's quarters hours ago. I'll show you where."

Vasill glanced toward Lane and she nodded.

"Don't move," Vasill said, then relieved the prefect of his sword, a dagger thrust into his belt, and another in his boot. Burdock kept his hands raised, eyes on Lane.

"It's not a trick," Burdock said.

"We'll see," Vasill muttered, moving in behind the prefect and nudging him forward. "Lead the way."

Burdock sidled past Lane, Vasill staying behind him, two other guards on his flank. Lane followed, catching both Cerelle's and Devon's gazes. Cerelle shrugged; Devon shook his head, his distrust nearly palpable.

They retreated back to the stairs, Burdock pausing to listen, but instead of descending to the foyer below, the prefect led them across to the opposite side, to another hall that mirrored the first. The path gave them an angled glimpse into the room beside the entryway, where Lane saw soldiers sitting around a table, drinking, the scraps of a dinner left on scattered plates and truncheons. One of them barked a laugh as they slipped by, but none of them looked toward the foyer.

Burdock motioned them forward into a corridor with lucent sconces and a few closed doors, but the hall was half the length, ending in a single door with a high polish.

Burdock paused and turned back. "This leads to the servant quarters. The hallways are smaller, along with the rooms."

"If you moved our people here," Lane asked, "why are there no guards?"

Burdock chuckled. "Oh, there will be guards, as well as servants. But not as many as you might think. Captain Silleac thought he could catch you on the Second Level, so after moving everyone, he set up a minimal watch here and took the rest down below. I warned him not to. I told him it was unlikely you'd be mounting a direct attack on the Fifth Level, that it would be stupid if you'd given up your position on the Second, but he's been anxious to catch you violating our pact."

"And you stayed behind?"

"I knew you'd come by stealth, that you likely already had a way into the manse, or at least within the walls. So I settled in to wait."

Lane still didn't know whether she could trust him, but she saw no other options. "How many guards?"

"Silleac left eight, but they may have been bolstered by the replacements from the barracks. The shift changed an hour ago."

Lane glanced at Vasill, who motioned to Mouse and three others. "Move fast. As quiet as possible. We'll be close behind."

Mouse nodded, then opened and slid through the doorway with the others. Vasill grabbed Burdock's arm, a dagger pressed into his side, then jutted a chin toward Sadie.

"Watch Lane. Keep her close."

Then they were moving, slipping through the door into the much narrower hall beyond, Vasill and Burdock in front, Sadie at Lane's side, the others behind. Vasill moved swiftly, prodded Burdock at the first cross corridor, the prefect murmuring right. The halls branched, simple doors appearing on all sides. Within moments, they passed a body, a gash in the soldier's neck, then two more at an intersection. Blood splashed the walls to either side, pooled on the floor.

The next two bodies were servants and Lane swallowed down regret, then they rounded a corner and Burdock said, "Those four doors, on the right." Three more dead soldiers lay sprawled out in the corridor.

Sadie stepped over the first and tried the door. "Locked."

"Allow me," Lane said grimly, hand already crooked.

The mundane lock and handle splintered with enough force the door juddered open a crack. Sadie thrust it all the way in to reveal Arch and Maupin, the tuller leader standing, braced for a fight. Both looked healthy and a wave of relief washed through Lane. She'd feared what they'd found when they'd raided the tower cells to retrieve Dalton.

"It's about time," Maupin mumbled, lowering his fists. Arch merely grunted in agreement as he stood.

Lane turned to Burdock. "You kept your promise."

"It wasn't easy. Silleac wanted to use more...severe methods of questioning."

"Lane." Vasill motioned to the remaining doors.

The next cell contained Dalton and Nic, both alert but looking as if they'd just been woken. Devon gave a strangled cry and rushed forward, plowing into Dalton before he could move. Devon sobbed into his shoulder, squeezing tight, then he pulled back and began checking him over—hands, fingers, face—motions frantic.

Dalton grabbed his arms to get him to stop. "I'm fine, Devon. I'm fine."

Devon expelled a harsh breath, then nodded, still trembling. He held on to Dalton, but dragged Nic into the reunion, the ex-gang member groaning. "No! Don't! It's fine, everyone's fine, it's not necessary!"

More of Lane's apprehension sluiced away as she shifted to the next door, revealing Picall and her mother.

A hot lump centered in her chest and tears pricked the corners of her eyes as her mother stepped forward and embraced her. She leaned her head onto her mother's shoulder, until her mother pushed her back gently and said, "Your father?"

Seizing control again, she completed the sigil over the last door. It juddered in its frame and swung open on its own, Raven and her father ready with raised fists. They both relaxed, her father sharing a tight nod with Vasill, who stood behind her with Burdock still in hand.

Then he faced Lane. "Do we have everyone?"

"Yes."

"Then let's go."

She nodded, then tensed as they heard someone approaching at a run.

Everyone with a blade or who had been a rebel or soldier stepped forward. Lane raised her hand, began a sigil, although she didn't have a clear sightline in the narrow hall.

Mouse rounded the corner, the other two guards behind him, one of them clutching his side, blood drenching his shirt from the wound down to his hip, held up by the other.

"We're out of time. Something's happening outside in the courtyard," Mouse said.

Lane hesitated, then realized everyone—including her mother and father—was looking at her. She drew in a steadying breath, then said, "Get us out of here, Mouse."

The entire group, nearly double in size now, charged down the hallway, a few of those that had been released pausing to pick up weapons from the Iandolan guards that had been killed. Lane stayed near the front with

Vasill, Mouse, and a few of the other guards. They moved fast, but were still trying to keep quiet. On the second turn, one of the doors ahead opened and a servant stepped into the corridor, then froze as she saw them.

Mouse darted forward, blade readied, but Lane barked, "No!"

The rebel smuggler had already twisted the woman around, knife at her throat. The cold, flat expression on his face belied his typical easy-going grin and Lane realized she'd never witnessed him killing someone. The juxtaposition between his two sides was jarring.

The woman's hands were clutching Mouse's forearm, the one holding the blade. Her breath came in heaves.

"Let her go," Lane said, stepping past Vasill. She spoke to Mouse, but kept her eyes locked on the terrified woman. "We're going to let her go back into her room and then we're going to move on. I don't think we need to worry about—"

Mouse slit her throat, the motion smooth, silent. The woman gagged, hands reaching for her neck even as Mouse laid her down on the floor.

"Move," Vasill ordered, thrusting Burdock forward. Mouse and the guards raced ahead, the others coming up behind, skirting Lane and the woman as she choked to death.

Someone halted behind her, touched her shoulder. "There's nothing more you can do," her father said. "It's done. And we still need to escape."

She turned to glare at him as the woman gave a final shudder and died.

"Lane?" Devon asked from behind her father and the sight of him with Dalton and Nic forced down her anger.

"Right."

She stalked after Mouse, Vasill, and the others, shoving the image of the woman from her mind.

When she reached the door out of the servant quarters, she found their lead group huddled in the hall outside, near the stairs. As she approached, Vasill said, "It's Silleac, in the foyer below."

She swore. Without stopping, she stepped around the corner to the stop of the stairs, facing down, then carved out the base sigil in the air before her, the double pyramid taking shape before her in pulsing blue lines. Behind, she heard curses and scrambling. Vasill appeared at her side, blade to Burdock's neck. Her father flanked her on the other side, a few others filing in behind where she couldn't see.

Below, Captain Silleac stood in the foyer with an array of Iandolan soldiers behind him, weapons drawn. All of them were soaked from the rain, dripping onto the cracked, tiled floor.

Silleac took a step forward. "There's nowhere to retreat. Surrender yourselves. Our little stalemate is over."

"Stand down, Captain," Burdock said.

Silleac transferred his glare to the prefect. "You aren't in a position to give orders."

"I told you not to send our men down to the Second Level. You should have kept more of them here."

"And you should have come down with me! You are the prefect, aren't you? Commander of the Iandolan contingent here in Luminesque? Loyal to Prefect Arctus and the Council? It's been difficult to tell, since their arrival. First you take hostages and make this ludicrous pact to let them free within Brovetto when we could have annihilated them at the gates. Then you balk at questioning the prisoners we have in hand, barely free up enough manpower for me to set watches on those running free in the city. You've blocked nearly every move I've made against them. So tell me, *Prefect*, are you loyal to Arctus and the Iandolan army?"

Burdock ground his teeth together, then said in a clipped voice, "I'm sworn to uphold the Founders Pact. I'm loyal to the citizens of the Crystal Cities. *All* of them."

Silleac's glare vanished. Silence hung for a moment.

Then Silleac said, "Martell, kill them all."

The older mage Lane recalled from their standoff in the barracks at the gates stepped out from the room to the right, already completing a sigil. Lane shouted, "Get back!" even as fire bloomed at the base of the stairs and roared up their length. She sketched out a defense, knowing she was already too late, and then someone grabbed her and yanked her to the side. Flames exploded against the back wall above the staircase and spread to either side. Lane was dragged to the floor as smoke billowed overhead, everyone yelling orders at the same time. She'd lost her hold on the sigil, the base collapsing. As the fire began to eat away at the back wall, she lurched to her knees, caught sight of Vasill, Burdock, Raven, and two guards in the opposite hall, the fire between them. But it had only taken hold of the wall, not the floor, had begun crawling across the ceiling. She could hear Silleac bellowing orders below.

"Pull back to the servants quarters!" her father yelled.

She heard those behind her retreating back down the hall, but she didn't follow. Instead, she shouted, "Vasill!" already sketching a sigil in the air. Just before she completed it, she stepped around the corner and released a torrent of fire down the stairs.

Silleac and a dozen of his men were already halfway up, but the captain and a few others dropped to the steps as the flames roared overhead, scorching the ceiling and the wall to one side. A couple of the other guardsmen weren't as lucky. Lane swore—she'd forgotten to angle the fire downwards—but before she could begin another sigil, Vasill snagged her arm.

"We're all across. Let's move!"

She hesitated, but movement caught her eye. Instinctively, she pulled back as Martell sent another wave of flame to the top of the stairs.

This second blast set the flooring ablaze, the back wall already char.

Lane followed Vasill back through the servant's door and slammed it shut behind her. When she spun around, she found Burdock, no one holding him, although Raven was close.

"Now what?" she asked. "How do we get out of here?"

"These are servant's quarters. We should have access to the kitchens, the lower storage areas, the delivery doors. But Silleac knows that as well."

"We came in through the delivery doors," Lane said, turning to Mouse, brow furrowing in distaste. "Get us back there."

He gave a mocking bow and then led the group down a different hall and cut left a short span away. On the other side of the servant quarter doors, Lane heard shouting, getting closer. They had a mage, she realized. The fire and door wouldn't stop them for long.

When she turned back, she found Burdock and Vasill waiting for her. "Let's go."

They caught up with the rest at the top of a narrow set of servant stairs leading down to the first level. At the bottom, Mouse led them right, into a corridor that Lane guessed ran the entire length of the back of the manse, arched entries to storage rooms to the left and right. The group fled down the corridor, Mouse in the lead, and had almost made it to the intersection Lane remembered passing through when they'd first entered the manse when Iandolan soldiers suddenly appeared. Mouse shouted a warning as the guardsmen saw them and bellowed a report to those behind. Vasill snatched Lane's arm to halt her as Devon turned around and said, "Go back!" motioning with one arm.

Lane spun, but halted at the bottom of the servant's steps. She could hear the pounding of booted feet in the hallways above.

Vasill pulled her back, placing his body between her and the stairs as he called out, "They're coming down the stairs!"

"Then we're trapped," her father said. He was looking directly at her.

Lane scanned all of their faces, huddled together in a tight group, as the Iandolan soldiers closed in from ahead and behind, and clenched her jaw. "Enough of this."

She pressed through the group, past Burdock, Raven, Cerelle, and her father, then stepped into one of the storage rooms. Crates and barrels were stacked to either side, a few opened, straw littering the floor. It smelled of musty hay, dirt, with a hint of something citrus. Lane focused on the back wall, raised her hand, and sketched out a sigil.

The cantrip crackled across the short space and blew the back wall out into the courtyard beyond. She stepped through the gaping hole into the drizzle before the largest chunks of stone finished clattering to the cobbles, waving the dust aside. Soldiers near the gates scrambled to form ranks as she moved to the center of the area between the back of the manse and the wall. Smoke from the fire started inside the manse billowed up from the roof into the night air, lit from beneath by flame.

"Should we retreat back the way we came in?" Devon asked.

"No. Have everyone gather around me." She began sketching another sigil, watching the guards as Devon ordered everyone close. As soon as everyone was near, she finished the sigil.

The shield began rising from the group before them, spreading out in a circle until they were surrounded, curving up and over them until it had created a dome that blocked out the rain. Similar to the dome that the rogue mage Terrial had erected around them on the quad at the Lyceum, this shield was more translucent. Its shimmer distorted the gathering soldiers in the courtyard beyond, but individuals could still be made out. Sound was dampened, as if Lane had stuffed wads of cloth in her ears.

She heard someone shift close behind her, then her father asked, "What are we doing?"

"Waiting."

"For what?"

Lane straightened as Captain Silleac emerged from the crowd, followed by Martell. "Him."

Silleac moved to within ten feet of the shield, Martell halting a step behind. The mage's hand was crooked. The soldiers stayed a good five feet beyond them, all of them reluctant to get any closer.

Lightning flared through the clouds overhead, although it took a long moment for the rumble of thunder to follow.

Silleac waited a heartbeat longer, then said, "You're surrounded. Time to surrender."

"So you can kill us or send us back to Iandolo and the Council?"

"It's what we should have done the moment you arrived."

"I've already been a prisoner of the Council. Or at least, one of the councilors. I didn't enjoy it. And I'm tired of being hunted and shunned and forced to hide. I'm tired of seeing my friends and family and those I love held prisoner or tortured or killed in an attempt to control me. So no more hiding. No more running. And no more accepting rules and boundaries placed upon me merely to keep me under control, to keep all of us under control. This ends here. You and your men will surrender and then you will remove yourselves from Brovetto, from Luminesque, entirely. You can return to Iandolo if you wish, or to any of the other provinces, if they will have you, but you cannot stay here. Brovetto will be free from Iandolo and Iridesque from this night forward."

Silleac began to laugh.

Lane raised her hand, began a sigil, Martell gasping and working at the same time. But he'd already had the base formed, only needed to finish the secondary half. He finished while Lane was completing her base.

Fire streamed forward, striking the shield and shooting up and over and around both sides, scorching the cobbles of the stones below. Those behind Lane shifted uncomfortably as the blaze continued. Lane waited until it sputtered out.

"My turn."

Lightning sizzled down from the clouds, connecting with the roof of the manse and the height of the wall to the other side. It danced across stone and roof, tiles shattering and pelting the soldiers below with debris. The guardsmen cried out, a few cowering, as the display lasted another breath, two, then died out, the afterimages of the jagged, white-hot streaks playing across Lane's vision.

"You don't have the upper hand here, Silleac," she said, once the crackle of the resultant thunder faded. "No matter that you have us surrounded. Unlike at the gates when we arrived, you have no leverage. Surrender, or the next strike won't hit stone and tile."

The muscles in Silleac's jaw twitched as he clamped his teeth tight, then he bowed his head, murmured something to Martell. The mage shook his head and when Silleac demanded something more he shouted, "I can't! She'll kill me first, before I have a chance to complete an attack!"

He backed away, glaring at Lane through the shield.

Before Silleac could decide what to do, Burdock stepped forward.

"Soldiers of Iandolo, this is your prefect speaking."

"Don't listen to him!" Silleac snapped. "He's clearly a traitor."

Burdock ignored him. "I order you lay down your arms and surrender. Gather all of our forces in the courtyard here or at the waygate."

"No weapons," Lane said from slightly behind him. "Only minimal supplies. Enough to get you safely to Iandolo. And they must bind Martell's hands behind his back and find Cole, the younger one, and do the same."

"You heard her," Burdock said. "Safe passage back to Iandolo, if you surrender now."

The soldiers shifted restlessly.

Burdock took another step forward and hardened his voice. "Stand down."

One of the lead soldiers took a step forward, then set his sword on the cobbles. He shot a death-filled look at Lane, but retreated to one side. After a pregnant pause, others began to do the same and Lane felt a tension in her shoulders ease. Silleac remained motionless until a few came forward to bind Martell's hands, then he spat on the ground at Burdock's feet. When he refused to relinquish his sword, his fellow guardsmen bound his arms as well and escorted him to one side.

Lane waited until nearly two-thirds of those in the courtyard had dropped their weapons before lowering the shield. With Raven and Vasill as escort, Burdock moved to oversee his men, speaking to Martell first, then some of the others.

Cerelle, Sadie, Devon, and the others gathered around Lane.

"Not exactly how I expected the evening to end," Cerelle said.

"The stalemate wouldn't have held much longer," Lane's father added. "You would have needed to take over the city eventually. It's the only way we'll be able to face the Council's army when it arrives."

Lane fought back a surge of irritation as her father moved to follow Burdock.

Cerelle chuckled and shook her head. "Maureen is going to be pissed."

"Who's Maureen?"

Lane sighed at her mother's question. "You'll find out soon enough."

"Hmm. You'll have to make certain any remnants of the government Iandolo installed here also leaves with the soldiers. It wasn't just the Iandolan army here."

"I can help with that," Maupin said, stepping forward, Picall at his side. "That is, if my fellow tullers are still around."

"Unsel and Vash and the others have been extremely helpful. They're all down in the Burn."

"We can take them down," one of Vasill's men said, "and bring back whoever wants to help."

Lane nodded, then frowned as she scanned the group. "Where's Mouse?"

The man who'd offered to help fidgeted. "He vanished as soon as you lowered your shield. He knows you aren't happy with what he did with the servant inside the manse."

She hesitated, then said, "I'll deal with him later then. Go. Tell everyone in the Burn what's happened."

She watched them lead Maupin and Arch away, but Picall stayed behind, shifting closer to Nic, Devon, and Dalton.

"You can go with them," Lane said.

"I'm not going anywhere," Devon said. "Not until they're outside the city." He motioned to the Iandolan soldiers. The others all agreed.

Then her mother touched her arm. "Burdock is returning."

Lane turned as the prefect halted a pace away, accompanied only by Raven now.

"Permission to send runners to gather the rest of the men down on the Second Level and those watching the Burn."

"Granted. What about Cole, the other mage?"

"He's down below. I'll have him bound before he's brought up here."

"Very well." She waited as he issued more orders, then said, "You realize you can't go with them. They'll execute you once you reach Iandolo, if Silleac doesn't manage to kill you on the way."

Burdock laughed. "I wouldn't survive beyond the closing of the gates. I was hoping for asylum here in Brovetto. I could be helpful in undoing some of the damage that's been done here."

Lane felt those around her tense, but she said, "I think that can be arranged. But first, let's make certain all of your soldiers make it out of the city."

For the next four hours, through the steady drizzle, her father, Vasill, Maupin, Arch, and all of their men herded the Iandolan army and the remnants of the government Iridesque had put in place into the plaza before the Iandolan waygate, where the refugees had first entered the city. The soldiers milled about and Lane could sense their anger, even standing on the ramparts over the plaza. But then Burdock called them to order, the soldiers forming up into ranks, and without fanfare, the gates were opened and they marched out of Brovetto into the coming dawn. The clouds had finally broken, stars peeking through, the horizon to the east barely beginning to gray. Lane watched from over the gates, her mother on one side, Devon on the other. The rest—Dalton, Nic, Picall—behind her.

When the last of the soldiers and the wagons of supplies left and the gates closed, Lane's shoulders slumped and exhaustion settled into her chest. She leaned forward onto her arms and heaved a sigh, her weight grinding her hands into the stone.

Then Picall asked, "What's that?"

Lane's head snapped up, searching the wayfare before her and the army already fading into the darkness, but she saw nothing.

"No, not the soldiers," Picall said, stepping forward. "That." She pointed toward the southwest, toward Iandolo.

Where the city would be, a faint white glow marked the horizon, pulsing as if with a heartbeat. Then it flared, a pillar of light streaming upwards into the heavens, fading out with distance.

"What was it?" Nic asked.

Lane knew, but despair had closed up her throat.

It was Devon who answered.

"That was the Warding placed over the waygate to Brovetto. Favian and the other mages have figured out how to release it."

PART II

THE
MANSE

Chapter Seven

"You've killed us all," Maureen Turing said.

The nominal governor of Brovetto sat in the makeshift meeting room inside the merchantile hall in the Burn, three other residents of Brovetto with her, all of them angry. Around them, Unsel, Vash, and a slew of her father's men were in the process of packing up their wagons, readying for the move up to the Fifth Level and the governor's manse. Some of those who'd settled into the area around the hall were also pulling up stakes, although a significant number of the refugees who'd come with them from Iandolo and had begun to settle into the abandoned Burn were going to stay.

Lane sat on the stone Cerelle had christened the Throne, her mother to one side, Devon to the other. All of them looked haggard, having only slept a portion of the morning after expelling Silleac and the rest of the Iandolan army from the city. Devon appeared distracted. Maureen and her escort had arrived shortly after they returned to the Burn, but Arrend had managed to hold them off until afternoon.

"We haven't—"

"You took a group into the governor's palace in violation of the truce and ended up destroying the governor's palace!"

Her shout caused Vasill and Lane's other guards to shift forward, but Lane halted them with a shake of her head before returning her attention to Maureen. But her mother spoke before she had a chance to respond.

"That's hardly fair," Varenov said. "She managed to pry the Iandolan army free from its siege of Brovetto. The city is free, something that hasn't been true for decades, if not hundreds, of years."

"And that's exactly what's going to get us killed. Did your daughter not tell you? I came to see her when you first arrived. I told her we were happy with how Burdock was handling his seizure of the city, that we'd come to an understanding with him and his men." She faced Lane. "I thought we had an understanding with you as well. You were to free those Burdock held and then leave the city. Not force all of the Iandolans out and bring the wrath of the Council down upon us."

"She didn't force quite *all* of the Iandolans out."

Maureen and her three compatriots—a man Lane vaguely recognized from the first meeting and two other women—spun on their seats as Burdock stepped forward, Arrend at his side. The proctor gave Lane a curt nod and then retreated. Lane had asked him to fetch the prefect as soon as he'd informed her Maureen was here.

"Burdock," Maureen said, by way of greeting, as he moved to stand behind Lane.

"I'm afraid I have to contradict the illusion you have of our arrangements before Lane's arrival."

"You said we would work together to bring Luminesque back. We were rebuilding the markets, repairing the agricultural fields. You pledged to fix the cistern system and bring water back to the lower levels—"

"It wouldn't have lasted. Captain Silleac had already sent reports back to the Council about what I was doing, without my knowledge, of course. I'd received orders from Arctus to cease all such actions. I ignored those orders, but Captain Silleac had been told to relieve me of my position, arrest me, and return me to Iandolo to face trial for insubordination if I continued. If Lane had not come to rescue the prisoners within the next few days, he would have been promoted to prefect and, I assume, all of those rebuilding projects would have been halted."

"He would have killed all of us under arrest," Varenov said, "and come after Lane next."

"Brovetto would have become a war zone."

"It's going to be a war zone regardless," Maureen said. "You've only bought us more time."

Lane gave a mirthless laugh. "Not as much as you might imagine."

Maureen frowned. "What do you mean by that?"

Lane drew in a steadying breath, already exhausted by the conversation, even though she hadn't participated much at all yet. "After escorting Captain Silleac and the rest of the Iandolan army out of the waygate, we noticed a bright flash of light from the direction of Iandolo."

Maureen shared a look with her followers. "Some citizens noticed the light as well. What was it?"

"The Warding that blocked the waygate to Brovetto," Devon said. "It's been taken down."

"Which means Iridesque now has access to the wayfare. They can send their army after us at any time."

"It could already be on the way," Varenov added.

Maureen drew breath to respond, but nothing came out at first. Her three companions shifted restlessly on their seats, horrified.

One of them—the man; Connor, Lane recalled—finally said, "What... what do you intend to do?"

"You have to leave," Maureen snapped. "Now!"

"That won't help," Varenov said calmly. "The problem isn't solely centered around Lane and Devon and the others. It's Brovetto and the Brovettans themselves." When Maureen began to protest, she raised a hand to halt her. "Obviously not all Brovettans, but the Council won't make a distinction. Those who've gained control of it have had enough. After what happened in Iandolo—with the revolts within the internment camps and the riots that started at our execution—I can assure you that the Council is now seeking retribution. They will be intent on destroying everything associated with Luminesque. It's likely any Brovettans remaining in Iandolo are being hunted down and executed in the streets. And now that the path to Brovetto is open, Havvelan will send Arctus and the Iandolan army here to eradicate it all. No more manipulations, no subtle power plays to seize control. Havvelan now has the excuse he needs to raze Brovetto to the ground."

The four Brovettans sat stunned for a long moment, before Maureen finally stirred and said, "But surely not all of the members of the Council would agree to such...slaughter. There are representatives from the other provinces..."

Varenov sighed. "How long has it been since the councilor who represented Luminesque was actually from Brovetto?" When Maureen didn't answer, she continued. "The political powers within Iandolo have been steadily replacing the official representatives from each of the provinces with people from Iandolo itself, people who do not have the interests of the province they represent as a priority. Instead, they favor Iandolo. It has been going on for years, perhaps decades. There were a few holdouts— Martov and myself, for instance—but whoever is behind it managed to kill Martov and put Havvelan in his place. They used my loyalty to Luminesque and my own daughter to place me on the executioner's block. Whatever faith you have in the Council is unfounded. It is nothing more than a façade for Havvelan and his ambitions now, and for whoever stands behind him."

Lane glanced over at her mother at the last statement, but turned her attention back to Maureen without comment. "What this means is that Arctus and the Iandolan army is coming. Would you rather have us here to help defend you? Or do you want us to leave?"

Maureen stiffened and glowered as Connor and the other two to either side traded concerned looks. "It seems we have little choice."

"Not if you expect to survive," Burdock mumbled.

She glared at the prefect, but otherwise ignored him. "What are you planning to do? How are you going to defend Brovetto? What do you expect or need from us?"

Lane closed her eyes in relief—she really hadn't wanted to fight Maureen in order to stay—then straightened her shoulders. "To be honest, I don't know yet. I don't know Brovetto. I've never lived here. My father and mother have some knowledge of the city, and Burdock has agreed to help us, but I was hoping that you, and perhaps a few of those with you, would be willing to advise us in the days ahead."

Maureen nodded. "I'm willing, and I believe I can convince a few others. It will help the residents of the city swallow these rather bitter pills you've brought us."

"And not all of our discussions will be about defending the city. We still need to survive until the army arrives and, hopefully, long after. Those projects that Burdock began? We intend to continue them. From what I understand, the situation with growing crops was not a problem of available land or weather, but rather water?"

"The cistern system and irrigation to the lower levels is broken. The previous governors said it couldn't be repaired."

"That was a lie," Devon said.

Maureen frowned. "What do you mean? It *can* be repaired?"

"Yes, it can," Lane said. "But it's more than that. Devon?"

"We used the irrigation channels to get out of the Burn and up to the Second Level without being seen. Along the way, we ran across one of the control panels. Some of the lucent used in the controls was shattered, but not all. It wasn't a random pattern. I'd wager someone intentionally shut down the water to the lower levels, reserving it for those above."

"It wasn't a malfunction with the pumps?" Connor asked.

"We didn't look the pumps over much on our way, but I didn't see any clear damage to any of them. We'll have to check, of course."

"I don't understand," Maureen said. "You said the lucent was shattered. How—?"

"Let us deal with that," Lane interrupted, before Devon could say anything. "But it can be fixed."

Maureen sat back, the tension in her shoulders loosening. "The majority of our agriculture was centered on the two lower levels, nearly all of it on the First. We've been managing it all at the bare minimum by using our own catch-basins and makeshift aqueducts, but if you can get the cisterns and irrigation working again…"

Behind her, Connor gave a shaky laugh. "We can grow our own food again, enough to feed everyone."

The other two women gave tentative smiles.

"You won't be able to get crops grown and harvested right away, of course," Lane said, "but the Iandolan army had a significant number of food, grain, and livestock on the upper levels that they didn't take with them. Once we've taken inventory, we'll be rationing that out to the citizens of Brovetto. We could use help organizing that as well."

Maureen hesitated, then stood. "Excuse us for a moment."

When Lane waved a hand in agreement, she and the other three stepped off to one side in a huddle and began an animated conversation.

Lane leaned slightly forward, eyes still on the delegation from the Brovettan citizens. "You can fix the water system, right, Devon?"

"I doubt it's as easy as repairing a few sections of lucent in that control panel, but yes, I believe I can."

"And what's your assessment, mother?"

Varenov shifted in her seat, her eyes on Maureen. "She's still angry, but the possibility of repairing the cisterns and offering up the food has mollified her."

"None of it will mean a damn thing if we don't figure out how to stop the Iandolan army when it arrives," Burdock murmured.

"One crisis at a time, thank you, Prefect."

She leaned back as Maureen and her little council broke apart and returned. They remained standing though.

"If what you say is true," Maureen said, "then Iandolo and the Council have been actively sabotaging Luminesque over the years—our water, our power, our voice. They have attempted to subjugate us. Such acts cannot be tolerated. It has been decided that we want you to stay, that we will help you defend Brovetto against the Iandolan army, if and when it arrives.

"In the meantime, Connor Vaughn will help oversee the repairs of the irrigation system—the cistern and pumps. Heather Brokaw—" she motioned to one of the women "—will help with the distribution of food and any other resources the Iandolans left behind. And I will advise you on the city and its defenses, with the aid of Sue Hicks, although I'm not certain what we'll be able to contribute that Burdock doesn't already know."

"The prefect may be aware of the military defenses, but I doubt we'll be relying on those completely," Lane said. "Recent experiences in Iridesque have convinced me that we'll need rather…unorthodox solutions if we have any hope of defeating the Iandolan army."

"We will do what we can." Maureen gave Lane a respectful tilt of her head, even if her mouth and eyes were pinched, and then began ushering the others out.

Lane stood and took a step forward. "How will we contact you once we've moved up to the Fifth Level?"

"Have your people ask around—the marketplaces, the ovens. We'll find you."

Then the group was gone.

"That could have gone better," Burdock said.

Lane faced him. "We got what we needed: control of Brovetto, at least for a time. And we will include them in whatever planning we manage to do. How much time do you think we have?"

Burdock shrugged. "Depends on how fast Havvelan manages to get Arctus and the army through the gates once they were freed. If they left immediately and had their resources lined up before they took the Warding down, they could be here in two weeks. If they forego the supply wagons and simply have the soldiers and mages march with minimal rests, less than that."

Lane hung her head, then gathered herself up again. "That doesn't give us much time to prepare."

"I doubt they send their army here on a forced march without ready supplies," Varenov said. "If they do, on the assumption that they'll be able to enter the city immediately upon arrival, they'll rethink that strategy once they run into Silleac and his men on their way back. At that point, they'll know they'll be facing closed gates when they get here. And they won't be able to simply blast their way through with their mages, because we have mages of our own."

"That's our main advantage," Burdock said. "The Iandolan army has been trained to use their mages to overpower whoever they face, because their enemies don't have mages. Once that playing field is leveled, even slightly, as with Terrial and the attack at the Lyceum, their typical strategies collapse."

"Especially if those mages know more or different sigils than they do," Varenov added.

"Except we might not anymore," Devon said, his quiet voice cutting into their conversation. He looked nauseous. Lane knew what he was thinking, but when Varenov and Burdock appeared confused, he said, "I told them about my research, remember? When they were holding me in the Tower? And we know they're already using some of what they learned from me. You said yourself they'd already started using cantrips before we fled."

"And I've also said that it might have nothing to do with your research. They saw Terrial using cantrips on the quad. They were likely trying to figure them out before Havvelan and Favian managed to get their hands on you." Devon didn't appear reassured, so Lane continued. "Regardless, at worst it makes the mage field level."

Devon stared at her a long moment, then turned away. "I need to finish gathering my stuff and figure out what to do about the cisterns."

"Devon, wait," Lane called out after his retreating back, but he had already slipped between the others packing up supplies in the hall.

"Let him go," Varenov said. "He'll be fine. He just needs to distract himself by doing something productive."

Lane sighed. "I thought he'd gotten over that already."

"That guilt won't ever go away, not entirely. It will always rear up and bite when you least expect it. But it will lessen. He's already handling it better than when we were on the wayfare on the way here."

Lane thought back to how Devon had wallowed in self-recrimination then, as he lay healing. "Still…"

Her mother drew her back toward where Cerelle and Sadie and a slew of others were gathering up their minimal personal effects. "You need to rest and focus on the move and what we intend to do after. Let Dalton handle Devon. They've been apart long enough I'm certain that's where Devon is headed."

* * *

Devon wound through the people packing up, out of the hall and into the practice yard, not thinking, not even aware of where he was going or why until he caught sight of Dalton giving lessons to the small cadre of

men and women lined up with practice swords before him. Alan stood off
to one side, watching, with Nic sitting on the rebuilt wall behind him.

He stormed up to Dalton, reining himself in at the last minute. He
wanted to grab the ex-guardsmen, crush himself into his chest, let all of
his guilt pour out of him as Dalton held him.

But he couldn't do that in front of everyone.

When he halted, a few paces away from where Dalton demonstrated a
move with his own sword, Nic hopped down from the wall and approached.

"What's wrong?"

Devon tried to answer, but he couldn't form words. Eventually he gave
an exasperated sigh and shook his head. "It's nothing."

Dalton glanced behind him, toward where they stood, but at a hand
wave from Devon he resumed his lesson.

Nic threw his arm over Devon's shoulder, drawing him away from the
yard. "Clearly it's not, or you wouldn't have come tearing in here like that,
all distraught and lost. Tell me what happened."

Nic settled him in near the communal oven, still within sight of Dalton.

"It was the meeting with Maureen, the representative of the citizens of
Brovetto."

"Did it not go well?"

Devon an impatient grunt. "As well as could be expected. They've
agreed to let us stay and help defend them, not that we would have given
them a choice. But after Maureen left, they started talking strategy—"

"And the mages came up and you latched onto the fact that you spilled
your guts while under extreme torture—both physical and mental—and
now you're riven with guilt all over again."

A surge of anger flooded the hollowness inside Devon's gut. Nic acted
like he had nothing to be guilty about. "You don't have to be condescending."

"I'm not being condescending, I'm being dismissive." At Devon's snort,
Nic rolled his eyes and faced him. "Listen, I'm not saying you shouldn't
feel any guilt—of course you're going to feel some—what I'm saying is
that wallowing in it, letting it overwhelm you, doesn't serve any purpose.
There's nothing you can change here. You were captured, placed in a cell.
They tied you to a chair, beat you senseless, mutilated you, and convinced
you they were doing even worse to Dalton. Anyone would have caved
beneath that. But setting aside whether you could have withstood all of
that pain, the fact is that you told them everything. At least, everything
you knew about how the mage system works. You can't take it back now.
It's done. There's no use in letting it eat away at you like this. All it's doing
is dragging you down."

Devon considered quietly, watching the training as it moved through its forms. He'd pushed the guilt aside when Dalton and the others were being held hostage by Burdock. Now that they were free, he'd fallen back on his previous anxieties.

He needed to move past them, needed to let what had happened go.

He drew in a steadying breath, exhaled heavily.

After a moment of silence between them, he asked, "What was it like?"

"Being held hostage?" Nic shrugged. "Nothing like what you described happening to you in the tower. We were questioned, sometimes forcefully." He pulled back his sleeve and revealed a bruise in the first stages of healing. "But we were fed, given water, allowed to walk the courtyard on occasion. Mostly it was boring. Lots of time to think. Too much time, actually."

"I'm glad."

They sat in silence, Devon watching Dalton and Alan as the two put those gathered through a series of formations, each paired with another. They wove through the group, making comments, adjusting positions— the placement of a leg or a hand or finger—then moving on. Their faces were stern, but they muttered words of encouragement now and then.

"Why aren't you out there?" Devon eventually asked, when it appeared the training was winding down.

"Oh, I learned to fight with the gangs. They couldn't train that out of me if they tried."

Devon grinned, then pushed away from the wall as Dalton approached. The ex-guardsman tousled his hair and pulled him in close, smothering him against his sweaty chest. Devon had missed the heady scent.

"Everything all right?" Dalton asked. "You were looking a little troubled earlier."

"Nic handled it." Dalton's eyebrows rose. "I find that surprising."

"Hey now! I can handle things, on occasion."

Dalton chuckled, but focused on Devon. "Training is finished for now so people can focus on moving up to the Fifth Level, those that are going anyway. Alan and the others did a good job while we were held captive. What did you want to do?"

"Unsel and Vash already have our stuff loaded in the wagons. We can do whatever we want."

"Hmm, I have some thoughts about that, but I think they're going to be preempted by whoever that is over there." Dalton pointed to where a man was searching the yard. As soon as he saw the three of them, his face relaxed in relief and he headed towards them. "Do you know who it is?"

Devon groaned. "His name is Connor. He's part of the delegation from the citizens that came to see us this afternoon." He pulled back from Dalton and stepped forward. "Were you looking for us?"

Connor halted a few paces away. "For you, actually. You said you could repair the lucent and restore the water, right? I'm supposed to help you."

"You mean watch me," Devon countered.

He fumbled with a protest for a moment, then gave up. "Maureen doesn't trust anyone, with good reason. Especially those who come from outside the city."

Nic and Dalton had edged in behind him. Dalton murmured, "Are you ready to do this? You haven't had much sleep in the last few days. Certainly not as much as we have."

Devon considered, but he doubted he could sleep even if he did attempt it, what with all of the commotion in the hall. "I'll need to grab some things from the wagons before we go."

"And I'll get Picall," Nic said.

Nic sped off to find the tuller while Devon, Dalton, and Connor headed back inside the hall to find Unsel. They ran into Vash instead, who told them where Devon's and Dalton's bags were stored.

As he rummaged through his satchel, making certain he had the lucent shards he'd scavenged from the nearby heap of debris, Connor said, "I thought we should start at the station where you said you found the damage, then maybe check the pumps close by to see if they've been damaged as well."

"Sounds good to me." He slung the satchel over his shoulder and looked at Dalton.

"I've got everything I need."

"Then let's go."

They met up with Nic and Picall outside the hall, then headed down the main thoroughfare out of the Burn, Connor keeping up a running commentary on how amazed he was at what the refugees had managed to do with the scorched section of the city in such a short time. It felt odd leaving the Burn without skulking through the drainage system or creeping through shattered buildings. Devon found himself searching the nearby ruins for Iandolan soldiers, even though Burdock had assured them that all of those who'd been sent to watch them in the Burn had been recalled. Or maybe it was simply habit from his time in the gangs in Iridesque when he was younger, or from hiding out in the lower levels after his expulsion from the Lyceum, or later, when he was helping the Brovettans escape from the internment camps.

It felt even stranger when they reached the ramp to the Second Level. By then, they'd joined a light crowd of others as they went about their daily lives—merchants hawking wares, customers haggling over prices, children shrieking in play as their parents worked or shopped around them. There were no guardsmen scattered among them, although Devon sensed wariness from everyone, and the streets weren't as crowded as Iandolo's either.

Brovetto was a mining city, so the ramp lay adjacent to the wall of the second tier, wrapping around its edge at a slow incline. As they climbed, Devon noted a second waygate—the one that led to Scintillesque—to the south, and that a significant portion of Brovetto lay to the north and east, away from the waygate to Iridesque. The northeastern part of the city held the majority of the agricultural fields, set up on rough, barren squares dotted with circular cisterns. In Iandolo, the water in those cisterns would have reflected the early evening sunlight, but here the cisterns were empty. The entirety of what Devon could see of the First Level looked dusty and deserted, as if it had been abandoned and returned to the Flatlands, even though, unlike the Burn, the buildings were intact.

"It reminds me of the Tull," Picall said, before catching Devon's gaze. "At least the outside of the tull."

Then they reached the Second Level and Connor cut back in the direction of the Burn.

"We weren't certain of the station you ended up coming through, but we narrowed it down to a couple of possibilities. Let me know if this is the right one," Connor said as they entered a small square with a dry fountain and a statue of a flock of birds. It looked completely different in daylight, vendors scattered around with either carts or thrown down tarps, produce and products on display, but Devon recognized the buildings that surrounded it. The scent of smoked meats and spices filled the air as they crossed to the small building that formed one side of the square and the door there.

Devon pulled the door open with a sharp heave.

"That should have been locked," Connor muttered.

"We weren't exactly concerned about security when we were here last."

They stepped inside the pump house, Connor closing the door behind them.

Nothing had changed much since they were here last, Devon noted. The trapdoor they'd come up through from below hadn't quite closed properly, jutting up slightly from the floor. The dust held their footprints and scuffling footsteps from before. The air was heavy with the scent of water, drowning out the spicier odors from the market, and only about half of the lucent lights from the control board still glowed with life. Devon pulled his green lucent lantern from his satchel and tapped it on.

He moved to the wall first, the others entering and fanning out to investigate the tight space. Dalton stayed close, letting Nic and Picall check out the pipes and valves and the trapdoor. Nic pulled up the door in the floor, Picall standing over him. They shared a glance, then Nic produced his own lucent lantern, flicked it on, and descended the ladder on the inside, Picall a step behind.

"Where are they going?" Connor asked. He'd kept near Dalton and Devon.

"To make certain the crawlspace is secure," Dalton answered.

Neither Dalton nor Devon responded to his raised eyebrows.

Devon leaned over the panel, tracing active lucent with one hand, mumbling to himself. Dalton pressed up close behind him, looking over his shoulder.

"Anything interesting?" he asked, his voice a rumble, his breath tickling Devon's neck. Devon shivered, even though he knew Dalton wasn't doing anything intentionally. It simply felt good having Dalton nearby again.

He waved with one hand. "It's complicated, but essentially the lucent paths here are a rough map of the pipes and channels in the immediate area that carry water from the cisterns to different parts of the city—the fountains, the fields, the sewers. The ones that are still lit up are active; the ones that are cracked or missing aren't. And some appear to be simply shut off."

Dalton stepped to Devon's side. "So all of this area isn't getting any water. They've been cut off."

"Exactly."

"It appears that most of the inactive areas are on the First and Second Level, if I'm reading this right."

Connor had come up behind them. "But lucent has been failing all over the city. Hardly any of it works anymore. Is it possible this was all just… random?"

Devon gave an unsubtle snort. "I don't think so. It's too…purposeful, too precise. Nearly all of the water distribution on the First and Second Level is gone, only a few sewer functions remaining. Everything headed to the fields has been severed. The cisterns have been left open, so that when it does rain, they won't capture any of it, it's simply funneled away, and other paths have lucent that appears whole but simply isn't active."

He shook his head. "No, this was done intentionally, but made to look like random damage."

"Can you fix it?"

He faced the Brovettan. "I can fix the lucent here. We need to check the pumps below to see if they've been damaged first, though."

All three moved to the open trap door.

Dalton knelt next to the opening. "What's the verdict?" His voice sounded hollow in the enclosed space.

"All clear," Nic answered. He sounded distant.

Dalton made Connor and Devon go first. They descended, the scent of water growing stronger, the walls damp with moisture. When they reached the end of the ladder, Devon turned immediately to the massive rounded door holding the water at bay, placing his hand on the lucent threaded through the hatch. He closed his eyes, sinking into the crystal and snaking through its layers in every direction, tracing it up to the control room above and down through the layers of rock that formed the foundation of the city.

"What's he doing?" he heard Connor ask, the voice dampened, as if he were underwater.

"Let him work," Dalton responded.

Devon withdrew from the lucent. "I don't see anything wrong here. The lucent is intact. Someone simply closed this door to stop the water from reaching the lower levels. Let's check the pumps I saw below."

They descended through the tunnel angled downwards, the stairs steep in this direction. After about fifty steps, Devon's lantern flickered and dimmed, but held. He touched the lucent to either side. Unlike the lucent in the door above, this lucent felt dead, although not from damage; he couldn't feel any flaws in the immediate vicinity.

He frowned.

"What's wrong?" Dalton asked.

He realized he'd paused, one hand splayed along a vein of blue. "I don't know. It's odd. The lucent here is undamaged, but isn't working. It's almost as if someone has turned it off. I noticed it the first time we passed through here as well."

"There were thousands of places in Iandolo where the lucent doesn't work anymore. Why is that odd?"

Devon hesitated, thinking back. "Because every instance I can think of in Iandolo where the lucent didn't work, it was because of damage. Maybe not to the lucent itself, but I could always trace backwards and find an area of damage somewhere along the way. I'm not seeing that here. Nothing close by anyway."

Behind him, Connor was breathing heavily and suddenly said, "I think I see the others. Their lantern anyway." He pointed, then pushed around Devon and headed downwards.

Dalton stepped up behind Devon. "I don't think he likes being underground."

They found Nic and Picall crawling through the massive hydraulic system Devon had seen on the first excursion into the tunnels. Both of the lanterns were flickering fitfully now, and both were much dimmer than they had been in the control room above.

"What have you found?" Devon asked.

Picall ducked out of a small chamber with at least ten pipes running through it, each branching off in a different direction toward the top before disappearing into stonework. She motioned vaguely with one hand. "We haven't found any sign of damage—no broken pipes, no machinery that appears shattered or jammed."

"There's general wear and tear," Nic said, appearing above them. He crawled out from a narrow pipe, held onto its edge, then twisted and dropped down next to them, brushing dust and grit from his hands. "Some rust and erosion, but nothing I can see that's significant. You'll have to check the lucent parts, of course."

Devon placed his hand against the nearest vein of crystal and closed his eyes. The others chatted and moved about, but he ignored them, taking his time.

When he emerged from the lucent, he found the others standing around him, Connor agitated, the others concerned. "What?"

"You were gone quite a while," Nic said.

It hadn't felt that way, but he did feel a rush of dizziness as he let his hand fall from the lucent. "I only found a few minor signs of damage to the lucent, nothing I couldn't fix along the way. The hydraulics here should be operational. There were some places farther out in the system that have either cracked or are missing lucent that will need more attention."

"Then," Connor said, a thread of hope entering his voice, "you can get water running to the lower levels again?"

"Let's find out."

He headed back up the stairs, the others following behind him. Dalton came up close and said, "Are you certain you want to try this now? You're looking a little pale."

Devon forced himself upward, his legs already protesting the climb. "I'll be fine."

Dalton hesitated, but dropped back slightly.

By the time they reached the ladder and the trapdoor, it felt like Devon's entire body was trembling. As soon as he emerged in the control room, he headed for the wall and began tracing out pathways. The others came up through with grunts, Connor with an audible sigh of relief, going to the door and stepping outside for a moment. Dalton, Nic, and Picall gathered behind Devon expectantly.

"This path here leads down to the large hatch holding the water back from the tunnel we were in," he said, tracing it out with one hand. "This is the tunnel down to the pump. This broken section of lucent must lead to the cistern in the Burn—"

"Which means this missing section leads to the fields beyond," Dalton finished.

"This path leads in the other direction, towards the waygate to Iandolo, but that's one of the places where there was some kind of interruption in the lucent. We'll want to find that and fix it at some point, but for now…"

He dug in his satchel, pulling out pieces of lucent he and Sadie had scavenged from the debris pile before the storm struck. Most were too small, mere shards, but he found one that should work.

He set it into the hollow in the wall where the previous lucent had been pried free, held it there with the palm of his hand, and sank into it. Concentrating, he reached out through the lucent to the jagged edge where the piece had been broken free, felt the paths there, reshaped them, until there was a shivering little snick of sound and the new piece merged with the old.

He heard Connor gasp behind him, the Brovettan starting to ask questions, but the others shushed him.

Devon focused on the other end, fused the new shard to the old, then shifted to the existing lucent that was cracked. It vibrated beneath his fingers as he repaired it, the cracks easier to fix than merging in the new piece.

He stepped back.

Even though the line was repaired, the lucent still hadn't lit up.

"Did it work?" Nic asked quietly.

"Not yet," Devon said. "The lucent path here is fine, but…"

"You said below that it felt as if the lucent had been turned off," Dalton said. "Maybe you need to turn it back on again."

He frowned, then thought of the massive door below, the potential he'd felt in the lucent there as it held the water back by keeping the door closed. He traced the paths on the wall to where the door would be, the lucent where the water was glowing a pale blue. There was a rounded node of lucent between the blue and the darkened lucent beneath it.

He paused, then tapped it, like they tapped their lanterns to turn them on and off.

The node flared once and they heard a grinding groan echoing up from the trapdoor. Within seconds, they could hear thousands of gallons of water gushing out of the opening below, spilling into the tunnel. All of them rushed to the trapdoor to listen as the roar of water increased, Nic barking out a laugh and shoving Devon's shoulder, Dalton grinning. Connor stood stunned.

Devon glanced back at the wall.

The path from the massive hatch to the pump lit up. He held his breath a moment as it stopped—

But then the repaired section to the Burn began to glow as well.

Chapter Eight

Devon winced at the high-pitched shrieks of children as they frolicked in the shattered remains of a fountain near the edge of the Burn. The once deserted area was thronged with people, both the refugees who'd accompanied Devon and the others from Iandolo and Brovettans from the upper levels as well. The former were filling water pouches and canteens and buckets from where water gushed from the ends of pipes protruding from broken stone; whatever the statue had once been was lost in the chunks of rubble both in and around the lip of the basin below. The later were coming down to verify the rumors that water had indeed returned to at least a portion of the First Level. The two groups were mingling, many pointing in the direction of the cistern, now full, and the barren fields beyond, talking animatedly, gestures sharp and succinct. Their faces were full of hope and wonder.

It had taken two days for the cisterns in the area to completely fill and the water to begin spilling out through the aqueducts to other parts of the area. During that time, Maupin and the tullers had fielded dozens of reports of leaks and places where obstructions had forced the system to overflow. Teams had been sent out and repairs made. Even here, at the fountain, Devon could see a section that had been hastily rebuilt and sealed. For the moment, though, everything appeared to be working properly.

Dalton draped an arm around Devon's shoulder, pulled him in closer. "You did good."

"I did what needed to be done."

Dalton kissed his forehead. "You did good, Devon. Accept it." He waved toward those gathered with his other hand. "I wager this is the first hint of real hope these people have had for years, maybe even decades."

"It is," someone said from behind them.

Devon turned, shaded his eyes with one hand, and made out Maureen's figure as she picked her way through the broken cobbles of the square surrounding the fountain. Sue Hicks, her aide, followed a few paces behind her, but that was the entirety of her escort.

"I'm surprised to see you here," Devon said.

"I came down to see what everyone was excited about." She halted beside them and took in the scene. "I see the rumors weren't exaggerating," she said under her breath, then faced Devon with an odd look. "You actually did it."

"You seem surprised," Dalton said. He'd stiffened defensively.

She eyed the ex-guardsman for a long moment. "You have to realize we've heard promises and pledges before, had our hopes raised, only to have them crushed when those promises are broken. It's nice to have one of them kept, for once."

"We're not finished yet," Devon added. "The part of the system we repaired only affects the Burn and a few of the surrounding areas. It doesn't quite reach the nearest fields. The system is going to need a ton of repairs and a thorough inspection of all of the control rooms, tunnels, pumps, and cisterns. This—" He waved at the fountain. "—this was simply a test run."

Maureen considered those gathered around the fountain. "The citizens of Brovetto thank you."

A moment later, she turned to leave, pausing to eye Devon. "Are you coming to the meeting with Lane this afternoon up on the Fifth Level?"

"No. There's too much to do down here. Besides, I'm not certain how much I'd be able to contribute to a war council."

"Says the man who brought down the Warding and halted an insurgency, not to mention started his own rebellion," Sue said.

Devon frowned at her. "Lane brought down the Warding. And what happened in Iandolo after...that would have happened with or without me."

"If you say so."

"Regardless, we'd certainly value your input at some point, Devon." Maureen gave him a terse nod and headed back toward where the market had been set up in Burn. It was doing a steady business now, with those from the higher levels arriving to see the return of the water.

Before Sue could follow, Devon caught her attention and asked, "Are there many large squares or parks in Brovetto? On any of the levels."

"Not as many as in Iandolo," she said, "but there's a square a few blocks in from each of the waygates and scatterings of parks on the levels as you climb the tiers of the city. Why?"

"Just…curious."

Her brow furrowed, but she shrugged and hustled after Maureen, catching up to her just before the market.

Dalton shifted away from him. "Why do I get the feeling that that question wasn't simple curiosity?"

"Because it wasn't. We have a little time before we're supposed to meet with Connor. Let's go see if we can find one of those squares she mentioned near the waygates."

They headed away from the broken fountain, through the market—passing Maureen and Sue looking at a display of pottery—and left the Burn. When they'd arrived, the areas around the Burn had been abandoned for the most part, even if the buildings were intact, but as they proceeded toward the waygate that lead to Iandolo, Devon noticed that a few people were already staking claims to some of the tenements and property. Like the lower levels in Iridesque, possession was equivalent to ownership. There, if you took hold of a room or building, as long as you could defend it, it was yours. The way a few of the men and women who were scouting out the buildings here bristled and glared at them as they passed, the same rule applied.

Then they neared the section along the main route from the waygate up to the Fifth Level. This section had never been abandoned—and had always had access to water. The barren streets and buildings filled up and by the time they reached the courtyard in front of the gates it felt like they were back in Iandolo. Except these streets were open to the sky everywhere, not just on the outskirts of each level.

They stood in the center of the courtyard, people weaving back and forth all around them.

"What are we looking for?" Dalton asked.

"Wardings. Or at least, their equivalent."

"You mean like the amber shard in the quad at the Lyceum?"

"Exactly. If Iandolo had them as last-resort mechanisms for emergencies, then it stands to reason the other Crystal Cities do as well. But I haven't seen one since we got here."

"Neither have I."

Devon gave Dalton a droll look. "You haven't exactly been roaming the city streets much."

Dalton grinned. Then he turned serious, scanning the courtyard—the barracks on one side, armory on the other. Devon couldn't help recalling the tension as Lane and the refugees faced off against Burdock and the Iandolo army when they first arrived and suppressed a shudder.

He focused on the cobblestones beneath their feet, the buildings on either side, the streets branching away in three different directions. Aside from the barracks and armory, the nearest buildings contained shops on the lower levels, residences above, stonework plain but with the occasional elaborate lintel or carved accent piece, even a mock column here and there. The streets were broad and a few industrious individuals had set up makeshift stands on the corners, selling root vegetables and roasted meats. It hadn't looked this busy when they arrived, but Devon supposed Burdock had had the place cleared long before they got to the gates.

"I'm not seeing anything that looks like a Warding," Dalton finally said.

"Me either. But Sue said there were squares nearby. Let's find one of those."

They asked a few passersby for directions and eventually found the square a couple of blocks away, off of one of the main thoroughfares. It was huge, taking up an entire block to the right of the main street, a low wall about waist height surrounding it, with four entrances along each of the streets on its four sides, each entrance covered by a low arch of stone. They entered through one of the arches.

If it had been a square in one of the busiest sections of Iandolo, the interior would have been crammed with tents and wagons and stalls, people crowding the market, jostling their way from vendor to vendor. The noise—a cacophony of haggling, shouts, shrieks, and laughter—would have flooded the area, along with spices, roasted meats, the tang of smoke, and an underlying scent of garbage and offal.

Here in Brovetto, the square wasn't even half full. The stalls were clustered near the center, spaced far apart, enough that the few customers roaming about could drift back and forth without fear of brushing up against anyone. Pickpockets would have a hard time finding marks and thieves would find it difficult lifting items from stalls; there wasn't enough going on to provide distraction, to draw the eye away from what they were doing.

"If it's like this everywhere in Luminesque, no wonder we haven't heard of any gang activity here," Devon said.

"We aren't here to shop…or steal," Dalton said.

They circled the area, checking out the walls made of stone, the arches, the few statues or sculptures that dotted the square on pedestals. Unlike most squares Devon knew of, this one didn't contain a massive fountain or sculpture at its center. There was simply the market. As they circled in toward the outer stalls, Devon's stomach growled. He hadn't eaten all morning and was focusing in on one of the carts with a sizzling array of smoked meat on skewers when he felt a change in the texture of the stone beneath his feet.

He glanced down, then reached out a hand to halt Dalton and said, "Look."

The wide stone pavers that blanketed the entire square had been replaced with the smooth, flat surface of a large chunk of amber crystal. Devon knelt down and pressed his hand to it, felt the tingling sensation he'd felt from the Warding in the quad back at the Lyceum, and grinned.

"This is it." He stood and paced back and forth, following the edge of amber, not paying attention to where he was going. He bumped into a woman, who gave him a scowl followed by a look of fear before hurrying away. Then he stumbled over the edge of a tarp a dealer had laid down to display his wares. The man gave him a dirty look at first, then caught sight of Dalton, lowered his head quickly, and ignored them.

Dalton grabbed Devon's arm and pulled him away. "You're attracting attention."

Devon glanced back at the vendor. "What do you mean?"

"We're clearly from Iandolo and, even though I'm not dressed as a soldier, I still have that bearing. We need to be more careful." Devon frowned, but Dalton drew his attention back to the amber crystal by saying, "So this is a Warding?"

"Yes, but not like any I saw in Iandolo or in Arrend's notes. All of those in Iridesque were like raw crystal, oddly shaped and faceted. This is… refined. Look, it takes up the entire center of the square! And it's flat and rectangular."

"It might not be underneath. But you're certain it's a Warding?"

"It's a Warding. I wonder if we've missed any others because they aren't like the ones in Iandolo?"

"We'll have to search for them some other time."

"Why is that?"

"Because we're supposed to meet Connor, for one thing. And then there's that."

Devon looked in the direction of Dalton's nod and saw a small group of three men and two women approaching, brows knit and expressions angry. They halted ten paces away. Dalton shifted so that he stood slightly in front of Devon as one of the men took another step forward.

"Who are you? And what are you doing here?"

"My name is Dalton, and this is Devon. We were part of the last group of refugees that arrived from Iandolo."

"We were checking out the market," Devon added.

"Didn't look like it to me," the man said. "Looked like you were more interested in the walls and the flagstones than the merchants."

A few of those behind him muttered in agreement. Like nearly everyone in Brovetto, they were thin and lanky, but with wiry muscle. None of them carried weapons Devon could see, besides their fists. But he'd grown up in the lower levels; he knew scrappers like these could be as dangerous as bulkier men, even without blades.

Devon placed a hand on Dalton's arm. "We were just leaving."

The man motioned with one hand and the four others began flanking them. "I thought we'd kicked all of you Iandolan soldier bastards out, but I suppose a couple could have escaped and hidden themselves away."

Dalton bristled. "Do you seriously think you can take me when I have this?" He patted the hilt of his sword.

A couple of the others faltered at that, but the man merely grinned. "I reckon five of us can take you."

Devon reached into his satchel. He didn't have a knife—he hadn't thought to replace it—but his fingers closed around a shard of lucent with a sharp edge. He drew it out, keeping his hand close to his body. Without a word, he and Dalton shifted so they were back-to-back, Dalton's hand now gripping his sword's hilt.

The group had nearly completed their circle when a woman shoved through the gathering crowd, stumbling out into the open at the edge. "Wait!" she cried out, catching herself. She was clothed in layers, a couple of shawls draped over her shoulders. She held up one hand, the other clutched to her chest. "Wait. I was one of the refugees. This man was one of those that led us here."

The five nearly surrounding them halted in uncertainty.

"And what about this other?" the leader said, gesturing at Devon.

The woman frowned. "I don't remember him, but he's clearly not a soldier. Look at him."

The man hesitated as those in the crowd began to murmur amongst themselves.

Dalton nodded toward the woman, then faced the group's leader. "We're going to leave now." He held out an arm in front of Devon and began to back them toward the remaining opening in the circle of would-be assailants.

The leader stiffened, as if about to order an attack, but the woman behind him said sharply, "If you hurt them, you'll have to answer to Governor Illea."

The man glowered as Dalton and Devon stepped outside of their circle, turned, and fled the square, moving fast but not running. Devon glanced back once as they reached one of the arches in the surrounding wall, but no one was following them. He slid the lucent shard back into his satchel.

"That was close," he said, his voice shaky.

"We forget that this city has been under Iandolo's heel for decades," Dalton said. "Most of these people have known nothing else. We'll need to warn Lane and the others—Arch, Arrend, Maupin…anyone who is clearly Iandolan. None of them should be traveling around the city without others with them. Other Brovettans."

Devon sighed and slowed, eyes scanning the streets. Not searching for Wardings this time, but watching the people again, looking for danger.

"What's wrong?" Dalton asked.

Devon shook his head. "Nothing. I'm…tired, Dalton. Tired of always running, of being forced to look over my shoulder. I've been doing that since I fled the Lyceum. No, since before even that really. I've been running and hiding and fleeing my entire life—in the lower levels as a gang member, at the Lyceum, afterwards in the streets being hunted by Favian and the Iandolan army, then the escape from Iridesque. It needs to end. *I* need it to end."

Dalton threw an arm over Devon's shoulder and pulled him in close. "It will end. We're going to make certain it does, here, in Brovetto. Now, let's go find Connor and see about repairing some more of the water systems for the First and Second Level."

* * *

Lane stood on the balcony of the room she'd taken in the governor's manse and watched the workers in the area of the courtyard below cleaning up the scattered stone debris from when she'd blown out the wall in the storage room so they could escape. Most of it was being hauled back to the ragged hole, to be used in the repairs, but some of it was being loaded into a cart, bound for the lower levels and all of the reconstruction going on there.

Someone knocked on the door to her rooms. When she turned, she saw Vasill enter, her mother a step behind.

"Councilor Varenov to see you, Governor," Vasill announced.

Varenov's eyebrows rose, then she stepped into the room. "I think we can dispense with the title of 'councilor' at this point. Besides, it leaves a bitter taste in my mouth." She headed toward Lane.

"And I'm not the governor," Lane added.

"Oh, but I'm afraid you are, daughter. At least in the eyes of most of those living in this city."

Lane wanted to protest, but knew it was useless. "Why are you here, mother?"

Varenov stepped out onto the balcony with her and looked down. "I've come to tell you that Maureen and her aide have arrived. Your father has sent them to the main hall, where he's set up one of the grand tables. He's also sent for Burdock; his men are bringing him to the meeting now."

"What about Devon and Dalton? I want them there."

"They're with Connor, working on restarting the water channels down to the lower levels. Nic and Picall are with the tullers repairing aqueducts and cisterns."

Lane's hand gripped the stone of the balcony hard enough her knuckles turned white. Her mother noticed, of course.

"Don't worry," Varenov said, smoothing out a fold on Lane's sleeve. "I've made certain you have some support in the room. Besides Vasill and myself, of course. Not that you need it."

Lane grunted and released her grip, brushing the grit from her hand. "Let's go then."

They stepped into the hall and moved toward the stairs. The scent of ash and char assaulted Lane's nostrils and she breathed shallow as they passed the section of the hall that had burned when she and the Iandolan mages had traded fire spells. The immediate area on the second floor at the top of the stairs was blackened and pitted, a few holes eaten through the walls and ceiling, although the stairs themselves remained stable and mostly unscathed. The foyer below was also charred, servants scrubbing the stone floor and walls as best they could. Lane wasn't certain where the servants had come from, but she did recognize some of the faces as refugees that had traveled with them from Iandolo, as well as a few tullers.

When she turned to enter the meeting rooms to the other side, she found Cerelle, Sadie, and Raven waiting.

Raven and Vasill traded curt nods. Cerelle straightened and said, "Everyone is waiting." Then she motioned into the room.

Lane hesitated, drew in a deep breath, and entered.

The room had once been a formal dining room, with wainscotting along the walls, a grand hearth against the right wall surrounded by shelving and cupboards. Most of the shelves were empty, a few of the cupboard doors askew. Cracks riddled the plaster above the wooden paneling. Wide windows lined the left, swaths of sunlight pouring in along the length of the table in the center of the room and glittering in the glass prisms of the chandelier overhead. Another set of double doors led into another room beyond the table, but the people seated and waiting captured Lane's attention.

Maureen had taken a place at the far end of the table, her aide to her left. Burdock sat to her right, two of Lane's father's men standing a few paces away, near the windows. He stood as Lane stepped into the room, bowing his head in a deferential nod. Maureen gave him a confused frown as Lane paused, then made her way to the chair opposite Maureen, even though that placed the entire length of the table between them. Cerelle settled to Lane's left, Sadie to her right, and Raven and Vasill took places behind her, against the wall. There were a few empty chairs between the two groups, but Lane's mother remained standing off to one side, near the hearth.

Tucked into a corner, Jillian held a stylus and board with a sheaf of papers on a small table to one side, her face intent.

Lane found the entire situation odd. The room was certainly more formal than the stone debris they'd used as seats in the merchantile hall in the Burn, but nowhere near the stateliness of the Council chambers in the towers in Iandolo. However, with Jillian in attendance—a Historian—the meeting took on additional weight, a heaviness Lane felt pressing against her chest.

Burdock remained standing until Lane took her own seat. But before she could begin, Maureen said, "I ventured down to the Burn this morning."

"And?" Lane asked, when she didn't immediately continue.

Maureen fidgeted in her seat, then gave a grudging nod. "Your man, Devon, did what he said he could do. The water was flowing again. The fountain was a shambles, but there was water. And already a market nearby. The cistern was full as well."

Lane couldn't suppress a smile. "I think he'd take offense at you calling him my 'man.'"

"What else would you call him? Your servant?"

Lane gave a small laugh and shook her head. "Certainly not that. He's…a friend. We've survived a lot together."

"Ah, one of those friends."

"Yes. And that's why we're here, isn't it? To discuss how we can all survive what's coming. Together."

"We aren't exactly friends. Yet."

Lane felt acutely aware of the scratch of Jillian's stylus in the silence that followed, but decided to take heart in the "yet." She shifted forward in her seat, set her elbows on the table.

"The Iandolan Army is coming. Even with unrest in Iandolo itself, Havvelan and the Council cannot simply let us go."

"Which is why I wanted you out of the city before anything could happen," Maureen snapped, then held up a hand and drew in a steadying breath. "But that has passed. And I recognize that, even if we had managed to force you out, it's unlikely anyone from Iridesque would have believed us. So yes, the Iandolan army is coming. What can we do about it?"

Lane turned to Burdock. "What are our defenses?"

The former prefect stirred. "The walls are clearly our best defense. Unlike Iandolo, Brovetto is built in tiers, because the city was meant to mine the tull it was built upon. The outer wall wasn't meant to hold people out, but to keep people in, safe from the edge of the tull and from the dangers of the Flatlands below. The only reasonable approach is along the wayfares, to the waygates themselves. Because of that, the only real defenses were built into the waygates. If they come any other way, the outer walls are vulnerable. As for the waygates, we can secure them, but the existing barricades are minimal. We can bolster them and fortify them as much as possible before the Iandolans arrive."

"Why are the defenses minimal? I would think—" Cerelle began.

But Burdock interrupted. "Because they were only intended to keep bandits and such out, not an army. There was no point in making them stronger. If the Iandolan army came, any defense was mote, because the Iandolans had mages. Nothing that could be built could stop their mages." He nodded toward Lane. "Think about how you escaped Iandolo. The gates were meaningless. The only deterrent you met were the other mages."

"But this time, we *have* mages," Maureen said. "We have you. And based on what I've heard from the refugees, you are equal to at least three or four of the Iandolan mages."

Lane frowned. "I was, perhaps. Before. But they've had time to learn. They were already improving before we fled."

"I'd still side with you," Burdock said, "based on what I saw in the courtyard when you were attempting to rescue your friends."

"And it won't be just Lane," Varenov said from the hearth. Those at the table turned toward her. "Don't forget that students from the Lyceum came with us when we left. Some of them are mages. They could be trained in the basics, at least." She gave Lane a meaningful look.

Lane shook her head. "Even with me at the reinforced waygates, it's unlikely I'll be able to hold them off indefinitely. They can bring dozens of mages against us. I can't withstand that much concentrated power, even with some help from the students with us, no matter how much training they receive. They're going to get through the waygates. What's the next line of defense?"

Burdock motioned to one of the guardsmen behind him, who brought forward a satchel. Removing a roll of paper, Burdock spread it out on the center of the table, motioning for chunks of stone and other knickknacks from the shelves to hold down the corners and edges. Everyone stood and gathered in the center of the table to get a better look.

"It's a map of the city," Cerelle said.

"Accurate as of ten years ago," Burdock agreed.

Maureen huffed. "So not that accurate at all." She pointed to a section. "That's the Burn, intact."

"It was the most recent map I could find," Burdock said, "and it suffices for what I intend to show you." He motioned to the area near the waygate to Iandolo. "If the waygate falls—"

"It will," Lane, Raven, and Cerelle said together.

Burdock waved the comment off in annoyance. "—then the next set of defenses will need to be set up in the courtyard and streets immediately behind it. Thankfully, whoever designed this city must have had defense in mind, at least partially. There's the main courtyard beyond the gates, the barracks and armory to either side, then the main thoroughfare that leads up to the ramps and promenade to the governor's manse above. That thoroughfare is twice as wide as the other two streets that branch off to either side of it, but the main strategic advantage to all of this is the buildings. They're all at least three stories tall and, what you may not have noticed when you arrived, they all have crenellations along the rooftops. The walls facing the courtyard don't have any entrances, except the main building directly across from the waygate—they're all along the streets— and the windows are tall and narrow. They're all made of stone as well, not lucent, which means—"

"Which means the courtyard beyond the gates is a massive trap," Raven said.

Burdock grunted. "It's what we call a murder hole. Line the wall and rooftops with archers—hells, stone debris or anything someone can hurl from the heights, even hot oil or pitch—and those that breach the gates are funneled right into the line of fire. The streets beyond do the same, forcing the attackers along set paths, at least until you reach the first cross-streets. But that first block—in any direction—is a long way away if you're taking fire from above."

"And after that?" Lane asked.

"Once the army reaches the rest of the city, it's a free-for-all. You can still attack from the rooftops, and they're still bottled up by the streets, but it's a maze. You can't defend it all, not unless you have far more bodies than we have in the city right now. You're going to have to focus on key places along the path to the Fifth Level."

"Such as?" Maureen asked, her tone brittle.

"The ramps leading up, for one. They're the only way the army can access the upper levels. Then there are strategic positions here and there throughout the city." He pointed to a few on the maps as he spoke. "It's likely that the army will pass through this park, for instance, if they take the most direct and easiest route to the first ramp. This intersection here would be easy to defend and costly to take, if we can force them down this street. There are a couple of dead ends here and here that could be used to our advantage if we can lure them in somehow." He leaned back from the map. "There are plenty of opportunities where we can hurt them on their path to the governor's manse, but once they push beyond the courtyard…" He raised both hands in the air. "Plans are meaningless after a certain point in battle."

Lane sat back in her chair, a hard yet hollow lump at the base of her throat. "You're saying that we can't stop them."

"They have the advantage of numbers. They have the advantage of training. They have mages. The best we can do with what we have here in Brovetto is hurt them. Hurt them so badly that they decide to retreat or to negotiate."

Lane thought about Favian and what little she knew of Havvelan. "They won't negotiate."

"Then we have to make them pay," Maureen said. She and her aide had been speaking quietly to each other off to the side, but now Maureen placed her palms flat on the table and leaned forward. "I've resigned myself to the idea that Brovetto will become a battlefield. It rankles and leaves a bitter taste in my mouth, but I see no way to avoid it. The only other option is to run and I know that most of Luminesque's citizens won't do that. So they will fight, using whatever is at hand. But you are wrong in one respect, Prefect Burdock." She turned to face him, and when her aide muttered "Maureen," low, in warning, she held up a hand to forestall her. "You have not factored in who will be defending this city. It will not, for the most part, be soldiers. It will be ordinary people, those who live here. Not only will they be more motivated because of that, of more importance, they know this city. Every part of this city."

"What are you saying?" Cerelle asked.

Maureen gestured toward the map. "This only shows the surface of the city—a ten-year-old city at that. You say that the ramps are the only way up to the Fifth Level, but that's false. From what I've heard, Lane, you yourself used an alternate route to gain access to the governor's manse to rescue those held hostage. There are other such routes—beneath the city, between buildings and walls, even to the Flatlands below. We can use all of these to hold them at bay. And we have another advantage."

"And what is that?" To Lane's surprise, Burdock's tone wasn't condescending, but rather respectful.

"We know what they truly want." Maureen faced Lane. "You."

Lane's gut tensed, but then, oddly released. Because it was true, she realized. In the end, Havvelan and Favian and the others were coming for her. She and Devon had upset their balance of power. They hadn't started it—Terrial had done that with the activation of the Warding at the Lyceum—but they had been the power behind nearly everything that had happened since.

She drew in a steadying breath, then said, "You're right. We should use that when we begin to implement our plans. I need to be seen, dangled in front of them, used to draw them out."

"It will be dangerous."

Lane nodded. "But necessary."

Burdock began rolling up the map. "Then we should get started. I assume you're willing to work with John Senn and his men to begin building up the defenses and preparing the citizens for the attack?"

"Of course," Maureen said.

"Then we'll begin by training anyone willing to be trained in how to fight. Everyone else we'll put to use fortifying the gates, walls, rooftops, and whatever other areas of defense we can find."

Everyone began preparing to leave, but Lane raised her hand. "I have one other thought." When they all turned toward her, she said, "What about the other cities?"

Maureen frowned. "What about them?"

"There are five other cities, all of them being affected by what's happening in Iandolo with the Council. The focus was always on Luminesque, but citizens from the other provinces were being subjugated as well. They were leaving Iandolo in droves, especially at the end."

"You think they'd come to our defense?" Burdock asked.

"Why not? Like Luminesque, their power within the Council has been subverted over the years. Their Councilors are representing them in name only, chosen by and subservient to Iandolo, not by the people in their respective cities. We should send envoys to each of the cities, explain to them that Luminesque is merely the beginning. Havvelan and the Iandolan army will come for them all eventually."

The room remained silent, except for Jillian's stylus, until even that quieted.

Burdock faced Varenov. "What do you think, Councilor?"

"Lane is correct: the Councilors from the other cities are mostly figureheads. A few have never even set foot in the province they represent. But the governments within the cities themselves are a different story. None of the other cities have been as troublesome as Brovetto, so there was no need to send governors to replace those already in power." She paused, considering. "It will depend on how loyal the governors are in each city, but I don't see why we couldn't ask."

"Then I'll have my father arrange two envoys, one each to travel the wayfares to Radimansque and Scintillesque, and from those cities to the other three," Lane said.

The others rose, Maureen and her aide departing first, Burdock escorted out by his keepers, to be returned to his rooms. He left the map behind.

"Do you think anyone will come?" Raven asked from Lane's side.

She stared at the tiers and streets of the city. "Even if they agree to help us, it's unlikely that they'll arrive before Havvelan and the Iandolan army. They have a lot farther to travel. We're going to have to do this alone."

"Then why send the envoys? Why bring up contacting them at all?" Cerelle asked.

"Because it will give the people hope," Varenov answered.

"Find Nic and Picall," Lane said to Raven. "I want them to be part of the envoys."

Raven nodded, but before she could leave the entire governor's manse shook, from its foundation up. Lane clutched at the table as the objects holding the map down juddered and skittered. Glassware trundled off shelves and crashed to the floor and shouts rose from elsewhere in the building. Dust and grit spilled down from overhead. A muted rumble from outside rose in pitch, then faded as the tremors died out.

Cerelle, Sadie, and Varenov traded glances with Lane from where they stood or crouched, holding onto a wall or a chair for support.

"Was in hells was that?" Sadie asked.

Two guards appeared in the doorway. "Governor Lane, are you all right?" one of them gasped.

"I'm fine." She straightened and brushed dust from a shoulder as she headed toward them. "Any idea what that was?"

The lead guard swallowed and shook his head. "No idea."

"Let's go find out."

They found the rest of the manse in disarray, servants shaken and uncertain. A few had begun cleaning up the damage—broken pottery and shards of glass from window panes. A sizeable crack had split one wall near the kitchens, plaster chunks littering the floor. Most took heart when Lane and the others appeared, but no one had an explanation.

Until they left the manse and were standing in the courtyard before the Fifth Level gates.

Lane was glancing around the yard, noting the confused looks on everyone's faces, when Varenov tugged at her sleeve. "Someone's coming."

She turned to see one of her father's men running towards them. He drew up short, clutching his chest as he caught his breath, one hand keeping his sword steady. He coughed, then gasped, "You need to come to the wall," already turning away.

She caught his arm. "Why?"

He coughed again, sucked in a breath, then said, "Because part of the Second Level has collapsed."

Chapter Nine

"What in hells just happened?" Devon asked, coughing as he sat upright. Chunks of stone and a few handfuls of silt fell off of his chest into his lap. Dust clogged the air, illuminated by the glowing lucent in the work station they had recently repaired and in the tunnels leading to the room. Dalton, already standing, reached down to help him up.

"I don't know, but whatever it was happened shortly after you activated the water pump."

They both paused to listen, but the pump nearest to them was still operating. Devon bent over the station, frantically checking pipelines in the various glowing lines of lucent.

"There!" He pointed to where a section of lucent was dim, the part beyond it dark. But not the filmy or speckled black of dead lucent. It simply wasn't activated. "That's on the Second Level, near the station we repaired this afternoon."

They shared a look. "Connor," they said together.

Before either of them could react, they heard someone running, coming from the direction of the thunderous rumble that had accompanied the shaking ground that had knocked them to the floor. Whoever it was, they were shouting. Dalton stepped in front of Devon until Devon recognized the voice.

"It's Connor! He's yelling, 'Shut it down!'"

He spun back to the work station, tracing out the dead line back to the first junction where he could stop the water's flow. He flicked the lucent off a moment before Connor stumbled into the station's room and gasped, "Shut down the Hanover branch, now! There's been a collapse! The water's pouring out into nothing, going nowhere!"

"Already done," Devon said.

Connor nodded and sagged against the wall, chest heaving. He waved them away. "Just give me a moment." He was covered with dust from head to toe, a bloody scrape near one eye. He pressed a hand over his chest, near his heart, and winced. When he saw their looks of concern, he said, "A chunk of stone from the ceiling hit me. There's going to be a horrendous bruise, but I don't think anything's broken."

"What happened?"

"I'm not certain. Everything appeared fine. I was monitoring the station near the Hanover branch when suddenly the ground began to quake. It knocked me to the floor. I managed to crawl to the main tunnel and get to my feet, but the sound was getting closer, so I ran. I could see parts of the tunnel collapsing beyond the station. I didn't make it far before the shaking stopped and the rumbling quieted. I ran back, but the station was dead and I could see sunlight through the tunnel on the other side." He paused to catch his breath. "You have to see it. An entire section of the Second Level is gone. Just…gone."

"Were any people hurt?" Devon asked.

Connor shook his head. "I don't know. It wasn't a heavily populated part of the city—it was on the Second Level—but there must have been people there. If there were, I don't see how any of them could have survived."

"Take us there," Dalton said. "If you can manage it."

Connor straightened with a cough and grimace. "I said I was fine."

Devon wasn't so certain, but Connor led them through the tunnel he'd come from. Dust and stone debris littered the floor, some chunks as large as Devon's head. Cracks lined the walls. In a few places, the ceiling sagged dangerously, but held. They passed the pumping chamber they'd worked on most recently, the lucent still glowing, water coursing through the pipes on either side.

As they drew closer to where Connor had been stationed, the lucent in the walls began to flicker in places. Devon didn't stop to repair them, too intent on keeping up with Connor. They moved into a section of tunnel where the lucent was completely dead, but up ahead Devon could see sunlight.

They emerged in the work station they'd repaired that afternoon, the panel of lucent almost completely dead. Only a few threads of lucent were still lit, all dim. One or two sputtered erratically. But beyond the station—

Devon edged forward, with Dalton and Connor to either side. He raised one hand to shield against the evening sunlight. They'd been working all afternoon in the lucent-lit darkness of the tunnels and pumping system and real sunlight made his eyes water. But his arm dropped when he saw the devastation.

A giant irregular hole had been opened up to the sky overhead, the edges jagged and clearly unstable. On one side, buildings had been torn in half, their interiors exposed. To their left, enough of the buildings had been taken that they'd simply caved in on themselves. Beneath, the layers of foundation for the streets and the tunnels and corridors of the pumping systems had been shorn off, mouths of pipes gaping open, some still spilling water into the emptiness below. A few sections of street and building had been undercut by the collapse. One such section gave way as they watched, a wall and stone cobbles tumbling down into the abyss.

Devon watched it fall, stepping up closer to the edge, Dalton laying a hand on his shoulder to halt him.

"We don't know if this section is stable or not," he said. "We could be standing on a plinth of rock jutting out over that sinkhole."

Devon nodded, but leaned forward to get a better look. He was four feet from the edge, but he couldn't see the bottom. "How could it be so deep?" he asked.

"We're a mining city," Connor said from behind them. He hadn't come as close to the edge as Devon or Dalton. "If I had to guess, I'd say that turning on the pumping stations and sending water down through pipes that haven't been used in years, maybe even decades, destabilized something and everything fell down into the mines below."

Devon felt nausea twisting in his stomach. "So we caused this?"

"Devon, we couldn't have known. If Connor is right, then those pipes carrying the water once worked fine. The neglect probably caused some to crack. Foundations shifted. The mines haven't been worked in years—"

"And once we turned the water back on, it leaked into the foundation, and then..." He couldn't finish. He bent over, sickened, and Dalton pulled him back from the edge. "I thought we were checking everything, repairing any cracks that we found."

"We've been doing that on the surface. Not underground."

"Then we need to start doing it underground as well!"

"That's...that's not always possible."

Devon looked up, ready to snap back, but caught himself when he saw Connor's reddened eyes, the tears that shimmered there unshed. The Brovettan wiped them away with one hand, his skin splotchy, face drawn.

Devon drew in a few steadying breaths to control himself, shoved the anger back, straightened. "We need to get up there, warn everyone to stay away from the edges before even more people die." His voice was ragged.

Neither Dalton nor Connor tried to stop him as he passed.

* * *

It took nearly an hour to find their way out, some of the tunnels they'd used to descend to this level either gone or caved in. By the time they emerged from a station house on the Second Level, seven blocks from where the sinkhole stood, the sun was beginning to set and storm clouds were boiling to the north, lit blue and purple from within by lightning.

Devon trotted toward the gaping pit of the collapse, Dalton and Connor a few paces behind, but they were halted from the edge by a thin crowd of gawkers held back by a line of guardsmen. Devon forced his way forward, until he stood before one of the guards.

"And where do you think you're going?" the guard asked, one hand held up to stop Devon from moving forward.

"I need to speak to Lane."

"He means the governor," another guard said from the side. When the first guard narrowed his eyes suspiciously, the second guard added, "It's fine. I recognize him from the governor's advising group. He's been working on the water system."

The first guard hesitated as Dalton and Connor stepped up behind Devon. As soon as he saw Connor, he relaxed. "All right then. Come on through. The governor and her advisors are surveying the damage from over there, about three blocks away. Stay away from the edge here. It hasn't been cleared yet and a ten-foot chunk fell away about half an hour ago."

He let the three of them through, a few of the gawkers protesting, until they saw Devon and the others heading to the right, not toward the edge. They skirted the line of guardsmen, who'd begun lighting torches as the darkness grew. Devon pulled his lucent lantern free and flicked it on.

They hit a row of tenements, cut right at the next street, then left, and cut through an alley, the edge of the pit now less than a block away. At the next intersection, they spied a group of torches at the end of the street. To the left, a building had been cut in half, jagged stone along its right edge where it had sheered away. To the right, Lane, her father and mother, Cerelle, Sadie, and a handful of guards were deep in conversation at the edge of a park, twenty feet from the pit. As they approached, one of the guards called out a warning, but Lane raised a hand to forestall them, stepping forward instead.

"Devon!" She pulled him in for a quick hug, Dalton as well. "We didn't know what had happened to you. We were beginning to think—" But she halted, lips pursed, then shook her head. "It doesn't matter." She waved toward the pit. "Do you know what happened?"

"I think we may have caused it."

Everyone turned towards him.

"What do you mean?"

"We think when we opened up some of the new pipelines, water leaked into the foundations, undermined them, and caused the collapse. We've shut off the main line leading to that section of the city, but we're going to have to check all of the remaining lines, tunnel by tunnel, pipe by pipe, for possible damage before I'll be willing to start them up again."

"I thought we were repairing the lines before reinstating them."

"Aboveground." Devon realized his tone had become belligerent, forced himself to add in a quieter voice, "We haven't been checking those underground."

"There will be pipes too small for us to check no matter how careful we are," Connor said. "There will always be some risk."

"But we'll minimize that risk as much as possible," Devon said vehemently.

"You don't know it was the water that caused this," a new voice said.

Devon spun as Maureen, her aide, and a couple of additional Brovettans emerged from the darkness behind them. She passed through them all, moving to the edge of the pit to stare down into its depths, her entourage hanging back, then faced them again.

"I've been helping to organize crews to rescue those trapped in buildings and in rubble near the edges of the collapse. There are still some being pulled from the debris here and there. None of them believe that this was caused by anything except the overmining and abandonment of the mines below. The Iandolans had us rip all of the lucent from the earth and send it to Iridesque as fast as possible. And then, when the mines were depleted, they simply left them. Few have been down there since. A collapse like this was inevitable."

She returned, halting before Devon, meeting his gaze. "Don't let this setback cripple you. The city needs water, needs those fields on the First and Second Levels to be productive. And you don't have time to waste being careful, not with the Iandolan army marching on our city." She looked around at all of them. "Get this city functioning again. The Brovettans aren't going to blame you as long as the water is flowing."

Then she nodded to Devon, motioned to the rest of her group, and vanished into the night.

Lane took her place at Devon's side. "You heard her. Be careful, but don't delay. She's right. We don't know how much time we have before the Iandolans arrive."

"About that," Devon said. "Dalton and I did a little exploring and found a warding in one of the plazas near the waygate."

"A warding?" She frowned. "I haven't noticed any wardings at all in this city since we arrived."

"That's because they're more refined here, more hidden. This one was embedded in the plaza's stonework, in the ground. There was a market set up on top of it. But if there are more of them—"

"—perhaps we can use them against the Iandolans," Lane finished. "Although that would have to be a last resort. As we saw in Iandolo, someone has to activate it, and that person is trapped inside it, along with everyone else."

"Unless there's a way to activate them from afar."

"Not that I'm aware of," Lane said.

"We know we can take the wardings down if we have to use them."

"In order to do that, I'd have to survive."

Devon's breath caught. He wanted to say, *Of course you're going to survive,* but he knew that wasn't guaranteed. They both knew it, after what had happened in Iandolo. If they didn't die during the fighting, if they were captured, Havvelan and Favian wouldn't keep them alive. There would be an immediate public execution, without trial.

Neither one of them would be allowed a reprieve.

The silence stretched too long. He tried to say something, anything, but his throat felt closed off. No sound came out at all.

Lane gave him a thin smile, placed a hand on his arm, said in a soft voice no one but he and Dalton could hear, "It's all right, Devon. I knew what I was getting into. I knew as soon as we fled Iridesque, as soon as I tore down the waygate. I accepted it a long time ago."

Her hand fell and she glanced toward the gaping emptiness of the pit, a thoughtful look on her face. "We should head back to the governor's manse. There's not much we can do here in the dark." Facing Devon again, she added, "And we should say goodbye to Nic and Picall."

Devon frowned. "What do you mean, 'Goodbye?'"

* * *

"Why in hells did you agree to go to Radimansque?" Devon demanded as he burst through the door to Nic's room in the manse. Nic sat on the bed, satchel between his feet, a stack of clothes and other essentials scattered around him. He'd just finished tucking in a shirt. Picall sat at a table, carefully oiling the wood of her crossbow. "And you," he added, facing her. "Scintillesque?"

"Lane needed us," Nic said with a shrug. He continued shoving things into his bag. "She said—"

Devon waved him silent. "I already know. She told me. Try to convince the other cities to come to our defense."

He felt Dalton press up behind him. "Can we come in?" the ex-guardsman asked. He held up a bottle of wine. "We paid a quick visit to Arch before we came here. It took some finagling, but he finally admitted he had a few reserves stashed away and let us have one."

By way of answer, Nic stood and grabbed the bottle. "I hear Radimansque has some extremely good wines." A thin knife appeared in his hand and he began working at the cork. As soon as it popped free, he took a heavy swig and passed it on to Picall before falling back onto his bed.

Devon shared a look with Dalton, then moved to Picall's table, taking up the bottle when she offered it. "What's gotten into him?"

"He thinks we're abandoning you all. Or that he's being sent away."

Nic snorted. "That's not it." He was lying on the bed, twirling the knife around in the air, flipping it from hand to hand.

Devon took a sip of the wine, made a face at how dry it was, and handed it over to Dalton. "Then what is it?"

Nic was quiet for a long moment, the knife flicking left, spinning, then right—

Until he snatched it in one hand and sat up to face them, heaving a long sigh. "It's this." He motioned around the room with the blade. "All of this. The manse, Lane as governor, you working to restore the lucent so the city will have water. I used to scrounge for food in the depths of Iandolo, even when I was part of Carbolen's gang. Dalton and Lane were merely students, Dalton a soldier. At one point, we were all fugitives, hunted by the gangs, the proctors, *and* the Iandolan army. Now Lane is ruling Brovetto. You're rebuilding it. And I'm—"

"You're being sent to recruit reinforcements, because we both know that the chances Lane and the rest of us can defend this city from Havvelan and Favian is minimal."

Nic met Devon's gaze and Devon saw the despair there. "I don't want this responsibility."

"None of us did," Dalton said.

"Well, I'm fairly certain Lane did, deep down inside. She was born into it, no matter how much she protested that at the Lyceum." He grinned and was heartened to see a tentative smile from Nic.

"Give me that bottle."

Devon grabbed the bottle from Dalton and handed it over, settling down beside the ex-gang member as he took another swallow. Nic made room, then grunted as he fumbled around amongst all of the clothes on the bed. A moment later, he produced something in one hand, handing it over to Devon. "I found this at the bottom of my satchel when I started to pack."

Devon held the red crystal up, the lucent wrapped in metal on one end in a spiral pattern, ending in a short cap and the jagged end of a stub of wood. "What is it?"

"The end of one of the staffs used by the Iandolan army."

"Let me see that," Dalton said, crossing the room to take it from Devon. He inspected it closely, then handed it back. "He's right. It's called a lithum. They always come in pairs—a red one and a blue one. The army carries them into battle, no matter where we go."

"I remember now. We saw them when the Iandolan army was being sent to Brovetto. Where did you get this?"

"During Lane and her mother's execution. When Carbolen set off the explosion, one of the mages carrying the staff was flung to the stage. He dropped the staff and the top broke off. I grabbed it and shoved it into my pocket, then later, during the insanity of rescuing you and fleeing the city, I moved it to my satchel and forgot about it."

"And Burdock didn't confiscate it when you were taken at the waygate?"

"I didn't have my satchel with me then. It was in one of the wagons."

Devon looked at Dalton. "What does it do?"

Dalton shrugged. "They never shared that with us. All they ever said was that both staffs had to remain with the army whenever we were outside of the city. It had something to do with the mages, not the soldiers. Maybe Burdock knows. Or one of the mages who came with us form Iandolo."

Devon laid a hand on the crystal. "Let's see what I can find out."

He sank into the crystal, slipping into the elongated facets and lines of structure within, just as he'd done to pick the lucent locks when he was part of the gangs. His perception of the others in the room dampened, but he heard them muttering, reacting to something he couldn't see or feel. But he stayed inside the crystal, traveling different pathways, mapping it out in his mind as he moved, as he'd done with the Warding when he and Lane were attempting to unlock it.

He recognized part of the structure—a lantern, like the green shard he carried around from the Lyceum—which made sense, because he'd seen the mages striking the lithum on the ground, seen them begin to glow. But that was near the center of the lucent. There were layers of nodes and connections surrounding that, interlocked in a much more complex pattern. He traced it out slowly, then stood back and surveyed it as a whole. The filaments that formed its foundation pulsed with an innate energy, sort of like the tension he'd seen in the structure of the Warding, but rather than feeling taut, these filaments simply felt...engorged. And no matter how he approached them, they refused to release the energy. Almost as if they were locked somehow.

"And I don't have the key," he murmured to himself.

It wasn't like the lucent locks he'd picked either. He didn't see any layers to traverse to release it.

He pulled back even farther, rotating the structure before him. It wasn't symmetric. Ovate, more or less, coming to points at the top and bottom, one half was indented, the "surface" rough, unlike the opposite side, where the energy was stored. The filaments were jagged, with crevices and peaks, like a mountain range.

"Or like the teeth of a key."

He pulled out of the crystal, taking a moment to center himself before glancing around at the others. They'd fallen silent and were all staring at him.

"What?" he asked. "What happened?"

"As soon as you entered the crystal, all of the lucent in the room brightened," Dalton said. "Not by much, but enough to notice."

"And as soon as you came back out, they dimmed again," Nic added.

"That makes sense," Devon said, setting the crystal on the table where Picall continued to clean her crossbow. "From what I saw, it acts like a storage device. There's energy stored in there already, but based on the configuration, I'd say it could hold a lot more, maybe ten times as much. Sinking into it probably allowed some of the energy to leak out."

"Why not all of it?"

"Because it's locked. There's another half to the structure—"

"The blue crystal," Dalton interrupted. "I told you they always come in pairs."

Devon nodded. "I'm guessing that, together, red and blue, the two create a pool of energy that the mages can tap into. To increase their power or..."

"Or give them power when they wouldn't normally have access to it!" Dalton said. He began to pace in the small room. "Remember when we descended into the mines below Iandolo, then out onto the Flatlands? Lane couldn't do anything. Even at the tull. Then, after breaching the waygate and escaping Iridesque, she couldn't do any magic again on the wayfare."

"She hated it," Nic said.

"But I know for a fact that the mages in the army could perform spells on the wayfare. I listened to a hundred stories from the men in my barracks who were sent to Brovetto after the attacks. They used lucent lanterns the entire way. The mages had small practice bouts when they rested at night!"

"Because you always had the red and blue lithum with you."

"The only problem is," Picall said, setting down her crossbow and picking up the red crystal, "you don't have the blue one."

"Which means this one is worthless." Nic lay back on the bed and put an arm over his eyes.

Devon stood and took the crystal from Picall. "Not worthless. Maybe I can figure out how it's made."

"If you do, the mages would be interested in knowing. From what I remember being a War student, they had few pairs of lithum. One of the main objectives of most of our forms, besides protecting the mages, was maintaining control of the lithum at all costs. I'm surprised you managed to get your hands on this one."

Nic sighed. "If you recall, at the time, the Pulpit was rather chaotic."

"I'll have to ask Arrend and the others from the Lyceum what they know about them," Devon said, still staring at the crystal.

Dalton took it from him, setting it back on the table and grabbing up the bottle. "Until then, we have this wine to finish."

Nic lurched up and reached for it, but Dalton snatched it out of the way with a laugh.

* * *

Lane entered her rooms in the manse to find her father waiting for her with two other guards. She halted a few paces inside the door, noted the tray on the low table with a decanter, glasses, and a platter of bread, cheese, and some kind of spread.

"It's been an active day, father," she said, continuing on toward the door to the bedchamber. Her escort settled in on either side of the outer room's door.

Her father sat forward and began pouring two drinks. "So I heard. And felt. I was down in the city when that section collapsed into the mines. Much closer than you were here."

Lane hesitated, hand on the inner door, then sighed and turned back. "What were you doing down there?"

"Scouting out locations for possible training yards for the citizens. And a few suitable buildings for your friends from the Lyceum."

She drifted toward the settee and chairs where her father sat. "We hadn't had the war council yet. How did you know we'd need training yards."

"We have no army, Lane, only a group of rebels led by me and my cohorts, a group of tullers led by Maupin, an ex-prefect of the Iandolan army with no soldiers beneath him, and the citizens of Brovetto. It wasn't that difficult to determine we'd need training yards." He handed over one of the glasses.

Lane swirled the dark amber liquid around and sniffed it. It burned her nostrils even without taking a drink. "Don't forget Arch's mercenaries."

Her father tossed his drink back. "Never," he gasped, setting the glass down. "They're going to be trainers, once we get started."

"And what did you find?"

"There are multiple squares and plazas on each level that we can use, besides the barracks and armories at the waygates. There's also a small complex of buildings on the Third Level for Arrend and the other college proctors and students. It's surrounded by its own wall and has a courtyard. The courtyard is paved in stone, but otherwise it's fairly close to the layout of the Lyceum itself. I've already had my men show it to Arrend and I believe he and the others are moving in as we speak."

"I'll go see them tomorrow morning then. You didn't have to wait for me here to tell me that though. You could have found me tomorrow."

Her father stood and came around the settee so that he stood before her. "That isn't why I came."

"Why, then?"

"Burdock told me about what was discussed at the war council, about the plans to use the city as our main defense—the streets, the secret ways between building, between levels. He wanted me to help him with the map, to chart out what the rebels knew so that we could make plans. But I'm not the one who knows the secret ways around Brovetto the best. We need someone else."

"Who?"

"Me," said someone deeper inside the room.

Lane spun to find Mouse standing at the doors leading to the balcony. One of them was open, so either he'd been on the balcony the entire time or had found his way there while they spoke.

The anger on seeing him was instantaneous. She narrowed her gaze and said, firmly, "No."

She handed her untouched glass to her father and turned away, but he grabbed her arm with his free hand to stop her. When she whirled back on him, he said, "He knows ten times more about this city than I do."

"He doesn't listen." She jerked her arm free. "He's reckless, careless, and far too free with the use of his blade."

"Lane—"

"He killed a servant for no reason when we came here to free you all!"

"I didn't hear you complaining about the soldiers we had to kill to get inside the walls," Mouse said. He hadn't moved from the balcony doorway.

"I didn't know about the soldiers until they were already dead!"

He moved into the room, to the low table, tore a chunk from the bread, and cut a sliver of cheese. "Would it have made a difference if you had known?"

"I would have told you to find another way."

"There was no other way. Except through the front gates. You knew that."

Lane grit her teeth and swallowed her response.

"Lane," her father said, "we don't need him to infiltrate. We only need him to show us the city's underground networks."

She fumed for a moment, glaring at the short rebel, arms crossed over her chest defiantly, then faced her father. "Use him for mapping, but nothing else. I don't trust him."

Chapter Ten

Lane stood on the threshold of one of the rooms inside the small complex of buildings that her father had found for the new college. Raven hung back a few paces behind her with another guard, one of the tullers based on his clothes and the deep tan of his skin. From within came the sounds of light conversation from the students waiting, punctuated with soft whispers and light laughter. From elsewhere within the building there were sounds of construction, of furniture being moved, mixed with curses and shouted orders.

Lane smoothed out the folds of her dress, but didn't move.

Raven stepped forward. "They're waiting for you."

"I know," Lane snapped, then drew in a steadying breath, let it out slow. "Sorry." She cast a look backwards, gave a wry smile. "After all of that heartbreaking time at the Lyceum—the dismissal, the flight into the lower city and the tull—I never thought I'd be returning, especially not as a proctor."

"Be thankful one of the proctors who wanted to flee Iandolo was a mage then."

Lane turned at the familiar voice approaching from down the hall and smiled. "Arrend! I haven't seen you in days."

"I've been busy here at the Collegium," he said, motioning around with one hand. "Ever since your father informed us he'd found it. We've got the dormitories set up already, and the dining hall, and have set aside a few rooms for classes. Some of the other proctors have already begun teaching students. Not just those that fled with us across the wayfare. A few others from Brovetto have come forward and asked to be taught. We've doubled our numbers already. I expect that will double again within the next few days."

Lane frowned. "Can we accommodate them all?"

"I believe so. Maureen's assistants, Hicks and Brokaw, have been extremely helpful stocking the kitchens and sending along anything else we need." Laughter broke from the room and he glanced inside, then turned back with a look of understanding. "Have you not introduced yourself to your students yet?"

"No."

"I see."

"I wasn't meant to be a teacher. Shards, Devon was the one who taught *me* how to use the sigils. He's the one who should be here."

"He's busy with the mines and water system." He touched her arm to draw her attention away from the door. "Lane, all teachers are nervous when they first enter a classroom."

"But I got expelled from the Lyceum. I never learned anything taught after the third year. I don't know what I should be teaching them."

Arrend shifted in front of her, so they were looking eye-to-eye. "Listen to me. This is not the Lyceum. It can't be the Lyceum and, if I have my way, it will never be the Lyceum. This Collegium will be better. I firmly believe that the reason you are as powerful as you are is because you *weren't* trained by the mages at the Lyceum. The mage proctors there, like Favian, have narrow vision. Their curriculum is too rigid, too set in its ways. But here, there are no rules yet. You can teach however you want. Except you have one thing you must keep in mind."

Feeling heartened, Lane gave a tentative smile. "What's that?"

"You have no time. The Iandolan mages are coming and these students need to be prepared."

Lane's smile gave out. "Right."

Arrend patted her arm again and began to walk away. "You'll be fine."

Lane straightened her shoulders, glanced back at Raven, then strode into the room.

Six people sat inside around a low oval table on an assortment of giant pillows. All of them fell silent and looked towards her, Raven, and her guard. They ranged in age from twelve to at least thirty. Most were between fourteen and twenty. The rest of the room was sparse, the walls bare, a single chest of drawers against one wall, an end table beside it. A pitcher of water and an assortment of cups were scattered around the table. There was no parchment to write on, no quills or bottles of ink, no slate with chalk at hand. The far wall contained a set of four arched doorways that led out onto a portico overlooking the courtyard at the center of the set of buildings. They might once have contained glass doors, but for now they were simply open. A fresh breeze skirled through the room.

The mage proctor from the Lyceum stood and gave a short bow. "Proctor Illea."

"No!" Lane said, more sharply than she'd intended. The mage proctor flinched. In a calmer voice, she added, "No, we don't have time for that. Call me Lane. And you are?"

"Dawn. Dawn Percy. And these five are Brigette, Daniel, Gregg, Serene, and Shian."

Lane nodded to them all. Brigette and Daniel appeared to be fifth years, Gregg fourth, so around seventeen or eighteen. Serene was younger, perhaps a second year. "I'm guessing all of you came from the Lyceum, except for you Shian. You're too young to have been at the college yet."

The girl stood, hands and fingers twisting together as she spoke, eyes wide. "My parents are from Opalesque. We…we fled Iandolo when the rioting began."

Dawn stepped up behind the girl. "We ran into her and her family on the wayfare. I'm not certain—we don't have a way to test here—but I think she'll be able to create the base form."

"There's only one way to find out," Lane said. She motioned for the two to rejoin the others in their seats around the table, taking her own position at one end, facing them. She raised her hand and crooked her fingers. "This is the hand position you need to use to begin the base form for the sigils."

Daniel rolled his eyes. "We aren't first years. We know the hand position."

Lane gave him a thin-lipped smile. "This isn't the Lyceum. And not all of you know the hand position. We're going to start from the basics, because some of what you've already learned at the Lyceum is wrong, and because not all of you are at the same level. If we're going over something you already know, then you can help the others who don't know it learn it. Is that understood?"

All of them nodded or muttered something Lane took as agreement, even Dawn. Lane closed her eyes briefly to calm herself, exhaled, then started again.

"This is the hand position needed for the primary sigil. The first two fingers are crooked like so, the others curled under, like a half-fist. This is what is taught at the Lyceum, but it turns out that this particular position isn't really necessary. If you perform the proper sequence, with the proper timing, even with one finger poised or even your entire hand, the sigil will appear. This crooked finger position has the advantage of stability and a certain amount of precision. If you need to be more precise, then you should switch to using a single finger."

Serene frowned. "They never taught us a single-fingered position at the college." Unlike Daniel's comment, Serene's carried no impatience or condescension. It was merely an observation.

"That's correct. But as I said, not everything the Lyceum proctors taught was correct. Their understanding of the sigils and its structure were limited."

"Is this how you and Devon Alamort managed to kill the Traitor Mage, Terrial?" Brigette asked, leaning forward intently. Both Daniel and Gregg also shifted forward, suddenly interested. Serene shrank back.

"Brigette," Dawn said, voice laced with warning. "I told you—all of you—not to bother her with such questions."

Lane raised a hand to halt her. "It's fine. I should have anticipated it." She focused on all six of them. "Yes, that is one reason we managed to defeat Terrial. She was trained by the Lyceum mages and only knew the basic structures that were taught there. She managed to experiment on her own while hidden in Brovetto and discovered a few new forms, like the cantrip, but she was blinded by the limitations the Lyceum mages taught. She never saw the true potential of the structure itself, because she never understood it. Not like I do. Not like Devon does."

Now Dawn was frowning. "What do you mean? The structure is fixed. The patterns of the sigils are fixed."

"Yes, the structure is fixed. But not the patterns."

"But they drilled us over and over at the college. This is the pattern. Repeat it exactly. Do not deviate. There were consequences if you did—lashings, beatings, sequestration. And I know the punishments were deserved. One of my friends accidentally messed up one of the patterns and died when the entire training room erupted into seething flame. Two other students and a proctor were also killed."

Serene looked horrified. "That can happen?"

"I heard about that," Gregg said with relish. "They said it was so hot none of them had time to scream."

"Gregg!" Dawn snapped, as Serene gasped. Shian hadn't reacted to any of it, simply taking it all in.

"To answer Serene's question," Lane said, raising her voice enough to override everyone else and capture their attention again, "such disasters can happen. But the reason they happened as often as they did at the Lyceum is because the proctors there didn't understand the true structure of the sigils and what it could do…and also carelessness among those casting the sigil. I'm going to teach you all the true structure and how to use it. If you're careful, and if you truly understand, then you shouldn't have any such accidents." She let her stern gaze drift over all of them, noting Serene's apprehension, Daniel's interest, and Dawn's skepticism. "Now, let's practice the two-fingered crooked hand position. Once I feel you've all mastered that, which shouldn't take long, then we'll move on to the pattern for the base sigil. That will likely take longer to master."

Daniel had straightened in his seat, Gregg following suit. "They didn't show us the base sigil until the third year and you're going to show us on the first day?"

"As I said, we don't have time. The Iandolan army is likely marching on Brovetto as we speak."

That sobered them all up.

"Now, crook your fingers, like so. Good, Daniel. And Brigette. Don't tense up so much, Gregg. Your form is fine but if you remain that tense the entire time your hand is going to cramp. Now help out Serene and Shian… although it looks like Shian is doing fine already."

She allowed them to help each other out as she walked around the table, occasionally correcting a finger placement or hand position. They practiced shifting from a natural stance into the crook for nearly half an hour, Lane emphasizing that they needed to practice the form at random until it became habit. They couldn't afford to spend time thinking about whether their fingers were in the correct place once those from Iridesque arrived.

Then she shifted to the base form, showing Serene and Shian the sigil and reciting the mantra to help with the timing. Her work with Devon helped here as she recalled how he'd managed to adjust her form until she got it correct. Brigette, Daniel, and Gregg already knew the base form, so she paired them off with Serene and Shian at random. Serene was anxious and terrified with her first few attempts, but after Brigette and Daniel created their own double pyramid forms, glowing a soft blue, and fireballs didn't spit from the walls, she relaxed enough she managed to produce her own in a matter of minutes. It took Shian longer, of course, because she hadn't been taught the mantra like Serene. The timing and placement of the nodes was brand new to her; Serene had already had some preparation.

As soon as all six of them had proven to Lane they could pull up the double pyramid with some accuracy, she shifted to explaining the structure itself.

"The double pyramid shape is composed of two sections that Devon named the Source and the Outcome. The four faces of the Source on the bottom control the four different aspects of whatever it is you're trying to create—namely direction, intensity, size and/or shape, and what type of construct you're making, such as fire, air, light, et cetera. After you set up the pyramids with the base form, you select what you need from these four regions. Your selections correspond to one and only one outcome in the upper pyramid. Once you've made your selections, you can't unmake them by dropping your hand or dispelling the double pyramids. Only someone else can counter your selection, or you have to complete another base form and make another selection to counter it yourself, which takes time. The trick is to become familiar enough with the faces of the Source pyramid so that you can make appropriate selections, and to be accurate in those selections in practice. A minor adjustment—missing a particular node or doing your selections out of order—can have drastic consequences."

"Wait," Dawn said, one hand gripping the back of a chair, knuckles white, the other held up to halt Lane's lecture. "Are you saying there's an inherent logic to the double pyramids? That it isn't just…random hand motions that make fire or lightning happen?"

"Exactly."

"But…" She waved her hand, pulled the chair back so she could sit in it, as if her legs had grown weak. "But at the Lyceum, the proctors all drilled into us that the sigils were sacred, that only certain hand movements would produce results. They never once indicated that there was a…a pattern behind them. It all seemed so random. Yes, if we didn't get the hand gesture just right, we'd—" she glanced at Gregg "—set the room on fire. Or worse. The sigils were a closely guarded secret. They were taught only once you'd convinced the proctors that you could be trusted."

"I only knew four of them," Daniel said. "And I was a fifth year."

"They showed you more in your sixth year," Brigette said, "but they made it sound as if those we learned were the only sigils available. Are you saying they were lying?"

Dawn laughed, the sound strained. "They were definitely lying. After you graduate, if you stay in the army or become a proctor yourself, they teach you more of them. More complicated versions of the ones you know and other new ones." She faced Lane. "But they never hinted that there were even more."

"I don't think they knew," Lane said. "This is why Devon's discovery of the true structure was so volatile, so feared. I believe Terrial stumbled onto some of the additional sigils herself, by accident. If she knew of the true structure, she would have been much more difficult to defeat at the Lyceum."

"She knew enough to nearly take over Iandolo," Brigette said.

Lane nodded. "Enough to be dangerous, yes. Which is why I keep stressing caution."

"So are you going to teach us how to use the Source?" Daniel asked.

Lane hesitated. She didn't like the eagerness in Daniel's eyes. And Brigette's. Both of them reminded her of Quinn back at the Lyceum. They didn't have her hatred, her unalterable conviction in her own importance or beliefs, but there was an underlying self-centeredness.

"Not today," she said. "We've been working for hours now. And I didn't bring my notes, nor anything to sketch with. We won't be working the forms in practice right away regardless. It's too risky. I'll want to make certain you understand the structure of the Source first." She turned to Dawn. "Can you find paper and ink for us to use next time? Or slate and chalk. And we should probably have someone design a model of the double pyramid shape for practice with sigils."

Dawn stood. "I'll see what I can do."

"Good." She glanced around at the six of them, certain she should say something more, but ended up turning and leaving without a word.

It wasn't until she was in the hall, halfway to the front doors of the Collegium, that her shoulders relaxed and the tension drained out of her.

"That wasn't as bad as you thought it would be," Raven said.

She shot the ex-Regular a heated glare. Raven simply laughed.

* * *

"This is an utter disaster," Devon muttered, picking his way through the debris at the bottom of the collapse. Dozens of people were crawling over the rubble looking for survivors who'd been buried, calling out and listening for any signs of life, although hope was fading. Maureen and her teams had managed to find a few overnight, hunting by lantern and lucent light, but Devon couldn't see how anyone could have survived this long. The debris was mostly pulverized stone, with only hints of a building's wall or patch of tiled roof here and there. In the harsh glare of daylight, everything looked so much worse. It left him hollowed out with lingering guilt and despair, hovering on the edge of tears, emotionally drained. He'd felt the same for hours as he, Dalton, Connor, and a team Connor had wrangled together combed the underground levels between the Second

Level and the base of the mine sealing off water pipes and scavenging any splintered or destroyed lucent along the way.

"Yes, but there's not much we can do about it now," Dalton said, "except mitigate the damage and figure out where to go from here."

Shouts rang out from the far side of the collapse and everyone in Devon's group halted and watched as people scrambled to a particular heap of stone. Men and women were frantically tossing rock to one side, someone shouting orders, and then those nearest the center of the activity lurched forward. A moment later, they pulled a body from the debris, the woman's arms hanging limp. She was covered from head to toe in grit and dust, with two dark splotches of blood on one arm and a leg. Devon thought she was dead until they held her upright and he could see her struggling to stand on her own. Two men slung her arms around their shoulders and led her off toward the makeshift hospital Mindell and Brokaw had set up off to one side.

"Well then," Dalton said. "There's a little sign of hope."

Devon watched as those left behind gave a weary cheer, hugged and clapped each other on the back, then began searching again with a little more enthusiasm. "I honestly didn't think they'd find anyone else alive."

Dalton turned toward Connor, adjusting the sack slung across his back. "Where are we on the mines and tunnels? How much do we have left?"

Connor pulled a ragged map from a pocket and unfolded it, turning it with a frown until it lined up with their position. "We've covered everything except a section near the western wall. I think."

"You think?" Devon asked.

Connor glanced up. "It's hard to tell if we've caught everything. The collapse affected three or four levels of the mine and the tunnels were a maze to begin with. Plus this map isn't necessarily the most accurate, it's just the most recent we could find."

"How old it is?"

Connor scanned its edge. "Twenty-two years."

Devon rubbed at his eyes with two fingers. "Let's check this last section, then we'll figure out what to do after that. We may have to go over everything again, to be safe."

A few of Connor's crew surrounding them groaned. Devon didn't blame them.

Under Connor's direction, they circled the edge until they came to the western side, the stone of the plateau Brovetto had been built on rising like a cliff face beside them. Loosened stone occasionally rattled down as it was dislodged, so they kept a good twenty paces back. Devon didn't see any tunnels that were accessible at this level—only a few a good fifty feet above—until they rounded an edge and found an opening half buried beneath a scree of stone.

"That's it," Connor said, consulting his map. "There should be a tunnel there, with access to some drainage pipes. We're deep enough that I doubt they're connected to the main water system though."

"We need to check," Devon said. "I don't want to cause another collapse."

They entered through the narrow opening, dirt and rock cascading down the scree's slope as they stumbled up over it. Inside, the tunnel shot straight back, clearly carved out of the plateau for the mines. They edged forward, wary of the fresh cracks that riddled the walls, but the supports appeared undisturbed and stable. Devon pulled out his lucent lantern and flicked it to light. A few others produced torches. The sounds of their feet scuffing the ground, kicking the occasional chunk of stone, and the rasp of their breaths echoed back at them as they progressed. The air was still filled with dust. Someone coughed, the sound shockingly loud in the confined space.

After a hundred feet, the tunnel opened up into a massive cavern like the ones Devon and the others had found beneath Iandolo during their escape. Devon briefly wondered if there were skrill here; hadn't Mouse mentioned them when they used the mines before to rescue Dalton and the others?

"The map says this is called Gunthor's Pit," Connor supplied. "It was one of the original mines in Brovetto."

"Where would the drainage pipes be?" Devon asked.

"Over here."

They cut diagonally across the vast empty hall until they reached the southern wall, then followed it toward the far corner. Their torches glittered on crystals in the floor and the ceiling about six feet overhead. Not lucent, or at least, not significant chunks of lucent, but Devon could practically smell the raw crystal that had been here before.

"I don't see anything," Dalton said when they hit the western wall. He glanced along both walls, then motioned with one hand. "Spread out. It might not be along the wall."

Those with torches spread out into the room, radiating out from the corner, everyone pairing up with someone with a light source. Devon stuck to the wall, holding his lantern high for Dalton and Connor, who stayed with him. A break in the wall's uniformity had begun to appear in front of them when a startled cry came from deeper in the mine.

"Connor! Come quick!"

The voice was more excited than apprehensive. Devon exchanged a look with Dalton, then handed him the lantern. "Check out what's up ahead. I'll go with Connor."

Dalton nodded and then Devon followed Connor into the darkness toward the torch waving slightly to catch their attention.

When they were about twenty paces away, Devon tripped over a chunk of stone that he couldn't see. Not a pebble or even a fist-sized rock; when he knelt down, cursing, his foot throbbing, it felt about head-sized. Ahead, he heard Connor stumble and hit the ground hard.

"Careful," he called out. "There are some sizable stones on the floor."

"A little late with the warning." Connor's voice didn't sound amused.

Devon stood and headed toward him, moving slowly and feeling ahead with his feet. "Say something so I can find you."

"Like what?"

That was enough for Devon to hone in on his position. Aside from some smaller debris, he didn't run into anything larger than what he'd tripped over. He ran into a scattering of loose stone a moment before he kicked Connor, still sprawled on the floor.

Reaching down to help him up, he asked, "Are you all right?"

"Nothing bruised but my ass."

Devon grinned and focused in on the torch still rocking side to side. The other torch had joined it, illuminating a wider circle strewn with large boulders, the rest of Connor's crew wandering among them.

"Let's move a little slower this time," Devon said.

Connor merely grunted.

They joined Connor's crew, Devon wondering what the fuss was about—all he saw were boulders—when one of the men with a torch raised it upwards and said, "Look."

Devon glanced up and heard Connor gasp at the same time.

Above, a cavity gaped, the space where the stone had fallen from clear. He assumed the nearby collapse had caused this one. But inside the cavity, glittering with an amber hue, was—

"Lucent," Connor whispered in awe.

"Raw lucent," Devon clarified. He recognized the jagged crystalline forms from the raw lucent he'd found at the Tull. "And quite a bit of it." If he'd found this much real lucent in Iandolo when he was scavenging in the lower levels, he could have lived off of it for decades.

"They must have missed it when they were mining this cavern," one of the others said, his voice excited. Devon understood. If anyone had found a cache of lucent like this before the break with Iandolo, before the attacks and the flight to Brovetto, they could have started their own business by selling it to the merchant houses in Iridesque.

Instead, Iridesque was marching on their city even now.

Devon wondered how deep the crystals went. If he could touch one, he could find out...

He shook his head. "Mark this location on your map, Connor."

"Already done," he said, charcoal snub in hand.

"We'll have to come back for it some other time. Right now, I think we found the drainage pipes along the wall just before you called us out here." He motioned to where the greenish tinge of his lantern hovered in the darkness. "Let's check those and get back to the main city. It's been an exhausting day."

The men and women grumbled, but they headed back toward Dalton, the torches making the extent of the cave-in here visible. Those with torches kept raising them to the ceiling, but they found no more veins of raw lucent anywhere on the way.

"What did they find?" Dalton asked as soon as they were close. He stood before a wide rounded opening in the wall framed with worked stone that angled down from the city above. Directly beneath it was a lipped basin more like what was found surrounding a fountain, but with a grate in the bottom, clearly designed to catch any overflow from the drain and siphon it deeper into the mines. A trickle of water ran from the opening, but stains marked along the drain's side indicated the waterflow could be fairly significant.

"Raw lucent. The vein was hidden in the ceiling and was exposed when part of the stone collapsed. What about the drain here?" He nodded toward the pipe and basin.

Dalton shrugged. "I don't think it's anything we need to worry about. It doesn't appear connected to anything affected by the collapse. As you can see, the water is still flowing."

"Any lucent?"

"I think there's some veins buried in the sides of the pipe."

Without comment, Devon stepped forward and felt around the edges of the worked stone until he felt a smooth section of the crystal. Closing his eyes, he sank into it, then followed the vein upwards. This drainage tunnel was narrower than the one they'd used to escape the Burn and reach the upper levels, but the lucent along its length functioned more or less the same. He traced it until he was satisfied Dalton was correct, then pulled himself back. When he opened his eyes, the lucent he'd touched still glowed a soft blue, trailing up through the darkness of the pipe.

"I didn't find any breaks in the lucent connection," he said, "so I think this section is secure. I think we're done."

Connor's crew gave a heavy sigh of relief and began chatting amongst themselves. A heavy tension left Devon's shoulders and a wave of exhaustion shuddered through him. They'd been crawling through the underground systems for hours. He needed a break and, as his stomach reminded him, something to eat.

"There's something else," Dalton said.

He groaned. "What?"

"Over here." Dalton led him and Connor further along the wall, away from the basin, leaving the rest of the crew behind.

Within twenty paces, another pile of stone debris emerged from the darkness, similar to what they'd found beneath the raw crystal deposit, except this appeared to be a collapse from the wall.

"Once I'd checked out the drainage pipe," Dalton said, "and it was clear you weren't headed back right away, I decided to see if there was another drain further along and found this. I thought it was simply another cave-in, but look."

He held up the lantern to reveal a gape in the wall above the stone.

"It's another tunnel," Devon said, moving forward and climbing the edge of the rockfall.

"I think the tunnel had been sealed, but the collapse dislodged the stone and opened it back up."

"Connor?"

The Brovettan scanned his map. He flipped it back and forth, pulled another sheet from his satchel and consulted it, then shook his head. "It's not on any of the maps I have with me."

Devon considered the opening, then crawled up the rockfall, stone slipping out from beneath his feet, and hauled himself up over the top. He dropped down into the darkness on the far side. "Give me the lantern."

Dalton climbed up behind him and passed it through, but didn't follow. "What do you see?"

"A tunnel. Man-made, but rough, as if it were carved out of an already existing natural corridor. Half of the walls have been untouched. And it's old. If it's not on any of Connor's maps, that means it came long before they were made, sealed off and then forgotten."

"Any lucent in the walls?"

Devon felt along the stone on either side, bringing the lantern close as well. "Nothing I can see or feel."

"It's possible it's from when the mines were started," Connor said from outside. "An exploratory tunnel or something. This was one of the original mines."

Devon stood and stared down the black corridor. The exhaustion he'd felt moments before had faded, replaced with an urge to check out the tunnel. The darkness pulled at him. He felt a light breeze brush against his face, as if something deep inside the plateau had been disturbed and woken.

As if sensing his intention, Dalton said, "We don't have time to explore it right now. We need to get back and report to Lane and Varenov."

Devon hesitated, then forced himself to turn back, Dalton helping him scramble out of the opening.

"Mark it on the map, Connor. We'll have to come back." He brushed dirt from his shirt and breeches. "There's something down there. I can feel it."

Chapter Eleven

Devon sank into the lithum held in his left hand and slumped back into his chair in the rooms he and Dalton shared in the governor's manse. He allowed himself to roam through the lucent, following the lines of tension that surrounded its core of energy. In his mind, that energy glowed with vibrant light, pulsing slightly, like a heartbeat. But it was contained, held in check, similar to how the lines of structure in the Warding in Iandolo had vibrated with tension, waiting for someone to unleash it…or release it so it could return back to its original form. For the Warding, he'd traveled the paths until he'd found that key, then Lane had unlocked it.

"There's a key here as well," he muttered to himself. "Somewhere."

He shifted his attention from the tension in the structure and the energy it held to the edges of the red crystal. One side was crumpled, like a wadded-up piece of paper, filled with ridges and valleys in a complex pattern, even though the surface of the lucent was faceted normally, its faces smooth. This was the key. Or the lock. The blue crystal was the other half. If the two of them were close enough together, the energy being held inside the crystal would be free to access.

But they didn't have the blue crystal.

He withdrew from the lucent and opened his eyes. Scanning the room, he found his satchel, reached to pull it closer, then upended it onto the desk in front of him. Chunks of crystal that they'd salvaged from the sinkhole and other scrap heaps throughout the city clattered onto the wood. He began sorting them, shoving smaller pieces aside, looking for one that was fist-sized, one similar in shape to the red lithum. But none of them were that large. He didn't think any of the shards they'd picked from the debris had been that large. He wasn't certain he'd seen or held a piece of lucent that large his entire life. At least, not outside of the wall of a building or a Warding.

He sighed, then picked up one of the larger pieces, one with a relatively large flat side. He cupped the purple crystal in his right hand, lithum still in his left, and closed his eyes again.

Holding the purple crystal up slightly, he traced the contours of the structure beneath, then switched over to the lithum. Picking one particular section of ridges and valleys, he focused on its shape, tried to memorize the angles and lines and nodes, then flipped back to the crystal. Keeping the lithum's shape in mind, he scanned the purple lattice inside the crystal, shifting and rotating it in his hand, until he found a section relatively similar. Not exactly the same—that would have been too fortuitous—but close.

Then, as he'd done when he created the rose lantern at the Tull, he tried to shift the structure of the crystal enough to match that one section of the lithum.

He felt the crystal vibrating in the palm of his hand, tingling against his skin. The structure resisted. Clenching his teeth, he pushed harder. Then, suddenly, the lines and nodes inside the crystal slipped and snapped into the new configuration.

He gasped and sagged back into the chair, his hands trembling. Letting them rest on the desk, he gave himself a moment to recover, breathing deeply.

When the trembling stopped, he ran his thumb over the surface of the purple crystal. Nothing had changed of the texture, but the color in the area he'd focused on had shifted. He thought. He couldn't be certain—he hadn't paid that much attention to the particular shade of purple when he'd started—but in that one area, it appeared to have a bluer tinge.

Encouraged, he leaned back and closed his eyes again. Picking a different area near the first, he fixed the image of the ridges and valleys in the lithum in his head, then found the same location in the purple crystal. Unlike before, he couldn't shift the lucent around until he found a region that matched. If the lock and key were going to work, he had to build from what he'd already crafted. The structure in the new location was significantly different than in the lithum, but he concentrated, pushing hard, the crystal's vibrations buzzing in his teeth—

Then the nodes slipped, as before, and a wave of exhaustion tingled through his body. He panted at the effort it had taken, breath slowing steadily. His arms had sagged into his lap, the two lucent stones held loosely in his weakened grip. He tightened his fingers around them both as he regained his strength, then shifted forward.

The purple of the second stone had definitely changed color, the patch of blue—actually more indigo—a little larger. When he sank into the stone, the section he'd attempted to alter had changed as well, although not quite to the shape he'd wanted.

But then he noticed his original alterations: the nodes he'd corrected had shifted again. Whatever he'd done with his second attempt had not only affected the new region, but the old region as well.

"Of course it wouldn't be that simple." He set the two pieces of lucent down and ran his hands through his hair, elbows on the desk.

"Talking to yourself again? I thought you only did that at the Lyceum."

Devon glanced up to see Lane standing in the doorway, Raven, Jillian, and a couple other guards behind her.

"Can I come in?" she asked.

"You don't need to ask," Devon said, straightening his slump and motioning with one hand.

Lane, Raven, and Jillian entered; the guards remained outside. Lane sat on the edge of Devon's bed, posture stiff at first, but then she sighed and sagged, head tilted back, and Devon literally saw the governor in her slip away, the Lane he knew from the Lyceum emerging.

Raven stationed herself near the door; Jillian shifted into a corner and, with an uncanny and slightly unnerving ability that he knew came from her studies as a Historian, faded away, stylus and note-board at the ready.

After a long moment of companionable silence, Lane shifted forward again. Her eyes scanned the room, falling on the lithum and the scattered crystals on his desk with a frown. "Where's Dalton?"

Devon turned his chair to face her. "He's down in one of the training yards with your father and Burdock, helping prepare the citizens of Brovetto for the coming fight. How go the rest of the preparations?"

Lane shrugged. "Moving forward." She glanced at Raven, who ducked her head out into the hall and spoke with one of the guardsmen there. The man trotted off. "Thankfully, Heather Brokaw is handling all of the supply issues—getting the resources for the training, supplying the new Collegium, making certain provisions are being stored for the eventual siege and being distributed in the meantime. Maureen and her assistant, Sue Hicks, are dealing with the citizens themselves—keeping them calm and focused. As calm as she can, anyways. I'm mostly dealing with organization and handling emergencies."

"Like the sinkhole."

"You aren't still blaming yourself for that, are you?"

"A little bit."

He expected her to protest, tell him it wasn't his fault, as nearly everyone else did, but instead she merely nodded. "I thought you'd still be working with Connor and his crew."

"We've spent the last two weeks nonstop checking and repairing what we could of the irrigation and water pipes on the Second Level after the sinkhole. Another round seemed pointless. So yesterday we turned the system back on in stages in that area, waiting an hour after each adjustment to make certain nothing else collapsed. Everything appears to be working normally. I'm sure there are leaks somewhere, probably down into the mines, but after we all released our collective held breath, I told everyone to take a few days off to relax."

Lane pointed her chin toward the crystals. "This is how you relax?"

Devon grinned. "It's research. You know I like research."

She stood, moving toward the desk. "What kind of research?" She picked up the lithum, frowning. "Why does this look familiar?"

"It's one of the crystals that the army mages in Iandolo carry around on their staffs. Remember? During one of the Brovettan raids, the students at the Lyceum were led from the quad by the proctors, two carrying one staff with a red crystal, the other with a blue one. Nic stole one during the attack at the Pulpit."

Lane snorted. "Of course he did."

At the door, the guard returned, carrying a tray of cups, a teapot, grapes, cheese, and a small knife. Raven took it from him and set it on the desk, shoving some crystals aside, before pouring each of them a drink. Lane twisted the lithum around in her hand as she absentmindedly sipped and ate a few grapes.

"And what have you discovered?"

Devon cut off a chunk of cheese. "That the lithum—that's what they're called—store power. Magical power. The reason the army takes a pair of these with them wherever they go is because it allows them to use their powers even when they're away from the city, like on the wayfares."

Lane's fidgeting with the stone abruptly stopped. "You're saying they can use their powers on the wayfare, when I couldn't, because of this?"

"No. They would need both the red and the blue one for it to work. Otherwise, you'd have been able to do magic on our way here, since Nic had this with him then. Without the blue one, it's just a lucent crystal."

"So it's worthless?"

"Not entirely." Devon took the crystal from her. "I can sense the power it contains inside, but it's locked. The blue crystal would act like a key, if we had it."

"Aren't you a lockpick? Don't you specialize in lucent locks?"

He gave her a droll look. "What do you think I've been trying to do?" He set it down on the desk. "I've been trying to pick it off and on for the past few weeks, since Nic gave it to me, but it's not like a lockbox or door. It needs that second half in order to make a whole. So today I started trying to create a second key, the same way I created your rose lantern."

"Based on your look when we arrived, it wasn't going well."

Devon frowned. "I wouldn't say that. It's just going to be harder than I thought. I'm starting with nothing. Well—" He lifted the red lithum. "—almost nothing."

"You started with nothing when you discovered the true structure behind the mage forms back at the Lyceum. I bet—"

She halted abruptly, her eyes going wide.

"You bet what?" he asked.

"I bet I know where you can find out more about the lithum."

"Where? At the Lyceum?"

"No, right here in Brovetto." She faced Raven. "We need to go to the Burn."

"Right now?"

"I don't see why not. We can check on the training exercises and the evacuation preparations on the way."

"I'll have to get additional guards for an escort if we're leaving the Fifth Level."

The two stared at each other a moment before Raven ducked her head, grumbled something beneath her breath, and headed for the door. She spat orders to the guards outside, who raced off in two different directions, before turning back. "The escort will meet us at the gates."

"Then pack up what you might need, Devon. Let's go."

Devon reached for the lithum and his satchel. "Is she like this all the time now?" he asked Raven.

The ex-Regular rolled her eyes. "All. The. Time."

Lane spluttered a protest as Devon grabbed a clutch of grapes to take with him. Jillian packed up her notes and followed.

They left the manse, passing through the courtyard where groups of men and women—a mix of citizens and refugees from Iandolo—were busy loading up wagons from the manse storerooms, a few already headed out the gates into the lower levels. Each wagon had four guards attached to it for protection, although Devon didn't think anyone in Brovetto would dare raid the supplies they knew were being hidden for the eventual attack on the city. Then again, he knew the mentality of those who lived in the lower levels of Iandolo—everyone was out for themselves. Some might think it better to take whatever they could, hunker down on their own, and hope they survived.

Once out of the gates, they descended to the Fourth Level along the curved ramp. The Brovettans on the streets here were sparse and everyone appeared on edge. Patrons were skittish, hesitant, taking longer to decide whether they wanted the wares, often barely haggling, agreeing too quickly to prices that were too high. At least in Devon's opinion. Vendors were tense, picking up on the unease. Everyone watched Lane and her escort pass with wary looks, many bowing their heads to whisper comments to their companions, others casting fearful glances toward the wayfare and Iandolo, as if suddenly reminded of what everyone knew was coming. Devon didn't sense open hostility, but there was definitely animosity.

They were a block away from Hargrave's Square when Devon heard the first sharp "Ha!"s coming from a hundred throats in unison at regular intervals. The volume increased until it became a shout when they rounded the corner of the last building and entered the plaza.

Hundreds of men and women were lined up in rank upon rank, each with their own wooden sword. Some weren't even mockeries of swords, just broom handles and, often, actual brooms. More or less as one, they would step forward, thrust, and yell, "Ha!" then retreat a step, shifting position before stepping forward with the other foot and doing the same. Burdock led the practice session, pacing back and forth on a makeshift stage at the front of the plaza, while men from John Senn's rebels and the other mercenaries scattered through the ranks, correcting position and form and generally yelling out insults and encouragement in equal measure. Most of the trainees looked intent but terrified.

Devon caught sight of Dalton about four rows back as Lane led them all toward Burdock, moving to the front of the stage, rather than mounting it.

"How goes the training?" she asked.

Burdock surveyed the field with a stern expression. "About as well as can be expected." Then he knelt down and said in a quieter voice that wouldn't carry. "Honestly, they're civilians. I expect half of them to cut

and run once they're face to face with the Iandolan army. And I won't
blame them when they do."

"Don't underestimate the will to fight when they're defending their
home."

"That's what will keep those that don't cut and run in their place."

"What about my father? I don't see him here."

"He's taken most of the more promising prospects and, with Mouse,
they're going through maps and memorizing back routes and hidden
passages and obscure mine shafts, learning the best ways to outflank
any soldiers on the streets. That's one aspect of our occupation here in
Brovetto that the Iandolan army failed at—finding all of those routes the
insurgents used to cut us off at the knees. They found some, but certainly
not all."

"I'm going to take that as a advantage for us then."

"Most certainly."

Lane watched the trainees for a moment, then said, "We're headed to
the Burn. Anything you need that I should pass on to Brokaw on my way?"

"Not at the moment."

She nodded and motioned Raven and the guards to lead the way out of
the square.

Shortly after they entered the Third Level, where most of those within
Brovetto lived. The streets grew more crowded, although the tensions
among the people didn't abate. Activity was more frantic and the overall
pervasive feeling was anxious. Most people glanced away when they saw
Lane, Raven, and the guardsmen. No one paid any attention to Jillian or
Devon, which was a relief. He'd been under too much scrutiny here in
Brovetto, because he was clearly Iandolan.

They passed the new college and when Devon asked why she wasn't
inside helping with the training, Lane waved a hand and said, "Dawn
Percy has them well in hand." Twenty minutes later, they came up on
the warehouse where Heather Brokaw had established her headquarters.
The building was massive, taking up an entire block. When they stepped
inside they found Heather standing at the head of a large table, Varenov,
Maureen, Sue Hicks, Cerelle, Sadie, and a score of others scattered around
it, all intent on the large map of Brovetto Heather was pointing at.

"—you see there are entrances at three key locations on the Third
Level, with a few smaller entrances scattered around the city. We need
to focus everyone's attention on those three locations first and use the
others to help pull in stragglers. Once the Iandolan forces know where
the Brovettan citizens are running, they're going to focus their attention

on those entrances. We'll have to seal them off and hope they hold. After that, we'll focus on using the smaller entrances and hopefully keep them hidden."

"I would hope that my daughter would keep their attention for quite some time. They aren't going to care about the general populace as long as she's distracting them."

"Speaking of..." Lane stepped up to the table. "Mother, what are you doing here?"

Varenov raised an eyebrow. "You expected me to sit in the manse and do embroidery? My stitching was never that good. I've been helping Heather Brokaw with the evacuation plans."

Lane motioned to Heather. "Once the people reach one of these entrances, what happens?"

Heather gave a nervous cough, then rallied. "As I said, we'll seal the doors to the three main entrances. We'll send out sorties from the smaller entrances to try to bring in anyone who was left behind. Everyone who makes it to one of the evacuation points will descend into the mines." She sorted through the stack of papers to the left of the map, pulling out one that Devon recognized as one of the mines. She set it overtop the city map. "We've set up the rallying point to be the Veridian Strike, one of the larger mines beneath Brovetto. It has multiple culverts off the main cavern for supplies and there's a deep pool in the far corner for water. We should be able to stay down there for at least a few weeks, maybe more if we ration harshly."

"Only a few weeks?" Cerelle asked.

"We're moving supplies in as fast as we can," Heather countered, "but the city was already barely functioning."

"Because the Iandolans were trying to starve us out," Maureen said.

"But the siege is going to last longer than two weeks!" one of the other women said. "Once the army arrives—!"

Lane cut her off. "We aren't going to retreat to the mines until the Iandolan army has breached the gates and managed to take the lower two levels. I doubt it will take longer than two weeks for them to capture the third. By then they will have been defeated or they'll have taken Brovetto completely."

That cast a somber pall over the group, until Lane drew in a deep breath and added, "That said, move as many supplies as you can into the mine. We don't know how many people will make it to the refuge, nor how long they'll have to stay. I'd rather be overprepared than under."

Heather gave a sharp, grim nod and she and the others leaned forward over the map, now discussing what other resources they knew of that needed transport. Lane moved away, but her mother caught her arm and pulled her to the side.

"You need to be careful with statements like that," Varenov said.

"I'm not going to gloss over the reality of the situation. They need to know what's coming."

"Yes, but they also need hope. If you take that away from them, then you've already lost the city, before the army even arrives. They will simply give up and hand it—and us—over to Iandolo."

Lane's jaw had set, but after a moment of staring at the floor she gave a curt nod. "I'll keep that in mind, mother."

Varenov gave Lane's arm a squeeze, then returned to the table. Devon fell into place at Lane's side as they left, turning toward the Burn, Raven and the escort surrounding them.

"Do you really think it will all be over within a few weeks?"

"Once they breach the gates and seize the lower levels? Yes. Burdock and my father keep telling me that we have a strong defensive position, that our walls will hold them off, that we can steal their strength through attrition as they try to take the city, but I hear what they are not saying as they plan and strategize and cajole each other. It all comes down to the fact that Iandolo controls the mages."

"But we have you."

Lane gave a wry smile. "And Dawn and the others. But I doubt Favian brings only a handful of mages to Brovetto. He's going to bring dozens."

Devon made to protest, but stopped himself. "After what you did at the gates when leaving Iandolo, you're probably right."

Lane said nothing.

The sun was beginning to set when they reached the Burn, casting the section where they'd taken refuge when they first reached the city in a deep golden light. Even so, Devon hardly recognized it. The cistern they'd used to sneak up to the upper level was full, the water glistening with ripples from the breeze coming off the Flatlands. The streets were bustling, people moving to and from the market, which was full of vendors. Smoke wafted up from the courtyard outside their impromptu hall, smelling of roasted meat and charred onions. There was still an underlying sense of tension, like in the upper levels, but these people had already survived the riots in Iandolo, had already seen chaos and destruction. They were more prepared...or at least more resigned.

Devon and the others had barely made it to the market entrance when someone shouted, "Lane!"

A tuller guardsman Devon vaguely remembered from their operations retrieving Brovettans in Iandolo pushed his way through a swath of Burners to reach them, waving a hand even though they'd stopped. Lane's escort tensed as he drew close, but she raised a hand and they backed down.

"Durran?"

Durran halted a short distance away and gave a curt nod to Lane and her guardsmen. "Neither Vash nor Rennick informed me you were coming. I would have sent someone to meet you."

"They didn't know. This excursion was unplanned."

Devon leaned toward Raven and asked, "How does she do it?" At Raven's confused look, he added, "Remember all of their names?"

Raven rolled her eyes and shrugged.

"I believe Vash is overseeing the fieldwork, now that the water is running, and Rennick—"

"Actually," Lane cut in, "we're here to see Gillian."

"The Historian?"

At the title, Jillian perked up, her stylus falling still. "Historian?"

Lane nodded. "Yes, the Historian."

Clearly confused, Durran motioned toward one of the buildings to the side of the market. "Certainly. She—well, she commandeered a wagon and moved it into the inner garden of one of the residences. Over here."

He bypassed the building Devon had thought they were heading toward, cutting through an alley onto another street, then turning again away from the central area of the Burn. Outside a hastily repaired wooden gate, he paused, as if about to say something, then shoved through the gate and ushered them into the garden inside.

At least, what had once been a garden. The stone pathways and a central stone fountain with a three-tiered basin remained, but there were no plants. The stone building inside was still stained with ash, but the inner courtyard had been cleaned. Lantern light shown in a few of the windows, even though Devon could see sections where the roof had collapsed, but Durran waved to the side, not the manse ahead.

Gillian had pulled the wagon up against the wall of the courtyard, its tiny back door open and an awning spread out overhead, supports staked into the dry dirt. The protective cloth ruffled with the breeze. A firepit had been built to one side, smoke skirling upwards, the supports of a spit on opposite sides. A flat rock protruded over the flames, covered with sizzling char and oil left over from cooking.

Gillian sat in a chair beneath the awning, puffing on a long pipe as she eyed their approach.

"Ah, my erstwhile student," she said to Lane. "Come to pick up where you left off?"

"Partially. Gillian, this is Raven, Devon, and Jillian."

"The warrior, the mathematician, and the Historian." She leaned toward Jillian. "Have you been keeping the Records? These are momentous times."

Jillian shrank back at first, the straightened, clutching her board and stylus close. "As best I can."

"Hmm. That's all that can be expected, of course." Her gaze shifted to Devon. "And you. Have you figured it out yet?"

"Figured what out?"

She leaned back, sucked on the pipe, then blew smoke toward the awning overhead. "I suppose if you had figured it out, you wouldn't be here searching for something, would you?" She focused on Lane. "And you *are* here to search for something, yes?"

"Remember at the tull, when I was reading the texts you had there?"

"Of course."

"One of them mentioned something about a 'node.' It allowed devices to work even when they weren't inside the city. Did you have that book with you?"

Gillian's eyes narrowed. "What makes you think I have any books with me at all?"

"You wouldn't travel anywhere without at least some of your books."

"Hmph. Well, I supposed that's correct." She set her pipe to one side and pulled herself up out of the chair. "Follow me."

She ducked around the wagon and into the small door in the back. Lane, Devon, and Jillian followed, while Raven and the others settled in at various points near the gate, the manse, and the garden.

"I couldn't bring everything," Gillian said, her voice muffled inside the wagon, "but I did bring what I thought might be important."

The interior of the wagon was packed nearly floor to ceiling with books, all neatly stacked, but filling up every available amount of space. Chests and trunks lined the floor and various trinkets and bangles hung from the rounded ceiling, including quite a few bunches of dried herbs. The scent that wafted from the open door was part must and part mint, or something with a strong sweet odor. Gillian ran a finger down a row of books, hunched forward, then gave a sharp, "A-ha!" and pulled a text out by its spine. Cradling it in one hand, she kept looking, procuring two more tomes before coming to the door.

They all stepped back as she descended the three short steps to the ground.

"I believe one of these is what you're looking for."

They shifted back to the area beneath the awning, Gillian spreading out a blanket over the rough ground, fussing that she didn't have enough chairs for everyone. She handed off the books to Lane, who immediately sat down and began paging through them, then produced a tea kettle and flask of water from somewhere, filling it and placing it on the stone over the fire.

Lane glanced up with a frown, then said in a quiet, warning tone, "Be careful with the tea," before returning to her reading. A moment later, she sucked in a breath and said, "Here it is," and handed Devon the book. "This passage, right here."

Devon read aloud, "'*Any object powered by lucent will function with a continuous charge unless that object is taken outside the network range. After that, it will remain powered until its battery has been depleted or until it is once again brought within network range. The exception, of course, is if someone is carrying a node, in which case the node will provide access to the network outside of the usual range.*'" He stumbled over some of the unfamiliar words and the odd stilted phrasing while reading, but otherwise it read like many of the mathematical texts at the Lyceum.

Lane leaned forward. "I think the lithum is one of these nodes."

"What's a 'battery'?"

"I don't know. Neither does Gillian. It's mentioned throughout the texts I've read, though, so it must be important."

"And this 'network'?"

"Same."

Devon stared at the passage, reading it over and over. "When we left the city, my lucent lantern was working and kept working...until we were at the tull long enough. Then it began to grow weaker. It got worse after I created your rose lantern. We went back to the city before it died completely."

"That must have been its 'battery' being depleted."

"These books are filled with diagrams of things from throughout the city—all of the cities actually." Jillian had taken one of the other books and now held it up for them to see. "It's one of the ells, with a train on the tracks. There haven't been operating trains within the city in decades." She traced a part of the diagram. "It shows how the train attaches to the ell, how the lucent powered it." She set the book aside and grabbed up the other one. "This one is a history of the Founder's Code, with all the rules of the Council in it. But it's nothing like how the Council is run today."

Devon reached for the book and Jillian drew it back, holding it to her chest protectively.

"Now don't be acting like one of those hideous librarians at the Lyceum," Gillian said, stepping between them to set cups and saucers down, then pouring from the tea kettle. "Why do you think I stole them from the library in the first place? They're to be shared, not hoarded."

Jillian glared for a moment, then reluctantly handed the book to Devon. But the Historian was right, the pages were filled with treatises and lectures on the rules and codes of conduct for the "integrated cities of the colony ships." He passed it on to Lane. "This is more your kind of book. Or your mother's."

He turned back to the one he held, reading the rest of the section Lane had pointed out, then flipping forward to pick up context. Lane focused on her book, while Jillian continued perusing the one with the trains in it. Gillian puttered with the fire, refilled their cups, and meandered out to hand some tea to Raven and the guards. At some point, one of the guards left and returned with some roasted fowl over smashed potatoes, the heavy seasoning and juices flavoring it all. Gillian made them set the books aside while they ate, afraid they'd stain the pages with their greasy fingers.

"So, what do you think?" Lane asked, licking one of her fingers clean and tossing a bone in with the other scraps. Night had fallen, the space beneath the awning lit with oil lanterns placed on the support poles. Raven sat with the other guards a short distance outside with their own meals.

"I think you're right, the lithum is one of their nodes. I don't understand half of the words they're using, even less of what they're discussing, but the context is clear."

"Anything in there to help you with unlocking the lithum?"

Devon grimaced. "Not really. But it did corroborate what I was thinking. I'm going to have to do it with brute force, if I'm able to do it at all. But there was something else in there that was more interesting, something that I think we can use against the Iandolan mages when they get here."

"The mages? What is it?"

"I'm not going to say, not until I verify what it says."

"And how are you going to do that?"

"By finding out what's inside that tunnel we uncovered in the mines beneath the city."

Chapter Twelve

Devon stepped up to the tunnel's entrance and once again felt a gust of stale air push past his face and an uncomfortable tug pulling him forward. Dalton stood behind him, a steadying presence. The workers had cleared away the pile of debris that had blocked the opening, although there was still a crunch of grit beneath his feet. He adjusted the strap of the satchel settled across his shoulder, heard the familiar chink of lucent rustling against each other from inside. He didn't know what he'd find, ultimately, but he had a good idea based on the book Gillian had grudgingly allowed them to take.

"Do you think there are skrill in there?" Dalton asked.

"I didn't until just now. Thanks."

They hadn't found any of the insectile skrill that lived in the abandoned mines beneath Iandolo here in Brovetto, yet, but then again, the mines in Brovetto had been active more recently. The skrill might not have had a chance to move in. But this passage was different. It had been sealed away. There could be anything inside there.

Taking a short breath, he stepped forward.

The sounds of the work crews in the cavern behind them immediately grew muffled, then faded away completely. He paused a moment to retrieve his lucent lantern, flicking it alight as they continued. Dalton kept close, his sword drawn, staying within the light.

For the first ten feet, the tunnel was clear, only a few loose pebbles scattered here and there, but once they'd moved beyond what the miners had cleared they encountered much larger debris. Chunks had fallen from the walls and ceiling, everything crazed with cracks. It was clear that the tunnel had been carved directly out of the stone, that it was not a natural formation, but the walls were far smoother and flatter than any technique the miners could currently replicate. Even with the cracks and debris, Devon was impressed with the durability and the uniformity of the structure.

The deeper they traveled, the drier the air became, the scent changing from must to dust. Devon found himself breathing shallowly through his nose, the air making his mouth parched and tickling the back of his throat. He swallowed compulsively and wished he'd brought a skin of water.

Then, around two hundred feet in, he sensed the tunnel opening up into a massive cavern.

He halted, holding the lantern up high, until Dalton nudged him from behind. Stepping to the side, the two of them stared up at the cylindrical structure within. Composed mostly of metal, it filled the center of the cavern, ascending up into darkness and descending into a pit beneath. A ledge of stone ten feet wide encircled the pit, with a metal walkway leading out over the drop-off to a door in the structure and a circular metal walkway with stairs to one side leading up and down. Devon could make out the shadows of other walkways above and below, where he guessed there were other doors. It reminded him viscerally of the Hub in Iandolo, except this pit had a central structure, like that beneath the three towers. He, Raven, and a few of the other Regulars had entered through the bottom of that structure to get into the towers to rescue Lane, a feat that made Devon's stomach clench and roll just recalling it. In fact, the longer he looked at this structure beneath Brovetto, the more it reminded him of that incident in Iandolo. The structure wasn't a single piece; it was composed of multiple sections, overlapping and connecting with each other. Pipes and chains jutted out and linked different sections. A few sections looked like lucent, although inactive...or dead, like most of the lucent in the Crystal Cities now.

"I think..." he began, taking a step forward. "I think this is directly beneath—"

Dalton darted to one side, stabbing downward just outside the reach of Devon's lucent lantern. A terrifying screech filled the cavern, echoing up and down the pit, setting Devon's teeth on edge.

Dalton reappeared, a skrill writhing on the end of his blade. He flung it to the ground and stomped on its head with a wet squelch. "A small one."

Devon shuddered. "But if there's a small one, there might be larger ones. Let's get inside this…axis, axle…before its mother shows up."

He hesitated at the metal walk, the darkness of the pit looming below. A stiff draft blew upwards, ruffling his hair. It smelled of desiccation. Swallowing back the nausea, holding the lantern high in search of skrill creeping down the chamber's walls toward them, he moved across to the doorway in the Axle. The walk juddered and groaned with his and Dalton's weight, rust flaking away and raining down into the pit, but it held. The door refused to give way though.

"Let me try," Dalton said.

"No, wait." Devon scrubbed at a lucent panel to the side of the door. "I think it's simply locked." He tapped the panel, which lit up slowly, a cool bluish white color that Devon had never seen in lucent before. He tapped it again, but noticed an indentation off to one side. "I think this is supposed to be a keyhole."

"We don't have a key."

"But you do have a lockpick."

Devon touched the panel and sank into the lucent, then frowned.

"What's wrong?" Dalton asked.

"Nothing. The lucent feels…ancient. Older than what we had in Iandolo, even in the towers or the Lyceum. But at the same time, the pathways are more refined. It's…odd." He felt a shift in the lucent, then a click. The door slid to one side about three-quarters of the way, pocketed in the wall of the structure, then ground to a halt with a metallic shriek.

Devon stepped through the opening, lantern held before him. Dalton gave the door a shove and it slammed all the way open, then he stepped inside.

They were in a narrow corridor that shot through the heart of the structure. A low vibrational hum permeated the air, tingling in Devon's feet. Lucent glowed ahead and he took a step toward it, but halted when Dalton caught his shoulder.

"Remember the skrill," the ex-soldier said, brandishing his sword, still wet with skrill blood.

Devon let him squeeze past, but followed close behind. He halted when panels and bands of lucent appeared on both sides of the corridor, some of them active, most of them dead, their threads streaked with black particles. He peered at the controls to one side as Dalton checked out the rest of the corridor ahead, returning a short time later.

"Nothing here but another door on the other side. What have you found?"

"I'm not certain. But look at how thick these bands of lucent are. If I'd found even one of these back in Iandolo when I was scavenging in the lower levels, I'd have been rich."

"What do they do?"

"Let's see if I can find out."

Devon reached forward and touched an active pale yellow band, letting himself sink into it, then traveled up its length until he hit a node where it branched into at least a dozen different pathways. Retreating, he headed downwards instead...and down...and down...

He pulled himself from the band, shaking his head. "It goes down deep. I never reached the bottom. Upwards, it hits some kind of node and branches out in different directions. If I had to guess, I'd say this section here is simply used for maintenance."

Dalton scuffed his foot on the floor, marring the thick layer of dust there already riddled with their footprints. "I don't think anyone has been in here to maintain anything in quite a while."

"No." He tapped one of the dead bands of lucent. It looked like it used to be blue. "That's why the lucent has been dying." He recalled what little he'd read of the book Gillian had loaned them. "We've forgotten how to maintain it. We lost that a long time ago. And it's finally caught up to us."

Dalton shifted uncomfortably, glancing around the narrow space. "Where do we go now?"

Devon desperately wanted to head downwards, to see where the bands of lucent began, but they didn't have time for that. It was too deep. "Up. I want to find this node."

They returned to the door they'd entered through, Devon attempting to close it with the panel, but it wouldn't budge. With a shrug, they began to ascend the metal stairs, Dalton first. The scaffolding protested, rust falling from every joint and surface, but it held. Three levels up, they heard the distinctive skittering of skrill from below, setting Devon's heart shuddering, but it was distant and sounded like it came from the stone walls of the shaft, not the metal structure. Still, he pushed Dalton to move faster. Ten levels up, they entered through another door, found a corridor similar to the first, so kept climbing. The higher they went, the more the bands of lucent were dead.

Then the scaffolding ended, hard up against a layer of rock. They opened the last door and found narrow stairs spiraling upwards on the inside, circling the interior, the core now mostly bands of lucent. The stairs leveled out at intervals, with maintenance panels along the walls.

Devon's legs were beginning to protest when the stairs spilled out into an open room with rock walls but a metal floor. Stations like the panel they'd found controlling the water flow surrounded the central pillar of lucent, which split and branched out in hundreds of different directions, plunging into the ceiling above.

"I'm guessing this is the node," Dalton said, staring up in awe at the sheer number of threads of lucent in every color overhead. It was impressive, even with the majority of them a sickening black. A few were flickering, already streaked but still functioning. A couple were pulsing in a steady rhythm.

"This is certainly the node." Devon moved toward one of the stations, raised a trembling hand over its surface, but hesitated. Everything was covered with a layer of dust. Everything from the metal to the stone to the lucent and the air reeked of age. He shivered with the thought that none of this had been touched in perhaps hundreds of years, sealed away beneath Brovetto generations ago, left and then lost, intentionally or not.

He flinched when Dalton asked, "What does it do?"

Rather than touching the panel in front of him, he pulled his satchel around and dug out the two books from Gillian, the one he'd looked at with the description of the lithum and the one with the illustrations of the train that Jillian had held. Lane and Jillian had taken the third, with the treatises on the Founder's Pact, to study. He laid them both out on the floor after sweeping an area clear, then sat before them and began paging through the manuals. "I remember seeing something like this in one of these. I just need to find it."

Forty minutes later, he sucked in a sharp breath and leaned back, his lower back screaming in pain at the movement. Twinges shot into his legs, which had grown numb and now tingled with renewed circulation. But he tapped the book, at a page that contained a diagram nearly identical to what they were seeing in the room. Sections of it were numbered, descriptions beneath and on the following pages. "This is it."

Dalton, who'd settled against the far wall to keep watch on the stairwell, came forward. "So what is it?"

"A '*Lucential Transient Junction.*'"

"And what does it say it does?"

"'—*distributes power from the central lucential pathways throughout the city, providing access to the energy to all levels and subdivisions attached to the junction.*'" Devon read more silently, then added, "The structure here is called the Core and it bores down to '*geo-thermal generators*' deep beneath the earth. That energy, whatever it is, is converted and transferred into the lucential pathways—what I'm assuming we call the lucent—and brought here to the surface, where we use it to power our lanterns, the irrigation system…everything. Everything that contains the lucent or relies on the lucent for power, including—"

Devon's voice choked off, as if he had no breath left in his body. He couldn't manage to suck in any air either. His entire body went cold in horror.

"Including what?" Dalton asked.

Devon forced his shocked body to draw in a breath, then gave a ragged exhale and said, "Including the magic used by the mages."

* * *

Lane threw up a shield a moment before the arrow of fire struck, the force of the blow staggering her back on the grounds of the training pit. "You need to focus, Brigette! Your sigils are sloppy! That should have been half that strength and the fire was in the wrong configuration. It should have looked like this." She sketched out the base sigil, began the secondary.

On the far side of the pit, Brigette's eyes went wide and she frantically began her own sigil. She finished it with a gasp as Lane unleashed her own fire. The ball shot toward Brigette at twice the speed of Brigette's arrow, flaring as it struck her shield, half engulfing the girl before sputtering out.

Brigette's nostrils flared. "How dare you? I wasn't ready yet!"

"You won't have the chance to get ready once the Iandolans arrive. Do you think they're going to wait for you to prepare yourself?" Lane set up her primary sigil, Brigette hastily following suit. "The Iandolan mages are relentless and vicious and, after our escape from Iandolo, they won't give us any mercy."

"You defeated them there. You blew open the gates!"

"Only because I knew more than they did. That isn't going to be true anymore. They know all about the double pyramid, the Source and Outcome. They tortured it out of us when they held us in the tower. The field has been leveled."

"You don't know that for certain."

"I know we can't go into the coming attack blinded." Lane snapped out a pattern, Brigette following her fingers with suspicion, crooked hand tracing out a counter, but she was too slow. With a cry of frustration, she abandoned the counter and flung herself to the side as spikes of ice pelted the ground where she'd stood. Lane had kept the radius of the attack tight, so nothing came close to hitting her, but still Brigette rolled into a crouch with a shriek, already preparing an attack. Her motions were sharper, more controlled this time.

"There you go," Lane said as she countered the fireball with one of her own, the two connecting a short distance in front of her. She felt the backwash of heat tug at her hair. "Now do it again. And again! Better. Much better. Your fire is smaller, tighter, more controlled, but also more powerful. Now change the shape. Go back to the arrow form. That was new. I hadn't seen that before. Do you remember how you did it? That's it. Closer. Well, that one was wild, forget that one. Focus. Shift your hand slightly. Not that direction, more left and deeper into that face of the pyramid. There! That's it! Now keep it coming. Memorize the shape and feel of the motions of your hand. You'll want to practice this form over and over on your own until it's instinct."

They volleyed back and forth, Lane deflecting or blocking most of Brigette's attacks as she experimented and adjusted her forms. A few of the attacks were close, singeing hair or washing her skin with heat. One burned a portion of her sleeve. When Brigette began to flag, Lane shifted and went on the attack, forcing her to defend herself, only relenting when Brigette cried out as a cantrip nearly caught her foot as she dodged.

"Enough!" she shouted, holding up both hands, even as Brigette finished the primary sigil. Lane was breathing hard from exertion, but Brigette was panting, unable to catch her breath. "Enough." For a moment, it looked as if Brigette would try another spell; fury pooled like liquid in her eyes. Again, Lane was reminded of Quinn back at the Lyceum. But eventually she nodded and relaxed, hands dropping, the sigil form dissipating.

Lane let the tension drain from her shoulders, then approached.

"That was a good session. You've come a long way in the last few weeks."

"I could be further along, if you were here more often. Dawn doesn't allow us to experiment," she said with resentment.

"Dawn teaches only what I allow her to teach."

Both turned as the heavy doors to the training field opened with a thick groan of old hinges. Dawn and Gregg entered. Gregg stared around at the wall—already scarred with fire and lightning and torn up with cantrips—to see if there was any new damage. Dawn headed straight toward Lane.

"Your father is here to see you. He's not in a good mood."

Lane frowned. "Do you know why?"

"He won't say. He has a contingent of five or six men with him. Not all of them look like guardsmen."

"I'll deal with them. Brigette, you should probably get some rest. I hit you rather hard today. And I assume you're here to work with Gregg, Dawn?"

"If you're finished."

Lane waved them toward the field. "Have at it."

She headed toward the gate, Brigette trailing behind. The young mage turned toward the dormitories as soon as they exited the training field while Lane closed the door, Dawn and Gregg already beginning to spar. Then she faced her father, noting Raven and her own escort off to one side. None of them looked relaxed.

"What's happened?"

"We may have a problem," her father said, and began to move toward the entrance to the new college. "My group has been mapping out every nook, cranny, corridor, and passage that we can find between the mines and the levels of the city, with the help of Maureen and her followers and some of the other citizens. Did you know there are extensive caverns leading all the way down to the Flatlands? Like those the tullers use to enter Iandolo. We'll have to keep an eye on them in case anyone in the Iandolan army or the Council knows about them. But the main problem is that we've found some locations that have been recently used."

They pushed out of the main gates of the new college onto the relatively crowded street.

"Recently used by who?"

"Mouse believes it's a group of Iandolan soldiers left behind in secret."

This brought Lane to an abrupt halt. "For what purpose?"

Her father shrugged. "We don't know for certain. But based on what we've found, where they've been hiding out…I'd say they've been following you."

"Me? What for?" No one said anything. Because of course the answer was obvious. Lane suddenly felt an uneasy prickle at the base of her neck, but fought the urge to glance around the street searching for someone watching her. Instead, she looked over those accompanying her father. "Speaking of, where is Mouse?" She couldn't avoid twisting his name in contempt.

"He's trying to track them down."

"Then where are we headed?"

"I was going to show you their most recent hideout, as far as we can tell."

"Very well."

They continued down the street, and for the first time in ages, Lane noticed how her escort, supplemented by her father and his men, had formed up around her, Raven to her right, her father to her left. They forged a path through the crowds, the people splitting and surging around them like water around a stone. Some of her protectors watched those on the street; others scanned the windows and rooftops on either side. Her shoulders itched with sudden sweat and she realized she'd become complacent here in Brovetto, even with the threat of the Iandolo army's arrival hanging over her.

The group cut into a much narrower cross-street a short distance from the college, then converged on an alley. It reeked of rot and piss, the cobblestones slick underfoot, but Lane ignored that. Her father opened a patched wooden door on the left side of the alley, two men entering before him, while two others stayed behind at the alley's entrance.

The room inside was dark and stifling. No windows and only a single small door leading into a cramped back room with a ladder, built into the wall, up to an opening barely a shoulder's width across. At the bottom of the ladder lay a body surrounded by a large pool of dried blood and a larger contingent of flies. Her father crouched beside it, hands resting on his knees.

"We heard this ladder led to a secret entrance to a tunnel into the mines, not unlike the one you used to get into the governor's manse to rescue us, so I sent a scouting party to investigate it." He grabbed the man by the shoulder and rolled his body back far enough Lane could see the crossbow bolt in the man's eye. "The soldiers—if they are soldiers—must have been here when the scouts arrived. When they didn't report back in, we came down and found Manning like this. Pinch is on the second floor."

He let Manning fall back, then ascended the ladder, Lane stepping over the body to follow. As soon as her head emerged into the even hotter room above, she saw Pinch, his head one its side, tilted toward her, eyes wide but lifeless. Blood had trickled from his open mouth and a fly landed on his cheek. He'd taken a crossbow bolt to the back. He was young, not even fifteen, with blond hair and brown eyes.

Lane clenched her teeth, then pulled herself up into the room, Raven and the others behind her. The stench of shit and piss assaulted her, coming from a bucket in one corner. Sunlight streamed in through shuttered windows, dust motes glowing in the air. When she approached, she noticed a few of the slats had been broken off, the remnants on the floor beneath. Easing up to the window, she could see the college across the street below, the main entrance far off to the right, but visible. From this vantage, she could see into the central courtyard and a few of the training rooms where they held classes. Daniel, Serene, and Shian were in the courtyard practicing secondary forms without using the base form first, the only safe way to practice when not on the training field. Other students were scattered about, studying, laughing, conversing. In one of the classrooms, Arrend was pointing to a slate as he lectured.

She turned back to the room, blinking as her eyes adjusted, then stepped away from the light. Bones littered the floor in another corner, along with other food scraps. No evidence of any kind of fire for cooking, but a few crates for seating were scattered about and rectangles in the dust against one wall suggested sleeping pallets had been spread out. A ragged opening in the back wall led to a stone tunnel that she assumed went into the mines.

"How many, do you think?" Lane asked.

"At least five, based on the tracks in the dust. Maybe six," her father said.

Raven had been scanning the room as well, had knelt next to the garbage in the corner, held one greasy bone in one hand. "I agree. I'd say they've been here for a week. Longer if they've been hauling their shit and garbage out every so often."

"You said there were other places like this?"

Her father shrugged. "We ran across a few boltholes that had clearly been used, but nothing raised our suspicions that it was anything other than squatters or refugees taking whatever shelter they could find. After Manning and Pinch, however, we reevaluated and noticed that many of the locations were near places you frequent or have been frequenting—the Burn, the gates to the Fifth Level and the governor's manse, the market on the Fourth Level, and now the Collegium."

"What can we do about it?"

"There's not much you can do," Raven said, "except stay vigilant. I'll add a few more guards to your escort, but after a certain point, more guards doesn't add much of a benefit."

Lane returned to the window, squinting through the slats. "And what about the college? What if they weren't spying on me in particular but the proctors and students themselves?"

She turned in time to see the skeptical look between her father and Raven.

"I'll tell Burdock to place some guards on the college," her father said.

Lane scanned the room again, then shuddered. "Raven, let's head back to the manse. I have an organizational meeting with Burdock, my mother, and Maureen in an hour." She faced her father. "Find these men. We can't afford to have them running loose around the city when the Iandolan army arrives."

* * *

"Do you think they're sending intelligence to Iandolo?" Varenov asked.

Burdock shifted in his seat at the table in the central hall of the manse. "I don't see how. No one is traveling the wayfare between here and Iridesque, and sending someone through Radminansque or Scintillesque would take weeks. Any report they'd receive would be long outdated by the time it arrived."

"I agree," Maupin said. He looked haggard from his excursion to the Tull. He'd been an unexpected but welcome addition to the meeting when they'd seen his caravan upon returning to the manse. "I'd guess they're here to do as much damage as they can from within, in whatever way possible. They'll likely try to report in as soon as the Iandolan army arrives though."

"We can't let them do that. They may know of our defensive plans, where we've retreated to in the mines, where our food reserves are."

"We'll find them," Burdock said. "Now that we know they're here."

"I'd feel more reassured if we didn't already know that the rebels led by John Senn managed to hide themselves within the city for decades with the Iandolan army searching for them," Maureen countered.

Burdock gave a wan smile. "Point taken. But the Iandolan army never attempted to map out every niche and cranny of the city, like we're doing now. We've already discovered at least three of their boltholes. I have men combing all of the known passages and rooms now. Some of them are being sealed off in preparation for the evacuation. My main concern is that the group isn't here to spy on our activities but rather to assassinate you, Lane."

No one had said it out loud until now, although Lane knew everyone had been thinking it since her father had shown her the room overlooking the college. Having the thought voiced sank a hot dagger into her gut and closed off the back of her throat. How had this happened? Only a short while ago, she'd been struggling as a third-year student at the Lyceum.

Her mother leaned forward into the silence. "That is the most likely reason they're here. Without you, Brovetto has no chance."

Lane gave an ugly snort. "This fight won't be won by just me."

"Not alone," Varenov said, "but you are the deciding factor."

The thought made Lane uncomfortable. "Speaking of, this meeting was scheduled to review progress. Since you've returned, Maupin, what do you have to report?"

Everyone turned their attention to the tuller.

"We brought as much food as the Tull could spare here to Brovetto. Heather Brokaw has already seized control of it, practically before we reached the gates. Gillian also had me bring more of her books. She said there might be some of interest to you, besides the ones you've already seen."

"Any report from Iandolo?"

"Nothing of consequence. The city was sealed after the riots, all waygates closed. The last of the tullers to escape through the mines beneath the city said the army had seized control of nearly everything, instituting martial law."

"Worse than when they were quarantining Brovettans?"

"Far worse. It has become dangerous to walk the streets. There are patrols everywhere, not just of soldiers, but mages as well."

"What about the Council?" Varenov asked.

Maupin shook his head. "As far as my tullers can tell, Haavelan, Arctus, and Favian have seized control."

"Are the other councilors still alive?"

Maupin shrugged. "If they are, they've been imprisoned in the towers."

"And the army?" Burdock asked.

"The last of the tullers left the city weeks ago. We've had no word from inside the city since. But as you likely already know, their mages managed to pull down the Warding that had engulfed the waygate to Luminesque and our scouts reported their army left the city along the wayfare within a week after that."

Burdock glanced at Lane. "More or less as we predicted."

"Which means…"

"Which means they'll be arriving any day now," Varenov said bluntly.

"Right." Lane tapped a fidgety finger against the table, then locked gazes with Burdock. "Where are the defenses at right now?"

"The wayfare and gates are locked down. The inner courtyard and marketplaces have been prepared. Have you made a decision on the Wardings?"

"We won't use them. It requires someone to activate them and, at the moment, the only one who can release the Warding after it's activated is me. I won't ask anyone to sacrifice themselves on the off chance that I survive what's coming."

"I thought Devon was the one who figured out how to unlock the Warding."

"He found the key, but he showed me how to do it through the bond we'd created. He could probably do it again, but he'd have to form a bond with one of the other mages. I'm not certain how long that would take. It isn't worth the risk. Plus, he can only do that if he survives the attack as well."

"Then we'll have the mages in training help us funnel the army into the streets and plazas where we want them to be. We'll try to contain them as much as possible."

"And everything is ready in Corinthian Plaza?"

"As ready as they can be." Burdock hesitated, then added, "You realize that no matter how much planning we do, no matter how prepared we think we are, none of it will matter once the fighting starts. War does not behave that way."

"I know. I've been told by many. But what else are we supposed to do? Simply sit and wait, with no plans at all?"

Burdock grunted. "I think we've done all that we can."

"The people of Brovetto are ready," Maureen said. "At least, as ready as they can be. Heather has done a good job wrangling supplies and Sue has prepared everyone for evacuation when the time comes. Those in training are ready to fight for their city." She paused, breath held, then let it exhale. "I know we treated you harshly when you first arrived, but I wanted to say that since then you've proven yourself—to me and to the others. The city hasn't been this cohesive and functional since before the governors the Iandolans put in place took charge."

"Even with the structural collapse and an army hovering outside the walls?" Lane said with a mock grin.

"Even then," Maureen repeated, remaining serious. "You've given the citizens hope again. Something to fight for. Stories of what you did at the gates when fleeing Iandolo have spread. Brovetto has faith in you."

Lane sighed. "Then let's hope that faith isn't misplaced."

* * *

Devon woke from troubling dreams with a start. He lay in the darkness of his rooms, listening to Dalton's deep breathing beside him. He heard nothing else, nothing that would have caused him to waken, but he was still restless. He rolled onto his back, Dalton rumbling and shifting, one arm reaching across his chest and pulling him closer. His breathing settled into sleep again with a rough snort and low snore.

Devon closed his eyes, tried to fall back asleep, but his mind bounced between the discovery of the Lucential Transient Junction and what it might mean, to the frustration with the lithium, to the continued work on the water supply...

Twenty minutes later, he sighed and gave up. Slipping from beneath Dalton's arm, he dressed quietly and made it to the door before Dalton said groggily, "Where are you going?" His partner had risen onto one elbow and now rubbed at his eyes with his free hand as he yawned.

"I can't sleep. I didn't want to wake you, so I was headed to the roof for some fresh air."

Dalton glanced around, clearly still not fully awake, then said, "Hang on a second. I'll join you."

He stumbled into some rough clothes and they made their way through the silent halls and up the stairs of the governor's manse to the roof. As soon as they stepped outside, Devon knew they weren't alone. A single figure stood at the edge of the rooftop, gazing out toward Iandolo, the city a sliver of light in the distance. Far to the left, lightning flared purple in a bank of clouds, too distant for thunder.

Devon knew it was Lane before she spoke.

"Couldn't sleep either?"

He moved up to her right side, Dalton beside him. "No. Something woke me, but I couldn't figure out what."

"Same here. But I think—"

Before she could finish, the sound of a single horn came from the direction of Iandolo. It was dulled by distance, fading away, but then sounding again. Lane's breath caught. Before the third peal could sound, a second joined it, sounding closer, louder, a little more urgent. Then a third, closer still. When a fourth joined in, Lane let her breath out slow and bowed her head.

"What is it?" Dalton asked.

"A warning," Lane said. She drew herself up, shoulders back. "We've run out of time. Our scouts on the wayfare have sighted the Iandolan army."

A fifth horn sounded, this one at the walls of Brovetto, at the gate, and then horns were sounding all across the city, melding into one long forlorn cry. It held, echoing through the streets, through all levels, until Devon could feel it vibrating in his chest.

And then it fell silent.

"The scouts farthest out will be racing back to the city," Lane said. "Once they're all back, we'll seal the gate. And then we wait for their arrival."

Behind them, people emerged onto the roof, Raven at the forefront with an array of guards behind her, then Lane's father and mother, Cerelle and Sadie, some servants, a few others. Raven headed straight for Lane.

"How did you slip past us? You shouldn't have been out here alone."

"I wasn't alone."

"Without a guard," Raven snapped.

Lane didn't answer.

Varenov moved up to Lane's left. "What were those horns?" It sounded as if she already knew.

"The Iandolans," Lane said. "They're hours away now. They'll probably be here by dawn."

This news sent a rustle of low conversation through those gathered on the roof, although Varenov merely nodded. Dalton placed an arm across Devon's shoulders; Devon found Lane's hand and gave it a squeeze. She gave him a tight smile.

Then Devon sought out her father's gaze. "Do you have a moment to talk? I think I have an idea."

PART III

THE
SIEGE

Chapter Thirteen

"Has anything changed?"

Lane turned as Dalton passed between Raven and Sadie and joined her on the parapet above the gate. "Not since they arrived this morning."

Dalton leaned out, hands pressed into stone. He was dressed as a soldier, sword belted to his side, although not in the colors of the Iandolan army.

Lane picked up a spy glass set to one side and tapped him on the shoulder with it. "Care to take a more distant look?"

He said nothing as he took the cylinder and extended it, training it out along the wayfare below. Lane had been using it all morning and didn't need to look anymore. It was pointless and would only increase the nauseous roil in her stomach and the anxiety she was desperately trying to hide.

The Iandolan army had arrived on the wayfare an hour before dawn, marching in from the distance, their magelights shining in the darkness, wavering like fireflies at first, barely discernible, but growing as they approached, until there was a line staggeringly long threading out toward Iridesque. The leading forces had halted a thousand yards beyond the gates, which Lane had ordered sealed as soon as the scouts who'd been arrayed along the wayfare to warn them of the army's approach had all returned. Lane had watched as the entire phalanx within sight had settled in, the drumbeats that had marked their progress fading as the sunlight strengthened. Tents had been erected, cookfires established. They were too distant to hear anything but the loudest of shouts, but Lane could imagine the cacophony of the chaos. Ordered chaos, though.

Through the spy glass, she'd seen a contingent of ten men and women step out to the front of the army and survey the gate and walls. Arctus was easy to pick out in full uniform, motioning back and forth with his arms. Haavelan stood ramrod straight, dressed like the wealthy merchant he was, not a councilor, listening, his face never turning from the gate. If he'd been closer, she might have been able to pick out the expression on his face. Next to them both stood Favian in mage robes, a military cut, not a proctor's. The seven others with them were a mix of soldiers and mages, all with high-ranking uniforms. Arctus was speaking more to them than Haavelan or Favian.

Even now, the thought of her old proctor made her hands ball into fists. The anger helped alleviate some of the sickening bile in her stomach.

"See anything of note?" she asked, unclenching her hands with an effort.

"They've got a lot of mages."

"Burdock said the same thing. He thinks they brought nearly all of them, maybe even those still in training at the Lyceum."

"I wouldn't be surprised." Dalton continued to scan through the spy glass, moving it minutely, pausing, then again and again. "It looks like they've got the soldiers and mages separated into cells, one mage for every...hundred soldiers. Close to that. How many mages do you think Iandolo had?"

"Maybe a hundred, including the fifth and sixth years at the Lyceum."

"Hmm. Always felt like there were more than that around."

"Not all of the first and second years make it to the third. And of course, the third year is the real test to see if you can continue."

"In any case, that means we're looking at maybe 10,000 in the Iandolan army. We have 3,500 here, counting everyone who's come forward to help with the defense. Three to one. But we have the advantage of walls, ground we know...sort of." He glanced away from the spy glass. "And you."

Lane had already discussed the numbers with Burdock and her mother. "Not all of those out there are soldiers or mages. There are support staff, caravans of supplies. Hundreds of others."

"True. The army looks larger than it actually is." Dalton lowered the spy glass, scanned the men and women on the parapet, the others lining the walls below to either side of the gate.

Everyone was tense, fidgeting and strained. Many were throwing glances up to Lane's position. It had been worse earlier, when the army had arrived; it had settled slightly since then. Possibly because Burdock and his chosen commanders had gone down to walk among the troops. She'd stayed because everyone else had rushed off to tend to preparations and those on the walls needed someone to focus on for reassurance. Her mother had gone to find Maureen and Heather Brokaw, certain that the citizens would need to be calmed down and told not to evacuate to the mines yet; only when the walls were breached would that be necessary. Maupin hadn't even made it to the walls, pulled aside by Burdock for a terse conversation before gathering up his tullers and racing out of the Fifth Level ahead of them. Her father had gathered his contingent of shady rebels and sprinted from the courtyard as well, after being pulled aside last night on the rooftop by Devon. And Devon—

Lane grabbed Dalton's arm. "Where's Devon?"

"I left him in our room, working frantically on the lithum."

"Alone?"

"Yes. Why?"

"Because he doesn't know when to stop and rest. I've seen him with the lithum. He'll—"

"Lane!" Raven barked. "Something's happening."

Lane jerked her attention back to the wayfare. Those protecting the walls all shifted forward as well. Below, another contingent had broken away from the front of the army, like that morning. Dalton handed over the spy glass without comment and Lane trained it down on those below.

"It's Havvelan, Arctus, Favian, and a slew of soldiers, none more than sergeants in rank. Two are carrying lithum staffs, red and blue, two are carrying banners."

"Those are parley banners," one of the soldiers behind them said. "They want to speak."

"About what?" someone mumbled.

Lane lowered the spy glass. "Let's find out."

She scanned the walls to either side until she picked out Burdock, the ex-Prefect watching her from below. He nodded when she signaled for him to meet her at the gate.

"Raven, chose an escort. No more than ten people in the party. We'll match their envoy. Dalton—"

"I'll stay with you. Devon can take care of himself."

Lane nearly protested, but caught the look in his eye. "Very well."

Raven, Sadie, and five other guardsmen led her and Dalton down to the gate where they joined Burdock. The ex-Prefect was giving out orders to the commanders that surrounded him, hundreds of others in their mixed army sprinting from the walls to positions around the courtyard. Dawn Percy stood off to one side with some of the mage students, all of them looking terrified and apprehensive.

Dawn stepped forward as soon as she saw Lane, her face calm, but her hands clasped together before her, knuckles white. "Brigette and Daniel are already on the walls. Where do you want the rest of us?"

"You've all studied the defensive plans?" Gregg, Serene, and Shian nodded. "Then take up your positions here in the courtyard. Remember, attack when you can, but your main goal is to help defend our forces from the mages if we're forced to retreat."

The three tore off, only Shian hesitating a moment. They split, Gregg heading for the barracks, Serene the armory, Shian straight for the streets and buildings opposite the gates. Shian's small form vanished among the militia scrambling to take up ragged form in the courtyard itself. Lane recognized the voice bellowing commands and curses in equal measure and picked out Arch's form directing the group, along with a bevy of mercenaries.

When she turned back, she faced Dawn. "Take up position on the parapet above the gate. That way you can help all five of our young mages."

"Of course."

She didn't watch Dawn's retreat, turning to Burdock instead. He finished giving out a few last orders, then waved anyone else approaching toward his commanders so he could focus on her.

"Ready to see what they have to say?" he asked.

"I'm fairly certain I already know."

"So do I, but maybe they'll surprise us and surrender." He waved to those guarding the gate mechanism overhead. "Open the gates!"

A heavy, echoing boom sounded inside the wall, followed by the grinding of gears. The massive gates began to creak outwards. Lane began moving before they'd opened wide enough to let one person through, the others following. Before she reached the doors, she raised her hand, fingers crooked, and traced out a sigil.

As soon as she stepped outside, the gates coming to a halt with enough room for three people to walk abreast, she paused and blinked, one hand raised to block out the late afternoon sunlight. A stiff gust blew sand across the wayfare before her. Havvelan, Favian, and the others had stopped a hundred paces ahead and were waiting.

Once her eyes adjusted, she moved forward, Dalton to the right, Burdock to her left, Raven, Sadie, and the others scattered around them in a rough circle. She could feel the heat of the stone beneath the soles of her shoes, the blistering sun against her skin. Sweat beaded on her forehead and shoulders. She remained focused on the envoy ahead, her back stiffening the closer they got. It wasn't until she halted twenty paces away that she realized her attention was fixated on Favian, not Havvelan or Arctus, that the anxiety that had roiled in her gut on the parapet above had been replaced with a white-hot anger. The smug expression on the Proctor's face only made that anger burn hotter.

"You did this," she said, before anyone had a chance to say anything. Favian's tight grin faltered. "You caused all of this. With your incompetence nearly twenty years ago and your petty politicking when you were forced to suffer the consequences. You created Terriel when you left her behind and you forged the destruction of the Council in your attempt to free yourself of the Lyceum. I lay all of the death and destruction that has happened and is to come at your feet."

Favian's smugness had faded into glowering hatred. He drew in a slow breath, fingers crooking into position at his side. "How *dare* you acc—"

"There doesn't have to be any more death and destruction," Havvelan broke in, taking a step forward to gain Lane's attention. "All you have to do is surrender yourself, Devon Alamort, Varenov Illea, and Raias Burdock for trial as traitors to the Founder's Pact—and hand over Luminesque—and the bloodshed will end."

Lane snorted. "Have you even read the Founder's Pact? The *original* Founder's Pact? I have. What the Council has been doing for decades, if not a hundred years or more, is subverting it, distorting the original intentions to their own ends. To *Iandolo's* ends. The other Crystal Cities and their representatives have been slowly suppressed and supplanted, until now the Council is controlled by only those who serve Iandolo. If there is even a Council left anymore. Where are the other Councilors, Havvelan? I don't see any of them here. You'd think more than one representative would have come for negotiations."

"Only one was necessary. The others are back in the towers in Iandolo."

"I hope their accommodations are better than Devon's or my own, the last time we were there."

"I believe Santigo Allemad has your old room."

The fact that he admitted it so readily told her all she needed to know about the Council members and the Council.

"So you've finally set all pretense aside."

Havvelan smiled. "Yes. And we've learned a few things since we last met."

He flicked a finger and turned, the two soldiers carrying the parley banners tossing them aside. At the same time, Favian's crooked hand lashed upwards and began the base sigil. Arctus and the guards drew up in formation around him.

He completed the sigil and a cantrip shot across the space between them, tight and condensed and much faster than any Lane had seen from the Iandolan mages after Terriel's attack had taught them the form.

It stuck the barrier she'd erected before exiting the gates, splintering into shards that fanned up into the air before dissipating.

"Did you really think I'd come out here unprotected?" she asked.

Favian gave a twisted smile. "You can't protect everyone."

Behind him, all along the wayfare, balls of lightning shot into the air, arcing upwards, trajectories aimed at the walls.

"No more time for posturing," Burdock shouted, and grabbed her arm.

He pulled her back toward the open gates, already starting to swing closed, as he shouted orders up to the parapet above. Lane let herself be drawn backwards a step or two, her arm raised to retaliate, but then let it drop and turned to run. Favian's laugh prickled at her neck as Dalton and Raven ushered her and Burdock through the narrowing doors, slipping through with the others a moment before they closed with a hollow clang.

"Above the gates!" Lane yelled, dashing for the stairwell inside the wall. She didn't wait to see if Burdock or any of the others followed. Bounding up the steps, breath held, she burst onto the parapet when the first balls of lightning struck.

The two nearest impacted Dawn's shield with a sizzling crack, jagged streaks of energy shooting off in all directions. But the shield held. Three others hit the shield Lane had erected on the wayfare before the gates. She felt her barrier shudder. To either side, dozens struck the walls or the shields erected by Brigette and Daniel. Lane was impressed that the two students held their ground, but then screams filled the air in the sections where there were no protections from Brovetto's mages. Stone cracked as the lightning gouged into the foundations left and right and flung men and women off the parapet. Lane hoped they were already dead as she watched the bodies fall down the escarpment, but then her attention was caught by Dawn shouting, "There are more incoming!"

Lane drew up to Dawn's side. "We can't protect the entire wall. There aren't enough of us. Let your shield go and target them individually."

Lane felt Dawn release her shield and she did the same, hand already crooked and tracing out a sigil. The first volley had been coordinated, but the lightning was coming at random now. She finished the first cantrip as Dalton arrived with Raven and Sadie, falling into protective formation around her and Dawn, although there weren't any immediate non-magical threats. She released two more cantrips into the sky before the first one struck the ball of lightning that had started its descent. The two spells collided with a sizzling crack and blinding flare of energy that made Lane flinch, but the lightning dissipated before reaching a target. Her second cantrip missed, crackling off over the Flatlands as the ball of lightning shattered stone from the parapet's edge, leaving a gaping crater. Lane swore. Her third caught the lightning a hundred feet from the wall.

Dawn had opted for a concentrated shield, the energy wavering into existence in the lightning's path. When the ball struck, the shield dispersed it like flour on a counter smacked with the palm of your hand. Tendrils of lightning shot out from the impact but faded quickly.

"Good idea," Lane said, switching from her cantrips to the shields as the volleys continued. "Keep it up. The shields are easier to place and more accurate. Save the cantrips for later."

They began to work in conjunction, Lane taking anything targeting the right side of the gates, Dawn the left. Brigette and Daniel continued using their shields to stave off as much as they could. Even working together, though, they weren't catching all of the lightning. Lane winced whenever she heard one strike, the screams that followed digging into her chest.

"Where's Burdock?" she asked between sigils.

"At the gates preparing for that," Dalton answered, then pointed.

Lane spared a glance at the wayfare, her stomach clenching when she realized the Iandolan army was already marching on the gates.

"Lane!"

She snapped her attention back to the walls, winced as three balls of lightning struck with a crack-crack-crack, all because she'd been diverted for a few seconds. Her jaw clenched as she ground her teeth together, then she raised her hand and began to trace a new sigil. "Change of tactics, Dawn. Time to go on the offensive. I'm raising a shield. I'll extend it as far as I can to protect the walls. I want you to target their mages. Give them something to think about besides attacking our walls."

Dawn didn't answer, tracing out a few more blocks to the lightning as Lane finished her shield.

Sigil complete, Lane closed her eyes, breath held, then let it out slowly.

The shield extended outwards from her hands, spreading swiftly, fifty feet to either side, a hundred, but then it began to slow, stretching another twenty feet, then ten, then easing to a halt. The edges of it were weak, thin as spider's web. It shimmered like a soap bubble, iridescent and fragile.

But it held as two balls of lightning hit near its center, Lane flinching as if they'd struck her instead. Another hit farther out, then three more in succession spread all down its length. One glanced off the tremulous edge and spun down toward the Flatlands, disintegrating as it dropped.

At least six more were arcing toward them now. She could sense them, even with her eyes closed.

"Any time now, Dawn," she said through clenched teeth. "I don't know how long I can hold this."

"Finishing up…now."

The spell snicked into place and Lane opened her eyes in time to see bolts of lightning flash down out of the clear sky and slam into the wayfare. She caught three flares, marching away from the wall, before the intensity of the white-hot bolts blinded her and she was forced to turn away. The sizzling crack of thunder bounced off the walls and back down to the Flatlands as the screams that had punctuated the beginning of the fight transferred from the walls to the wayfare. Lane held tight to the shield, the incoming balls of lightning still raining down, but only two new ones joined the fray from the wayfare.

"Again!" Lane shouted, but Dawn was already completing another sigil. She glanced down toward Daniel's section of wall to find him attempting to extend her shield, but too late. Two more balls of lightning hit the parapet, just outside her shield, and she grimaced. On the other side, Brigette had taken their lead and placed smaller shields before those coming in outside of Lane's barrier. Only one made it through their defenses there.

The stone beneath Lane's feet began to shudder. At first, she thought it was caused by Dawn's second attack, the thunder rumbling through the parapet, but then she realized it was the gate.

She let her shield fall and took a step forward to find the Iandolan leading forces a mere thousand feet from the gates. But then men and women began pouring from the gates below, led by Burdock and a contingent of thirty men on horseback. They charged with an indistinct battle roar, the two forces meeting with a clash of blades and bodies four hundred feet from the gates. There was no order to the attack, simply mayhem as men slashed and pummeled, the two lines merging into chaos.

"They're starting to build shields," Dawn said to one side.

Lane shifted her gaze farther along the wayfare, to where jagged lightning now slammed into shields. A few of those shields gave way under the impacts, but most of them held. "At least they're not launching more lightning at us." She looked back down at the melee before the gates.

Dalton appeared at her side carrying a crossbow, Raven, Sadie, and a few others arriving with the same.

"You keep an eye on the mages," Dalton said. "We'll watch the gates. If it looks like Burdock and the others will need you, I'll let you know."

She hesitated, but there was no way she would be able to keep her eyes on everything. "I'll try to keep the mages busy."

Dalton nodded, then leaned over the parapet, arms propped on elbows, and aimed into the fray below.

Lane drew back to give them room, Dawn pulling back as well. "Keep up the barrage of lightning. We need to keep them occupied."

"Why didn't they have shields up to begin with?" Dawn asked. "They have more mages. They could have protected themselves and sent volleys at the wall at the same time."

"I think they were trying to overwhelm us with that initial attack. Overwhelm *me*. I don't think they expected us to have any other mages ready to defend Brovetto except for the two of us. Remember, the others were just students to them, not yet ready for any of the advanced magework." She raised her hand. "Let's see if we can't whittle down their mage advantage a bit more. I think Brigette and Daniel can handle anything that slips by us for a moment."

She scanned the nearest section of Iandolan soldiers for the formations she'd seen at the Lyceum in the training sessions, the ones designed to protect the mages during battle. She spotted one close to the front lines—too close. She'd risk hitting the Brovettan forces. She wondered briefly if they were protecting Favian, if he were on the front lines, but without the spy glass she wouldn't be able to tell at this distance. She doubted Favian would put himself in that much danger. He'd stay farther back. But not too far back, maybe...

"There."

She sketched out a sigil, matching Dawn's, but with more precision. Lightning crackled, striking the center of the formation she'd picked out, but encountering a shield. She swore, her hand already moving, lightning hitting another formation farther back, then another and another. Her fifth lightning strike blasted through the shield and slammed into the bodies and stone beneath, soldiers flung to the sides, most staying inert. But she didn't linger, didn't *want* to linger, already picking out new formations. Those on the wayfare had begun to shift though. She wasn't certain why. A reaction to their attack? Pulling back supplies to protect them?

"Raven," she barked, catching the ex-Regular's attention. "There's movement within the army behind the front. See if you can figure out what they're doing."

Raven fired her crossbow, then snatched up the spy glass, peering through it intently. Lane kept up her barrage, cycling back to the formations closest to the front, but the shields here were stronger, meaning their most powerful mages were closer to the city, the weaker ones in back.

"It's their mage formations," Raven reported. "They seem to be merging together in pairs."

"Why would they do that?" Dawn asked.

Lane swallowed a curse. "For protection, as you said. Two mages working together, one to create a shield, the other to attack. Dawn, break off and start a shield for the gates now!"

Lane completed her own sigil and began another immediately.

She'd nearly finished when the air before the gates a thousand feet up erupted in a sheet of fire. It fell from the heavens, flames roiling as if in a maelstrom. Dawn cried out in triumph a breath before the fires engulfed the parapet, Lane jerking away from the heat, losing her form, as the flames poured over Dawn's shield like water, flowing off to one side. The men and women around them cried out in terror, most of them ducking or throwing themselves to the stone beneath their feet. Lane sucked in a harsh breath, choked on the smoke that now filled the air, but staggered to the edge of the parapet.

The shield didn't extend to the wayfare before the gates.

The fire fell onto the men below, screams erupting instantly, figures flailing, some tumbling off the edge to the Flatlands below, burning as they fell, as the stench of charred meat drifted up with the smoke. Lane covered her mouth and nose with one hand, suppressing the urge to retch, her hand already in motion. The smoke stung her eyes and tears blurred her vision, but she didn't need to see perfectly to know that more fire would fall from the sky.

"Dawn—" Her chest spasmed with a fit of coughing, her voice already raw. "—protect the people above the gate! I've got the wayfare!" She hoped Daniel and Brigette knew to keep their own sections safe.

Her new shield snapped into place a moment before a second sheet of fire descended. It draped like an arched tunnel over the wayfare, flames running down its sides and then falling toward the desert beneath. The fighting hadn't stopped, but the fire and shields kept those on the parapet from firing their crossbows. Another sheet of fire hit Dawn's barrier, the drafts tugging at Lane's hair as Dalton pulled her back from the edge.

The heat was worse than the sun, as if they were inside a clay oven, the air turbulent and dry, the smoke getting thicker. Lane desperately wanted water, her throat parched and scratchy.

"Burdock's losing ground on the wayfare," Dalton shouted over the turmoil. "He may need help with a retreat."

"I can't drop the shield or they'll all be incinerated."

"Dawn—"

Lane was already shaking her head. "She's the only one keeping *us* alive."

Dalton's expression became grim as he searched for a solution and came up empty.

"Lane," Raven interrupted, her voice strangely calm, "they're trying something new."

Lane and Dalton glanced to the sky where Raven indicated. Sheets of flame were still descending in regular intervals on the walls, but between those attacks they could see fireballs arcing into the air, like the balls of lightning before.

"I don't understand," Lane said. "They're too high. They won't hit the walls. They won't even be close."

From behind them, Sadie said, "They aren't targeting the walls." When they turned, she added, "They're targeting—"

"The city," Lane finished in horror.

The group on the parapet fell silent, all eyes tracking the fireballs—ten of them—as they reached their apex and began to descend. Lane's chest constricted, her hands clenching into fists at her sides. She spun, searching to see if there was a pause in the sheets of fire that forced her to keep the wayfare covered, but there weren't. Burdock's men needed the shield or they'd all die. Not even Daniel and Brigette were getting a reprieve. She turned back to the city, strode to the edge of the parapet there and leaned into her arms.

There was nothing she could do, not without sacrificing Brovetto's defenders.

The first fireball hit, somewhere on the Second Level, a hollow crump sounding from that direction while a pillar of flame rose from the location, tendrils of smoking debris arching away from it. As the flames died back, black smoke began to billow outwards in a thick column as buildings caught fire. Three more fireballs landed in quick succession, the remaining six following suit, scattered across the bottom three levels—one near the Burn, two in the mostly uninhabited areas to the east, but the rest in populated regions near the gates. Lane drew in a ragged breath, winds from their own conflagration battering at her.

"They've launched four more," Raven reported. "No, seven."

Lane stiffened.

"They don't care about the city," Sadie said from Lane's right side. "Just as they didn't care about the Brovettans they placed in the internment camps in Iandolo. They don't need us."

"They intend to kill us all," Dalton said. "No quarter, no surrender, no mercy. Like the parley, any diplomatic resolution, any offer of a treaty, will be a trick. They came here to destroy all of Luminesque, by any means necessary, because they don't need us."

Lane pushed back from the wall. "Then we need to stop them, by any means necessary."

She returned to the side overlooking the wayfare and the gate, scanning the battlefield below as it stretched toward the horizon, ignoring the crumping sounds from behind as the fireballs continued to fall. The fighting was relegated to the wayfare, except for the work of the mages. There was only the one approach.

"Any means necessary," she whispered under her breath. Then: "Dawn, I'm going to drop the shield over the wayfare. Do whatever you can to cover both the parapet here and the wayfare below. Start your sigil now."

She waited until she could feel Dawn initiating the base form, her movements shaky but practiced. When she started the second form, Lane began her own.

It was simple. It was blunt. But she put all of her frustration and anger behind it.

As soon as she finished the second half of the new form, her shield over the wayfare below fell away. Dawn's barrier had already gone up, a flat plane tilted over the parapet and the gates below like an awning, so that what fire it caught would sluice down to the wayfare below. Lane approved. Hopefully Burdock pulled his men far enough back to be under its protection.

Her cantrip splintered the air before her and shot toward the army below. It expanded as it traveled, the size of her fist when it formed. By the time it hit the center of the enemy forces on the wayfare, it was ten times that size.

None of the Iandolan mages saw it coming.

It lashed into the soldiers, men sliced and diced and torn asunder, screams cut off practically before they could form, blood and body parts flying. Lane swallowed back bile, but the deaths were only secondary; collateral damage.

The real target was the wayfare itself.

The cantrip plowed into the elevated roadway's surface with a grinding shriek of shattering rock, shards thrown up in all directions, like an explosion. But the cantrip didn't stop, churning through stone, flinging chunks of rock and people aside as it pressed forward. And it still grew, expanding as it ate away at the platform. The Iandolan army in the area began to panic as they realized their mages couldn't stop it. It gouged deeper, had already dug a hundred-foot path through the center of the roadway. Its diameter was now the same width as the wayfare. No one in that section could escape it.

And then it hit the support, the plinth of stone that held it up over the Flatlands.

Stone cracked and shattered, the sound shuddering deep into Lane's chest, reverberating in her bones. Beside her, Dalton swore in awe and Dawn muttered what sounded like a prayer. And still the cantrip ground on. Atop the wayfare, the Iandolan soldiers near the plinth suddenly realized what was about to happen and began to run.

"They're too late," Sadie said, the words layered with grim satisfaction.

The cantrip reached the far side of the plinth, spat boulders the size of buildings out the other side, then began to dissipate out over the Flatlands.

The wayfare held for a breath…two…stone falling away from what remained of the plinth, from sections of the elevated road…

Then, with a thunderous crack, a section of the wayfare a thousand feet in length fell away, carrying a sizable chunk of the Iandolan army with it.

Chapter Fourteen

"What have you done?" one of Burdock's commanders spat. "The wayfares have stood since the Founders built them four hundred years ago! Now you've destroyed it! How do we get to Iandolo now?"

"We don't," Burdock said as he entered the room.

Lane, Dalton, Raven, Sadie, and the rest of her escort had abandoned the parapet as soon as they realized the collapse of that section of the wayfare had caused the Iandolan army to pull back and halt the attack on the city. Now Lane gulped down water to ease the burn in her smoke-scorched throat, coughing slightly. Her back ached; her neck, her shoulders. Exhaustion had overtaken her as soon as she sat down in a chair. She couldn't stop the trembling in her hands.

She'd been ignoring the commander's tirade, but was thankful Burdock had arrived.

She focused on the commander. "We'll find a way to Iandolo if necessary... *if* we manage to win this war. And if we don't, it won't matter anyway."

"The governor is right," Burdock said, emphasizing her title. "If she hadn't torn up the wayfare, the Iandolan army would already be inside the gates. As it is, it still took far too much effort to defeat the portion of the army that was stranded on our side of the wayfare after its destruction. I've just come from the gate. We've subdued those that are left and have incarcerated them in the Armory."

Lane gave a wry smile. "How appropriate." Then she frowned. "Were there many of them?"

"There were when the wayfare collapsed, but they refused to surrender even though escape was impossible. We had to fight them to a standstill at the edge of what's left of the road. Even then, some of them threw themselves over the edge rather than give up their swords."

Lane bowed her head, sick to her stomach at the thought. But she knew the horrors would only get worse.

"It's bought us a reprieve," Burdock continued, pouring himself a cup of water and gulping it down. He ran the back of his arm across his forehead. He looked weary and battle-worn, face covered in sweat and grit and flecks of blood. His uniform was torn in places, matted with even more blood, and he reeked.

"I don't think it will be as much of a break as you think," Lane said carefully.

"What do you mean?"

She glanced at Raven and Dalton. "I think…I think it's clear that the mages have learned from Terriel's attack on the Lyceum and what they managed to torture out of Devon in the towers when he was captured. They're using the Source in new and different ways, with Outcomes that they never even considered before recent events. We could see it in the attacks today on the walls. We'll have to check with Dawn Percy and the others, but I don't recall them using balls of lightning before. And their fireballs were larger and had more range than I've ever seen. Only some familiarity and practice with Devon's structure for magework would have allowed them to produce those effects." She drew in a steadying breath. "But it's more than that."

Burdock had set down his cup and crossed his arms over his chest. "What?"

"Raven and Dalton will back me up on this, I believe." She leaned forward. "When the attack began, the mages and the soldiers were set up in their standard formations. They have these newfound powers—or at least, the powers they had have been expanded—but they didn't consider how to change their formations. The majority of that is because they've never had to face other mages. They're used to dealing with regular men and women, so they separate their mages—to protect them; if a unit is compromised, they only lose one mage at a time—and surround them with soldiers. That's how the fighting started. But once we'd traded volleys for a while, they realized that formation doesn't work well against other mages."

"How so?"

"Because it's difficult to attack and defend at the same time. It takes time to perform the sigils. Some of the forms produce an effect that remains on its own, leaving the mage time to work on another sigil, but these usually fade fast. If you want the effect to remain, you have to keep focused on it, which means you can't produce another spell. If you're working alone, you have to make a choice—attack or defend. But if you work in pairs or as a group—"

"You can do both," Burdock finished for her.

Dalton stepped forward. "Because they've never faced off against other mages, they didn't think of this. They relied on what they already knew. But in the middle of the battle, once they were put on the defensive, they adapted. They merged their cells, so there were at least two mages in each, one for attack, one for defense."

"When they launched the assault on the city, ignoring the walls, and we couldn't stop them because they had one mage in each cell protecting the others…that's when I resorted to the cantrip that destroyed the wayfare. It was the only thing I could think of at the time." She said this to the commander, who did not appear mollified. Burdock may have cowed him into keeping silent, but it was clear he still didn't agree with her decision.

Burdock didn't seem to notice. "I don't see how this relates to them pulling back and giving us a break from the fighting."

"Because Favian—and I assume it's Favian in charge of the mages—may be ambitious, self-absorbed, and unscrupulous, but he's not stupid. He adjusted quickly to the realities of battling mages. I assume he'll adapt his newfound powers to deal with the destruction of the wayfare as well. I can think of at least two possible solutions using the Source without even trying."

"But you're more familiar with it, have been practicing with it longer," Raven said. "It will likely take them longer to come up with even one solution."

"Probably," Lane said. "But after seeing what they can do already today in the field, I'm not going to count on it. I think both sides underestimated the other today."

"How did you underestimate them?" Burdock asked.

"I underestimated their depravity. It never crossed my mind that they would ignore the walls and target the city."

"They clearly hoped to take the walls and gate quickly. They only targeted the city when that failed."

"So what should we do now?" Dalton asked. "Just wait?"

Lane considered for a moment, then stood. "No. Tell Dawn to pull Gregg, Serene, and Shian back from their posts around the courtyard. Have them pair with Brigette, Daniel, and Dawn on the walls, one for attack, one for defense. We can learn from experience as well." She turned to Burdock. "Set up watchers and runners. Have them keep an eye on the Iandolan army, in particular, what they're doing regarding the broken wayfare. I want regular reports."

"And what about you?"

Lane hardened. "Oh, I intend to stay on the wall—to back up our defenses when necessary, but mostly to go on the offensive."

"Very well. I'll get the orders sent."

Burdock and Dalton left in a rush. Lane was turning to Raven when Sadie stepped forward. She'd noticed the young Brovettan fidgeting in the background both above the gates and here inside one of its meeting rooms. But she was difficult to read, always restless, always with a dour look or scowl. "What is it, Sadie?"

"I was wondering if there were somewhere else I could be assi—"

She cut off as they heard running footsteps in the corridor outside. Raven tensed, but then Cerelle burst into the room, face red, breath coming in gasps as she lurched to a halt and bent over, hands grasping the table for support.

"Cerelle, what—?"

"Riot at the...mine entrance. Citizen's...are panicking. Your mother... needs your help."

When Cerelle began to collapse, Sadie leapt forward to support her, holding her sister up by draping her arm over her shoulder. Lane made to help, but Cerelle waved her away, coughing as she tried to catch her breath.

Lane turned to Raven. "Get us an escort." She glanced at Cerelle and Sadie, then shook her head. "No, get us a carriage. Cerelle's in no condition to walk or run and we need to get there fast."

Raven began snapping orders, guards running from the room. Lane poured another cup of water and handed it off to Cerelle as soon as she thought she'd recovered enough to handle it. The Brovettan took a tentative swallow, then a heavy gulp when she didn't immediately spit it back up.

"Can you move?" Lane asked.

When Cerelle nodded, they headed for the door and the courtyard below.

"What can you tell me?"

Cerelle drew a steadying breath, coughed once, then said, "When the attack began, some of the citizens showed up at the mine entrance where they've all been told to evacuate. But your mother was there already, and Maureen, and the two of them, along with Heather and the guardsmen assigned to the mines, convinced them all that it was too early, that they should return to their homes until the gates fell, as planned." Cerelle broke into another fit of coughing, but she'd begun regaining her strength, no longer leaning so heavily into Sadie.

Lane could already tell where this was going. "But then the fireballs began to hit the city."

Cerelle nodded. "Everyone panicked, demanded that we open the mines now. When I left, your mother and Maureen were holding them off, mostly because there weren't that many. But I passed people racing for the entrance on my way here, saw the looks on their faces. If someone doesn't get down there—"

"I understand."

They spilled out of the left side of the gatehouse into the courtyard to find Raven waiting, a carriage with four horses pulling up before her. She shouted at the drivers as she snatched open the door, Sadie helping Cerelle inside. Lane climbed in after as Raven snapped, "The Veridian Strike mining entrance. As fast as you can!" She pulled the door closed behind her, Lane's last glance outside catching at least four soldiers leaping onto the footers built into the sides, holding themselves upright with handles near the roof.

* * *

When the mages started their attack on the wall, Devon felt it. Like when the Brovettans attacked Iandolo, way back when he was a student at the Lyceum, he felt the magework as a thrum in his chest. He glanced up, concern for Dalton, for Lane, threading through his body, even though his rooms in the governor's manse had no windows. He nearly set the crystal he was trying to forge into the key to the lithum aside to go join them. But there wasn't much he could do to protect them. He was no mage; he had no fighting skills. He was a mathematician, a seeker of patterns, of order amidst chaos. The best way he could help would be to recreate the lithum battery.

Especially since everything Favian and the other mages knew about the Source came from him.

The guilt that he'd been able to suppress by working constantly since their arrival in Brovetto surged forward and he bowed his head, his chest tightening so much it was hard to breath. Images from his time in the towers of Iandolo, under Arctus', Favian's, and Havvelan's hands shuddered through him.

He'd caved under the torture and told them everything he knew.

He allowed himself to wallow in the guilt for a moment, the thrumming in his chest continuing, then he sucked in a steadying breath, closed his eyes, and pulled himself out of it.

"Lane discovered new things when we were at the tull," he reminded himself. "But if she's going to have any chance at all, I've got to finish this key."

He shoved the thrumming sensation from the fighting into the background and focused on the purple crystal before him, the red half of the lithum on the desk. Except the crystal wasn't exactly purple anymore. It had shifted into a deep indigo after his more recent adjustments.

Body already trembling from the effort, he focused on a new section, comparing the surface there with the surface on the red lithum, noting the peaks and valleys, then choosing which elements of the purp—no, indigo— crystal he wanted to modify. He focused, easing the nodes inside the crystal into their new positions. He'd learned a few things while practicing over the last few days. The crystal was easier to manipulate if he used a more delicate touch, less brute force. Also, he'd started to get a feel for what changes each adjustment would make to the structure as a whole. He'd been able to make significant progress. But every now and then, a change resulted in an unexpected and disastrous cascade that set him back rather than pushed him forward.

Teeth clenched against the vibrations the changes caused, he felt the nodes slip into their new positions. A wave of fatigue washed through him and he placed his hands on the desk to steady himself until it passed. He inspected the crystal again—lighter now, but blue rather than purple—and grunted.

He picked another section and did it again.

In the middle of another alteration, the thrum in his chest intensified enough to catch his attention, making him lose focus. The crystal shuddered and he pulled back, but not before it shifted into a new pattern. This time, he nearly passed out. When he checked the crystal, he'd lost at least ten percent of the progress he'd made that morning. He swore—his exhaustion not giving the words much force—and sagged back into his chair, rubbing his eyes with his fingers.

Then he noticed the thrumming had halted.

He sat up, focusing on the direction of the gate and the wayfare to Iandolo, but felt nothing.

Surging to his feet, he tried to race for the door but stumbled, staggered, and collapsed to the floor. His body felt drained, more than he'd thought. Like that time at the Shandy Quad's bar when he'd been drinking all night and felt fine, but when he stood up to head back to the Lyceum he hadn't been able to stand upright. Someone had to catch him and ease him to the floor, then had handed him a glass of water.

He groaned and bumped his forehead against the floor a couple times, then eased his hands beneath his chest and pushed upright onto hands and knees. He held that position for a long shaky moment, lightheaded, then pulled his feet beneath him and stood.

He immediately began to fall again, but aimed himself at the door, catching himself on the frame. Using the wall for support, he managed to half walk, half drag himself down the hall and into the main corridor before one of the servants found him.

"Heavens and hells, where do you think you're going?" she exclaimed, then shouted, "Mari, get over here!"

"I need to…get to…the rooftop," he gasped, appalled at how out of breath he was considering the short distance he'd managed to come.

"Don't fret none, my lord, Mari and I will get you there."

Mari, another servant, but younger and more robust, stalked around the corner, hands wringing a towel. "What are you going on about, Darcy, there's a war—" She cut off and swore when she saw him, lurching forward to take his arm. "You shouldn't be out and about, my lord, you're as pale as bone!"

"Roof," he said, waving with one hand. "And I'm not a lord."

With each beneath one of his armpits, they navigated the corridors and stairs up to the roof. Emerging into the blinding sunlight, the first thing Devon saw were the columns of smoke rising into the blue sky.

"The edge."

Darcy and Mari led him to the roof's edge, where he'd stood the night before with Lane as the horns sounded the Iandolan army's approach. Darcy gasped, one hand covering her mouth in horror, but neither servant let go of his waist.

"Have they already breached the city?" Mari asked.

"No."

"But it looks like half the city's on fire!"

"Look at the wayfare."

Mari's arm on his waist clenched tight, but her voice was surprisingly steady. "It's collapsed."

"I'd wager Lane took it out to stop the Iandolans."

Mari muttered a curse that was awed and reverential.

"Should we be heading for the mines, my lord?" Darcy's voice trembled.

"Don't be daft," Mari scoffed. "We haven't heard the evacuation bells yet."

Devon considered. He couldn't see the mine's entrance from here, nor the streets around it, especially with the smoke blocking most of the view, but they'd never considered destroying the wayfare during their planning sessions. They'd thought the focus would be on the gates, but clearly Havvelan and Favian had targeted the city instead.

"Don't wait for the bells," he said, drawing back from the wall. "You'd better leave for the mines now."

"But, my lord, the governor said—"

"They aren't attacking the gates," Devon said, the words curt. "They're hitting the city. Just look! You aren't going to be safe unless you get to the mines."

Darcy and Mari shared a look.

"All right then," Mari said. "We'll get you down to the courtyard and grab a carriage."

Devon shook his head. "No. Go without me. I need to finish what I've started, moreso now than ever. Get me back to my room and then go."

Neither Mari nor Darcy said anything, nor did they move, but his legs were more stable now. He stepped back, ducking to pull out from beneath their support, and they let him go. He made it three steps before he had to stiffen to steady himself, but he didn't fall. He'd reached the door leading down into the manse when they both appeared at his side again to help him. He heaved a sigh of relief.

Once back in his room, he collapsed into his chair. Some of his strength had returned, but not much. He drew in a steadying breath, then reached for the indigo crystal.

"Is there anything we can get you?" Darcy asked.

He turned to find them both still standing in the doorway, worry etched into their faces. Not for themselves, he realized, but for him.

He gave them a reassuring smile. "I'll be fine. Now go, or you won't reach the mines in time."

"But you see, my lord, we know what you did for us, working on the aqueducts and starting up the water and everything. That's more than the Iandolans ever did. Oh! Sorry! I know you're Iandolan yourself, but—" Flustered, Darcy cast a panicked look at Mari, who stepped forward.

"What she's trying to say is, it doesn't feel right us leaving you here by yourself and fleeing to the mines after all you've done to help Brovetto, when you aren't Brovettan yourself. It seems...ungrateful."

Devon didn't know what to say. He hadn't thought about what the Brovettans would think of him, of his work, he'd only worked. Because he knew he was the only one who could repair the lucent. And he'd needed the distraction from the aftermath of the torture and his own guilt. But now, his slip into self-pity earlier felt petty and trite.

He held up the crystal. "I need to finish reforming this crystal. It's part of a pair and it may be the only thing that saves us from the Iandolan army, from their mages in particular. I'm the only one who can do it, but...it drains my strength, far more than I thought it would, and I'm not certain I'll be able to finish it in time." His voice cracked and he sucked in a breath to steady his emotions. "Even if I do, none of it will matter if the citizens of Brovetto are all dead. You need to go to the mines. It's the only place you'll be safe. There's nothing you can do to stop the Iandolan mages."

They stood in silence, until Mari said, "Very well, sir."

He returned his attention to the crystal, aware of a hushed conversation in the hallway outside, followed by silence. He nodded to himself. Not that some company wouldn't be appreciated, but really, what could they do to help? Nothing. Only he knew how to alter the lucent. It was up to him.

He sighed and settled in, turning the crystal in his hand until he found the spot where he'd left off. Concentrating, he began to slip the nodes into a new position—

Darcy appeared in the doorway, bearing a tray of sliced meats, cheeses, and fried mushrooms and onions. Mari stood behind her with a decanter and glasses.

"You said the...whatever you're doing...drains you," Darcy said, then pointedly set the tray down on his desk. "We brought you fortifications."

"Some more liquid than others," Mari added from his other side. She poured a glass, the scent of strong alcohol filling the room, and handed it over. "This is something the cooks have been brewing up in the cellars. It should perk you right up."

Devon held it for a long moment, then sighed and took a sip.

He coughed and spluttered. It burned all the way down.

"What is it?" he gasped, his voice hoarse.

"Something new," Mari said smugly, setting the decanter aside. "What do you think?"

Devon did feel a little more invigorated. He took another sip. It burned just as much as the first. "It's...interesting."

"Then don't mind us. We're here to make certain you finish…whatever you need to finish."

"Even if we have to slap you to keep you conscious," Darcy added.

Mari grinned, leaning forward onto the desk. "So get to work."

* * *

The carriage lurched to a halt on the outskirts of the square in front of the mining entrance. Raven opened the door and leaned outside, but didn't step out. Lane could hear the roar of a thousand voices all shouting at once, although she couldn't pick out anything coherent. But the tone was raw and panicked, laced with fear and terror. The air coming in through the open door was tainted with smoke, enough to make her eyes tear up and scratch at her throat.

"Can you get us closer?" Raven yelled to the drivers.

Lane could see the stone side of a building through the door, a straggle of people passing by, all headed toward the mining entrance.

Raven cursed at whatever the driver said in response, then glanced down into the carriage. "We're going to have to go the rest of the way on foot. Lane, you're with me. The rest of you spread out around her with the guards outside the carriage. We'll keep it close and tight."

Everyone agreed and then Raven was pulling her out into the space between the carriage and the stone wall.

She'd thought the crowd was loud from inside, but once she stepped to the cobbles it tripled in volume, rebounding off of the buildings on three sides of the square and the stone façade of the bluff that held the mining entrance. It stretched up to the Fourth Level, a nearly sheer sheet of rock, the massive mouth of the mine carved into its base, sealed by weighted stone doors. Lane had caught a glimpse of a thin line of guardsmen holding back the horde of people pushing forward as she stepped from the carriage, but she couldn't see over the crowd once she was on the ground.

Raven, Cerelle, Sadie, and the four guardsmen closed in tight, shoulder-to-shoulder, as Raven ordered the drivers to wait. Then they began pushing forward.

As soon as they cleared the carriage, they were caught in the ebb and flow of the crowd. Some of those nearby noticed who they were and tried to step aside, but most were too focused on reaching the mining entrance. Their utter terror bore down on Lane with the weight of stone, tasting of the ash and char as tatters of the smoke from the burning city blew across the square. But she noticed that no one was fighting; no punches were being thrown. And no one appeared to be getting trampled underfoot.

These were families and businessmen and workers all simply trying to shove their way forward. It hadn't degenerated into a full-on riot

Yet.

Ten minutes of jostling later, Cerelle turned to Lane and shouted, "We aren't making much progress! We're mostly being shoved back and forth near the same position!"

"Then we need to try something different," Lane said. "Try to hold here for a moment."

She raised her hand, fingers crooked, and Raven, Cerelle, and Sadie pushed away from her to give her some room. She traced out a sigil as fast as possible, finishing a moment before someone stumbled into Cerelle, who jolted her arm. But the sigil had been cast.

White light began to fall from the sky above their position in streaks, like rain, then started to drift toward the mine's entrance. Those surrounding them gasped and drew back, although the light faded before it would have hit anyone in the crowd. It had the intended effect though. People quieted and began to draw back from the light, allowing Raven and the others to push forward, Lane in their midst. The crowd parted in a straight shot toward the mining entrance and the chaotic fervor of those gathered calmed.

By the time they reached the haggard line of guardsmen, pushed nearly flush with the mining doors, the entire square had settled. Restless still, but no longer in turmoil.

"Thank the Founders you got here in time," Maureen said, her voice calm but with frayed edges. "They were on the verge of overwhelming us. Nothing we said could calm them, not once the city started to burn."

Her mother stepped forward and embraced her briefly, holding her shoulders after with both hands. "What happened at the gate?"

"Something unexpected." She gave them a short rundown of the attack, ending with her destruction of the wayfare. Both Maureen and her mother raised their eyebrows at that. "I'm afraid it's only bought us a little time, though. And I think we're going to have to alter our plans."

Varenov sighed. "Burdock has been warning us that no plan survives the first battle."

"He has."

Lane looked over her shoulder at the square filled with the citizens of Luminesque. Most were watching them silently, although the restlessness had begun to escalate as they talked. There was a low susurrus beginning, a rustling as people began to fidget and shift.

"We thought the siege would last for weeks," Lane said, turning back to her mother and Maureen, Heather standing behind them. "It won't. Not if they're attacking the city directly."

"What do you need us to do?" Heather asked.

"We're going to have to open up the mines now," Lane's mother answered.

Lane nodded. Her mother turned to Maureen and Heather, giving out orders, the three already moving toward the guardsmen waiting on either side. Lane faced the square. "I need some height."

The nearest guardsmen glanced around, then scrambled to stack some crates to one side of the mine up before her. The burgeoning rumble from the crowd died out as she climbed atop them.

"Citizens of Luminesque," she said, using a sigil to carry her voice to everyone present, "as you know, the Iandolan army has arrived." A wave of fear roiled through those gathered. "We thought they would focus on breaking the gates and that that would take time, but as you saw, after an initial attempt at the gates, they targeted the city instead. I and the mages who traveled with me from Iandolo as refugees protected the city as best we could, but we are outnumbered. We've hurt them enough for a reprieve, but that won't last long. Because they've chosen to hurt you, the people of Brovetto, we've decided to take advantage of this pause in the fighting to open up the mines early." A roar of hope rose and those nearest began to surge forward. Lane raised her hand, fingers crooked, face stern, and boomed, "But only if you proceed in an orderly fashion! I *will* seal this entrance if I have to!"

Those in the front halted, eyes on her hand. From behind, a hollow, echoing boom sounded as the stone door separated and began to grind open. Lane held steady, staring the crowd down, but even her threat didn't keep them from pressing forward. The guardsmen held them back as best they could until someone shouted from behind, then they pulled away.

The crowd streamed forward, parting around Lane's makeshift stand, a few of those passing calling out in thanks, reaching out to her, some sobbing in relief. Raven and the others kept them back enough they couldn't touch her. Her mother, Maureen, Heather, and others herded them into the opening, offering encouraging words, reminders about where to go, and an occasional reprimand.

Lane lowered her arm and glanced down at Raven. "We need to go."

The ex-Regular nodded and helped her down, Cerelle, Sadie, and her guardsmen forming up around her again. They headed against the flow, angling toward the side of the square, where the pressure wasn't as great.

Halfway across, the bells signaling the evacuation to the mines began to peal out over the city, starting close, but spreading quickly. New people were already beginning to stream into the square, most running, looks of shock on their faces. Fathers were carrying children, mothers had baskets on their hips, others were carrying trunks between them. Most had stuffed essentials into satchels slung across their backs.

Cerelle and Sadie had climbed into the carriage, still standing where they'd left it, when they heard the first screams.

"What's happening?" Lane asked, searching the square for trouble. But the crowd had paused, people looking back, arms raised, fingers pointing toward the sky. Then everyone turned and surged toward the mining entrance.

"Look," Raven said grimly.

Lane rounded the carriage and stared in the direction of the waygate to Iandolo.

Fire balls were once again being flung into the city, the first few intercepted by Dawn and the others at the wall, but at least two others made it through. Lane watched in horror as one of them exploded within blocks of the square, a plume of debris flung upwards with a roar.

She spun on the drivers of the carriage. "Get me back to the wall. Now!"

Then she leapt inside, Raven a heartbeat behind her.

Chapter Fifteen

"What's happening?" Lane demanded as soon as she reached the parapet above the waygate. Dawn and Shian stood at the edge, hands moving through forms, one attempting to intercept the fire balls being flung from the far side of the breach in the wayfare, the other protecting those on the parapet with a shield. Shian, the youngest of their mages, was holding up remarkably well, considering, her face taut with determination. Between Dawn, Shian, and the other two pairs, most of the fire balls were being countered. Dalton and Burdock watched from behind, both of them radiating pent-up frustration. Lane understood. At the moment, this was a mage war, but she thought their time would come here shortly.

In the background, the peal of a hundred bells heralded the evacuation to the mines.

Burdock turned as she approached. "Most of the Iandolan mages have resumed their attack. They're paired up for attack and defense, so Dawn and the others haven't been able to do much about whittling down their forces. However, not all of them are focused on hitting the city. Look." He motioned toward the wayfare below and handed her the spy glass he held.

Lane moved up next to Dawn, who shot her a quick glance without pausing in the formation of her sigils. Lane noted lines of exhaustion already beginning to form. She wondered how much she and the other mages had managed to eat during their brief respite after the collapse of the wayfare. Then she focused on the Iandolan army.

It was obvious what Burdock wanted her to see, even without the spy glass. A cluster of the army stood near the edge of the broken section of the wayfare. Through the glass, she could see at least eight mages, one of them Favian. Two of them were actively protecting those gathered with shields. The rest were soldiers, including Prefect Arctus. They were arguing, Favian jabbing his fingers at the missing part of the wayfare, a few of the mages gesturing in response, Arctus standing back with his arms crossed. The rest of the soldiers were shifting about nervously.

Favian pointed at one of the mages, who stepped forward reluctantly, then traced out the second half of a sigil in the air before him. Since he hadn't started with the base sigil, nothing happened, but Lane grunted in recognition. After a few iterations, two other mages attempted to trace out the same sigil, Favian slapping their hands away when they made a mistake. Lane flinched each time, remembering Favian's impatience, vitriol, and condescension from when she had been a student at the Lyceum, learning beneath his tenure. Of course, he'd been teaching her specifically so that she'd fail, to garner political favor among her mother's rivals. She'd always thought he'd singled her out for his hatred, but perhaps not.

After long moments of practice, the three stepped forward, working in sync until Favian either grew impatient or felt they were close enough to make an attempt for real. Under his direction, all three began the base sigil, followed by what they'd just practiced, each holding steady as soon as the spell was complete.

Before them, in the open air before the jagged edge of the torn wayfare, flat shields began to shimmer into being. Unlike the shield she, Shian, and the others were using to protect them from the mage attacks, however, these shields were thick, nearly the same thickness as the wayfare itself. They butted up against the edge of the stone ten feet in front of the mages themselves, but the shield itself was straight, so there were gaps were the two met. The shield extended out from the wayfare about ten feet, only about one tenth of the missing section, but as soon as the shields steadied, Arctus motioned one of the soldiers forward.

"Oh, no," Lane breathed. She felt someone settle in beside her, but didn't stop watching through the glass.

The chosen soldier didn't move for a moment, seemed about to bolt, but then one of the others nudged him forward. He approached the makeshift shield bridge reluctantly, looked out over the edge of stone. The shield was mostly transparent; Lane got vertigo imagining the drop down to the Flatlands below that the soldier could see. He straightened back up, shrugged his shoulders in fatalistic acceptance, then stepped out onto the thick shield.

It held, the man's relief obvious. He turned back, but Arctus motioned him farther out. He took another step, then another, now over halfway across the shield bridge the mages had constructed. With his next step, however, his foot began to sink into the shield. With a cry that Lane could see but not hear, he twisted and leaped for the crumbling stone edge of the wayfare behind him, the shield bridge the mages had constructed falling away beneath him. His chest impacted the wayfare and his hands scrabbled for purchase as his body weight pulled him backwards. Lane took an involuntary step forward, her breath caught in her throat. One of the mages abandoned his hold on the form and lurched forward, snagging one of the soldier's arms a moment before he would have slipped over the edge. He hauled him back onto the wayfare, both men collapsing from the effort.

Favian simply stood over them both before turning back to the rest of the mages.

"He's lucky," Burdock said on her left. "They've lost eight men in previous attempts."

"You'd think they'd secure the volunteer with a rope so if he does fall they can catch him," Dalton added. Lane hadn't heard him approach from behind.

She lowered the spy glass. "I don't think either Favian or Arctus care how many are lost. They may even think it's motivating for the mages."

"Did you see enough to give us a timeframe on when they'll be successful?" Burdock asked.

"They're close to figuring out how to use the shields to construct a bridge. They're focusing too heavily on thickness, not on structure. A brute force approach. Not surprising, since they're new to manipulating Devon's Source to yield specific Outcomes."

"How long until they hit the waygate again?"

Lane glanced toward the horizon, shocked to realize that it was nearing dusk. It didn't feel as if the entire day had been spent on the fight, even though Burdock had warned her that time slipped by faster than it seemed during a battle. "I'd say you have two hours…three at most."

"Will they attack at night?" Dalton asked.

"They have before." Burdock leaned forward onto the parapet as the mages below prepared to make another attempt, then pushed back abruptly. "I'll warn the forces below."

He retreated, passing through Raven, Cerelle, and Sadie on his way. Beyond, one of the fire balls that had slipped through their defenses exploded near the Burn.

"We should pull back to the secondary defenses," Raven said.

"No," Lane answered, "not yet. We need to buy the citizens of Brovetto enough time to reach the mines."

Raven waved a hand, as if she'd expected nothing less.

Lane turned to Dawn. "Do you need a break? I can take over for a bit."

Dawn's jaw clenched. "I can hold on for a little longer."

"Good." Lane faced the wayfare below. "I want to give them something else to think about besides that bridge."

She raised her hand, fingers crooked, and traced out a sigil.

A river of flame fell from the sky, surging down the length of the wayfare, starting with the group surrounding Favian. Screams rose, faint with distance, indicating she'd caught at least some of them off guard, but when the smoke and fire cleared Favian and his mages were still alive, frantically erecting additional shields for protection. Arctus' soldiers were scrambling. Lane sent another wave of fire, then another, before switching to a hail of deadly ice shards. While shields shaped correctly could shunt fire aside easily, it was more difficult to protect against hundreds of individual blows. Each ice spike would be felt and would weaken the mage holding the shield in place. She continued the ice barrage for a moment, then began throwing cantrips. The first was like the one she'd used to tear the wayfare apart, an attempt to widen the breach she'd already caused, but Favian must have anticipated the attack. It struck the shield his mages had constructed at the edge of the wayfare with a hideous sizzling crack that echoed out across the Flatlands. Some of the mages stumbled or were flung back, but the shield held. She flung a second directly at Favian himself, but didn't wait to see if it landed, sending other smaller cantrips down the length of the army. Most were intercepted by shields, but not all.

"It's having an effect," Dawn said. "They aren't throwing as many fire balls now."

"Keep intercepting whatever they're throwing at the city as best you can, but if you get a break from that, help me with the army."

"With pleasure."

The exhaustion had bled from Dawn's voice and her hand motions were reinvigorated as she launched into an attack similar to Lane's. Beside her, Shian also appeared encouraged, the slump in her shoulders lessening. She took a moment to reestablish her shield over the parapet.

The back and forth continued as the sun sank into the horizon, the shelf of a storm painted orange and purple in the light. Stars began to appear overhead, and the moon rose. Lane's arm and shoulder began to ache from all of the motion. She'd been forced to practice for hours at the Lyceum, and had practiced long hours with those here in Brovetto, but nothing like what she'd done today.

When she began to wonder if she could continue, Dawn suddenly said, "The fire balls have stopped."

Lane finished her sigil and let her arm drop. It was dark now, the only light coming from the stars, the fires in the city behind, and the magelight and fire on the wayfare below. Dawn followed Lane's example and let her own arm fall, massaging it with her other hand, wincing at the pain. Shian kept her shield steady though.

After a few moments, both Brigette and Daniel halted their own attacks from the walls on either side. Lane remained wary, but no further fire balls or cantrips appeared from the Iandolan army. She could see their shields shimmering with reflected light, both from the moon and their own fires.

Lane shook out her arm. It felt lose, without strength. She wasn't certain she could lift it again if she had to.

"Do you think it's over?" Shian asked.

"For now, perhaps. We can hope."

Dawn suddenly wavered and Lane caught her before she could collapse. Cerelle and Sadie stepped forward in the torchlight and took her.

Lane looked down at Shian, the young mage barely keeping herself upright. "We're all exhausted. Go with them, get some rest. Tell the other mages as well. I'll stay here and keep watch."

"But—" Shian began to protest, but Lane halted her with a look.

"You were defending the walls much longer than I. Go."

Shian ducked her head, then retreated with Cerelle, Sadie, and Dawn. Raven and Dalton joined her at the parapet's edge, Dalton scanning the Iandolan forces with the spy glass.

"Shian's right, though," Raven said, "you are exhausted."

"I'll be fine."

"Weren't you the one suggesting Devon was pushing himself too hard?" Dalton said.

"I don't have a choice."

"Devon feels the same way."

Lane didn't respond. She knew he was right. She and Devon were both stubborn. "What do you see?"

"They've retreated from the edge of the breach. I think they're pulling back for the night."

"Let's wait and see if Burdock agrees."

"I do."

The ex-Iandolan Prefect emerged from the darkened stairwell into the light. He motioned for the spy glass and Dalton handed it over. They all stood in silence as he surveyed the army on the wayfare.

After long enough for Lane to begin thinking he'd changed his mind, he lowered the glass.

"They've returned to their camps. I'll keep a rotation on the walls, of course, but I think we should order everyone to rest. It's been a stressful day, even if none of those on the walls saw any real fighting."

"Agreed."

Burdock turned to her. "That includes you."

"Of course. I'll wait another hour, to be safe."

"Hmmm." He faced Raven. "Keep her to her word."

Then he stalked off, already giving orders.

* * *

"Wake up!"

Someone slapped Devon, hard, his head rocking back from the blow. He groaned, tried to pull himself up out of the exhaustion, tried to pry open his eyes. "I'm…"

"Wake up! You said we didn't have time for this!"

The second blow—or was it the fifth? He felt as if he'd been struck more than a couple times—landed harder than the first, but it sparked a burst of anger. "I'm awake, damn it!"

He forced his eyes open to find Mari standing over him, hand poised to hit him again. She grabbed him by the jaw and cocked her head, staring him in the eye, then grunted in apparent satisfaction.

"Took longer that time to pull you out of it," she said, stepping back. "A lot longer. Darcy went off to get you more to eat. She'll be back in a second. You need to keep working." She set the dark blue crystal—not indigo any longer—into his lap and wrapped his hand around it before moving off.

With effort, he pulled himself further upright from the slump he found himself in before his desk. His head throbbed and he couldn't hold it steady as he reached for the red lithum to one side. He couldn't seem to lift his arm either, so his fingers dragged across the surface until they bumped into the lucent. He hung his head, but managed to roll it into his grasp, then rallied enough to lift his head and start to focus.

But something had changed.

"Something's different," he murmured.

The mystery helped him center himself, the exhaustion fading. He knew it was only temporary; he'd reached the point where nothing helped anymore—not food, not whatever alcohol Mari had brought, nothing. Soon, not even Mari's slaps would be able to draw him out of it. His body needed sleep. He couldn't endure much more of this.

Mari must have heard him, for she shifted closer and said, "The evacuation bells have stopped. I think the attacks inside the city have stopped as well. I haven't heard any explosions in the last fifteen minutes."

As soon as the mystery was solved, his body began pulling him back into unconsciousness, but he shoved the sensation aside, focusing on the lithum before him. "Someone should go check to make certain."

"Darcy will let us know."

He nodded, already sinking into the crystal in his fist. Over seventy percent of its surface now complemented the red crystal, enough that the two were beginning to interact slightly, a sympathetic vibration he could feel when he held one in each hand. And the transformations were getting easier, as if the two crystals *wanted* to be compatible.

Choosing a new area, he focused, the vibrations spreading through his body, singing in his bones, stronger now, more painful. A cry of anguish began low in his throat, grew, forced out through his clenched teeth, until the nodes inside the crystal slipped and eased into new positions. He cut the cry short with a yelp, fell forward onto the desk, gasping. Consciousness wavered, his vision fading in and out. He heard Mari approach, her footsteps somehow getting farther away, then he snapped into a moment of clarity and found her cradling his shoulders, rocking him back and forth. Tremors coursed through him. He couldn't get them to stop.

He sobbed, tears streaming down his face, the two crystals clutched close to his chest in a death grip. Mari stroked his head, told him to hush, that it was all right. But he couldn't stop sobbing either. It was too much. He couldn't do it. It had drained him, depleted him, and still it wasn't enough. This weariness, this utter exhaustion, these uncontrollable shudders and emotional turmoil, it reminded him of something. He'd experienced it before, somewhere. He'd felt it all before...

In the towers in Iandolo, when he was being tortured. Havvelan, Favian, and Arctus has pushed him and pushed him and pushed him, until he felt like this—disoriented, lost, alone. He'd fought them until this moment...

And this had been the moment he'd caved.

He sucked in a sudden, stuttering breath and the sobs cut off sharply. His chest ached as he held the breath, as he realized he was on the verge of giving up again, as he'd done then. No, not giving up. Giving *in*. Letting the exhaustion win. Letting the trauma wash through and claim him. Back in the towers, he'd told Favian everything. All that he knew about the Source and the Outcomes and the structure behind the magework. Everything. He'd betrayed Lane and Dalton, Arrend and Nic, all of those who'd helped him escape the Lyceum the first time, all of those who'd come to rescue him from the towers.

He couldn't betray them all again here.

He expelled the held breath in one large gasp, as if he'd been underwater and had just broken the surface and found fresh air. Mari pulled back as he sat forward and held the two crystals before him. He was still weak, still trembling, but the tremors that had wracked his body had halted.

Mari squeezed his shoulders. "Are you all right?"

He turned to face her. "I will be. Once I finish this."

He focused on the two lithum, compared their surfaces, noted that each one emitted a faint glow now. They were almost paired up, a little over ten percent left to go.

Gathering himself, he sank into the blue one, sank into the vibrations of each, pulled in his last reserves of strength…and *pushed*.

The nodes began to slide into place, almost before he willed them into their new position, but it required so much energy. He fed it everything he had, dredging up more, and more still. The surface shifted faster and faster, nodes snicking into position without any effort on his part now, the two syncing up on their own, until suddenly everything was…perfect.

He sagged back, completely spent, heard Mari cry out and dart forward as the two lithum slipped from his listless fingers. Darcy returned as Mari caught them, gave a yelp of shock, nearly spilling the tray of food she'd brought. She set it aside with a clatter as his eyes began to shutter closed. He couldn't move. His breath was slowing. Darkness surged forward.

He could barely hear Mari and Darcy speaking, their voices coming from a great distance.

"Did he do it? Did he finish?"

"I suppose so. Look at the two glow."

"But is he…is he dead? He's so pale. Is he even breathing?"

Something pressed hard into his neck. "He's still got a pulse, but it's unsteady."

"What do we do?"

"Go find someone."

"Who?"

"Anyone! Anyone with more authority than us! A healer if you run across one."

Footsteps pounded away, followed by faint shouts for help.

Then someone leaning in close, even though he felt far, far away.

"I'm sorry, my lord." A chocked sob. "I'm sorry I pushed you."

And then the darkness took him.

* * *

Lane jolted out of sleep to the roar of thunder and the sound of screaming. She shot up from her pallet inside the barracks to find the room in chaos, soldiers shouting and scrambling for armor and weapons, Raven shoving through the lot to get to her.

"The bastards figured out how to build the bridge under cover of darkness!" she shouted. Lane could barely hear her, even though she'd pulled in close. "They're attacking the waygate! All hells have broken lose out there!"

With Raven's help, Lane dragged herself from the pallet, still groggy, and began making her way across the frenzied barracks floor.

"What's making that noise?" she yelled.

"See for yourself!"

Raven flung the barracks door open and Lane flinched back as a lightning bolt struck the center of the courtyard beyond, stone splintering, the sizzling crack of thunder instantaneous. Dozens of bolts were snapping down out of the sky into the city, coming from a boiling sea of cloud cover. Based on the continuous thunder, Lane would guess dozens more were lancing down throughout the city.

Behind, the soldiers who'd finished dressing pressed up against them.

"Out of the way! We need to get to the gate!" the sergeant in charge bellowed.

"Through that?" Lane faced him, saw him flinch back when he recognized her.

Two more bolts shattered stone cobbles in the courtyard. The sergeant grimaced, but settled back, hands raised to either side to keep his men from pressing forward. "What do you suggest?"

Lane risked a glance toward the gate, the entire courtyard lit in blue-white flashes, then pulled back.

"There are men huddling in close to the gate. I think whoever is up on the parapet is shielding them from the lightning. I can get you to that position, but then I need to find Burdock and see what's going on."

The sergeant nodded. "Do it. We'll figure it out from there."

Lane stepped to one side of the door, hand already in motion. Lightning struck again thirty feet away, pelting her with shards of stone, but the sigil was complete. "Go now!"

The sergeant belted out an order and the entire contingent of soldiers surged past her. Raven and Lane joined them, Lane glancing upwards to see bolts hitting the shield she'd placed over the entire courtyard. Others trapped in other buildings took advantage and either fled or rushed toward the protection of the gate.

When she'd crossed the courtyard, Lane found the sergeant. "Everyone here?"

"If they aren't, then they're on their own," he answered.

She nodded and let the shield go, lightning instantly striking the center courtyard again.

Raven was holding the door to the stairwell. They leapt up the steps, pausing at the top to ascertain whether the mage on duty still had a shield erected. Gregg was standing alone at the back of the parapet, arm raised, face strained with effort. Lightning pummeled his shield from above. Burdock paced behind the soldiers leaning over the wall. Beneath the continuous roll of thunder, Lane heard the sounds of the army below attacking the gate.

Lane headed toward Burdock. "What happened?"

"They perfected their mage bridge."

"And we didn't notice?"

"The clouds covered the moon and we didn't notice the fog concealing that section of the wayfare until too late. Not until the lightning began. They kept it close and tight. None of the mages on duty noticed the use of magic."

Lane leaned out over the edge of the parapet between two soldiers. Below, Arctus' forces had crowded up to the gate, halting fifty feet away, carrying torches and accompanied by mage lights. Torches tossed from the wall littered the wayfare immediately before the gate, and the lucent embedded in the gate had been activated, providing additional light. A cylindrical mage shield covered the Iandolan army and the wayfare. A few of the Brovettan soldiers lining the walls were taking pot shots at them with crossbows, but it wasn't effective.

Farther out, where the fog Burdock had mentioned was dissipating, she could see the reconstructed wayfare, the section she'd destroyed now glowing with the silvery blue sheen of a shield. Beyond that, there were pinpricks of blue light where the mages were creating the sigils for the lightning. Too far to distinguish the mages in the dark, even with a spy glass.

To the east, beyond the storm front, the sky was beginning to lighten with dawn.

When she turned back, Cerelle, Sadie, and a slew of new soldiers emerged from the stairwell. She didn't see Dalton anywhere. Frowning, she said to Burdock, "They were standing there when you arrived?"

"According to the guards on watch, that's the position they were in when the fog began to clear and they were first noticed. They've held that position for the last fifteen minutes, since the lightning began."

"Why? It doesn't make sense."

Before Burdock could answer, one of the soldiers beside them grabbed her arm and snapped, "Governor!"

She spun in time to see a group of five mages, Favian in the lead, emerge from the front of the army, spread across the width of the wayfare.

Lane began a shield sigil a few breaths before the five mages raised their hands, fingers crooked, and began their own spells. Lane finished hers with a gasp, the shield beginning to form before the waygate. But the others finished their cantrips moments later.

The shield was only half formed when the cantrips struck, blocking Favian's and two others. The rest made it through, grinding into the gate with ear-piercing shrieks of metal and wood that sounded even above the thunder. Lane held her shield and shouted, "Where are the other mages?"

Burdock leaned in close to her ear to be heard. "We've already sent for them!"

She wouldn't be able to hold the shield against five, not if they concentrated their power.

Below, without conferring, Favian and the two closest to him began another cantrip, centered on her shield. The two mages on the edges of the wayfare focused their attention on the walls outside her shield.

"They're targeting the walls!" Burdock bellowed, men already scrambling. "Fall back to the courtyard! Pull back to the secondary positions!" When he faced forward again, he said to Lane, "We'd already taken nearly everyone off the walls because we couldn't protect them from the lightning. Not with only one mage on duty."

Lane couldn't respond, too focused on the cantrips below. Favian's hit first, followed closely to the other two. She felt the blows shudder through the shield, but it held. The other two cantrips slid past and gouged into the walls to either side, rock crumbling and cascading down to the Flatlands below with a rumble she could feel in her feet. Some of the soldiers cried out in alarm at the tremors coming up through the stone. All five mages were already completing their next spells.

She should have made her shield wider. But she'd had no time to think, only react.

The barrage of cantrips hit and she flinched as her shield wavered. Raven came up to her other side and said, "I don't think Gregg can hold his own shield much longer."

She spared a glance back, keeping her arm steady, and caught the stricken look on Gregg's face. His arms were trembling, his skin sheened with sweat.

Another round of cantrips hit her shield and she gasped.

"Burdock! Get everyone off the tower!"

"We can hold until the other mages arrive—"

"No, we can't. Get them moving now! Send everyone to their positions around the courtyard. Cerelle, Sadie." The two Brovettans stepped forward as Burdock began shouting orders, men falling back from the parapet's edge toward the stairwells on either side. "Find the other mages. Tell them to report to their secondary positions. Then stay with them. Protect them."

Both ran for the steps.

"Lane!" Raven warned.

Behind, Gregg gave a strangled gasp and collapsed. Raven lurched toward him, caught him before his torso hit the ground, and shouted, "There are still people on the parapet!"

With a curse, Lane let her shield covering the gates go as lightning bolts began slamming into the parapet on all sides. Men were flung back from the explosions. Lane began another sigil, completing it with a stab of her finger, then bolted for the stairwell. Raven hitched Gregg up and dragged him for the steps as the temporary shield Lane had erected blossomed overhead. Grabbing Gregg's arm, Lane and Raven heaved him up and hauled him off the parapet, crowded in on all sides by men and women fleeing the walls. They spilled out onto the edge of the courtyard, soldiers breaking toward the buildings on all three sides even though lightning bolts still lanced down from above.

Lane pulled up short, shifting Gregg over to Raven. As she began another sigil, she asked, "Where's Dalton?"

"Cerelle said something happened to Devon. Someone from the governor's manse came to get him during the night."

Lane pursed her lips. "Do we know what?"

Raven shook her head. "No, the messenger refused to say."

Lane thought she knew, but she couldn't let her concern distract her. Spell complete, shield forming over the courtyard, she grabbed for Gregg again.

To the side, the waygate groaned and shuddered, wood and lucent splintering. A large chunk of metal, one of the braces, clattered to the stone of the courtyard.

Burdock appeared out of nowhere and hefted Gregg's limp body up over his shoulder. "Go, go, go!"

They sprinted across the courtyard, Brovettan soldiers surrounding them as they abandoned the wall. The gate gave another grinding moan of protest, chunks of stone falling from the parapet above. Soldiers stumbled and were picked back up. Ahead, those that had already reached the streets that branched off of the courtyard were erecting the barricades they'd prepared. Burdock headed for the main building, directly across from the waygate, Lane on his heels. Beyond, the city was still being pummeled by lightning, the storm clouds roiling above.

They staggered into the shelter of the building, soldiers holding the doors. Burdock handed Gregg over to a group of Brovettans, who carted him off to rooms deeper inside, then turned back to the door. Guardsmen were still fleeing the gate, which shuddered again.

"We aren't ready yet," he said. "Our forces aren't in position."

Lane stepped forward. "Then let's see if I can't buy them some time."

She started the basic form, the double pyramid forming out of scintillant light before her, then began the secondary form. The same form she'd used on the parapet the day before.

The cantrip formed over the fleeing men, air torn and distorted as it sped toward the waygate, growing as it went. It plowed into the already weakened doors, shattering lucent, churning through wood and bending metal, until a critical point was reached and the entire waygate exploded outwards. Debris flew onto the wayfare and the Iandolan army waiting beyond. But the cantrip didn't stop. Through its distorted field, in the diffuse early morning light, Lane saw the army lurch back, soldiers scrambling to get out of the way, realizing the cylindrical shield would not protect them if the cantrip entered at its mouth. The mages at the forefront flinched back or cowered, hands raised to protect themselves, all except Favian.

He began the basic form, unrushed—he couldn't rush, or the form would fail—then launched into the secondary as the cantrip bore down on him, its edges churning into the wayfare now. Lane held her breath—

But the shield formed around Favian and the mages to either side a heartbeat before the cantrip struck. Its force flung all three back, but the cantrip splintered as it passed over them. The two mages on the outer edges of the wayfare weren't so lucky, torn to shreds as it twisted through them. The cantrip entered the cylindrical shield, began tearing into the army itself, the screams horrifying, but the edge of the shield disrupted the energies and the cantrip began breaking apart, whorls of fractured reality spinning off in all directions.

At Lane's side, Burdock gave her a stunned by respectful look. "You destroyed our own gate."

"They have too many mages. They were going to breach it soon anyway." She turned her back on the destruction. "Let's use what little distraction this will cause and prepare the courtyard."

Chapter Sixteen

In the blank void, Devon felt the touch first. Before that, there was nothing—no sight, no sound, no feeling. Nothing. But with the touch… sensation. A disturbance that brought him back to himself.

He cursed it for a moment. That nothing had been calm, soothing even. Now, other thoughts were encroaching. Thoughts and aches and pains and a weariness that felt embedded in his bones. He wanted to retreat back to the void, but the touch…

No, the caress. A hand tracing down his cheek, from hairline to jaw.

Dalton.

He opened his eyes, his entire body willing him to sink back into the void, but Dalton crouched over him, face close, twisted with raw pain that transfigured into a tentative smile that morphed into grief.

The hand touching his face slipped behind his head and Dalton leaned forward and kissed his forehead.

"I thought you were dead," he rasped, throat thick with phlegm, expression contorted with unshed tears. "When they came to get me— when I arrived—you were barely breathing and your heartbeat—" He choked off and kissed him again, this time on the mouth, and held his head against his shoulder.

Devon tried to respond, but his words were muffled by Dalton's shirt. Dalton held him a moment longer, body trembling, then laid his head back on the pillow. For the first time, Devon became aware he was laid out in his bed, the room lit with a strange purple light.

"What was that you said?" Dalton asked.

"I said you're smothering me."

Dalton barked a laugh as he sat back, shaking himself, visibly seizing control. He scrubbed his face with his hand and stood, pacing. "That's the second time you've scared me into thinking you were dead. When I first saw you at the towers, when we pulled you from the cell—" He cut off again, then rounded on Devon, pointing a finger. "You can't do this to me anymore. I can't take it."

"I can't promise anything."

Dalton's hand dropped and he swore.

Devon became aware of a low rumble, like thunder. He frowned and tried to sit up, his torso barely rising from the bed. "What's going on?"

Dalton looked in the direction of the waygate. "There was a break in the attack after Lane destroyed part of the wayfare, but it appears to have resumed. The city is being riddled with lightning. I don't know what's happening at the waygate."

Devon twisted and tried to sit up, Dalton reaching out to steady him. The effort left him breathless. "We have to help."

"You're in no condition to do anything."

"You don't understand." He waved a hand toward the desk, where the red and blue lithum were both glowing with a steady pulse. "I fixed the lithum. We can use it now."

"I saw it when I arrived, but I don't see how—"

"The hub! Don't you remember finding the hub? We have to tell Lane. And John Senn and the others!"

Dalton laid his hands on Devon's shoulders. "Calm down. You're becoming agitated, which is only going to exhaust you further. Now explain it to me, slowly."

Devon drew in a steadying breath, let it out slowly. "When we found the hub, I said that it controlled everything related to the lucent, including magework. When I told Lane and the others, we came up with a plan. But it would only work if I could finish repairing the lithum."

"What's the plan?"

"The biggest advantage the Iandolan's have is their mages, right? The idea is to get the Iandolan army trapped in some part of Brovetto...and then turn the lucent off. Shut it down completely, from the hub."

"Turn it off."

"Then the mages won't have any power."

Dalton pondered a moment. "Including Lane and the others."

"That's true. Unless I fixed the lithum. It stores power. If I managed to get it repaired, and somehow got it to Lane, then she'd have a source. She'd be able to deal with the Iandolans while the lucent was inactive."

Dalton was pacing now, thinking. He pointed at Devon. "Except the Iandolans also have lithum. Every battalion has one."

"Which is where John Senn and the other rebels and mercenaries come into play. Once they know the lithum has been repaired, they're going to use all of the byways and tunnels and secret passages throughout the city to target and take out as many of the lithum in Iandolan hands as they can while they march on the city. They only need to get one part of each pair—either by seizing it or destroying it—to render it useless."

"It's unlikely they'd be able to disable all of the lithum in the Iandolan army."

"How many of them are there? There can't be that many. I don't think the mages at the Lyceum know how to construct them. They're using the same ones crafted hundreds of years ago. Some of those must have been lost through the ages, or failed, like all of the lucent seems to be failing."

Dalton hesitated. "I don't know. Now that you mention it, I've only ever seen a dozen or so in one place, when the army was gathering to march on Luminesque."

"I don't think there's as many as you've been led to believe. But it doesn't matter. Lane's father said he and his group would take out as many as they could find. As long as we get those nearest to Favian when I turn off the lucent, he'll be powerless. As will most of the rest of Iandolo's mages. But in order to do it, I need to get down to the hub."

Conflicting emotions flitted across Dalton's face—concern, protectiveness, fear, and loss—but his shoulders finally sagged. "All right. I'll get you down to the hub. Somehow."

"No, you won't."

Both Dalton and Devon turned to the open door to Devon's room in surprise. Arrend stood in the corridor just outside, with Darcy and Mari behind him, both fretting. The ex-Lyceum proctor's back was rigid with purpose.

Arrend stepped into the room. "You can't take him to the hub, Dalton." He reached for the two lithum pieces. "Someone has to get these to Lane, and in the process inform her father that the plan is in play. Otherwise, none of this matters. I don't believe we can trust anyone else but you. At least, not anyone who still remains in the governor's manse that they'll believe." He handed the two crystals over, then turned to Devon. "I'll make certain Devon gets down to the hub...wherever that is."

"But he can barely sit up, let alone walk," Dalton protested.

"We'll manage. Mari, go see if you can find a wheelbarrow or handcart. There should be something like that in the courtyard, if they weren't all taken down to the mines when they were sending down supplies."

Mari nodded and rushed off.

Dalton faced Devon, a skeptical look on his face.

"You need to get those to Lane. Then help her father take out the Iandolan lithum."

"But—"

Devon reached out and took hold of his hands, still clutching the two crystals. "I'll be fine. I'm likely heading into the safest part of the city. I doubt Favian knows of the hub or how to access it."

"That doesn't make me feel better."

With effort, Devon stood up. "Go. I don't trust anyone else with the lithum."

Dalton's eyes narrowed and he gave a rumbling growl of discontent before leaning forward and giving Devon a short kiss and turning to Arrend. "Keep him safe."

Then he left.

Devon waited until he heard Dalton's footsteps fading down the hallway outside, then gasped and sagged toward the bed, his legs collapsing beneath him. Arrend caught him with a grunt.

"You shouldn't have wasted energy standing up," Arrend said.

"He wouldn't have left if I hadn't." Arrend began to ease him back onto the bed, but Devon halted him by clutching his arm. "No, don't. We don't have time. Darcy!"

Darcy entered the room, hands twisting together with nervous energy. "Yes, my lord? What do you need?"

"Help me to the door. Arrend, gather up those books. Put them in the satchel and bring it with us. I'll need them to figure out the hub once we get there. Then, both of you, help me get down to the courtyard."

* * *

"What's happening?" Lane asked, coming up behind Burdock who stood at the front of the building overlooking the courtyard, Raven shadowing her. From over his shoulder, she could see debris littering the area near the gate, thrown there by her cantrip, a gaping maw where the gate had once stood.

"Hard to say," Burdock said. "We don't have a vantage on their position any longer and they're using a screen to keep us from seeing what's happening on the wayfare."

He handed her the spyglass and she squinted through its lens. But Burdock was right. There was a shimmering wall of blue light obscuring the wayfare about a hundred feet out along the wayfare. "It's called Paterni's Wall," she said, handing back the spyglass. "It was one of the first sigils I cast, once Devon showed me what I was doing wrong with the base sigil. Something all fourth years learn—simple, but effective at hiding army maneuvers when necessary."

Burdock grunted. "I remember it being used during training and on the field, but I never knew what it was called. The mages always liked their secrets."

A bolt of lightning flashed down in the middle of the courtyard, spitting up scorched stone with a crackle of thunder, but no one flinched. The barrage of lightning had continued for the last few hours, although at a lesser rate than during the main attack. Once everyone had settled into position around the courtyard, Lane had dropped the shield to conserve energy. Their runners between the defensive units could mostly stay hidden inside buildings, with only a few moments of exposure when they dashed across a street or alley.

"How's Gregg doing?"

"Recovering. He mostly needs some rest, something to eat." At a look from Burdock, Lane added, "He'll be ready when he's needed, I'm certain."

Burdock tensed. "That might be sooner than you think." He motioned toward the breached waygate.

A thick fog was spilling through the opening. Before Lane could react, lightning began pummeling the area nonstop, the resultant thunder shuddering in the stone beneath their feet. Burdock began shouting orders, men who'd been waiting, tense and already battle-weary, springing into action, taking up positions near windows and doors, gathering around the main entrance. No one stepped outside yet. It would have meant instant death. Lane could feel the hairs on the back of her arms and neck standing on end from the electricity prickling the air.

Then the intensity of the lightning cut off as one of the other mages—Brigette, most likely—erected another shield over the courtyard. As soon as the deadly bolts ended, Burdock's men rushed out to the barricades that had been erected around the entire edge of the courtyard.

Lane snagged a young runner's arm. "Find Gregg. Wake him if necessary." As soon as the boy nodded and dashed off, she followed Burdock out to the barricade.

Above, lightning slammed into the shield, splintering into an eerie cascading lightshow that would have been beautiful if it weren't so deadly.

Lane prayed the shield would hold, but turned her attention toward the fog that now smothered the entire front half of the courtyard and continued to flow outwards. It had built up so high that it obscured the entire wall. The muted sounds of an approaching army could be heard through it, distorted and twisted so that sometimes it appeared far away, other times so close she felt she could reach out and touch one of their soldiers. She could sense the unease of the men around her, so stepped up to the front line near Burdock.

"Enough of this," she said, raising her hand, fingers crooked.

As soon as she finished the sigil, a gust pushed past her, followed by a sudden stiff wind that tore into the fog, shredding it as it pushed it back out through the gate and up and over the wall. The leading edge of the Iandolan army was abruptly exposed, the men near the front halting in surprise as their screen vanished, then raising arms to protect their faces as the wind became a gale, picking up dust and debris and throwing it into their ranks. Lane herself staggered forward as it pushed at her back, steadying herself on the barricade made of upturned wagons, barrels, tables, chairs, and whatever else had been at hand. Raven grasped her shoulder and pulled her back and down, lower to the ground, the rest of the Brovettan soldiers huddling close to the barricade around them.

Lane leaned in close to Burdock's ear to be heard over the torrent. "I don't have that much practice with wind!"

Burdock didn't answer as the gale intensified, shutters and roofing tiles and other pieces of the buildings around them ripping free in a deadly hail. Parts of the barricade began to groan, the table at Lane's back trembling under the onslaught.

And then the wind cut off, almost as abruptly as it had arrived, windborne pieces clattering to the courtyard.

Lane gasped, realized she was panting, her heart pounding hard, her hands sweaty. It wasn't quiet—lightning still hammered at the shield overhead—but it felt still, as if everyone were afraid to move.

She glanced toward Burdock, then both of them glanced up over the barricade.

The Iandolan army had hunkered down onto the cobbles, most of them lying flat, a few crouched, but they were beginning to stir. Toward the back, beneath the arch of what had once been the waygate, she could see the battle robes of mages and a few of the lithum staffs.

Favian rose from a crouch among them.

Lane lurched upright with a surge of anger, her base form already begun. Favian noticed her and began his own sigil, shouting something

Lane couldn't hear. She loosed her cantrip as Burdock began bellowing orders.

Her spell plowed into the front ranks of the Iandolan army, soldiers screaming as those behind panicked and flung themselves out of the way. She'd aimed it directly at Favian. Halfway to him, she caught another distortion out of the corner of her eye, a cantrip cast by one of the other mages, then a jet of fire shot toward the gate from the armory. At her side, Burdock roared, "Stay behind the barricade! Don't move into the courtyard! Let the mages handle this!"

Favian completed his spell and a shield appeared, angled so that it caught her cantrip and deflected it upwards and over the army. It slammed into the wall to the right of the waygate, chewing into stone, boring a hole as large as a cart before it burst out the far side.

Lane swore, although she'd expected nothing less, then snapped her hand back into position for another sigil. The other mages near Favian were already dealing with the thrown cantrip and fire. Near the front ranks, a Prefect ordered the Iandolans forward and they began to advance again. Lane pelted them with shard of ice the size of her arm, until someone threw up a shield to protect the soldiers. She switched to fire, sending flowing flames across the cobblestones at their feet. From behind the barricade, Burdock's men pulled out crossbows and began picking off soldiers at random. Crossbow bolts rained down from the roofs of the buildings on either side as well. Gregg appeared, haggard but with a grim nod, and settled in at her side to protect her.

The courtyard descended into chaos, the Iandolan army advancing slowly, the entire square subsumed in screams and moans and shouted orders. Lane remained focused on Favian and the mages, trying to keep them all on the defensive, giving them no time to launch anything at the Brovettan army huddled behind the barricades. Her fellow mages did the same. But some attacks went astray or were deflected by Favian and the others. A cantrip—one of their own or one of the Iandolan mage's, Lane couldn't tell—ground into one of the buildings at the edge of the courtyard, stone and mortar showering down on those below before the entire top front of the building collapsed outwards, crushing the leading edge of the Iandolan army in that area. A plume of fire erupted above the Brovettans to Lane's left, settling on the men and women there. Heated air blasted into Lane's face, reeking of burning flesh and making her eyes sting and tear up. She scrubbed at her face with her free hand, not pausing the sigil she'd been attempting. Smoke billowed from various fires, obscuring the advance, along with sheets of fire, layers of fog, and wavering Paterni's walls.

Yet the Iandolan army gained ground inexorably. In a breech in the magical attacks clouding the air, Lane saw more soldiers entering through the hole where the waygate had stood, including more mages.

When the Iandolan front was only fifty feet away from the barricade, Burdock grabbed her shoulder to get her attention and leaned in to mutter, "It's time."

She shared a glance with Gregg, then both of them faced the courtyard and began identical sigils. As soon as they finished, a wall of flame erupted from the stone twenty paces from the barricade in an arch that covered half of the courtyard. They heard the Iandolan soldiers curse and fall back, but Lane and Gregg were already moving, retreating back into the building behind them, then bolting up the stairs to the upper floors, followed by Raven and a guard of ten men. She heard Burdock ordering the retreat behind them.

But the time they'd reached the roof, half of Burdock's men had already fled into the streets, headed toward the next set of defensive positions scattered throughout the city. Parks and squares, bottlenecks and streets suitable for ambushes—whatever they'd been able to find that had a strategic advantage. All designed to spread the Iandolan army out among unfamiliar terrain and give the Brovettans an edge, but all organized to lead everyone back toward a central location on the Third Level.

Lane moved to the edge of the roof and stared down into the courtyard below. The Iandolan army had reached the barricade and Burdock and those left behind were engaging with swords and pikes and spears, holding their ground. Overhead, the barrage of lightning strikes had lessened, the shield still holding. Lane assumed it was because a significant number of the Iandolan mages had moved from outside the wall into the city, their battle robes easy to pick out among the ranks below. She noted they were working in pairs now, even a few triples, which was not how they'd been training when she was a student at the Lyceum. The other four mages from Brovetto were keeping them busy.

Gregg moved up to her side and she glanced up, noting it was already afternoon. It didn't seem like they'd been fighting since dawn, and yet she felt the exhaustion.

Hopefully, they'd get a reprieve in a moment, if not a rest.

"Ready?" she asked.

Gregg nodded and raised his hand, finger crooked. He began his sigil, while Lane focused on a specific section of the courtyard and began her own.

Gregg finished first, a shimmering blue wall forming in the center of the courtyard and expanding outwards to either side, until it stretched from armory to barracks and reached nearly to the shield above. It completely blocked their view of the demolished waygate and the wall. Below, the Brovettan mages cut off their attacks and Lane heard Burdock bellow the order to retreat, although she couldn't make out the words. The Brovettan defenses pulled back almost as a single unit, abandoning the barricades, running into the streets and into the buildings on all sides. The Iandolan soldiers were left standing in confusion, most of them spinning back to face the wall Gregg had erected.

Lane finished her sigil, the cantrip forming above the Iandolan army beneath the building, not as large as the one she'd used to destroy the wayfare or the waygate, not as draining, but it didn't need to be. The distortion headed downwards, at an angle, toward the base of Gregg's wall. The Iandolan soldiers who noticed it began to shout and point, those in its path scattering out of the way. A few Iandolan mages—both in its path and to either side—began sigils, but none of them would have enough time to finish before the cantrip struck.

Including Favian.

She saw the proctor in the middle of the soldiers beneath her position as soon as she finished the cantrip and let her arm drop. He glared up at her, then raised his hand to begin a sigil.

Except he wasn't aiming at the cantrip.

She snatched Gregg's arm and pulled him back. "We have to go!"

They raced for the door leading to the stairs, Raven taking note and shoving the rest of the escort down below. The ex-Regular stayed behind. As they reached the entrance, Favian's cantrip plowed into the top of the building. Lane screamed, "Run!" and shoved Raven and Gregg into the stairwell, glancing back to see the cantrip ripping through the edge of the roof, stone pulverized. She ducked into the stairs and tore down behind the other two, the entire building trembling around them. Rocks the size of her fist and smaller began raining down from above, bouncing down the stairs, pelting her back. Gregg cried out and flinched as one struck his shoulder, but he didn't stop moving.

Then the entire building shuddered and lurched, throwing all three of them into the wall to one side. Gregg stumbled and fell, Lane reaching out to catch him and keep him from falling further. Once steadied, she pushed him on, stone dust beginning to fill the stairwell.

Her cantrip had struck the courtyard.

Coughing, they spilled out onto the ground floor into their entourage of Brovettan soldiers. A few of them called out and Burdock appeared.

"Are you all right?" At Lane's nod—she couldn't speak, her throat too dry and coated with dust—Burdock ordered them back into the depths of the building, away from the gate, into the city.

As soon as they began to move, Lane caught sight of the courtyard through the raised dust and tatters of Gregg's blue wall. The entire center of the courtyard had collapsed down into the mines below, taking a significant portion of the Iandolan army with it. Only those who'd been at the edges, closest to the buildings and the barricades, had survived. And those outside the wall, of course. How many did that leave? She couldn't be certain. But while the shield above still held, the lightning bolts and the growl of thunder had ended.

"Did you take out Favian?" Raven asked.

She scanned what little area she could see through the building's entrance. "I don't see him." Her voice sounded like gravel, harsh and raw. "But somehow I doubt he was close enough to the center of the courtyard to have been caught in the collapse."

"Then we'd better get moving," Burdock said. "This will give us a reprieve, but I doubt it takes them long to recover and regroup."

"No, it won't. And now that they know how to create a bridge, the collapse won't slow them down much. Whatever army they have left outside—"

Burdock nodded. "Will be moving into the city within the hour."

They all shared a grim look, Lane certain they were thinking the same thing.

They'd planned the retreat on the assumption that they'd have hours to reach their new positions, that it would take the Iandolans at least that much time to find a way to circumvent the gaping hole in the courtyard. But now...

"It's going to be a free-for-all in the streets," Raven said.

Chapter Seventeen

"We have to make it down to the Third Level," Devon said as he, Arrend, and Darcy reached the stairs leading to the foyer of the governor's manse. Devon's arm was thrown over Arrend's shoulder for support, Darcy on the other side. "That's where we can access the hub."

"That may not be as easy as it sounds," Arrend answered.

He grunted as Devon took the first step, nearly toppling all of them over. They managed to steady each other. Then Arrend grabbed the handrail and they took the next step at the same time.

They were ten steps from the bottom when the double doors into the foyer swung wide open, revealing Mari at the handles of a pushcart, two of the citizens of Brovetto left to guard the manse's gate with her.

"This was all we could find," Mari said as she steered it toward the bottom of the stairs across the stone floor.

"It's fine." Devon reached the bottom step and Darcy and Mari took him from Arrend's grip and eased him into the cart. The box-like bed reeked of cabbage and leeks and dried earth. It operated like a wheelbarrow, except there were two wheels up front instead of one. Devon sagged into its embrace and Darcy tossed the satchel of books on top of him. "Who are these two?"

Mari grabbed the handles of the cart, lifted, and rolled him toward the door. "Guards. We can't go out into the city without some form of protection. And helpers. You're heavier than you look." She halted at the door.

Outside, the courtyard was littered with debris—crates and carriages and other detritus left behind from the push to relocate supplies to the mines, plus chunks of stone piled to the sides from the damage done since they'd arrived. Scorch marks riddled the cobblestones and lightning flares illuminated the sky in every direction. Inside, the resultant thunder had been muted, but here it growled at them from every direction. As they hesitated, one of the bolts struck the wall surrounding the manse's level, tearing a chunk of stone from its edge with a sizzling crack.

"It's not as bad as it was earlier," Arrend said. "They appear to be concentrating their attack on the waygate right now."

Sweat prickled Devon's skin, but he drew in a steadying breath. "We're going to have to risk it. Mari, get us to the courtyard gate."

"Yes, my lord."

She lifted and shoved forward, Devon thrown back and nearly losing hold of the books as they juddered forward. The sound of the battle grew louder, even over the rattling of the cart, but Devon was forced to focus on hanging on as they charged across the yard to the gate. He could hear the others shouting as they ran, but couldn't make out the words.

Then they were beneath the gate, Arrend, Darcy, and the two guards joining them a moment later, all gasping for breath. Arrend moved to the far side, where the ramp that led down to the Fourth Level began. He stared down at the city, then motioned them all forward. "Look."

Mari moved the cart close enough Devon could see.

Below, the courtyard of the waygate was concealed by a shield sustaining a barrage of lightning attacks. The waygate and walls surrounding it were filled with craters and holes. The wayfare beyond was concealed by a bank of fog.

Fire bloomed in dozens of locations throughout the city, plumes of smoke rising from every level. One entire section on the Third Level was an inferno. A new Burn. And yet, even with the lightning still raining down at random, and the sounds of destruction echoing up from below, the city was beautiful in the late morning light; a clash of light and shadow.

"Something's happening at the waygate," one of the guards said.

Devon glanced back to see the fog being torn and ripped away, as if by a fierce wind, exposing the wayfare beyond. It was packed with the Iandolan army, spread down its length into the distance. Although he could see a section appeared to be missing, the soldiers there marching across what appeared to be thin air.

"They've breached the waygate," Arrend said.

"Then we need to move, threat of lightning or not. Mari?"

She grunted as she lifted the back end of the cart, then spun them toward the ramp leading down to the Fourth Level.

As they began the descent, he thought he spotted something on the horizon to the south, but before he could call anyone's attention to it, they hit the decline and he had to concentrate on not falling out of the cart.

* * *

Dalton dodged through the everyday items—trunks, clothes, even a few pieces of furniture—that had been abandoned in the streets as the citizens fled for the safety of the mines. He tried to keep to the shelter of the buildings as much as possible. His breath dragged in his lungs and his arms and legs were tingling with numbness, but he couldn't stop to rest. The two pieces of the lithum thudded into his back with every step, reminding him of what was at stake if he didn't find Lane and her father.

He rounded a corner and ground to a halt, chest heaving. Ahead, the entire end of the street was engulfed in flames, the smoke thankfully billowing away, to the west. He could feel the heat from the inferno even half a block away.

He swore. "No way I'm getting through that."

Based on the smoke plume, the blaze covered multiple streets. He'd have to go around.

Backtracking to the last intersection, he chose a street parallel to the fire, keeping it to his left as he ran. He saw no one here on the Third Level, although he had run into a few people on the Fourth huddled in whatever shelter they'd found. Everyone near the fire had likely fled once it began to spread. But Senn was supposed to be directing his men from near here. He hoped he hadn't been forced to relocate.

Four blocks later, and two diversions, he finally rounded the fire. Two blocks beyond that, he entered the stables where Lane's father had set up shop.

The entire section of stalls was empty.

He spat a curse, then caught a flicker of lantern light from beneath the door leading to the building set behind it. He heard voices a moment before he burst through the door.

John Senn looked up from where he and a covey of men were looking over the maps they'd created of the city. Dozens of others were tossing supplies into crates. Four men near the door tensed and began to draw weapons until they recognized him and relaxed.

"Dalton." Senn looked confused for a moment, but then his eyes widened. "Did he finish it?"

Dalton moved to the table. "He did."

Senn straightened with a grin. "Then we have a chance." He motioned to his men. "We're in the process of relocating. That fire is getting far too close. You caught us just in time. But now that we know, we can change tactics."

Wrapping one fist on the table, he said, "Listen up! Our orders have changed. We're going to head down to the First Level and we're going to engage the Iandolan army directly, but—" He held up a hand, cutting off the Brovettan rebels' growing shout. "—our goal is to take out as many of their damned staffs as possible. They're called lithum and they come in pairs, one red and one blue. Together, they allow the mages to perform their magic, even outside the city. You need to steal them or destroy them, I don't care which. And you only need to destroy one of the pair; without its mate, the other is useless. If we can take them all out before Lane is driven to Fargrave Plaza, then we all stand a chance of surviving this attack. So grab what you can and meet back up at the Yolk Tavern on the First Level. We'll coordinate from there."

His men gave curt nods of agreement and then began filing out of the room in pairs and groups of three.

Senn turned to the man next to him. "Set the signal so that the others below know to begin as well."

The man took off at a run.

"Others?" Dalton asked.

"Maupin and his tullers, along with the rest of my men. We placed them all in multiple groups around the city at strategic points that the Iandolan army will likely pass through on their way up to the governor's manse." He glanced at Dalton's bag and lowered his voice. "Do you have them with you?"

Dalton nodded.

"Then we'll have to get you to Lane. Harlan, Wane, you're with me and Dalton. No matter what happens, you have to get him to Lane." Both men fell into position around them without a word.

The room was mostly empty now, the last few rebels clearing out as Senn gathered up the maps and papers spread out on the table and stuffed them into a satchel. They headed for the door and passed through the stable beyond.

Outside, the fire had gotten closer, no more than a block away. The air radiated with heat and smelled of smoke and char. Ash and embers fell from the sky. Dalton raised his arm to cover his mouth and nose, the others doing the same.

"We need to get to the edge of the Third Level so we can see what's happening at the waygate!" Senn yelled over the roar of the fire and thunder.

They headed off, away from the fire, but angled toward the main thoroughfare that would take them to the ramp leading down to the Second Level. Halfway there, they ran into citizens who'd stayed behind in their homes or businesses but were now fleeing the flames as they spread. Senn's rebels were herding them toward the main road as fast as they could move them. The lightning attack had shifted toward the waygate, although they couldn't see what was happening there yet. Sporadic bolts still landed inside the city, making progress in the open dangerous.

When they reached the thoroughfare, the gates to the Second Level ahead suddenly lit up in bold greens and purples, the threads of lucent woven through them coming alight. The men and women ahead of them reeled back in uncertainty, but Senn's men urged them on. Above the gates, two spheres of yellow lucent blazed forth like miniature suns. The sight was shocking here in Brovetto, where working lucent was so rare, but Senn grabbed Dalton's arm and dragged him forward, yelling, "That's the signal!"

As he passed beneath the blazing arch onto the ramp, Dalton wondered when Devon had had time to repair the lucent. Then again, maybe it hadn't really been broken, merely unused. And he had had his hands full helping Burdock's men training the citizens in even minor combat techniques these last few weeks.

Ahead, the waygate blazed with white-purple lightning, pummeling the shield over the courtyard. As they watched, though, a cantrip tore into the roof of the building opposite the waygate, the entire front section caving into the floors below. A rumble of destruction followed after a moment, the delay between sight and sound eerie.

Then the ground beneath them shook, the tremble reminiscent of the collapse of the mine weeks before. Dalton caught himself against the pillar of the arch above, glancing up when dust and sand sifted down and struck his neck, but the tremor ceased after a couple of breaths. Below, the frenzy of lightning halted, only a scattering of bolts left throughout the city. The shield remained though, blocking their line of sight to the courtyard.

The roar of crumbling and cracking stone echoed up from below, building slowly, but far louder than the rumble of the collapsing building.

Senn faced him, expression grim. "They collapsed the courtyard into the mines below."

"What does that mean?"

"The waygate is lost. The battle has entered the city now."

Dalton eyed the area around the courtyard, but it was too distant and the angle too great to pick out movements in the streets. But with the courtyard caved in, surely the Iandolan army would be delayed getting into the city, right? He turned to ask Senn, but Lane's father had already headed down the ramp.

They descended to the Second Level, Senn's men breaking into groups, some sprinting away in odd directions, most leading the citizens toward the secondary access points to the mines where everyone else had sought shelter. Senn stood in the center of the plaza at the bottom of the ramp, gazing toward the waygate.

Dalton came up behind him. "What now?"

"With the loss of the waygate and the courtyard, it's going to be difficult finding Lane. She could be anywhere."

"The plan was to have the Brovettan citizens scatter, but lead the Iandolans to Fargrave Plaza on the Second Level. Our best chance of finding Lane would be to head to the plaza."

Senn stared out into the surrounding buildings, then finally sighed, shoulders sagging. "Agreed. If we try anything else, we'd only run into her through blind luck." He glanced to the side and Dalton could see the anguish etching his face. He was, after all, Lane's father. "Let's hope she makes it off of the First Level."

* * *

Devon was nearly thrown from the cart at the bottom of the ramp from the Fourth Level down to the Third when Mari suddenly dropped the handrails and the back legs thudded into the cobbles and skidded a few feet. His satchel bounced from his grip and popped open when it hit the ground, the books and papers inside sliding out. A few of the papers were caught in the heated winds from the fire and blew into the smoke-filled air. Darcy, Arrend, and the two guards scrambled to catch them as Mari doubled over, hands on her knees, coughing harshly.

"I'm all right," she gasped between breaths, her voice raw. She waved at the ash falling from the sky. "It's the fire. I just need...a moment." She broke out into another fit of coughing, sinking to her knees.

Devon glanced at the plumes of black smoke, tainted orange-red from the fires beneath. His skin crawled with urgency, but he said, "We'll take a rest here." He glanced back at Mari. The servant's arms were trembling from the exertion of pushing the cart, even though the other two guards had spelled her multiple times as they crossed the short stretch on the Fourth Level from one ramp to the other.

Arrend knelt down and picked up the spilled books, adding the pages brought to him by the others before handing the satchel back. "I don't think we saved all of the loose pages."

"That's fine." He nodded reassuringly to Darcy, even though he didn't know what would be important once they reached the hub. "It's the books that matter most now."

They paused to stare out at the conflagration that consumed a large section of the Third Level ahead, the heat from the inferno palpable, even though the main fires were blocks away. Flames could be seen rising into the sky in a few places, and the sound of crackling and splintering wood could be heard through their roar. The gusts from the disturbed air tugged at Devon's hair and clothes, his throat already raw from the smoke.

Arrend suddenly stilled. "Listen."

Devon frowned. "What am I supposed to be listening to?"

"The thunder. It's stopped."

They all glanced at the sky overhead. The lightning and thunder that had been so consistent that it had faded into the background was absent, not simply lost among the raging sounds of the fire.

"What does that mean?" Mari asked in a ragged, broken voice.

Before anyone could answer, the ground beneath them shook, the tremors escalating enough that Devon grasped the side of the cart to steady himself before they began to fade. A moment later, the sound of grinding stone filled the air, loud enough to smother the crackle of the fire.

They waited as it died out, breaths held.

"What was that?" Darcy ventured.

"Nothing good." Devon faced Mari. "Are you ready to move?" When she nodded, he motioned to one of the guards. "Take over for now. Let her recover."

They headed off into the Third Level, skirting the fire, Devon giving directions as they moved. The smoke grew thicker, the pulsing heat hotter, until they were forced to cover their mouths with arms or cloth torn from their clothing.

But when they turned left onto one of the side streets, they were forced to a halt.

"It's an inferno," one of the guards muttered in shocked horror.

Ahead, the buildings on both sides of the street were ablaze, the flames and smoke ragged and torn by the winds, the entire corridor a whirlwind of bright embers. A few of the structures had partially collapsed, the debris strewn across the cobbles still on fire. Besides the crackling of fire, they could hear the groans of stressed wood.

"Is there another way down to the hub?" Arrend asked.

"The only other route I know of is through the Second Level mining collapse. We'd have to go all the way down and then back up again."

They traded looks.

"Then we'll have to go through."

"No way in any hell," one of the guards said, then bolted back the way they'd come.

The second guard hesitated, then took off after him without a word.

Devon looked at Darcy, but the older servant merely straightened her back. "Forget those bastards. I'm not leaving."

Mari gave a curt laugh. "And you aren't going to get very far without me."

"I can probably stand..." Devon tried to push himself upright using the side of the cart, but after a moment of initial strength, a wave of exhaustion passed through him from his toes to his head, leaving him lightheaded. He slumped back into the cart. "Or perhaps not."

Arrend squeezed his shoulder, eyeing the street ahead. "We'll have to move fast. Cover your heads with whatever you have at hand. Did anyone bring any water?"

Mari shook her head. "But there was a fountain a short way back."

"Here." Arrend gathered up the cloth they'd been using to cover their mouths and handed them over. "Soak them in water, if you can."

Mari took off, not quite running. They were all exhausted, Devon realized. They wouldn't last much longer.

"The entrance to the hub is only a few blocks away," he said.

No one said anything, the three of them watching the fire rage, spreading to another building and moving closer as they waited.

Then Mari reappeared, a bucket in hand. Water sloshed to the cobbles as she set it down and began pulling out their soaked rags.

"Hang them over your head and shoulders!" Arrend yelled.

Devon snatched the cloth Mari handed him, the satchel with the books tucked close to his chest, and draped the dripping mass over his head, taking one edge and wrapping it over the lower part of his face. The water was blessedly cold against his skin, already raw from the heat. He felt the water permeating his clothes where it touched him, but before he could shudder from the sensation Mari picked up the cart handles and they ran for the flames. The sound of the fire grew into a horrific cacophony of destruction that hit them from all sides as they dodged the fiery debris on the street. Embers stung Devon's face and smoke bit at his eyes, but he held the satchel tight with one hand, steadying himself with the other. A curtain entirely aflame ripped free from an upper story window and fell across their path, but Mari ran right over it without pause. Darcy screamed and Arrend shouted something, but they were behind him. He couldn't see them, couldn't hear what the proctor had said.

Then the entire façade of the building ahead of them cascaded down into the street. The cart lurched as Mari attempted to turn, but it was too sharp. Devon only had time to tuck his body into a ball as he was rolled onto the hot cobbles. He tumbled once, twice, heard Mari land with a grunt and a clatter of the cart, then came to a halt a few feet from the edge of the collapse. Heat—like that of an oven—pulsed against his face from the bricks.

He barely had time to gasp before Arrend was pulling him back with Darcy's help. As they loaded him back into the cart, he noticed burns on Darcy's face and hand, her soaked shawl missing. But as soon as he landed in the cart, Mari was shoving him forward, around the destroyed façade, and into the street beyond. Through flames, he could see the small building that served as the entrance to the hub and he shouted and pointed. Mari headed straight for it, plowing the cart's wheels over whatever debris was in the way. Arrend raced ahead and flung the door open, ushering Darcy through. A smoke-choked breath later, Mari plowed through with the cart.

Behind, something in the building across from them gave a bone-shaking snap and the side of the structure began to bulge outwards. Darcy cried out and both she and Arrend shoved the heavy door closed a moment before the building caved inwards. The small building they'd entered shuddered, dust sifting down from above.

With the door closed, the noise from the fire was muffled, making the interior eerily quiet. It was also significantly cooler than outside. The three standing sank to the floor, backs against walls, breaths coming in heaves smattered with coughing. Devon pulled the cloth from his head, surprised to find it mostly dry. Any of his skin that had been exposed was hot to the touch, likely burned, as if he'd stood out too long beneath the sun.

He tried to speak, but broke into a bout of coughing, his throat dry. He worked up some spit and swallowed, then tried again. "I think we're safe enough in this building for now," he managed, voice cracking. "I think it was made by the Founders."

The others looked around the small room. Like the water control room Devon and the others had found when they escaped the Burn through the cistern tunnels, it was square, with a panel of lucent against one wall, a few of the pieces of lucent glowing, and a large rounded opening opposite the door. Once Arrend had caught his breath, he stood and wandered toward the opening.

"Be careful," Devon said. "There's a pit in the floor on the other side with a stairwell winding around its side leading down to the hub. There's a lucent panel on the wall to your right. Touch the blue button."

Arrend hit the button and lucent lights flickered into life inside the other room. Darcy and Mari both gasped.

"The lucent works," Darcy murmured.

"This building was sealed from the inside when we found the hub," Devon said. "I don't think anyone has been in here in hundreds of years."

"I'd agree," Mari said, motioning to the layer of dust on the floor riddled with tracks. Some were from them, but there were clear tracks leading from the pit and the stairwell from when Devon and Dalton were here days ago. With the lights on, they could see old cobwebs in the corners of the ceiling, water stains on the stone, and other signs of long disuse.

Arrend was at the railings on the edge of the pit. "There's no way we're getting the cart down there."

"No." Devon pulled himself to the edge of the cart again. "We're going to have to walk."

He heaved himself upright, ignoring Mari's protest, using the cart edge for support. Weariness washed through him, like before, but he closed his eyes and fought it. For a heartbeat, he thought he'd pass out. If he hadn't had a hand on the cart, he would have fallen, but the dizziness receded.

He faced Mari and Darcy, both standing at his side, ready to catch him. He gave them each a grim smile. "We need to get moving. It's already starting to get hot in here."

* * *

"Lane!" Burdock shouted. "They're already starting to outflank us!"

Lane shot a glance in the direction Burdock pointed. Two blocks away, down the side street, she could see the Iandolan army fighting a group of Brovettan resisters. A clawed hand gripped her gut as the Brovettans broke and retreated.

"Keep moving! We have to get to the Second Level before they cut us off!"

Burdock nodded and passed the order through the ranks.

On the side street, the Iandolans caught sight of them and headed their way. Beneath her breath, Lane muttered, "I don't think so," and raised her hand, fingers crooked. She sent a cantrip down the street, angled to one side, then followed it up by another to the other side. The first gouged into the base of a tenement, ripping through its foundation enough that it sagged and began to fall into the street. The second did the same to a building with a bakery on the ground floor, its upper floors crumbling down on top of the first building, blocking the street.

Someone grabbed her arm and she spun, hand still raised, Raven flinching back and letting go.

"We have to move," she said. "They're right behind us."

As she spoke, the men behind them blocking the end of the street gave a warning cry, splitting down the middle as a cantrip plowed through the gap. Gregg stood farther back in the intersection, near the mouth of the next block, a shield already forming to shunt the cantrip up toward a sky now beginning to darken toward dusk. Gregg looked haggard, face gaunt and strained, but the shield held.

The gap closed as soon as the cantrip passed, but the Iandolans had clearly advanced during the distraction. More and more of the Brovettan forces were filling the intersection.

Without a word from her, Burdock yelled, "Fall back to the next intersection!"

Lane was already on the move, running toward Gregg's position, Burdock, Raven, and the closest men forming up around her. They raced through to the next intersection, the sounds of the fight behind amplified by the narrower street. Clashes could be heard on all sides, some distant, punctuated by the rumbling roar of collapsing buildings and the ear-grating churn of cantrips through stone. It was mind-numbing, the adrenaline from the attack long ago peaked and now settled into a sense of normalcy. The sounds of destruction had dulled and were now shunted into background noise.

They continued for another two blocks, defending and holding as long as possible, sealing off any avenue of approach where they spotted Iandolan forces by destroying shops and apartments or throwing up hasty barricades with whatever was at hand. The Iandolans were on both of their flanks now, as well as behind.

Then they spilled out onto an open marketplace surrounded by a low wall and pocked with burn scars and craters from the fire and lightning attacks earlier. Burdock hustled Lane, Raven, Gregg, and their escort through the wide arch and into the empty market, only a few tattered and collapsed tents and a scattering of carts left behind. A few vendors had abandoned their wares in their flight toward the protection of the mines.

They were halfway across when someone shouted, "Prefect Burdock! Iandolan forces to the left!"

"To the right as well!"

Burdock swore. Lane turned to the left, hand raised, but the attackers had already reached the end of the street. The Brovettans had barely managed to contain them at the opening. Behind, they were pushing into the market square, while to the right there weren't enough Brovettans to hold them back at all.

"Run!" Raven ordered, then shoved Lane toward the only remaining opening on the square, the street leading toward the ramp to the Second Level. She stumbled, but caught herself and charged toward the street, Raven on her heels. Burdock pushed Gregg after her, bellowing for those nearest to protect their backs. He turned toward the fighting, rushing toward the right, sword raised.

She didn't see the outcome because she tripped and sprawled across the slick surface of the amber at the center of the plaza. Raven and two of Burdock's guardsmen hauled her upright and they dashed toward the far end of the market, pulling out ahead of the main force. Gregg had sprinted out ahead of them, through the arch and across the street into the next block. He turned and gestured for them to run, scanning behind them, eyes widening.

As she neared, she heard him mutter, "We aren't going to make it."

She ground to a halt and turned back.

The marketplace was already being overrun. Iandolans were pushing the Brovettans back on all fronts. The Iandolan soldiers from the three main streets had advanced far enough to join forces. She could see mages among them, prefects and their accompanying men with the red and blue lithum crystals burning with light. One or two of the groups with lithum only had one staff, the other missing. As she watched, a contingent of Brovettans suddenly surged forward into one such group carrying lithum, two men targeting one of the staff holders. They took him down, his cry lost in the general noise of the fight. The men smashed the blue crystal on the flagstone before being overwhelmed. She thought she recognized one of them as a Tuller.

"They're going to overrun us even if we bolt for the ramp right now," one of the soldiers said. His rank appeared to be captain.

Gregg suddenly straightened, eyes on the center of the marketplace. "Go. Take her as fast as you can to the ramp. I'll delay them as long as I can."

"What are you going to do?" Lane asked.

Gregg met her gaze. She couldn't interpret what she saw there before he focused on the captain. "Go!"

The captain and his men began herding Lane down the street, Raven pulling at her arm. When she resisted, Raven said bluntly, "We don't have time for this. Move! Or none of us are going to survive!"

Lane turned and ran, Raven and the guardsmen keeping pace with her.

Behind, she heard the fighting continue, getting louder as the armies converged on the mouth of the street. They fled through the next two intersections without pausing as the sky darkened overhead. Yet it didn't get truly dark. Too much of the city was on fire. Too many sections were being consumed by flame. The sky overhead was filled with smoke lit from below, as if it had become overcast.

The street began to angle upwards toward the gates and the beginning of the ramp to the Second Level. The group slowed from the incline, everyone already exhausted from the battle at the waygate and courtyard, plus the hours of retreat afterwards. Her breath burned in her lungs. Her sides ached from exertion. She couldn't think, her mind running in chaotic circles. The collapse of the wayfare beneath her cantrip. The explosion of the waygate. Favian's face looking up at her on top of the building above the courtyard. The roar of the building collapsing around her. The frantic withdrawal into the streets and the sudden combined Iandolan army invading the marketplace square. All of the images, all of the sounds, cycled over and over through her head, ending with Gregg's last order to run. Run where? The Iandolans were closing in. Their strategic plans had crumbled to dust around them. Where could they go? What could he do to stop them?

And then it hit her.

She came to an abrupt halt just before the gate to the ramp and turned back. Raven halted twenty paces beyond her, on the first part of the ramp.

"What are you doing?" the captain gasped, his men stopping, some of them bending at the waist to catch their breath. "We can't stop. We need to keep going."

She stared down the street behind them, the Brovettan army pushed back farther than she'd expected, the Iandolans behind them. They packed the roads and intersections for as far as she could see, but her gaze was on the distant marketplace, where she'd stumbled and fallen.

Onto amber.

"No," she whispered. "I said no."

A flash of amber light blinded her for an instant, but she blinked and caught the amber warding that had been inlaid into the center of the square expanding, surging upwards, enveloping the square, then the next block and the next. It happened in the space of a breath, like when the amber Warding at the center of the Lyceum quad had been activated. This Warding wasn't as large, but within seconds the light solidified into a cube of amber, sealing everyone and everything in a three-block radius of the market inside.

Including Gregg.

Around her, a few of the guardsmen gasped. A few stumbled backwards in shock.

"I said no," she repeated, her voice cracking.

A door slammed open and she turned, slow, so slow, still stunned by the activation of the Warding. Four Iandolan soldiers, their uniforms dirty and stained, charged out of one side of the gatehouse, swords drawn, faces locked in intense determination and hate. She recognized one of them: Captain Silleac, Burdock's second. She'd outpaced her escort. Not by much, but enough. And Raven was too far ahead. She didn't have time to react, didn't have time to raise her hand or to complete a sigil, and her guards were behind her, too far away to intervene.

Silleac swung. She jerked back instinctively, but felt the captain's blade slice into her side, low, near her pelvic bone. She cried out at the white-hot, silvery pain.

Then someone slammed into Silleac from the side, a blur of black and gray and tan fabric, a knife descending into the Iandolan's neck.

Lane hit the cobblestones hard and rolled to her side, a breath hissing through her teeth. Silleac landed with the sound of deadweight, the man atop him yanking the knife free and snapping his head toward her.

"Mouse?" she gasped.

The rebel lurched upright and faced the other Iandolans, but Raven and her escort had already reacted and were cutting them down around her. Mouse glanced back at her, gave her a jaunty grin, and then fled into the shadows of the gate.

"Governor!" the captain cried, kneeling by her side. Her hand had clamped itself to her side, but she could feel blood slicking her fingers, soaking into her clothes. "How bad is it?"

She panted a moment, then grit her teeth. "I don't know."

The captain reached for her. "You'll have to move your hand so I can take a look."

When she did, his eyes widened and he swore, his voice hoarse. Then he clapped her hand back in place and shouted for some cloth, his hands already undoing his belt. Raven arrived with a wadded-up shirt, which he folded and slapped onto her side, using his belt to secure it into place. When he shifted her to get it under her, she nearly passed out. The bolt of pain when he tightened the belt shocked her back from the edge.

A guard appeared. "Captain, not all of the Iandolans were trapped in the Warding. We have to keep going."

"She's losing a lot of blood," he responded, and looked to Raven.

The ex-Regular surveyed the street behind them, then the ramp. Her jaw clenched. "We're going to have to move her."

She knelt at Lane's side, but when she lifted her, Lane passed out.

Chapter Eighteen

"This is it," Devon gasped. He let go of the railing on the stairwell with one hand to point, Arrend holding him up with the other, but his knees gave way beneath him almost instantly. Behind, Mari and Darcy sucked in a sharp breath, but he caught himself before collapsing completely. Once he'd regained his footing, he nodded at the doorway ahead. "That's it."

"Get the door open if you can," Arrend said, and both Mari and Darcy rushed forward. Darcy carried the satchel of books. Devon had given Mari his dagger in case they ran into any skrill and his green lucent lantern to guide them. Devon had managed to descend most of the spiral stairway in the pit, but his energy had begun to flag once that had ended and the stairs penetrated into stone. That tunnel had felt endless, but they'd finally reached the hub.

Or the Core, as the book called it.

After an initial struggle, the door gave way and the two servants stumbled into the chamber beyond, drawing up sharply when they saw the column of multi-colored lucent, both dead and alive, and the branches that shot off into the ceiling in all directions. Even though Devon had been here and seen it before, the sheer magnitude of the lucent used tightened his chest. His fingers itched to snap off a piece and flee with it tucked protectively against his body, a resurgence of his life in the lower levels of Iandolo both before and after Carbolen's gang.

He waved toward the massive column of lucent in the center. "The consoles are over there, surrounding the lucent."

Arrend escorted him forward, moving slowly, while Mari and Darcy wandered around the open room in awe, reaching out tentatively toward the strands of lucent above.

"Here," Devon said, then sighed. "I should have thought to bring a chair. You'll have to set me down on the floor. Darcy, bring me the books. Spread them out on the floor. Arrend, you can help me. Some of the pages are marked, but I never got through all of them. You can look for sections that seem to refer to this node while I read over the parts I've already found."

"I can read a little," Mari said uncertainly.

"I can't read at all," Darcy added, already pulling the books from the satchel.

Devon considered, then caught sight of the opening leading downwards that he and Dalton had come through when they originally found the hub. "It might be better if you both watched that entrance, keeping an eye out for skrill. And close the door we came through so we don't have to worry about them coming from that side."

Mari appeared relieved and immediately moved to the opening to the stairs leading downwards, taking a moment to peer down into the darkness with a shudder. Darcy closed the door behind them.

Arrend handed him a book. "Lean up against the console. It will help preserve your strength. I'll get whatever books you need next." He picked up another book and began leafing through it, his brow creasing as he read a few lines. "The sentence structures and format of this is odd. And so many...words I've never heard of before. What exactly am I looking for?"

"Anything that tells us how to shut the entire system down."

Arrend's head shot up. "Shut what down?"

"Everything. Including the mages' magic."

Arrend's eyes widened. It was the first time Devon had ever seen him shocked. But it didn't last long. He waved a hand at the Core. "As soon as you want to try something, let me know."

"We can't try anything until we get the signal from Lane."

"What signal?"

Devon gave Arrend a steady look. "We'll know it when we feel it."

Then he opened the first book.

* * *

Dalton, John Senn, and the few men and women that accompanied them trotted into Fargrave Plaza and halted, some of them bending over and gasping to catch their breath. Stretching across a two block by two block area, it was one of the widest squares within Brovetto, studded with small sections containing trees and bushes and assorted flowers and a few small fountains. Most of the plants were struggling, the fountains dry, the water for both shunted toward the agricultural sections of the city. Barricades had been erected across the streets leading toward the ramp to the Third Level, and stacks of trunks and barrels had been placed at certain positions on the plaza, as if debris had been cleared and shoved to one side. Scars from the Iandolan lightning riddled the plaza, including one tree that had been split in half.

They'd approached from a side street, the three-story school that had been chosen as their fallback position to their left, in the center of the long row of buildings facing the plaza on that side. The entrance was surrounded by more barricades, fronting steps that led to the massive double doors behind a portico with columns and a large balcony overhead. The windows on the lower level had been boarded over, but those above that looked out on the plaza had been left open.

"I don't see any guards," Senn grumbled.

Dalton looked up at the smoke-blackened night sky above. "They're probably inside, keeping out of the path of the fireballs and lightning… and whatever else may come from the sky."

"Still, there should be some sign of them. Unless they've abandoned their post."

Dalton caught some movement in one of the upper windows. "I don't think they have."

Senn didn't answer, merely motioned everyone forward. They angled toward the school, keeping in the open so that they'd be seen by those on watch, but eyeing their surroundings. It was unlikely any of the Iandolans would be here yet, but with the waygate breached they couldn't be certain. There was more than one way up from the First Level to the Second.

When they were a hundred feet from the school, a group of men stepped out onto the portico, most with crossbows held at the ready.

"Identify yourselves!"

The group drew to a halt and Senn moved forward. "I'm John Senn, the leader of the Brovettan rebel group."

The leader stepped forward, as if to get a better look, then said, "You'd better get in here before more of that lightning comes from the sky."

Those on the portico relaxed.

They wound through the barricades and up the steps, Senn greeting the leader with a handshake.

"Any news?" the leader asked.

"The waygate has fallen and from what we saw before descending to the Third Level, the courtyard as well. The Iandolans are on the way. What about here at the school?"

"Nothing except the fireballs and lightning. Thankfully the fire never struck close by, but the lightning drove us indoors." The leader nodded to where some bodies were laid out to one side, covered in sheets. "We lost a few men to that. Some citizens also showed up after those attacks ended and we sent a few men with them to get them safely into the mines. Otherwise, nothing else."

"No sign of the main forces from the waygate?"

"Nothing yet."

Senn glanced toward the plaza. "They'll be coming. We need to prepare for them."

They entered the school, the main hall beyond the doors wide with doors off to the left and right wings and stairs on either side leading up to the upper level. Whatever furniture had been in here before had been shoved up against the wall, the heaviest to either side of the main doors in case they were needed as a barricade. Tables and chairs had been set up in the center of the hall, but the back was covered with pallets.

"I have men in all of the dormitories upstairs with windows facing the plaza, armed with crossbows and incendiary devices. We've set up the back rooms here as a makeshift infirmary and we're using the kitchens for food of course."

At the mention of food, Dalton's stomach rumbled. He realized he couldn't remember the last time he'd eaten anything.

Senn noticed. "Bring us whatever you have ready in the kitchens right now. Make certain your own men have eaten as well. And double whatever watch you have up above. I don't think it's going to be long before the Iandolans arrive. Everyone else should get some rest."

The leader looked surprised. "But…they weren't supposed to be here for days yet."

"Plans change."

Senn commandeered a table and began setting up, his men clustered around him. Dalton moved to the back of the room, settling onto one of the pallets, while the activity throughout the building began to pick up, like an anthill that had been disturbed. Someone brought him a cup of thin soup, which he scarfed down without tasting, then he leaned against the back wall.

The next moment, he startled out of sleep as men began to shout.

"Incoming! They're Brovettans!"

"Looks like the entire force from the waygate! Or what's left of it."

"Move, move move! Secure their flanks! Barson, take Copper Street. Neill, the west corner. Wasson, Millett Street. Go, go!"

The hall was packed with men and women all moving at once, bustling about, groups heading out the door into the plaza. More men than Dalton had thought were in the building. He made to stand and his entire body screamed with aches and pains and twinging muscles. He'd been asleep longer than he'd thought, certainly more than a moment. He staggered to his feet, rotating his neck and shoulders to work the kinks out, grabbed his satchel, and searched for Lane's father.

Senn stood near the door, hustling men through onto the portico. The doors were flung wide open, the square outside still dark. But now torches and fires were being lit throughout the school, the surrounding buildings, and out on the plaza itself. He moved toward the door, the room beginning to empty.

On the opposite side of the plaza, Brovettans were spilling out of the streets into the empty space, most heading straight for the school without looking back, others fanning out to either side. They were rushing, but also clearly exhausted, movements sluggish. A few stumbled, but rallied. The men from the school sprinted out to either flank, taking up formation and covering the retreat. The buildings beyond were backlit by the pulsing orange-red fires on the First Level.

"Our attempts to keep them delayed and distracted on the First Level seem to have failed," Senn said, as more and more entered the square.

Dalton didn't respond, but a cluster of those fleeing caught his attention. "What's that? It looks like—"

"They're carrying someone," Senn interrupted, suddenly alert. "Can you see—"

"It's Lane!"

He spun and shouted, "Healers!" but they were already arrayed behind him, at least a dozen people, with helpers, including Mindell and his daughter, Aver. Tables had been shifted out of the central aisle and Dalton suddenly realized the pallets beyond served a dual purpose—sleeping mats for those needing rest and pads for the wounded.

Then Raven and the men carrying Lane were scrambling through the door, everyone shouting. Mindell pressed forward and with one look ordered them to set Lane down on one of the tables. He shoved everyone aside and dragged his daughter to the table, reaching to tear the clothes around Lane's wound apart. Queasiness roiled through Dalton's stomach at how saturated Lane's clothes were with blood as he and Senn pushed forward through those crowding around. When Mindell gently pulled the makeshift bandage someone had tied around Lane's waist aside and fresh blood welled up, he nearly vomited.

"The wound is deep," Mindell said, his voice achingly calm, "but I don't think it hit anything vital. We need to staunch the flow and suture it up as soon as possible. Get me water, clean cloths, sutures and a needle, and some of the poultice to help coagulate blood and halt blood flow. Now! The rest of you tend to any other wounded brought in." He glanced around at the crowd pressing in close. "And for the Founder's sake, give us room!"

Everyone backed off a few steps, but few left. Some of the other assistants appeared with a bucket of water and arrays of utensils. Mindell began washing the wound clean, more blood welling up, then handed that task off to his daughter so he could begin applying the poultice. He slathered it on thick, putting a compress over it, another assistant holding it in place.

Senn broke through those gathered and halted at the head of the table. When Mindell made to protest, he spat, "I'm her father."

Dalton came up behind him as he reached forward and brushed the hair from her forehead with a trembling hand. "She's so pale."

"She's lost a lot of blood," one of the assistants said. Mindell was too focused on checking the wound and applying more poultice.

Dalton moved around Senn, out of the healers' way. One of Lane's arms was dangling from the side of the table and he grabbed her hand and squeezed it before placing it across her chest. It was cold, but he could feel a faint pulse.

"The bleeding has slowed," Mindell said. "We need to tie this up now." He snatched up the already threaded needle and leaned forward, pinching the sides of the wound together, and began to sew.

Dalton's stomach flipped as the needle pierced skin and he was forced to look away, his breath hitching. He noticed Raven standing to one side, watching Mindell work intently, her jaw set, eyes angry.

"What happened?" Dalton asked.

"I was too far ahead." Her voice was thick with self-incrimination. "We were running and she stopped and I didn't notice…"

A commotion at the front entrance drew Dalton's attention and he touched Senn's shoulder. "It's Burdock."

Senn glanced up, then back down at Lane.

"There's nothing you can do for her right now," Aver said. "Go. We'll take care of her."

Senn hesitated, then reluctantly backed away.

The two of them headed toward Burdock, the men stepping aside before them. They met him halfway to the doors.

"How is she?" he asked immediately.

"They're working on her," Senn reported. "The healers said they've got the bleeding under control. They're stitching her up now."

Concern etched his face and, for a fleeting moment, hopelessness. But then it was gone, a grim, stolid mask overtaking it all. "We need her."

Neither answered.

"What happened?" Senn asked.

"The Iandolan forces figured out how to cross the collapsed courtyard faster than expected. They've been riding our ass ever since. We pulled back to the marketplace, but they were going to outflank us. I sent Lane ahead with Raven and a contingent of guardsmen. They said they were ambushed at the entrance to the ramp to the Second Level. My guess is it was the group of Iandolans we knew were hiding in the city but couldn't find, apparently led by Silleac. I'm not certain how he made it back into the city, since I escorted him personally onto the wayfare when we kicked the Iandolan forces out of Brovetto, but he was here. The only reason Lane is still alive is because of Mouse, according to Raven. He came out of nowhere, killed Silleac, who'd attacked Lane, then vanished. The others took out his accomplices."

"Mouse had been sent to hunt them down," Dalton said.

"He didn't do it fast enough, did he?"

They all looked back to where Mindell was still working on Lane.

"What about the Iandolans?" Senn finally asked, to break the silence.

"According to my men, Gregg activated a Warding in the marketplace. He waited long enough that as many of the Iandolans were in the square as possible, and as few of our own men. It's bought us some time. The Iandolan army halted at the bottom of the ramp and is regrouping. The other Brovettan mages took out portions of the ramp behind us as we retreated, but that won't slow them for long. The Iandolan mages learned quickly from the collapse of the wayfare and the courtyard."

"Then we have time to set up Fargrave Plaza as Lane suggested."

Burdock's eyebrow rose, his gaze shifting to Dalton. "Then Devon has managed to activate the lithum?"

"He has."

Burdock absorbed this information as more and more men entered the hall. Most of them were wounded and were supported or carried to the waiting healers, the pallets in the back already filling up. Some had been triaged into the back rooms. Dalton saw a few that were likely already dead where they lay.

When Burdock turned back, his shoulders had stiffened. "Then get everyone into position. But we all know that Havvelan, Favian, Arctus, and the rest won't listen to any of us other than Lane. If she isn't there to face them when they arrive…"

* * *

"I found it!" Devon announced, startling everyone, including himself. His voice sounded overly loud in the confines of the Core's chamber. In a softer tone, he said again, "I found it. Or at least, something that might work."

Arrend shifted closer, looking over his shoulder. The books and papers were scattered around them, a couple discarded as useless, like the one dealing with the original Founder's Pact and the laws established to govern the cities. "What have you found?"

Devon pointed to a header. *"Emergency Shutdown of the Core."*

"That would seem appropriate. Can we do it from here?"

Devon scanned the directions beneath. "I think so. I recognize some of these diagrams depicting panels." He read some more, tapping the pages, then glanced toward the consoles. "Help me up."

With Arrend's support, he stood, leaning heavily on the console. He set the book to one side, opened to the correct pages, scanning back and forth from the console to the diagrams. "This one doesn't match. We need to find one that looks like this."

Arrend stared at the fine lines and circles of the picture, each section labeled with words that made no sense to Devon or his mentor. After a moment, he nodded. "I'll look this way, you take the other direction."

Darcy had come up behind them. "Let me help."

With Darcy's aid, Devon managed to make it to the next console, and the next, but neither were a match. By the third, Arrend called out, "Over here!"

They circled to Arrend's position, passing Mari guarding the door on the way. Arrend stepped aside as Devon arrived. "Is this it?"

"I think so." Devon reread the directions, all the way to the end, flipping pages back and forth. Then he began pushing buttons. After the third, lucent in the Core at the center of the room began to light up. As he proceeded, others began to turn off. A few flickered, their light dim, and often a button appeared to do nothing. Devon assumed those corresponded to threads of lucent that had burned out.

Then he reached for the last button, an innocuous pale blue set on the right edge of the console, but hesitated. His hand was trembling.

He glanced up at Arrend. "This is the last one. According to this, if we push this next, it will shut down the Core. All of the lucent within Brovetto will die and, if the books are to be believed, all of the magic as well."

"Then shut it off," Darcy said. "That's what we came here for."

Devon withdrew his hand. "No, not yet. We have to wait for the signal."

* * *

On the school balcony overlooking Fargrave Plaza, one of the men near Dalton's and Burdock's position stirred.

"Prefect, they're coming."

Both Burdock and Dalton rose, a rustle of movement from the other men spreading out from their position. Burdock gave curt orders to a slew of waiting runners, who departed without a sound, heading for the lines of men who'd arrayed themselves throughout the school and all along the barricades below. Although the warning was likely unnecessary. Dalton could see movement among the men. They'd already noticed what was happening on the far side of the square.

Iandolan soldiers had appeared on the main streets leading into the plaza, a uniform line completely blocking each road. But there they'd halted. From their vantage, Burdock, Dalton, and those around them could see a sea of men behind them, lined up rank and file, all in the Iandolan maroon and white uniforms. Dalton recognized the formations from his training at the Lyceum and knew there would be mages interspersed throughout.

As if sensing his thought, wavering blue shields began to form in the middle of the plaza, eight of them, starting at various points in a long line across the entire square. They expanded from a single point, but by the time they'd finished, they created a single curved wall that arched up over the back half of the plaza, protecting the men as they began to march forward.

Burdock looked at the evening sky, the sun ready to set in less than two hours. "It took them less than a day to reorganize and reach the plaza." He gave Dalton a look that he couldn't interpret. "Go tell Lane, if she's awake." Then, to everyone on the balcony in general, "And someone find our remaining mages!"

Dalton headed into the state room behind the balcony—what he thought had been the school's dining hall, now filled with soldiers hastily preparing themselves for battle—then down the stairs to the main hall still flooded with wounded. After stabilizing Lane, Mindell had moved her into one of the side rooms, out of sight of the rest of the army. Rumors of what had happened had already spread, but Burdock insisted that hearing a rumor and seeing Lane herself lying near death were completely different monsters when it came to morale.

He entered the room to find the four mages—Dawn, Brigette, Daniel, Serene, and Shian—waiting inside. Shian huddled in a corner, body shaking with silent sobs, Serene comforting her. Brigette leaned against the wall just inside the door, arms crossed, jaw clenched. Dawn and Raven stood behind Lane herself, faces pensive. Daniel crouched near Lane's table, head in his hands, but rose as soon as he saw Dalton. His eyes flashed in anger.

"How did this happen?" he demanded.

Dalton glanced at Raven, surprised she hadn't already told them. But she seemed to have retreated into herself.

He focused on Daniel. "When we took over Brovetto and sent the Iandolan forces away, they left behind a small group of men…or smuggled themselves in somehow after. They remained hidden, well enough we couldn't find them once we knew of their existence. They simply waited for an opportunity." He moved forward, glancing at Lane. Her eyes were closed, her breathing steady. He couldn't be certain, but her skin didn't look as pale as it had before. He glanced at Raven, then Daniel again. "They're all dead now."

Daniel clenched his jaw in grim satisfaction, but that fell away, revealing raw pain edged with panic. "What are we going to do? She's more powerful than us. And Gregg is trapped in the Warding. The five of us won't be able to stop the Iandolans alone."

Dalton was about to answer when someone grabbed his hand, the grip light and fumbling. His gaze shot down to the table to see Lane watching him intently before her expression broke into confusion.

"Where—?" she muttered, her voice no more than a wisp of sound.

Raven lurched forward, but halted, bowing her head.

"Brigette, fetch one of the healers," Dalton ordered, even as his hand closed around Lane's and relief rushed through him like a gust of wind. Shian shot up and stumbled to the edge of the table with Serene, her sobs now loud. She reached for Lane, but Serene held her back. Daniel had staggered back a step, his head lifted up as he sucked in a deep breath to steady himself.

Lane tried to lift her head. "What—?"

"Don't," Dalton said. "You're gravely wounded. Don't move unless you absolutely have to."

She laid her head back down, but frowned at all of the others as Brigette rushed in with Mindell and his daughter.

"Back off," Mindell demanded, shooing all of them aside as the two rounded the table and began checking Lane out from head to toe. They pulled the blanket covering her aside to inspect the bandages over the wound, muttering to each other, felt Lane's forehead, checked her eyes, her pulse, listened to her breathing.

After a long moment, Mindell turned to Raven and Dalton. "She appears stable. Don't do anything to make that change." To his daughter, he said, "Stay here, just in case."

As soon as he left, Lane caught Dalton's attention with the wave of a hand. "What's happening?" She appeared much more focused, much less confused.

"You were attacked—"

She cut him off. "I know that. What's happening now? We're at the school, right?"

"All of our forces have retreated to the school. Those that could. We've manned the barricades and settled in. But the Iandolan army just arrived."

Lane shifted, casting glares at Dawn, Brigette, and Daniel. "Find Burdock. He may need you."

"Burdock's up on the balcony," Dalton said.

The three mages left, Brigette with a roll of her eyes.

"What are the Iandolans doing?" Lane asked.

"They've erected a shield across the back half of the plaza. When I left, they were marching onto the square."

"Then there's no time left." She shot a look toward Serene and Shian. Shian had stopped sobbing. "You both know what to do?" They nodded. "Then go. Stay hidden. Don't let any of the Iandolan mages see you. And remember, cast close to your target. You aren't trying to kill Iandolans, you just need to take out your target."

Serene grabbed Shian by the shoulder and they left the room at a run.

"What are they supposed to do?"

"It doesn't matter. Hopefully we won't need it, but I'm afraid—" she cut off with a gasp. She'd tried to sit up while Dalton was turned and now clutched her side with one arm, her upper body supported by the other.

Dalton swore and Aver spat a curse and lurched forward.

"Governor, you can't move! You'll reopen the wound. You don't have the strength yet!"

"There's no other choice," Lane said, swinging her legs off the table so she sat at its edge. She reached for Dalton's hand, clutching it so tight he hissed in pain, then glanced at Raven.

"Help me up."

"I failed you—"

"We don't have time for this!" Lane spat, then softened. "You can't be everywhere, all at once. Now help me up."

Raven hesitated, then gave a sharp nod and moved to Lane's other side. Aver was still cursing.

Lane caught Dalton's gaze. "If the Iandolans don't see me on that balcony, they'll attack without hesitation. This is our last chance to end this, our last chance to break them. If we don't stop them here, Brovetto will fall."

Chapter Nineteen

Dalton and Raven carried Lane up to the state room and the glass doors leading to the balcony over the portico below, Aver trailing behind. Lane grit her teeth against the agony, sweat breaking out across her entire body. Her side throbbed like a beast with its own heart. Mindell's daughter grumbled inaudible protests the entire way after ordering one of the other healers to fetch fresh linens and more poultice. By the time they reached the outer room, blood had soaked through Lane's clothing and she could feel that the stitches had popped.

"Set me down here," she ordered between ragged breaths. They settled her onto the floor, the soldiers already crowding the room shuffling back and away, leaving them a wide space to work in.

"We shouldn't be moving her at all," Aver spat as she ripped the saturated linens aside and inspected the wound. "She needs to rest—"

"I need to end this war," Lane interrupted, voice sharp even through the pain...or perhaps because of it. "In order to do that, I need to stand up and walk out onto that balcony. I need everyone on that plaza to be convinced that I am whole. I cannot stagger. I cannot collapse. And above all, they cannot see any blood."

Aver stared at her, then said in a quiet but serious voice, "It may kill you."

"Then so be it. What do you need to do to make that happen?"

Aver didn't have a chance to answer. Mindell stalked in, eyes fiery with anger, with two others trailing behind him with supplies.

"What's the meaning of this?" he began. He drew breath to say more, his anger focusing on Dalton and Raven, but Aver leaped up from Lane's side and cut him off with a slew of hushed words.

As they conversed, Lane reached out and grabbed Dalton's hand, hard enough he winced. She drew him in close. "You're here. Does that mean Devon succeeded with the lithum?"

"I have them here," he said, and patted the satchel strapped over one shoulder.

Relief flooded Lane's body, pushing the pain back for a few blissful moments. "Then there's a chance this will work."

Burdock came in from the balcony. "Brigette and Daniel are on the balcony. Dawn is below. Where are Serene and Shian?"

"Moving into position."

"Then you intend to go through with this?"

"It's the only chance we've got. If we don't stop them here, they'll overrun the city."

"Then you should know that we've spotted activity on the wayfares from both Radimansque and Scintillesque."

The hope that flared choked off her breath. When she finally managed to speak, her voice was thin and hoarse. "What color banners were they flying?"

"We can't tell. They're too distant. And it's dusk. We won't be able to tell before nightfall."

Lane's shoulders slumped. "They'll never get here in time. We're on our own."

"Why would the banners matter?" Dalton asked.

"When I sent Nic and Picall to talk to the other cities, I told them—if they managed to convince them to return with an army—to fly Brovettan colors. If they aren't bearing green and gold…"

"Then they're here in support of Iridesque," Burdock finished.

"Governor."

All three of them turned to face Mindell's stern expression.

"My daughter has explained the situation. I don't agree with your decision, but will abide by it regardless. Are you certain you wish to do this?"

"I am."

"Then so be it."

Lane couldn't tell whether he'd chosen her exact words from a few moments before on purpose or not. The healer had already motioned the others forward. They forcefully moved Burdock, Raven, and Dalton aside, taking up positions around Lane's body, Mindell near her wound.

He pulled something from one of his pockets and held it up, catching Lane's gaze. "Chew this. Don't swallow." He shoved it into Lane's mouth.

Lane began to chew. It had an acrid, acidic taste, like bark, that filled her mouth and trickled down her throat. After a moment, her tongue began to tingle and go numb. She nearly spat it out in a panic. "I cansh shalk! I mussh be abbo sho shalk!"

"The numbness will fade in a few minutes, now chew!"

Lane glared at him, but kept chewing. The bark was slowly being reduced to pulp and the numbness was creeping down her throat. Mindell began to administer to her wound.

"Some of the stitches have pulled. We'll have to replace them. The bleeding isn't that bad. The poultice is working. Hand me that needle and those sutures."

He looked at Lane. "Can you feel this?"

Something tugged at Lane's side. "Shush a shug."

"Good. The bark's working. Spit it out."

Lane turned her head to the side and spit the gross, pulpy mess to one side. Before she could complain about it, Mindell shoved something else into her mouth.

"Chew."

Lane grudgingly bit into the new tidbit and was pleasantly surprised. It tasted a little like cinnamon and mint, sharp and biting. Its prickling scent assaulted her nostrils. Also, the numbness in her mouth and throat was beginning to fade, as promised.

At her side, Mindell was working furiously, focused. He demanded the poultice, more sutures, a swipe of the wound that produced a bloody rag, but not as much blood as Lane had expected, linens, more poultice. Lane felt only a few pulls and some pressure now and then. The numbness had seeped into her body, the pulsing agony she'd felt as Dalton and Raven had carried her reduced to a dull throb.

And then Mindell sat back and heaved a sigh. He wiped sweat from his forehead with his upper arm, his hands too bloody.

He faced Lane. "Reach into my right pocket. There are a couple more of those second chews in there. Take them. If you start feeling the pain again, use another one. I wouldn't use more than three. They're not as effective as that bark I gave you first, but they won't cause the numbness."

Then he leaned in close, the disapproval tainted now with concern. "Make this worth it."

He stood, someone handing him rags to clean off his hands. He gave Lane one last worried look, then departed.

Lane let her head fall back to the floor and closed her eyes. An utter calm washed through her. Whether it was resignation or an effect of the chews she couldn't tell. It felt like that time Gillian had given her the tea, only more intense. All she wanted to do was sleep, but her entire body was tingling with energy.

When she opened her eyes, Dalton was leaning over her. "Are you all right?"

She tucked the chew into a corner of her mouth. "I feel more focused, less distracted. But it also feels like I'm hovering just outside of my body."

"Is there any pain?"

She considered. "Yes. But it's...distant."

Burdock leaned forward as well. "The Iandolan army has filled the plaza. Or at least, their half of it."

Lane sighed. "Then we'd better get this started."

She reached up, her arms' motions oddly...elongated. As if they were farther away from her than normal. She braced herself for the same agony as before when Raven and Dalton lifted her to a sitting position, but there was only an initial twinge that was absorbed by the general dullness that permeated her. She still gasped, as if her body were reacting to things her mind was longer attached to.

"Ready to stand?" Raven asked.

She nodded.

The twinge was stronger this time, but once she was upright and stable, it faded as before, subsumed.

Raven and Dalton hung close to either side, ready to catch her if she wavered. But once she was on her feet, she became...centered.

She clenched her jaw, focused on the open doorway to the balcony, where she could see Brigette and Daniel and a scattering of soldiers dividing their attention between her and the plaza below.

Then she stepped forward.

The Fargrave Plaza was utterly quiet, dusk already casting it in shadow as the sun set. Torches lit the Brovettan barricades on either side of the building and lined the edges of the balcony, casting the Brovettan half of the plaza in a fiery light that was echoed by the still raging fires throughout the city on all sides. Torches were being used by the Iandolans as well, but there was a profusion of lucent lanterns throughout their forces in varying shades of green and blue and purple, along with bright white orbs that floated high overhead. Lane searched the Iandolan ranks looking for the paired lithum, but saw only a few.

When she reached the ornamental stone lip of the balcony, she glanced down to scan the Brovettan army and caught sight of her father, standing next to Dawn. He gave her a nod from his position at the front of the outer barricade. Thousands of other faces were turned up to her as well and she noticed a ripple of motion passing through the ranks as word spread. But she didn't have time for a rousing speech to strengthen her own forces.

Instead, she turned her attention to the Iandolans.

They filled the entire back half of the plaza, battalion after battalion of them, on the far side of the shimmering shield they'd erected. She knew most of them had been trained at the Lyceum, but not all. Not after Arctus, Havvelan, and Favian had initiated the recruitment program during their purge of Iandolo of the Brovettans. A significant number of them would be brawlers and gang members, toughs and rogues. But it didn't matter. The Brovettans were outnumbered at least two to one, likely more. Lane doubted all of their forces were here in the square.

And that didn't take into account their mages.

Raven and Dalton settled into position on either side of her. Burdock remained behind her. Brigette and Daniel stood apart, at the far corners of the balcony. Both of them gave her a nod indicating they were ready. Their job would be to shield her from any attacks, if they came.

To the far west, the sun sank beneath the horizon with a glorious display of burnished orange thrown up against the clouds. Between the buildings to the southeast, where darkness had already settled onto the Flatlands, she could see a trail of fiery light shooting back toward Scintillesque—an army marching on Luminesque. She didn't dare turn to see if she could spot the second army marching from Radimansque to the northwest. Her attention needed to be on the plaza, on the army already here.

She spat the chew that had lost all of its flavor toward her feet, raised her arm, hand crooked, and started a sigil to amplify her voice. On the far side of the Iandolan shield, the army reacted. Men tensed, shouts rose, muted by the short distance and the shield. In the forefront, where she suspected Arctus, Havvelan, and Favian would be, another shield rose before she'd finished. Someone must have had the base sigil already cast, ready and waiting. This new shield enveloped only a small group of men, perhaps twenty in all.

"Favian will be there," Dalton said.

"Havvelan as well," Burdock added. "But not Arctus. He wouldn't want to be constrained by the shield."

Lane ignored them.

"Welcome to Brovetto, Havvelan. And you, too, Favian." Her words boomed out over the square, easily heard by everyone. "But I'm afraid I'm going to have to ask you to leave."

Some of those around her chuckled and there was a wash of quiet laughter from the Iandolan army. Lane kept her eyes on the group inside the smaller shield, saw movement.

A moment later, Havvelan responded, his voice no doubt augmented by Favian.

"I'm afraid you've misread our intentions. We won't leave until this rebellious, Founder-forsaken city is burned to the ground, along with all of those in it."

"We won't let that happen. *I* won't let that happen."

Havvelan snorted in contempt. "And what do you intend to do about it."

Lane raised her left hand. Not crooked; not tracing out a sigil. But it was signal nonetheless.

To the left, behind the Iandolan shield, a cantrip suddenly formed less than thirty feet above one of the mismatched stacks of furniture and debris that were scattered around the plaza. Those Iandolan soldiers near it shouted in fear and began to scramble. Even through the shield, Lane could see a couple mages attempting to stop it. But the cantrip wasn't targeting the soldiers or the mages.

It angled nearly straight down, to the base of the jumbled furniture.

Within seconds, it grew to twice its size and then struck the flagstone of the plaza, gouging into the ground, throwing up chunks of rock in all directions as it continued to expand, sinking deeper and deeper. The stone debris turned from the dark gray of flagstone into the ochre and sandstone that formed the heart of the butte the city rested on, and still it ground deeper. The tortured sound of disintegrating rock continued—

Until something deep beneath the plaza gave way.

A roughly circular area surrounding the stack of furniture sagged, those standing on it lurching to keep their feet.

And then it simply collapsed downwards into the mine below.

Screams rose from the gaping hole, its edges widening as more gave way, as more fell into the gap, but then the screams cut off and a tremendous crack of stone hitting stone erupted from the sinkhole. The ground trembled, a shudder Lane felt through the building beneath her feet. To either side, both Brigette and Daniel were completing sigils, new shields being thrown up at the edges of the plaza, covering the streets, cutting off the Iandolan army's escape. A plume of rock dust belched from the sinkhole, its edges now frayed, chunks continuing to slip free and fall, even as the Iandolan soldiers nearby scrambled to get away in panic. A roar erupted from the Brovettan lines, men shouting and pumping their fists into the air. Inside the Iandolan lines, mages began targeting the shields spanning the streets, their attacks splintering, ineffective.

Lane lowered her arm.

"You cannot escape!" she said, raising her voice over the cacophony, still amplified.

Her own men quieted, as did the Iandolans. Their mages halted their attempts on the shields. But they were riled now, their forces shifting back and forth.

"You cannot escape," Lane repeated. "The only way out of the square is forward. You'll have to lower your shields and surrender yourselves to us, or lower your shields and fight."

Someone inside the smaller shield below shoved their way forward.

"You expect *us* to surrender to *you!*" Havvelan bellowed. "*You* are the ones who defied the Council! *You* are the ones who escaped rightful custody after the attack at the Lyceum and then hid within the lower levels of Iandolo. You're the ones who fomented rebellion after the quarantine, the ones who started the riots after being caught and sentenced for execution. Iandolo descended into chaos because of you, a rebellion that took weeks to quell!"

"And how many citizens of Iandolo—no, of the Crystal Cities—did you kill to bring order to the city?" Lane countered. "How many Brovettans did you murder while ostensibly rounding them up for your quarantine? How many did you subdue here in Brovetto itself over the years? Don't pretend that all of this is because of two Lyceum students who were merely trying to graduate. Two Lyceum students who helped you subdue the attack on the Lyceum and Iandolo itself. This has been going on since long before we were even born. We've been in Luminesque long enough now to see what you've done.

"For decades, Iandolo has mined Brovetto to its core, hollowed it out, stole all of its lucent for your own purposes. And then when the mines ran dry you began stripping it of the lucent already in use. You sabotaged the water system, pillaged the infrastructure, left the citizens here with barely enough to survive. There's little to no lucent left here. Barely any life, because of you. Because of those like you who infiltrated the Council and turned it toward your own ends.

"You could have left us alone. Let us *go*. No one here—not Devon Alamort or myself, not my mother or father, not any of the local citizens who assumed the role of governor when you took its own governor away—none of us wanted any of this. But you and your arrogance, your petty jealousy and wounded pride, you couldn't let us all slip away. You had to come and seek vengeance and retribution."

Lane paused, her breath heaving, her heart thundering in her chest. She didn't think it was whatever the healer had given her. The frustrated words had spilled out from some inner source that had been dammed up for weeks, months, perhaps years. Since the Lyceum. Since Favian and Quinn and Devon's disastrous challenge. All of that pent up pressure had finally released.

As her heart and breath calmed, she realized the plaza had quieted.

It was broken by Havvelan's laughter.

"You think we could have left you here? Only the young would be so naïve. Brovetto has been a thorn in our side for a hundred years! If we'd left you here, that wound would have festered. You would have come for us eventually. You would have—"

Lane threw up her right hand and, on the plaza, a new cantrip formed, targeting another one of the piles of debris. As before, it angled down, growing and expanding, then eating into the flagstone, churning through rock into the foundations of the square. The Iandolans nearby attempted to flee, but they were packed too tightly together. There was nowhere to run.

This time there was no warning, no sagging in the center. The area simply dropped, taking the pile of furniture that had been erected as a marker and at least a hundred Iandolan soldiers with it, including one of the pairs of lithum. The stone struck the bottom of the mine beneath with another ground-shaking roar and plume of rocky dust.

As the cloud began to settle, Lane said, "You forget that this entire city was built over mines."

"And you forget that we have mages!" Havvelan spat, enraged.

Burdock shouted a warning to the Brovettan men at the same time Lane saw the Iandolan shields collapsing. Brigette and Daniel were already creating sigils in response, but cantrips, sheets of fire, and balls of lightning were already forming. The Iandolan mages had been one step ahead.

"Get down!" Dalton shouted.

Lane had barely begun to turn when he slammed into her from the side, both of them dropping beneath the edge of the balcony's stone railing a moment before a fireball slammed into it a few feet from where she'd been standing. Flame roared over them, searing Lane's skin, but Dalton took the brunt of it, teeth clenched as he lay on top of her. It lasted an eternity, then Raven was there, smothering the flames in a frenzy.

Dalton gasped and looked up at Raven. "Is it out?" At her nod, he relaxed and shifted to one side of Lane. "Are you all right?"

Lane did a survey of her body. The pain in her side had begun to pulse again, the chew wearing off, but it wasn't unendurable yet. "I'm fine. Are you?"

Dalton twisted so she could see his back. "You tell me."

"You're clothing and the armor you had underneath are scorched, but intact. Mostly."

He hissed as he moved. "It feels like its melted into my skin." He met her gaze, attention shifting. "How did you get those cantrips behind their shields?"

"I didn't. Serene and Shian, with a few guards as escort, positioned themselves in the buildings on the other side of the shields." The balcony beneath them shuddered as another section of the plaza collapsed. "They waited for my signal. But I think they're letting loose now."

Something struck the upper floors of the school, debris raining down to the left of the balcony as glass windows throughout the building shattered. Raven, Lane, and Dalton covered their faces, listening to the tramp of feet as orders and curses and screams flew back and forth. After the tinkling of glass ended, Lane looked up to find the corner of the school missing.

But then her gaze shifted higher and the bottom of her stomach dropped away, as swiftly and deeply as the collapsing plaza.

"Oh, no," she breathed.

"What is it?" Raven asked.

"The gateway at the top of the ramp that leads to the Third Level…"

"What about it?"

"It's lit. The lucent there is lit."

She dropped her gaze back to Dalton.

"Devon should have turned the power off by now. The lucent—the magic—should be dead or dying.

"Something must have gone wrong."

* * *

A sustained shudder trembled through the Core chamber, dislodging stone from the ceiling and stirring up dust. It sent vibrations up through Devon's hands where they rested on the floor. One of the books he'd been referencing fell from the console. The Core itself jangled, crystal lucent jostling against each other, the sound like wind chimes in a faint breeze.

"What was that?" Darcy asked.

"The signal."

Devon pushed himself to his knees, then to his feet. Dizziness washed over him as he stood, his vision fading, but when Darcy made to help him, he waved her away.

He focused on the console, began checking the settings against what it said in the book, even though he and Arrend had been over them a dozen times while they waited. "Lane just collapsed part of the Fargrave Plaza. That's the tremor we just felt. And now it's our turn."

He glanced up. Both Arrend and Darcy had drifted closer, were standing at either shoulder. Mari watched from her position at the door.

At a grim nod from Arrend, he tapped the last lucent button in the sequence.

Nothing happened.

"Is that—is that it?" Darcy asked. "Did it work?"

Devon frowned. "Something should have happened."

He and Arrend glanced up at the Core. The threads of lucent that had been lit before were still pulsing faintly.

"I'd think the lucent here would be powered down as well," Arrend ventured. He met Devon's gaze. "Something's wrong. It didn't work."

Devon began flipping through the pages of the manual. "It can't be. We checked this a hundred times. We did exactly what it said!" Panic began to set in. "If we don't get this turned off, Lane and the rest will have to stand up against all of the Iandolan mages. They'll be overrun. This is their only—"

Arrend laid a hand on his arm and Devon went still. "I don't think there's an issue with the sequence. I think it's the Core itself. It's old. And it's been abused and misused and forgotten for decades."

They both looked at the strands of lucent before them, a significant number of them dark. Dead. Like so much of the lucent in all of the Crystal Cities.

"I never checked the pathways," Devon said to himself.

Without waiting for a response, he slapped his hands onto one of the bands of lucent, a pale green, like his lantern. He dove into it, hesitated a moment before heading down, down, down—

And hit a crack in the lucent, the pathway partially blocked. He swore, but focused on that section, as he'd focused on the purple shard in order to change its form to create the lithum. With a push and a shivering hiss, the crack reformed and the pathway cleared.

But still nothing happened.

He spat another curse and dove deeper, found nothing more in that vein of lucent, so returned.

His eyes snapped open—he hadn't even realized he'd closed them—and Arrend immediately asked, "What's wrong?"

"Some of the lucent pathways are blocked. I've cleared this one. I'm going to have to check the rest."

"What about Lane and Burdock and the others?"

"They're one their own for now."

He selected another band, blue this time, and began another search. Instinct told him the issues were somewhere down below, but when the blue strand was clear for a significant length of time, he checked upwards, just in case. Nothing. He resurfaced, switched to a darker blue, and began again.

This one had several cracks, which he fixed as quickly as possible. Unlike forming the key for the lithum, these changes weren't as draining, which was good because he'd barely regained enough strength to stand on his own. As he worked, he heard Arrend snapping a book open, followed by the flicker of pages. Darcy murmured something. Mari answered. But he couldn't spare the attention to listen to the words.

He snapped back, moved to select a new strand of lucent, but Arrend halted him.

"There are hundreds of bands of lucent here. You won't be able to fix them all, especially those that are completely dead. We need to focus on the strands that are related to shutting the system down." He pointed to the book. "There are only twelve that are referenced here for that. You've already repaired one of them. Work on this one next. I'll identify the others while you work."

Devon merely nodded, slapping his palm against the pale purple band Arrend had indicated and began the next search. More cracks, a significant one that nearly cut it off from the network completely, deep, deep down the shaft where they stood. That one took more effort to repair, his hands trembling when he finished. He made fists to get them to stop, then began work on the next, another green, then a blue, a pale yellow, another verging on orange. Two of them were fine, the others had minor cracks. Thoughts of Lane and Dalton intruded as he worked. What was happening on the plaza? Had they realized yet that the plan had failed? Were they still bargaining with Havvelan and Favian? Or had the fighting already broken out?

Were they already dead?

He'd begun to sweat, his palm slick as it dropped away from the smooth surface and Arrend pointed out another strand.

"This is the ninth one," the proctor said.

Devon didn't acknowledge the comment, merely sank into the dark red lucent and searched.

When he emerged again, another tremor rumbled through the chamber, more violent than the first.

If he'd had any doubts before, he now knew: "The fighting has begun."

Arrend pointed to another strand. "This one."

The tenth was easy, a few minor flaws in the crystal, the eleventh a little harder. He emerged from it with a gasp and leaned forward onto the panel before him to steady himself, but managed to say, "Last one. Which one is it?"

Arrend pointed, a grim expression on his face.

It had once been a cobalt blue. Now, it was completely dead, its lucent flecked with black particles up and down its length.

Devon's gut clenched. None of the others had been dead.

But he'd repaired dead lucent before.

Stealing himself, he slapped his hand onto the lucent and began to search. It was like swimming through muddy water, the black particles obscuring his vision. But he could sense the structure of the lucent as he moved. It was still there, still viable, it had simply been cut off somewhere. If it had been Iandolo, he would have said someone had found a segment of the strand exposed and broken it to free it, to sell it in order to survive, as he'd done so many times in the lower levels as a gang member…and even before that. But this wasn't Iandolo. And none of these strands had been exposed, at least not where anyone could easily find them. That had to mean that if there was an interruption in the lucent, it was—

"There," he muttered. He lingered a moment, felt around its edges. The pathways were completely severed. He couldn't tell if a chunk had been snapped free or if it had simply cracked across the entire strand. It didn't matter. He'd found it.

He pulled himself from the lucent. "I've found the break. But I can't fix it from here. We have to head down, about four levels. There are access panels on each level." He spun toward the door leading downwards, then halted. "Grab my satchel, with the lucent shards. We may need them."

Then he headed toward the door. He moved without thought, adrenalin surging through him, and only staggered a little at the beginning before gaining his balance. Fatigue washed through him, but not as badly as it had in the manse after creating the lithum.

At the door, he turned to Darcy. "Stay here, at the consol." At her stricken look, he added, "In case someone needs to press that final button again to get this to work."

She nodded and raced back to the panel.

Then he, Arrend, and Mari were moving, Mari holding his lucent lantern high to guide them down the stairs encircling the outside wall, the lucent Core in the center. They reached the door, the ground tremoring again on the way, and passed out onto the stairs circling outside the central shaft. Three levels down, he entered the short corridor passing through the center, found the band of cobalt blue lucent, and checked their progress.

"We're close. Another level or two down."

Neither Mari nor Arrend responded, merely hastening down another level, then two.

The door to the corridor slid open with a grinding sound that made Devon wince, but it opened fully. He dodged inside as soon as he could, found the access panel for the lucent, and slapped his hand against the appropriate band.

"The part that's broken is just overhead," he said, removing his hand and attempting to peer upward along the thread. Mari shifted closer so he could use the light from the lantern, even though some of the bands of lucent inside the panel were already lit.

When that failed, he thrust his arm up along the thick column of lucent.

"I've found it. There's a section here that's shattered." He closed his eyes and tried to picture what his fingers were feeling. "There's a sizable chunk missing. It must have broken free and fallen down inside the paneling here."

"Can you fix it?" Arrend asked.

"Only one way to find out. Hand me the satchel."

Mari pulled it from her shoulder and he began to root through the pieces of lucent he'd collected from the scrap heaps in the Burn and other parts of the city since they'd arrived. Most were too thin, too small.

He finally pulled out a dusky violet-colored piece, hefted in one hand.

"It'll have to do."

He shoved his arm back up into the paneling, twisting the violet piece of lucent around until it fit into the missing crevice in the lucent, then sank himself into the strand.

He repaired the shattered pieces from the original band first, then focused on the new piece. It didn't quite fit, a little too large, but he began fusing it in place, merging the structure of the original crystal with the new, aligning the appropriate pathways from top to bottom. The violet crystal had some extra pathways he didn't need, and he began sheering them off, separating them from the main band—

And suddenly the cobalt blue thread of lucent surged with power, brightening with a flash, pulsing as the vibrational hum that had always been present in the corridor increased, buzzing in Devon's teeth. He jerked his hand out of the paneling and shook it, as if it had gone numb, even though there hadn't been any kind of shock, only a mild tingling sensation against his skin as it activated.

"Did it work?" Arrend asked.

"I don't know. The lucent thread is active now, though."

"Let's find out."

The three of them raced back up to the Core, burst through the door to find Darcy standing over the console. She startled as they spilled into the room.

"Has it stopped?" Devon barked.

"I don't think so."

"Then hit the button again!"

Darcy slammed her hand down on the button—

And all of the threads from the level of the console and above went dark.

Chapter Twenty

"Hold the line!" Burdock bellowed as Lane threw up a shield before the balcony.

Seconds later, a ball of lightning slammed into it, crackling as it broke apart. To either side, Brigette and Daniel were protecting the line below, helping Dawn. On the plaza, the Iandolan soldiers had rushed forward and were engaging their lines at the barricades, men screaming and dying everywhere. The plaza had descended into chaos. The only portion of the army that hadn't moved were those inside the shield that protected Havvelan and, Lane assumed, Favian and those with him. It still remained in the center of the square, the two gaping holes from the collapses around it. Lightning and fire and cantrips were being flung left and right, with Brigette's and Daniel's shields barely holding it all at bay.

"We need to go on the offensive," Lane muttered to herself, still holding her shield.

As she said it, a cantrip formed over another one of the markers and began to bore downwards. Warnings were shouted and soldiers began scrambling away, the plaza more open now that the Iandolan shields were down.

Not all of them made it.

Another collapse took out a chunk of the plaza, but this time some of the Iandolan mages reacted. The cantrips and fireballs began targeting the surrounding buildings, those that had been behind their initial shield.

Lane swore. "They've figured out we have mages on their flanks!"

With a roar, the front of one of the buildings fell outwards, exposing the rooms within. Lane didn't know exactly where Serene and Shian had gone, but she prayed they were still safe.

She needed to give them a chance to escape.

"Burdock, Dalton, Raven, everyone on the balcony! I'm going to drop my shield!"

Her hand was forming the base sigil as soon as she let the shield go. Something slammed into the school above them, men crying out as debris fell behind her, but she ignored it all, concentrated on her sigil, selected the nodes for what she wanted—

And let it go.

Fire bloomed above the plaza, a sheet that expanded in all directions until it covered at least the back two-thirds—

And then it dropped.

Shields popped up in sections all across the square, mages hurrying to protect themselves. Many of the magical attacks on the barricades and the buildings faltered.

The massive sheet of fire landed with a whoosh, the flame flowing like water in every direction as it encountered the shields and was forced into new directions. It funneled between them all, incinerating those in its path that had been too slow or had been caught too far from one of the Iandolan mages.

"Gods," someone nearby murmured.

Lane was already creating a new sigil. Before the fires she'd unleashed had faded, a crackling ball of lightning appeared over the army. It sizzled and sparked—

Then spat bolts down into the shields and stone below.

"That one's new," Dalton said at her side.

"The only thing that's kept us alive since we escaped the Towers in Iandolo is that I know more about how the magic works than they do, even after what they tortured out of Devon. I can still surprise them."

Another cantrip appeared, gouging down into the mines below, and Lane huffed in satisfaction. At least one of her two youngest mages was still alive.

"I'll try to keep their mages distracted. You three should focus on the barricades."

"Of course, governor," Burdock said. Lane grimaced at the title, but he'd already turned away, shouting at the men behind them to descend to the lines below.

Dalton and Raven didn't move.

"Go with him," Lane said through clenched teeth. The ball of lightning was weakening. Fewer bolts were being thrown. "There's nothing you can do from up here."

A sudden spasm of pain shot through her side and she hunched forward around it with a gasp, the spell lost. The ball of lightning exploded, sparks cascading down in a fountain of light, but she barely saw it out of the corner of her eye as she collapsed forward. Raven caught her and settled her to the stone.

"Nothing except protect you," she said.

Lane fumbled for her pocket as Brigette stepped in front of them, hand moving, her face a rictus of concentrated anger.

"I've got it," she said. "Daniel, cover the line."

"Done!" Daniel barked, shifting closer to them as well.

Beneath their looming figures, Lane's hand closed on one of the chews the healer had given her.

"The pain is returning," she said, then shoved it in her mouth. Cinnamon-mint flooded her senses as she began to chew.

"You've started bleeding again as well."

Dalton held up blood-slicked fingers, the blood appearing black in the coruscating flashes of lightning and fire that surrounded them.

Lane gave him a grim smile. "I don't have anything to take care of that."

To the side, a purplish light flared and began to grow in intensity.

All three of them stared at it in surprise. It was coming from Dalton's satchel.

He snatched it up and folded back the flap.

Inside, the red and blue lithum were both glowing much brighter than before, each one flaring with sporadic pulses.

Understanding struck and Lane's head snapped up toward the top of the building, toward the gate at the top of the ramp to the Third Level.

The lucent there was dark.

She grabbed Dalton's hands. "The power is off. Devon's done it." She glanced down at the lithum, then back up at Brigette and Daniel, both still casting or holding sigils. "And the lithum is working." She caught Raven's gaze. "Lift me up."

With her help, she stood, braced against the stone balustrade, and surveyed the plaza. Brigette and Daniel were keeping up the attack, forcing the Iandolan mages to defend or be killed. The shield above the lines must be coming from Dawn below. On the barricades, the Brovettans were mostly keeping the Iandolan army at bay, although in a few sections they'd either broken through or one of the mage attacks had created a breach. Burdock and her father were engaging Arctus in the area before the balcony.

But it was the lithum out in the square that held Lane's attention. Like their own, it had brightened and was flashing with each use by one of the nearby Iandolan mages. There were only a few of them left; she counted five. The shields of those mages not close to a lithum were beginning to flicker. As they watched, one of them failed completely. A fireball fell into the undefended area and exploded, the mage within flailing about like a torch before collapsing to one side.

Two more failed, lightning taking out those mages, then all of them. The only shields that remained were those within a few hundred feet of one of the Iandolan's lithum. Brigette and Daniel began targeting those alone. Their lithum flared as they defended themselves against the assault, but Lane noticed that their lithum was dimming. The flares weren't as bright. The stored energy each lithum contained was being drained away.

Soon they'd have nothing.

She glanced down their own lithum. It may have faded, but not by much. Possibly because there were only four mages draining its power. There were at least a dozen out on the plaza using the Iandolan lithum.

She pushed back from the balcony, only a slight twinge of pain coming from her side. The chew was working.

"Enough," she said.

Daniel halted, but his hand hovered before him, only the base sigil completed.

Brigette continued to cast, her eyes locked on the plaza, on the shields. Her lips were pressed thin, her eyes squinted in rage.

Lane stepped in front of her and grabbed both of her wrists, interrupting a sigil. "I said enough!"

Brigette growled, eyes narrowing, and fought to free herself, but Lane held on, digging her fingernails into skin, until Brigette gave a frustrated cry and wrenched free. She stood there panting, but the intensity of her rage had drained away. She wiped at her mouth with the back of her arm.

Satisfied, Lane turned back to the plaza. The mages were holding their shields as best they could, even though there was no one attacking. The army itself was still pummeling the barricades.

Lane raised her arm and drew a single sigil.

Thunder boomed over the square, the air shuddering beneath the sound. Men and women on all sides cried out and clapped hands to their ears. Stone shivered. The fighting at the barricades died down to only a few scuffles, and then even those ended as everyone realized there were no fireballs or lightning arching through the skies, no cantrips tearing into buildings or the ground or flesh.

An odd quiet settled, broken only by fitful coughs, moans, and the uncomfortable jostling of confused men.

Lane stared down at where Arctus and the men around him had paused. He glared back.

"It's over," Lane said.

The Prefect barked a derisive laugh. "And what makes you think that?"

Lane waved toward the center of the plaza. "You've lost your mages."

Arctus spun, as did many other Iandolans on all sides. Behind, the remaining mages still huddled under their own protection.

One of those shields flickered and went out.

Dawn let her own shield above them all fade.

"Impossible," Arctus spat.

"Send someone to find out from Favian himself," Lane said. "Or go yourself." Then she straightened. "Or better yet, we'll all go."

She caught Burdock's gaze and received a nod, then turned her back on Arctus. "Dalton, bring the satchel with the lithum. Brigette, Daniel, and Raven, come with me."

She retreated off the balcony, through the inner hall and down the stairs to the front portico. The school had taken a beating—walls cracked, chunks of stone and plaster littering the floor, dust floating everywhere. The healers and wounded in the main hall below watched her pass with wide eyes, those that were conscious anyway.

She half expected Arctus to have ordered the Iandolans to continue the attack, but when they stepped out beneath the balcony to where Burdock had assembled an escort composed of himself, her father, and twenty other men, Arctus had ordered his men back from the barricades. Both sides were tense, hands gripping the handles of their blades in anticipation of a resumed fight, but for now, everyone held steady.

Lane ordered Dawn to stay behind, as a precaution, then headed directly toward Arctus, Burdock and the others falling into position behind her. Brovettans pulled parts of the barricade aside to let them through, then closed it up behind them.

She halted ten paces from the prefect.

"You're wounded," he said, nodding toward her side.

She glanced down at bloodstain on her clothing, spat her chew onto the ground, and said, "It's nothing."

He grunted, suspicion touching his eyes.

"Shall we?" She motioned toward where the shield surrounding Havvelan and Favian still held. There were only five shields left now, three near Favian and two others off to one side near where one of the Iandolan lithum still burned, although its colors were dim.

Arctus grimaced, but he turned and moved toward the shield. His men parted before him. Lane didn't see him issue any orders, but twenty-six soldiers fell into step with him, to match her own escort. She followed, keeping her distance. As they passed through the Iandolan line, the soldiers shifted restlessly, some even stepping back. She kept her eyes forward though, judging their distance from Favian and the other shields.

Fifty paces away, she halted abruptly. Arctus didn't notice until he'd reached the shield. He spun, hand going to his sword, but when Lane didn't react, he paused.

"We'll wait here," Lane said.

"Wait for what?" he asked.

"That." Lane jutted a chin out to the mages behind him.

When he turned, one of the three shields near Havvelan and Favian flickered and died, the mages and men inside shrinking back. One of them— the mage who'd been struggling to hold the shield up, Lane assumed— collapsed to the ground. As she did so, the second shield failed, which left only Havvelan and Favian's here. They were close enough now she could see them inside, could see the red and blue glow of the lithum with them.

To the side, the other lithum died, the shields near it collapsing. Everywhere on the plaza, groups of soldiers and mages stood in bewilderment, uncertain what was happening, uncertain about what they should do.

Arctus stared at the last group, jaw hardening.

"It won't be long now," Lane said, voice soft.

Then the blue lithum inside Favian's shield began to flicker. He spun toward it, watched in horror as it flickered again, returned but much dimmer—

Then went dark. Its red pair followed suit.

And within a breath, the shield that had protected Havvelan, Favian, and a slew of additional mages and soldiers faded out.

Favian took four angry steps toward Lane. "You did this!" he spat. "How did you do it? How did you steal our power?"

"I didn't steal your power. Devon did."

Favian swore, the words vicious and guttural. "We should have killed both of you the moment he sent his challenge to the board at the Lyceum."

Lane lifted her chin. "If you had, then Terriel would have succeeded in her seizure of Iandolo. You'd be locked inside the Warding even now. Don't forget it was Devon and I who freed you. Devon and I who confronted her on the quad and defeated her. And all of that happened *after* you'd expelled us from the college."

"*You* were expelled. Nothing more serious happened solely because your mother was a Councilor and she vowed to keep you within the towers where we could keep an eye on you. *Devon* fled, became a fugitive. If he hadn't, it would not have gone so easily for him."

"I'm certain it wouldn't."

She fixed her attention to Arctus. "As I said, you've lost your mages. Favian has verified it. What do you intend to do now?"

"Seize her!" Favian shouted. "Seize them all! We can end this right here if you simply take them and execute them here on the plaza."

Lane faced him, raised her hand, fingers crooked, and began the base sigil. Favian sucked in a sharp breath and lurched back as if struck. Some of the closest mages gasped, began to murmur amongst themselves.

"You can see it, can't you, Favian? The double pyramid. The base structure of all of our sigils."

"That's not possible," he muttered. He raised his own hand, began his own sigil, but nothing happened. No double pyramid formed. He tried again, and the murmurs increased.

He was too far away from the lithum Dalton carried.

"What does it mean?" Arctus asked.

"Yes, Favian," Havvelan added harshly. "What does it mean?"

Favian let his hand drop, but didn't answer.

"What it means," Lane said, "is that *we* still have access to the power that is the heart of magecraft. *We* can still rain down fire upon your heads, or call down lightning, or send a cantrip through your front lines." To either side of her, Brigette and Daniel began their own sigils. "What it means, is that for the first time in recorded history, Iandolo is without mages to protect its army, to protect its city."

Havvelan, who'd remained half hidden amongst the others in their group, now pushed forward, stepping up to Arctus. "It doesn't matter. You can't possibly have many mages. Maybe a dozen, at most. And your 'army' is composed of ragtag rebels and citizens who barely know how to hold a blade. The Iandolan army has been training for decades. We can overwhelm you long before your mages can take us all out."

"That's likely true," Burdock said. He didn't move forward, leaving Lane, Brigette, and Daniel at the forefront, arms poised to cast. "But have you had a chance to check out the wayfares from Radimansque and Scintillesque? There are armies approaching along both routes. You can see their fires from here. And I'm willing to wager that none of you asked them for aid. We did. They aren't coming here to reinforce your position. They're coming here in the hopes of destroying you."

The look shared between Arctus and Havvelan confirmed Burdock's guess, but Lane had turned her attention back to Favian.

"Besides," she said, "I don't need to defeat your entire army. All I need to do is defeat you three. I can do that here. One fireball, to incinerate you all."

Favian scoffed. "You're bluffing. You don't have the spine."

Lane snorted, then said in a perilously soft voice, "You forget, Favian. Devon and I had Terriel on her knees at the Lyceum. The battle was over. We didn't have to kill her, there at the end. I was the one who finished it. Do you think I won't do that now, to you, to someone who has manipulated and wronged me since the day I set foot in the Lyceum?"

Lane was shocked at the vehemence of her own words, even uttered so quietly. Her arm was trembling, her body more than willing to complete the sigil and kill him. Kill them all. The pain this one man had caused—to her, to Devon, to all of the Brovettans in Iandolo that had been quarantined, and all of the citizens of Brovetto who had been forced to deal with the consequences of his failure twenty years before—all of it for the sake of his politics, his arrogance, his quest for power. She hadn't realized how strong her hatred of him had grown, how much it had eaten away at her over the years.

But he must have seen something of that hatred in her eyes, because he said nothing.

"You deserve to die for what you've done," she said, almost too softly to be heard.

Then Dalton laid a hand on her shoulder. Nothing more.

The tension drained out of her body with a small shudder. She let her head drop, drew in a steadying breath, and then dismissed Favian, as if he were nothing.

When she raised her head, she focused on Havvelan and Arctus.

"What's it going to be? Will you surrender? Or do we continue fighting, with our side the only one with active mages and an extensive knowledge of this city?"

"With two armies of reinforcements on the way," Burdock added.

Arctus considered, watching the three mages, hands still raised. But he finally nodded. "The Iandolan army will stand down."

"Traitor," Havvelan spat, as Burdock and the rest of the escort moved forward to seize the councilor, prefect, and Favian.

Behind, a rumble of dissatisfaction rolled forth from the Iandolan army, but Arctus raised a hand to quell it, then gave orders to the soldiers with him to spread throughout the other commanders. They dispersed at a run, only one remaining behind.

Then he faced Lane. "Where would you like to hold the army?"

"They can remain here in the plaza for now."

He nodded to his remaining commander. "Assume command and see that the others follow their orders. Those within the city are to report here. Set up camp. There's to be no aggression toward the Brovettans unless in self-defense. Send word to those still on the wayfare that they are to remain there until further orders are received." He eyed Lane. "Have them send in food and supplies. We don't need to be a burden on the Brovettans."

Burdock whistled and more Brovettans came running to help secure the plaza. The Iandolan soldiers grumbled, but they obeyed their commanders, pulling back even farther from the Brovettan lines.

Lane watched for a long moment, then let her arm fall. To Brigette and Daniel, she said, "Stay here. Be ready to use the lithum, if necessary. But mostly, make your presence known. Dalton, leave the lithum with them."

Dalton peeked into the satchel, where the two lithum glowed with faint light. "They're not as bright as before. I don't know how long they'll last."

"They've lasted long enough, I hope."

He slung the satchel over Brigette's shoulder.

Then Lane and Dalton approached Favian, Raven standing protectively at her shoulder.

All three—Arctus, Havvelan, and Favian—were on their knees now, surrounded by Brovettans.

"This isn't over," Havvelan said as they came near. "It won't be that easy taking control of Iandolo."

"Oh, I don't know," Lane said. "I think, with the mages taken out of the picture, the other cities might find it in their best interests to support us."

"And what do you intend to do?"

Lane's eyes narrowed. "I intend to return the Council to what it was meant to be, to what the Founders intended. Each member will be an actual representative of each city, there with the interests of their city in mind. No more councilors who owe fealty to Luminesque and Iandolo only."

"You'll never be able to control them."

"I don't intend to control them. They'll keep each other in check. That's how the Founders wanted it."

"You'll never be able to control the mages," Favian spat.

Lane frowned. "You assume there will be mages left when we're done. I'm fairly certain that what we did here in Brovetto, we can also do in Iandolo and the other cities."

"You wouldn't dare."

"Why not? I wonder what the Crystal Cities can achieve without the threat of mages hanging over them for a while. It might be more than you think."

"You won't be able to survive without your power for long."

Lane smiled. "Probably not. I've grown used to it now. And to think, for the first three years at the Lyceum I was afraid that I'd never be able to use that power. But that was all because of you." She knelt down in front of him, even though it sent a twinge of pain through her side. She wondered if she had another chew. "You should have simply accepted your position at the Lyceum, left the Council alone."

"If you and Devon and your mother hadn't interfered—"

"No, we weren't the ones to stop you. You failed because you never took the time to understand how the magic actually worked. In fact, you actively disregarded it when Devon tried to show you in his challenge. Even after you tortured him to find out what he knew, you didn't really take the time to understand what he told you. You simply used it, as bluntly as possible. That's the only reason we managed to hold you off here as long as we did. The magic isn't a hammer, it's a blade."

Favian spat on the ground in front of her.

She sighed and stood. "You're never going to understand."

It looked as if he were going to respond, but she turned away, moved swiftly back to Brigette and Daniel, both of them watching the activity on the plaza. They'd been joined by both Serene and Shian. Lane embraced them, glad to see both of them alive. Then she headed toward the barricades and the battered school.

"This isn't going to be easy," Dalton said. "I don't know how those in Iandolo are going to react. I don't know how we're going to keep the army in check. I don't—"

"I know," Lane interrupted, then placed a hand on her side, felt the wetness there. "But right now, I need to see Mindell." She reached into her pocket, but there were no more chews left. There *should* have been more; they must have fallen out. She began to move faster. "Whatever he did to get me this far is—"

The spasm of pain drove her to her knees ten paces from barricades. Dalton knelt down next to her, arm across her shoulders, began to shout for help. Raven stood over them, hand on her blade.

She clutched at her abdomen, said through gritted teeth, "Get me…get me inside…"

The next spasm overwhelmed her and she felt herself falling forward.

She never felt herself hit the flagstone of the square.

Chapter Twenty-One

"—but I think she's coming around."

Lane recognized Devon's voice and opened her eyes, blinked. The world was a murky wash of sunlight and blurred figures. She could tell she was lying down in a bed, blankets pulled up to her chest, her arms atop them, her upper body supported by pillows. The blurred figures were moving, a group off to one side whispering to each other, a single person to the other side, standing back, another sitting next to the bed.

"Devon? Is that you? Are you alive…or are we both dead?" The words came out as a croak, her throat dry, her lips parched.

The figure next to the bed leaned forward, but even when she blinked the face remained washed out and unrecognizable.

"It's Devon. And we're both alive. Here, take a drink."

She felt the lip of a cup pressed against her mouth and managed to swallow a little bit of water. Her throat instantly felt better.

"What's happening? Where's…Burdock?"

The figure standing back shifted forward, took her hand up in his as he leaned forward. "Burdock is preparing to meet with the arriving army from Scintillesque."

Lane's hand tensed, squeezing involuntarily. "The banners…are they green and gold?"

Dalton—she recognized his voice as well—squeezed back. "Green and gold. Same for those coming from Radimansque.

"And Arctus? Havvelan? Are they—?"

But her blurred window on the world was narrowing. She strained to keep it in focus, to keep herself present.

"I think we're losing her," Devon said.

Then the murky sunlight shuttered.

* * *

"And she's gone," Devon said, leaning back and setting the half-empty cup of water to the side.

Dalton laid Lane's hand back on the covers gently. "What do you expect? She overextended herself on the plaza, kept herself going only through the drugs the healers gave her. When those wore off, she crashed." He drew in a shaky breath and said in a quieter tone, so that the others in the room wouldn't overhear. "When she collapsed before the portico of the school on the plaza, I thought she was dead."

"She should have been."

Both Devon and Dalton started at Raven's words. Devon had forgotten she'd taken up position near the headboard and hadn't left since Lane had been carried up here to the manse from the plaza. Burdock had explained what had happened at the ramp, the attack by the Iandolan assassins, how Lane had been hurt. He could tell Raven blamed herself for not anticipating it and protecting Lane.

"I think you're overacting," Devon said. "You couldn't possibly have stopped them. You were fleeing the army. No one expected the Iandolans to be at that gate."

Raven eyes hardened. "I should have expected it. But they surprised us. Surprised *me*. If Mouse had shown up one breath later, she'd be dead."

"But she's not. And even after, she managed to halt the army at Fargrave Plaza."

"She's stronger than she looks," Raven said.

"Yes, she is." Devon stood. He'd been resting since the stand at the plaza, but creating the lithum and then repairing the Core had taken so much out of him he was still shaky. "She always has been the strongest of us all."

Dalton laid a hand on Devon's shoulder. "We need to get down to the waygate. The Scintillesque army is almost here. Burdock is waiting for us."

Devon drew back with a sigh, then faced Raven. "None of what happened was your fault."

Raven dropped her gaze to Lane, then turned away.

Shaking his head, Devon headed toward the others in the room: the mages Daniel and Serene, and Lane's mother and father.

"Did she wake up?" Varenov asked.

"For a moment. Not long."

"What did she say?"

"She asked about the city."

"Of course she did," Senn said, glancing toward his daughter. "I wouldn't have expected anything else."

"I should have called you over—"

Varenov cut him off. "Nonsense. We have all day to sit with her. You, on the other hand, need to take care of Brovetto."

A cold shudder ran through Devon's body from head to toe. "What do you mean?"

"She means that you're the one everyone is going to turn to, as long as Lane is...unavailable. That's why Burdock called you down to the waygate. And that's why we're here now. To give you our reports."

"But I didn't do anything—"

Varenov's chuckle cut him off this time. "Everyone knows you cut off the magic, and gave Lane the lithum so she could still use it. Your servant friends Darcy and Mari made certain of that. That's the only reason Lane managed to bring Havvelan, Arctus, and Favian to their knees. As far as the citizens of Brovetto are concerned, you both saved the city. But don't worry. I'm certain that once Lane regains her strength, attention will shift back to her. For now, though..."

Senn took over. "I'm here to report that the Iandolan army has been contained and, aside from a few isolated scuffles and fistfights amongst the soldiers, they have behaved themselves. No attempt has been made to break free from the plaza, and they've restricted themselves to the roads we've established between them and their supplies on the wayfare. It helps that the only way they can reach the wayfare is if one of our mages is with them and they have the lithum. Otherwise, the army is trapped here in Brovetto. Arctus, Havvelan, and Favian have been detained and are sitting in their cells here in the manse as we speak. Havvelan and Favian have spent most of their time demanding to see Lane or raving about the injustice of it all. Arctus has mostly been brooding, with little to say. We are going to have problems with them when it comes time to return to Iandolo, though. We don't have the manpower to keep them controlled. And who knows what reception we'll get when we finally reach Iandolo itself."

"What are Burdock's thoughts on that?"

Senn shrugged. "We haven't had much of a chance to talk recently. We've both been busy with keeping an eye on the Iandolans."

Devon sighed. "I'll ask him when I see him at the waygate." He faced Varenov. "And what are you supposed to report on?"

She smiled. "The citizenry of Brovetto, of course. They have tentatively begun leaving the protection of the mines, although many of them are finding their homes destroyed, either by fire or lightning or quakes. Many buildings were damaged, if not destroyed, to the point where they likely aren't safe. For those in such situations, we're having them return to the mines for shelter and food. Heather Brokaw has retained her role as resource allocator. Maureen Turing and Sue Hicks have taken on the organization of clean-up crews and repairs, although that's in the early stages. Connor Vaughn has already rounded up the group you had working on the water systems and is currently repairing whatever damage that has sustained in the battle. He's focusing on irrigation and drinking water for the city first. Thankfully, the water supplying the mines was not affected, so we have a ready source there."

"It sounds like the two of you have everything handled."

"For the moment," Senn said.

"What do you need me for?"

Varenov took his arm in hers and led him toward the door. "We need you to heigh it on down to the waygate and greet the Scintillesque army as a proxy for Lane."

"Why can't you do it? You were a Councilor. You know how to be a diplomat." He couldn't quite keep the fear and desperation from entering his voice.

Varenov patted his arm and let him go. "Because we're going to take your place at our daughter's side, in case she wakes up again."

Then she abandoned him and Dalton in the outside corridor, closing the door to Lane's rooms behind her.

Devon stared at the guards outside the door, then Dalton, who wrapped his arm around Devon's neck and dragged him down the hall.

"Come on. We need to go join Burdock."

* * *

Devon had never been to either of the other two waygates in Brovetto. The one that led to Scintillesque wasn't as large as the one to Iridesque, maybe three-quarters of the size, with fewer architectural decorations around the sides and atop the parapet. Fewer threads of lucent on the doors of the gate itself as well, although it was hard to tell with all of the lucent in Brovetto turned off at the moment. Not that the lucent would have been lit had the Core been active.

Burdock was waiting inside the gate with a retinue of a hundred soldiers, mostly made up of citizens, since any of the Brovettan forces with actual military experience had been assigned to watch over the Iandolan army.

The prefect turned from his seat on a horse, the animal prancing in agitation, as Devon and Dalton's carriage came to a halt in the significantly smaller courtyard inside the gate. A soldier rushed forward to open the door, stepping back to hold it for them.

Devon glanced at Dalton, who said, "After you."

Devon shot him a glare.

As soon as he disembarked, he headed for Burdock, the prefect turning his horse to face them.

"About time you arrived," he said. "The Scintillesque army is almost here."

"I was with Lane."

Burdock's eyebrows rose. "Has she woken?"

"She came to for a moment, enough to ask about you and the city, but then she went back under again."

Burdock nodded. "Still, that's a good sign. In the meantime…"

A horn blew a fanfare, interrupting what he'd been about to say. He spun back to the gates as it faded.

"They're here," he said, as the gates began to creak open.

With a curt order, the soldiers formed up around them, straightening postures and weapons. Devon was impressed, given that a month or so ago most of these men and women had been shopkeepers and farmers and servants. They had a different sheen to their faces now. Hardened. Scarred. They hadn't come out of the battles unscathed.

He wondered how many of them would be able to return to their previous lives.

On the far side of the gates, the leading edge of the Scintillesque army appeared, two figures on horseback surrounded by a slew of soldiers in the orange and gold colors of the city of Watt, although all of the banners they carried were the green and gold of Brovetto. Those banners flapped fitfully in the breeze coming off the Flatlands, gusting into Devon face, carrying dust and grit with it. He watched the two in the lead, realized it was a man and a woman, but they halted on the edge of the city, where the wayfare joined with the plateau Brovetto was built upon. Devon searched the men and women in the leading entourage, but didn't see Nic anywhere. He fidgeted.

"Are you ready?" Dalton asked beneath his breath.

Devon sucked in a steadying breath and walked forward at Burdock's side, the prefect's horse moving steady but slow. At the cusp of the gates, perhaps a few paces outside, they halted.

"Welcome to Luminesque," Devon said, his voice sounding overly loud, even though it wasn't. "My name is Devon Alamort. The governor, Lane Illea, couldn't attend your arrival, although you'll meet her later if you wish. I assume, since you're flying the Brovettan colors, that you're here to aid the city against Iridesque and the Iandolan army?"

Everyone on both sides tensed, soldiers shifting hands towards weapons, horses jostling as they picked up on their mounts' emotions. Even with the banners, it was possible this was a trick. Nic wasn't supposed to have warned them to use the green and gold banners unless they'd agreed to help Brovetto, but he could have been forced to tell them.

"Not the most diplomatic opening," Burdock muttered.

"I don't do diplomacy," Devon answered. "Everyone knows that."

The woman at the front nudged her horse forward and everyone stilled.

"I've heard of you. You're the one who collapsed the Warding at the Lyceum, then proceeded to kill the one who'd attempted the Brovettan coup. And yet now you're here in Luminesque, defending the Brovettans themselves?" She tilted her head up slightly. "There is a story there."

"One that I'm willing to tell."

She nodded. "I am Lorellen Swelt, governor of Watt, and yes, we've come to give aid." Her gaze shifted from Burdock and Devon up toward the city. There were still plumes of smoke from errant fires that hadn't yet been put out, and clear damage from the battle could be seen in multiple locations, although the worst of it was hidden. "I don't hear any fighting." She looked at Devon. "It would appear that we've arrived too late."

"Too late for the main battle, perhaps, but not too late to be of use. We have managed to force the Iandolan army's surrender—"

Lorellen's eyebrows rose in surprise and a murmur ran through the Watt army.

"—but that was only the beginning. We're going to need your help, and your army, if we want to reshape Iandolo and the Crystal Cities. But that's something you should be discussing with Lane Illea, not me. Can we escort you to the governor's manse?"

Burdock spoke up for the first time. "Your army can take up residence in the barracks and the area surrounding this gate. In fact, we'd ask you to take control of the gate, if you wouldn't mind. At the moment, our resources are scarce and we need the men currently manning the gate elsewhere."

"Of course." She motioned her companion forward. "This is Commander Geralti, the...prefect, if you will, of our forces."

"Very well." Burdock passed out new commands as the Watt army began to move forward, Lorellen turning to Geralti and issuing orders as well. Then he turned back to Devon. "I'll remain here and sort out the army with their commander. Are you all right taking the governor up to the manse without me?"

"I'll be fine."

He nodded and his horse sauntered off toward Geralti. Lorellen had dismounted and now approached with a hooded figure to her right and an escort of five Wattan soldiers. The two armies were beginning to merge around them, the tense silence from before now a rising roar of conversation and the tread of booted feet.

"I believe you know my companion," Lorellen said as she approached, waving to her side.

The figure to her right threw back his hood and said, "Surprise."

"Nic!"

Devon lurched forward and they hugged each other, Nic laughing, Devon on the verge of tears. He hadn't realized how much he'd missed his old bartending friend, even if he had been a spy for Carbolen's gang. When he finally pushed back out of Nic's tight hold, he noted the ex-gangmember looked older, more haggard and worn, with wrinkles around his eyes and the corners of his mouth. Even though he was smiling, turning to embrace Dalton, there was an edge to the joy.

"It's good to see you," Dalton said, stepping back. "And you managed to convince them to support Brovetto!"

"That was the assignment," Nic said, then leaned in close, although he spoke loud enough for Lorellen to hear. "Not that it was easy."

Lorellen chuckled. "Initially, we ignored him, thought he was mad. But he was...persistent. And persuasive."

"It helped that Wattan traders and citizens began returning from Iandolo with stories about what Havvelan and the Council had done to the Brovettans before Lane destroyed the waygate and fled to Luminesque. All I had to do was convince everyone that Scintillesque was next, unless they did something about it right now."

"Even then, it wasn't easy," Lorellen added. "Not everyone in Watt was willing to take the risk."

"Well, I'm relieved you're here," Devon said. "We'll need your army, along with Radimansque's, to help us with Iandolo itself, as I said. But I'll let Lane explain all that. She's the one who has a plan as to what will happen with the Council and the cities after that."

"And what does she intend to do?" Lorellen asked.

It was asked lightly, but Devon could sense the guarded fear behind the question.

"She intends to return the Council to what the Founders meant it to be," he said.

Lorellen frowned at that, not understanding what he meant. Because no one remembered the Founders Pact, not as it was originally written.

But they would find out.

He motioned toward the carriage. "If you'd come with me?"

"Of course."

And they headed off toward the manse.

* * *

The meeting with the governor of Radimansque two days later went nearly the same, except with a waspish reunion between Nic and Picall, the two of them bickering as they broke off from the group and headed off toward the Burn, where Picall wanted to reconnect with her tuller friends and family. The governor of Radimansque was more reserved and less committal, but Devon and Dalton convinced him to speak with Lane while his men settled in at the waygate.

After that, the governors of the three cities retreated behind closed doors with Varenov, Burdock, and John Senn. Devon found himself wandering the manse, then the courtyard outside and the walls. Dalton took shifts as a guard on the Fifth Level, in the manse, and watching over the Iandolan army. Devon still had bouts of weakness from working with the lithium, so didn't dare work with Connor and his crew on repairs throughout the city. In fact, Lane and Dalton forbade him from working with them. After a moment where he nearly passed out on the stairs, he grudgingly agreed they were correct.

So he settled into the room he shared with Dalton at the manse with his notes and his books, sending Jillian to find Gillian and return with more.

Darcy and Mari checked in on him constantly, bringing wine and food. Nic and Picall visited, each sharing their experiences traveling to Watt and Balnis and their troubles convincing the governors to support Brovetto.

It felt like he was back in the Lyceum, shuttered away in the dorm, working on his challenge.

And then, a couple of weeks after the arrival of the governors from Scintillesque and Radimansque, someone knocked on door, which was odd, because it was open. Darcy and Mari simply walked in now. Nic and Picall burst in without warning.

He turned from the pages of the inner workings of the Core and found Lane standing at the entrance.

He stood abruptly, the chair falling onto its side with a clatter. "You're walking!"

Lane grinned, then grimaced. "Somewhat. It still hurts like hell."

He reached for his chair to offer it to her, but a servant darted into the room from the hall with one for her, placing cushions on the seat and arms. Lane settled into it with a sigh, then motioned to Devon. "Sit. We need to talk."

He frowned, but took a seat, marking his place in the book. "What do we need to talk about?"

Lane didn't answer right away, casting her gaze over the scattered papers on his desk. "What are you working on?"

"Multiple things. This is Arrend's research about the Wardings, what I still have of it. We still have to take down the Warding that Gregg erected. These are all notes about the Core and the lucent and how it all works." He picked up another book with dozens of slips of paper sticking out of the pages. "And this references many of the same kinds of nodes and junctions we've worked with here in Brovetto, but in Iandolo. They have their own Core, it seems, and it's connected to all of the other Crystal Cities and their Cores. A central hub of some kind."

"So we can turn off the mages' access to magic in Iandolo as well?"

"Theoretically."

"And turn it back on again?"

"According to these books. We can test that out here, in Brovetto, whenever you're ready."

"Not right now. We need to keep Favian and his mages under control for the moment."

She shifted uncomfortably in the chair, settled into a new position, then looked Devon in the eye.

"I've been discussing how we're going to change the Council with the other governors, returning it to what the Founders originally envisioned, and they seem to think that the other cities will agree with the changes. It places the power more directly into each governors' hands. But it isn't going to be easy. Havvelan seized control before he left, imprisoning the other Councilors, if they aren't actually dead already. He has control of the military...or at least Arctus does. Arctus appears willing to work with us, and with your help we can eliminate the threat of Favian and the rest of the mages in Iandolo. If we confiscate as many of the completed lithum as we can find, and recharge them before we head to Iandolo, then we'll have the advantage, like we do here now.

"But that isn't going to be enough. We'll only succeed if the people of Iandolo support the new Council. We've seen what the general populace can do if they get riled up, when we were fleeing Iandolo before. None of the governors want those kinds of riots in the city if we try to take control."

"I don't think you'll have to worry about the citizens of Iandolo," Devon said. "In general, the people in Iridesque don't care who's running the city, as long as they can live their lives without disruption, as long as they have food and water and no one is raiding their homes and arresting them—or killing them—in the streets. I doubt your new Council will be doing that."

Lane smiled, although it was strained with bitter memories. "No, we don't plan on that."

"Then what is it you think you need, especially from me? You appear to have everything else covered."

"Not quite. We can handle the food and water and safety of the citizens, but their lives are still being disrupted because of the lucent...or rather because the lucent has been dying."

She left the statement hanging and it took Devon a long moment to realize what she was saying. When he did, his chest tightened in shock and no small amount of fear. He could feel his heart thudding hard in his chest. His throat had tightened, to the point he found it hard to breath.

He leaned forward, his chair creaking in the stillness. "You want me to...repair the lucent? In Iandolo. All of it."

Lane waved toward his stacks of papers and books. "You've already started researching it. And we already know you can do it. In fact, as far as we know, you're the only one who *can* do it. You repaired the elevators into the Brovettan quarantine zone. You repaired the water system and the threads of the Core here. You've done dozens, if not hundreds, of smaller repairs since the Lyceum."

"But an entire city!" He meant it as an incredulous shout but it came out a strained gasp. He sat back into his seat. "An entire city."

"And not just Iandolo..."

He stared at her. "All of them. Brovetto, Watt, Balnis...all of the Crystal Cities."

"All of them." She let the idea settle for a moment, then added, "Think about what happened when you repaired the water system here in the Burn. Think about how the people reacted and what it did to revitalize Brovetto. If you do the same for the Crystal Cities, perhaps with the new vein of lucent you found in the mines below…"

She didn't have to finish. Devon could see it in his mind's eye. It would stabilize all of the violence, all of the hatreds, all of the petty disputes that the cities had sunk into over the years. It would prove to the citizens of the Crystal Cities that the new Council intended to help them, *all* of them, those in the lower levels as well as those in the towers.

But could he do it?

He turned toward his papers, to the books. Research was one thing— notes and diagrams and thoughts scribbled out on pages. Actually affecting change, making the repairs, and on such a scale…that was another.

It had only been a few weeks and he was already feeling restless. Bored. Even with his research.

He turned back to Lane and smiled.

"When should I get started?"

About the Author

JOSHUA PALMATIER is a fantasy author with a PhD in mathematics. He currently teaches at SUNY Oneonta in upstate New York while writing in his "spare" time, editing anthologies, and running the anthology-producing small press Zombies Need Brains LLC. His most recent fantasy novel, *Crystal War*, concludes the fantasy series begun in *Crystal Lattice* and *Crystal Rebel*, although you can also find his "Throne of Amenkor" series, the "Well of Sorrows" series, and the "Ley" series still on the shelves. He is currently hard at work writing his next fantasy and designing the Kickstarter for the next Zombies Need Brains anthology projects. You can find out more at www.joshuapalmatier.com or at the small press' site www.zombiesneedbrains.com. Or follow him on Blue Sky at joshuapalmatier.bsky.social or on X as @bentateauthor or @ZNBLLC. And check out the Zombies Need Brains Patreon and online magazine ZNB Presents at www.patreon.com/zombiesneedbrains.

www.ingramcontent.com/pod-product-compliance
Lightning Source LLC
Chambersburg PA
CBHW031208020726
47499CB00002B/531